# WHAT OTHERS ARE SAYING

## About *The Road Unveiled*

"I had eagerly awaited the follow up to *The Persistent Road*, and Tim Bishop did not disappoint me. *The Road Unveiled* captured my heart with its timeless story of love, friendship, loyalty, and a journey on roads I now want to travel. I hope he quickly writes the next book in this series!"

—PATRICIA BRADLEY
*USA Today* bestselling author

"In *The Road Unveiled*, Tim Bishop takes the reader on a remarkable journey with characters in search of God's will. His use of imagery and suspense makes this cycling adventure come alive."

—BARBARA TUCKER KETCHUM
Author of the award-winning *Driving Timmy's Car*

## About *The Persistent Road*

"*The Persistent Road* is a beautifully written story of tragedy and triumph. It's a simple, straightforward narrative of the complicated nature of love, loss, and faith. This is a journey well worth taking."

—ACE COLLINS
Christy Award-winning author

"A convincing story of how even the hardest of hearts isn't hopeless. Expect a wonderful but intense journey on two wheels, one that is both difficult and freeing. Great book!"

—BETH PATCH
Senior editor/producer for CBN.com

## About *The Persistent Road*

"*The Persistent Road* is an enjoyable and unexpected story that tackles tough spiritual questions. If you enjoy engaging, faith-based stories that take you on a journey, this book is a good choice."

—**Katie Powner**
Christy Award-winning author

"Tim Bishop's *The Persistent Road* will draw you in and keep you turning the pages and telling yourself, 'just one more chapter' until the very end. It's a book I'll read again and again."

—**Patricia Bradley**
*USA Today* bestselling author

"Written with immersive descriptions and deep reflection, *The Persistent Road* takes readers on a journey through the marvels and wiles of both nature and the human condition. More than a novel, it's hope on paper."

—**Katie Shands**
Author of the award-winning *Finding Franklin*

"*The Persistent Road* is not only an engaging celebration of the human spirit but an insightful reminder that God can create miraculous outcomes even when all seems lost."

—**Chris Carpenter**
Managing editor for Crossmap.com,
a division of *The Christian Post*

"Original, eloquent, memorable, replete with deftly crafted characters and many an entertaining plot twist, *The Persistent Road* showcases author Tim Bishop's genuine flair for the kind of narrative-driven storytelling that keeps the readers fully involved from start to finish. Highly recommended."

—**Midwest Book Review**

# THE ROAD

## UNVEILED

A NOVEL

# TIM BISHOP

OPEN
ROAD
PRESS

Thompson's Station
Tennessee

In loving memory of Frannie Bishop.
I'm so grateful I got to be your son.

# CHAPTER 1

The Eiffel Tower in Paris would have been more appropriate. Or floating a boat through a canal in Venice. But Lauren Baumgartner would make the most of this. After all, the setting was her doing, not his. Three weeks since bicycling out of Portland, Oregon, she was just glad her fiancé had flown in to surprise her.

Jeffrey Maddox laced his fingers through hers as they strolled beneath a banner in the center of Missoula, Montana. It read *Big Sky Hikers Extravaganza*. On the other side of a crowd-control barrier, the July sun beat down on vendor tents of recreational outfitters, outdoor clubs, travel companies, and local merchants lining either side of Main Street.

Live music blared from the stage at block's end. Goosebumps prickled Lauren's arms.

"Katrina and the Waves," Jeffrey said.

Lauren beamed. "'Walking on Sunshine.' I love the lyrics."

"What are they again?"

"They're about reuniting for more than just a short visit. Which means true love." She squeezed his hand.

Jeffrey nodded. A closed-lip grin widened his cheeks.

Though clean-shaven, the trace of his dark beard matched the shade of his wavy black hair. His chocolate eyes looked ahead, aligned with his square chin and prominent Adam's apple.

"Even if I could stay, I don't have a bicycle."

Right. But as they walked past a vendor tent for a local bicycle shop, Lauren pointed to it. And snickered.

Jeffrey smirked and shook his head.

"Young man, would you like to try the challenge?" An older man stood in front of the next booth with an axe in his hand.

Jeffrey looked over. "I haven't been called that in a while. What challenge?"

The man flicked his head toward the log beside him. "Chop through this in ten seconds and win a free T-shirt for the missus."

A rush of blood warmed Lauren's cheeks.

"A few others who haven't come close gave you a head start." Behind the man's orange hunting cap hung shirts with screen-printed images and cute captions.

"Okay."

"Be careful," Lauren said.

Jeffrey handed the man a five. "I got this."

When Jeffrey took the axe and straddled the log, his biceps bulged from underneath his skin-tight shirt. With two mighty swings the piece broke in half merely from the force of the blows.

"Whoa!" The man stood back and eyed Jeffrey. "I've never seen that before."

Jeffrey returned the axe, dusted off his hands, then side-hugged Lauren. "Which do you like?"

They were heavy cotton and would increase her hefty load once on the road, but she couldn't turn him down. She pointed to a pink shirt with a grove of pines embossed on it in black. The caption read *Stand Tall.* "Do you have this in women's medium?"

The vendor pulled a shirt from under the counter. "Here you go."

"Thank you." Lauren slid her hand into the crook in Jeffrey's arm and squeezed it.

A half hour later inside a restaurant, Jeffrey handed their menus to the waiter, who departed for the kitchen.

Lauren looked at Jeffrey from the corner of her eye. "So, 'Counselor for the Great I Am,' how's work going? Any new cases?"

"Defending another church that had to let a staff member go."

"Why'd they let him go?"

Jeffrey leaned forward. "It was a her. She came out as gay."

"Was she in leadership?"

"She was counseling people."

Lauren grimaced and shook her head. "Don't churches have a right to employ people who agree with their doctrine?"

"You would think so. This one's going to be a biggie." Jeffrey placed his elbow on the table and cupped his chin. "So it's been a few weeks. What's traveling on a bicycle been like?"

"It's incredible. You wouldn't believe how beautiful it is out there. You not only see everything at a much slower pace, you hear the rushing waters of a mountain stream, the cry of birds overhead. You smell the evergreen forest . . . or lavender fields and feel the wind against your face. I wish you could join me."

"It must be spectacular." Jeffrey scratched his arm. "But duty calls . . ."

Of course it did. His job mattered. Lauren ran her hand through her long strawberry-blond hair. His sacrifices would soon be hers too. The adjustment had begun to take root.

"That guy you introduced me to . . . what was his name again?" Jeffrey said.

"Doug . . . Doug Zimmer."

"Is he a good travel partner?" With his lawyer eyes Jeffrey examined hers.

"Yes. He knows a lot more than I do about bicycle maintenance . . . He's been through a lot lately."

"Are you ever afraid?"

"Oh no. He's safe."

Jeffrey twisted in his seat. "No, I meant traffic, wild animals, crazy people."

"No, not really."

He cleared his throat. "Are you still planning to go all the way across the country?"

Lauren widened her eyes and nodded rapidly. "It's now or never. Atlantic Ocean, here I come."

A wrinkle formed on Jeffrey's brow.

They finished eating and wrapped up their conversation. Among other things, they'd discussed Jeffrey's work, the places Lauren had been to, and the people she'd met.

Jeffrey pulled a business card out of his wallet and handed it to her.

The forward motion of his hand tweaked her heartbeat.

"Tell your friend Doug that I'd like to talk with him. He sounds like a good guy."

"Yes, he is." She had no idea why Jeffrey wanted to talk to Doug, but she took the card and tucked it away. Then she placed her hand on top of his. "It's so good to see you. I've missed you."

Jeffrey squirmed. "I missed you too. And, yes, so good to see you." Then he broke eye contact with her. And pulled his hand away.

"Jeffrey, what's wrong?"

"What do you mean?"

"You've been fidgeting since we sat down."

He sighed. "There . . . there's something I need to talk to you about."

"Okay."

"You've been off on this fantastic journey, and, well, I'm not. I'm living life, doing good work, and engaging with people."

"It'll only be a few months before I'm home. You were the one who didn't want to set a date."

"Yeah, I know. But . . . it's just that . . . I mean . . ."

"Jeffrey, what's wrong?"

"I—I wonder about us."

Lauren leaned forward. "What do you wonder about us?"

"To be honest, I get lonely."

She glanced to the side. "What's that supposed to mean?"

Jeffrey leaned back. "It just makes me wonder. I haven't seen you in . . . how many weeks?"

"Is there someone else?"

Jeffrey looked away.

"Jeffrey, tell me."

"Look, don't make this out to be something it isn't, okay?"

"It's another woman, isn't it."

"No, not really. It's just that . . . you go on this big adventure and expect me to answer your every phone call and check in with you every day. I have things going on. And we're three time zones apart."

"Two now . . . You haven't answered my question."

"What question?"

Lauren drew in a deep breath. "Is it another woman?"

"I told you, not really." He glanced sideways.

"What's that supposed to mean?"

"There is a woman I've met who, well, it's just made me wonder about us. It's hard to know. Lauren, you can't have a relationship without relating. I'm just not sure about things. You're never around . . . Do you wonder? . . . About us, I mean."

"I hadn't until now." Lauren looked around the restaurant for the restroom. "If you'll excuse me."

Jeffrey grimaced and tossed his head, looking away.

Lauren got up and walked to the restroom.

Upon exiting the stall, she approached a sink.

A woman with long, flowing black hair, who was washing her hands beside Lauren, caught her eye in the mirror. "I couldn't help but notice. You and your boyfriend make such a stunning couple."

Lauren summoned a smile. "Thank you for saying that." But did Jeffrey's character measure up to his appearance? Her blood simmered as it pulsed through her neck.

Jeffrey's problem was other women couldn't keep their eyes off him. And he was too polite to ignore them. Sooner or later some bimbo would come along and snatch him up. What was he doing coming out here to dump this on her? How could she continue her adventure with this hanging over her head?

But then, trekking through life alone again . . .

The woman pulled a napkin from the basket between their sinks, wiped her hands, and left.

Lauren and Jeffrey had been so close before her trip. And so close to becoming one. But was he just another man who wouldn't be there when she needed him?

When Lauren exited the restroom, Jeffrey was staring out the window.

As she sat, he started, then looked at her, his face drawn. "Look, you mean the world to me. I hope you know that. You always will."

Lauren studied his eyes. "But you're not sure. Jeffrey, I hardly ever hear from you."

"That's not true."

"I called you after the accident, and it took over a day to hear back from you." Her heart hammered. "It could've been *me* who was hurt . . . It was traumatic, Jeffrey. And where were you?"

"I'm sorry, but . . ." He dropped his head and shook it. "I'm just wondering. Can't you understand that?"

"Well then, you don't have to wonder anymore." Lauren worked the ring off her finger and set it in front of Jeffrey.

He raised his hands to chest height, palms out. "Lauren, don't. That's not what this is about." He picked up the ring and set it in front of her.

"Oh, isn't it? Forty-five years old, never married, with more past girlfriends than you can count on fingers and toes."

"That's not fair."

"Isn't it?"

"I haven't been seeing anyone, Lauren. I've remained true to you. I'm just trying to figure out where we're at right now. Would you rather I have said nothing?"

"I'll tell you where we're at. If you can't figure this out, I'll do it for you." She picked up the ring and slapped it down in front of him. "Now take it."

A couple at the table beside them looked over, then resumed their conversation.

Reluctantly, Jeffrey placed the ring into his pocket. He shook his head, his brow furrowed.

Lauren's eyes moistened. She lowered her voice. "This can't be God's will, Jeffrey. He doesn't play hide-and-go-seek with our desire for someone to love us. You knew I was taking this trip, and you agreed to it. Now you're changing your mind." Lauren sniffled.

"Well, you're right about one thing."

She looked up at him, wiping the tears from her eyes.

"God doesn't play hide-and-seek with us."

"Then why do I feel like my heart is on a yo-yo string?"

"I'm trying to be honest with you. I only want the best for you."

"Then why don't you ever call me back?"

Jeffrey fiddled with his napkin. "I do, but . . . well . . . sometimes, I'm in the middle of something."

"For a day and a half?"

"You know I have a busy job. I can't just drop everything every time the phone rings. People are depending on me. That's why they pay me."

"You and your job."

"You've known about my job for years. You know how important these cases are for the Kingdom. Do you want to see the rights of the unborn continue to be trampled on? What about those who are being persecuted for their faith? Most lawyers wouldn't touch those cases, or if they did, they wouldn't understand what to do with them. Is there something about my job you can't embrace?"

"Yes, there is."

"And what's that?"

"You're married to it."

"Lauren."

"Don't *Lauren* me." She got up, reached into her zip pouch, and threw a twenty-dollar bill on the table.

"No, Lauren. Come on."

"No, you come on." She raised her chin and turned to leave.

"Don't you want a ride?"

"No." She snatched the pink T-shirt from the booth seat, shoved it into his chest, and stormed out of the restaurant.

# CHAPTER 2

The first ten minutes of Lauren's walk through town were a blur. Perhaps Jeffrey was right. Maybe it was unfair of her to expect him to return her calls the first possible minute. And he *was* doing important work. After returning from the mission field and before surrendering much of her heart to him, she'd celebrated what good work he was doing. His biggest fan.

Christians *were* getting trampled in the court of public opinion, let alone the court of law, and Jeffrey was doing something about it. Should she stand in the way of that? Why couldn't she be more supportive?

But she'd always been leery of Jeffrey and the many women who'd had an interest in him—and he in them. How come he'd never married? Was he merely a playboy in a lawyer's suit?

Maybe this was all her fault. Fifteen years in Uganda had kept romance at a distance. It seemed whenever she got close to someone, things would blow up. And then there was her

9

secret. If Jeffrey ever found out about that, there's no way he would marry her.

Lauren wandered the downtown streets of Missoula until her adrenaline burned off. The festive surroundings did little to alleviate the tightness in her chest.

While checking on Freddie, a fellow traveler who'd been admitted to the hospital, Lauren reconnected with Doug. Eventually they departed for their hosts' home. Brother Jim Covington, a pastor at a local Missoula church, and his wife, Maggie, had welcomed Lauren and Doug with open arms.

Doug remained downstairs with Brother Jim while Lauren and Maggie went up to the room where Lauren had slept the night before and sat on the bed. Her stomach hadn't stopped churning.

"What's on your mind?"

The sound of an older woman's voice triggered more emotion. Maggie's tone sounded like Lauren's mother's voice the day Tommy Delano had pushed her off the jungle gym. Her mother couldn't console her now—not even by phone—but she was grateful Maggie could.

With her short, curly hair dusting the back of her red knit top, the petite but round woman got up to close the door and returned to the bed, wrapping her arm around Lauren. "That's okay. Let it out."

After composing herself Lauren took a deep breath. "I just broke up with my fiancé."

"Oh dear. How long had you two been engaged?"

"Going on a year. We were due to be married after I finished my ride across the US. But we've known each other much longer."

"How long?"

"Twelve years."

Maggie grimaced. She'd been so jovial when they first met. But now her brown eyes reflected the sorrow pouring from Lauren's aching heart.

"We met at a church in Virginia, where I'm from, and corresponded while I was still serving at the orphanage in Uganda. Then things seemed to click when I furloughed."

"What happened?"

That was a good question.

"I don't know. We're drifting apart. He's become lax at returning my calls. And me, I don't know. I just don't know. To tell you the truth, I feel a little relieved . . . though I do love him."

"You've been through a lot . . . With all the cycling, the accident, and now this."

"I feel so . . . so lost. Like I've lost my best friend."

"Oh, I'm so sorry, Lauren." Maggie cradled Lauren in her arms.

"And my—maybe my last chance to have a family . . . I guess I'll always be single." Another wave of emotion spilled out.

Maggie waited until Lauren gathered herself. "How old are you?"

"Forty-two . . . I had more kids than I knew what to do with in Uganda. But none of my own. And now this."

"There, there." Maggie patted Lauren's leg.

Lauren hadn't experienced this type of comfort in over two decades. She'd just begun her sophomore year in college when the tragedy that changed everything happened. And had her parents not been delivering her to school, they might still be alive.

"Is it him or me, Maggie? I just don't know. Why are these things so complicated? Why doesn't God just spell it out?"

"He's always teaching us. And loving us. No matter what. He lets us choose so we can learn His ways, but He won't allow us to go over the cliff without His safety strap around us."

"Jeffrey is such a good man. But I always wondered if he would ever really commit to a woman. He's so handsome . . .

women find him irresistible. He's had so many girlfriends but never married."

"Lauren, are *you* afraid of commitment?"

"I—I don't think so."

"Marriage is a big deal. You likely won't find yourself cycling for weeks on end once you marry."

Lauren laughed. "That's why I'm out here now, before I get married." She burst into tears. "And now I'm not. I'll never get married."

"You must be exhausted. You've not had a good night's sleep in how long?"

"Yes, you're right." Lauren caught her breath. "I must admit, it's been a while. It's hard to sleep when there's so much excitement around you."

"Why don't you take a nap, Lauren. Sometimes when we push ourselves beyond our limits, we crash. See if some rest helps."

"Thank you, Maggie. I'm so grateful for how you and Brother Jim have helped us."

Maggie smiled. "You're blessing us in the process. We're so glad you're here . . . Does Doug know you broke up?"

Lauren chuckled. "Poor Doug. I about collapsed in his arms and drenched his shoulder with my tears. I'm so glad he was there."

Maggie smiled. "Sleep as long as you need to." She closed the door behind her as she left the room.

Four days later, with her phone pressed to her ear, Lauren looked out the window of her room at the Covingtons', mountains zigzagging the horizon.

"Why haven't you returned my calls?" Jeffrey said.

*Really? He doesn't get it.* She'd been busy trying to support Freddie, who'd gone out of his way to help her. Furthermore,

Doug was struggling over his recent losses and trying to find himself. But Jeffrey was more concerned about *his* world in the Washington Beltway.

Lauren cleared her throat. "I'm sorry, but I had lots of things to tend to . . ."

"Yeah."

*Does he really expect me to console him?*

"What could be more important than us?"

"A date in court to defend *Ruggles versus Newark, New Jersey?*"

"You know that was an important case."

"Yes, you're right . . . Aren't you at least going to ask what's going on here?"

"Sure, what's going on?"

Five minutes into their conversation, an urgent matter on Jeffrey's end interrupted them. Lauren embraced his cause of defending Christians in court but . . . "You can feel free to call when you have more time to talk, but I can't guarantee I'll have a signal. I'm leaving here tomorrow. Goodbye."

Doug walked into Lauren's room at the Covingtons' and stared out the window. Roads he would soon pedal swirled around those beautiful mountains. Traveling alone had its benefits, but the empty pit in his stomach suggested he wasn't ready to part ways with Lauren.

Jeffrey certainly didn't want him to. Doug had already talked to the "Counselor for the Great I Am." He seemed a principled man, though not as lofty as the moniker on his business card characterized him.

"Are you planning to leave tomorrow?"

Lauren nodded. "Yes. What about you?"

"Uh-huh."

She jammed her laundered bike shorts into a stuff sack.

"It might be safer to stick together," Doug said.

Lauren looked up and tilted her head. "Are you going through Yellowstone?"

"Oh, I've heard stories about Yellowstone."

"Do tell."

"Well, you know, bears—grizzly, that is—and lots of cars. Maybe not easy to find places to stay. Then there's RVs with less-than-professional drivers."

"God will protect me." She reached for another piece of clothing on the bed.

"Are you really thinking of going there?"

She nodded, then squeezed one of her tops into the stuff sack and worked it down. "It was one of my reasons for coming on this trip."

Doug would never go through that park on a bicycle unless they'd closed the road to motorized vehicles and exterminated the bears and wolves. Brother Jim and a few of his parishioners had warned him not to travel there. As had the guy at the bicycle shop.

He compared the route through Yellowstone on his Bicycle America map to the instructions on a sheet of paper in his hand. "We can still travel a few days together."

"I must admit, it's fun to have someone to talk to and enjoy the scenery with." She looked up, raised her eyebrows, and pointed a folded pair of bike shorts at him. "And you do know a lot more than I do about bicycle maintenance."

"On my visit to Bicycle America, they gave me an alternate route east. It ends up in the Black Hills of South Dakota, but I can get you to Yellowstone that way too."

Some of the alternate routes would put them on the interstate where frontage roads were unavailable. He'd take his chances there, with plenty of services not far from the highway.

A woman like Lauren . . . well . . . any woman shouldn't be traveling alone. He remembered when he'd first met her on the road, her flowing ginger locks, her trim physique. Maybe she didn't understand what a target she was for unscrupulous men.

The bike shop attendant had explained a quicker route out of the Rockies—and presumably bear country—from Missoula to Great Falls. *"Once you're east of Lincoln, it may bore you to tears. You might see a pronghorn or two, but, other than deer, that's about it. And traffic on Route 200 moves at land-speed records."* If it were up to just Doug, that's where he'd go.

But, no, he couldn't leave Lauren alone.

"Spectacular scenery, yes, but I'm told those bison will decide for themselves where to roam. They cause traffic jams and slow travel for hours. Then after the park, if you stay on this route"—he jiggled the Bicycle America map—"you end up having to go over Hoosier Pass. That's eleven thousand feet." He couldn't imagine pushing his recumbent to that altitude.

Lauren kept packing.

It wasn't just the wildlife in Yellowstone that bothered Doug. Accommodations in peak season could be scarce on such short notice, with throngs of tourists enjoying the geysers and seeking out grizzly bear sightings. More power to them when they could do so from the safety of their vehicles.

"Brother Jim said you're required to camp at approved campsites only. Not sure how far apart those are."

Lauren took a deep breath. "I'll think about it."

Booking ahead might work if they knew where they were going and when they would get there. However, such rigid planning didn't take into account bad weather, unplanned repair jobs, special side trips, or connections with interesting people, should their free spirits lead there.

Of course, skirting Yellowstone came with no guarantees either. Park boundaries only appeared on maps and didn't limit bears, wolves, bison, and big cats from roving wherever their wild, unbridled hearts pleased.

Despite plenty of bicycling since starting her trip in Portland, Oregon, a month ago, Lauren felt the same jitters she had then. When she walked out of her room at the Covingtons', she would leave her safe haven and venture back into the unknown.

She'd met Doug three weeks ago. At sixty years of age he was old enough to be her father, but he was still young enough to enjoy the adventure and provide companionship and support. She could help him continue to recover from losing his wife, Ruth. If traveling together didn't work out, plenty of alternate routes crisscrossed the countryside. And it *was* a free country.

Goodbyes weren't easy for someone who, at a young age, hadn't been able to say goodbye to her own parents. That was twenty-two years ago but seemed like yesterday.

"Did you get all your things from your room?" Maggie, shoulder height next to Lauren, wore baggie jeans and a red sweatshirt with a grizzly bear embroidered on the front.

"I think I have everything. We travel lightly." Her comment, of course, didn't take into account her violin, which Doug had reminded her didn't lighten her load.

He walked into the kitchen and addressed their hosts. "I can't thank you enough. I'll never forget you."

"That goes for me too," Lauren said.

Brother Jim, a giant of a man, stroked his beard, then nestled Maggie to his side. "It was all our pleasure."

"Did you get water for the road?" Maggie broke Brother Jim's grasp long enough to grab the bunch of bananas from a bowl on the table. "And, here, take these with you."

Lauren held out both hands to receive them. "Thank you. I think we have all the water we need for now." Then she gave Maggie a long hug. "I'm going to miss you."

Doug embraced Brother Jim and then Maggie.

The foursome exited to the backyard, where Doug's recumbent and Lauren's upright touring bicycle rested against the house.

Lauren placed the bananas into a front pannier.

With his forefinger Brother Jim pushed the frame of his glasses to the bridge of his nose. "Could I say a prayer for you before you leave?"

"Absolutely." Doug leaned his recumbent bicycle against his thigh, his hand gripping the top of the seat rest.

Lauren nodded.

"Dear Heavenly Father, as Doug and Lauren hit the road, may Your peace follow them, may You protect them, and may You bless them as they commune with Your beautiful creation. Thank You that Maggie and I had the privilege of participating in their adventure, even from the comfort of our home. May You help them understand better the depth of Your love. We praise You for the work You've been doing in their lives. And for Lauren, bind up the hurt that comes with breaking up with her fiancé. Lord, grant her the desires of her heart as she delights in You and waits on You. Thank You that she loves You so much and wants to do Your will. In Jesus's name, amen."

Brother Jim looked at Doug. "Don't forget that fundraising job I told you about."

"I won't, Brother Jim. Thank you so much for your vote of confidence."

After another exchange of hugs Doug led Lauren out of the Covingtons' driveway and, in minutes, to the outskirts of town, where the majestic Montana landscape pulled them into a world of beauty, mystery, and undiscovered treasures.

# CHAPTER 3

Lauren had ridden the interstate a short distance in Oregon, and it wasn't her idea of enjoyment. Travel on Interstate 90 in Montana started much sooner than she expected.

Tractor trailers whizzed by topping eighty miles an hour. The deafening rumble shot tremors up her arms. To avoid the powerful draft and the potentially severe consequences of driver inattention, she followed Doug to the far right over a collection of big-rig shrapnel.

Within fifteen minutes Doug slowed to a stop. "My tire's flat."

He leaned his bicycle against the guardrail. No sooner had he unloaded his panniers and removed the rear wheel than a Montana state trooper pulled to the shoulder and turned on his flashers.

"Howdy. Need some help?"

"Hello, Officer," Doug said. "We appreciate the cover. I'm about halfway through. Should be only another ten minutes tops."

"Are you two sure you want to ride the interstate?"

Lauren sent a wry smile Doug's way.

Wheel in hand, Doug worked the tire back onto its rim. "Not as sure as I was before we left."

"Once you make it to Drummond, you may want to consider a ride through Flint Creek Pass on Montana Route 1. It's not a wide road, but the traffic won't bother you there. Plus you'll have some great views."

"Oooooo!" Lauren said.

"Thanks. We'll check into that."

The trooper chatted with Lauren as Doug completed the repair. "Just so you know, we've had two cycling fatalities in the past month on I-90." His finger wagged toward the travel lane beside them. "This here is a drag strip. The motorists want to get from point A to point B as fast as they can, and they're not concerned about your safety. Be careful."

Her stomach sank further. She didn't need convincing.

"Thank you, sir," Doug said.

Two and a half hours later they exited onto a frontage road. The constant whir of high-speed traffic diminished as they cycled into a pastoral setting.

Lauren's pace had slowed for the past few miles. Nature's bell was ringing louder with each pedal stroke, but no services were in sight. "I need to stop."

"Stop? Okay, if you say so. Right here?"

"Yeah. I need to go to the bathroom." Yesterday she'd tucked away the thought of how this might work while traveling with Doug, but the time had now arrived. "Would you mind going up the road?"

"Sure, but don't you want me to hold your bike?"

"I'll manage."

Doug continued riding while Lauren stopped. She grabbed a roll of toilet paper, a clear, ziplock bag, and an ultralight trowel from her handlebar bag. Then she laid her bicycle on the roadside grass. With all the gear hanging from the bike, maybe he had a point about holding it.

"Watch out for snakes!"

Lauren ventured toward a small stand of trees, scanning the tall grass to avoid a step she might regret.

When she reached the leafy partition and turned around, she waved off Doug in the distance so he would look the other way.

He obliged.

With no cars in sight she relieved herself and bounded like a deer back to her bicycle, eager to depart before anyone stopped.

An hour later they rolled into Drummond at dusk and stopped at the Flint Creek Motel. A lit *Vacancy* sign slowed her heartbeat.

They parked their bicycles and walked into the office.

"Got any rooms?" Doug said.

"You're in luck. One left."

Lauren's stomach sank. "Is there a campground nearby?"

"Depends how you define nearby . . . *and* campground." The gray-haired man chuckled. "Judging from your attire, I don't suppose you want to go ten miles in the dark. You could check out the town campground, but I wouldn't recommend it. It's right across from a bar. If you came from the interstate, it was right on the corner." He looked at Doug. "I wouldn't want *my* wife anywhere near that campground."

Doug smirked.

A fresh dose of sweat dampened Lauren's brow. "You don't have another room, do you?"

"No, ma'am. And the other places in town are full."

"How many beds do you have in that vacant room?" Doug said.

Lauren jumped in. "No, that's alright. Let's go check the campground. I'm sure it will be fine. I feel like sleeping under the stars tonight."

"Okay, if you insist. Thanks, mister."

"Do you want me to at least hold the room for you in case you change your mind?"

"No thanks," Lauren said.

Doug followed her outside. "Are you sure you want to do this?"

"Do what?"

"Set up camp in the dark across from a bar?"

"Oh that. Of course he's going to say that. He wanted to sell his last room."

"Why don't *you* take the room, and I'll go tent across from the bar."

"Really? That's thoughtful of you, but I can't let you do that."

Wrinkles formed in Doug's forehead.

"Come on. Let's go check it out." Lauren mounted her bicycle. "You ready?"

Doug climbed on his recumbent and the two pedaled back toward the interstate.

As the sun dipped below the horizon, the outline of a sign on an open parcel of land across from a few businesses masked a small portion of the burnt-orange sky, a final scene of a magnificent sunset in the Wild West.

The sign grew in size as they cycled toward it. Squinting, Lauren read *Town of Drummond Campground. Camp at your own risk. No facilities.*

It appeared they would be the only two campers this night.

"Are you still sure?"

Lauren looked across the street. "Good thing a bar's there. I may need the bathroom before bed."

"Want to go over now before setting up?"

"No, let's set up first."

Doug grimaced. "And leave all our stuff over here unattended?"

But what else could they do? She'd take her chances. If she ran into trouble, Doug would abandon camp after ten or fifteen minutes and check on her. "We can go in shifts."

Doug sighed. "That's not gonna happen."

With no time for more debate, they scurried to unload gear and set up their tents. They placed them ten feet apart toward the back of the campground, well off the road, but not hidden from view. And well within earshot of the clamor inside the bar.

A half hour later the tents were set up with inflated mattresses and sleeping bags inside, all done with headlamps.

Among other gear, Lauren's violin case sat on the ground. She couldn't leave it there. Maybe take it into the bar with her? No, that might be awkward or invite trouble. She could put it in her tent with her other valuables, but what vagrant wouldn't first look inside a tent at a vacant campground? Twenty feet behind her tent, near the edge of the clearing, the dark, tall grass beckoned. Of course!

When she returned to tend to her remaining gear, Doug said, "You aren't going to leave that over there, are you?"

"Don't tell anyone."

"I wouldn't want you to forget it."

Lauren grinned. "Not a chance. It's coming to bed with me when we get back."

A gibbous moon cast a sheen on their tents, competing only with the light from a solitary streetlamp and the security lighting from off-hours businesses nearby. The campground's floodlight was apparently out of order. They tossed their valuables into their tents, locked the two bikes together, and headed to the bar to eat and use the facilities.

Lauren watched from across the street as Doug opened the door to the bar, peered in, then motioned her to come while he lingered in the doorway.

A sign hanging from the ceiling pointed to the restrooms. Amid the smell of alcohol arose that of charbroiled burgers. A dozen customers were inside, a few of them talking back and forth across the room.

Lauren hastened to the ladies' room. The eyes of a cowboy seated at the bar escorted her as he swiveled on his seat, a handgun stowed in the holster on his hip. She ignored him.

Instead she focused on the sign—a cowgirl with legs crossed—above a crescent cutout on the knotty-pine door. Reflective glass plugged the hole in the rickety door.

When she pulled the handle to open the door, she froze. Pinups of nude male models stared at her, as many of them as it took to cover the interior walls, overlapping one another to maximize the skin exposure. Only a small mirror and an oversized soap dispenser above the tiny sink, grimy from neglect, interrupted them. To avoid looking back at the beady-eyed men, she glanced down at the cracked linoleum floor and closed the door, securing the latch and dropping the hook lock into place. She could touch the opposite walls at the same time but would keep her hands to herself. Two-inch gaps above and below the door guaranteed lack of privacy.

On the other side of the door she could hear Doug getting sucked into some banter. "Mister, I'll ride your bike for ya tomorrow if you want a day off . . . as long as your friend comes along." Apparently Doug ignored the comment. However, she wondered about the look on his face. She continued staring at the floor and listening.

Another voice piped up. "Where ya headed?"

"East," Doug said.

"Need a place to stay tonight?"

"No, we're all set. But thanks."

A moment later she heard Doug's voice again. "Are you still serving food?"

Another man, presumably the bartender, said, "We have a few burgers left. That's about it."

"Okay. Let me check when she gets out."

Supper sounded good, but would they have to eat in the bar?

She finished up, unlatched the door, and pushed it open.

Four sets of male eyes met hers as she strode toward the entrance.

Doug, however, had sat at the bar. "Want a burger?"

"Can we get it to go?"

Doug looked at the bartender, who looked at Lauren. "Sure. How would you like it?"

"Medium rare, please."

"Same for me," Doug said. "Have a seat."

Lauren walked over and sat on the stool beside Doug.

Before they could begin their conversation, the man whose eyes had walked Lauren to the restroom got up and meandered over, stopping right beside her, his body swaying.

Nausea threatened to supplant her hunger pangs, so she avoided eye contact with him.

But Doug did not. "Can I help you?"

"Yeah. I wanna talk to your friend here."

"She's busy."

"She don't look busy to me."

"Jason, settle down," the bartender said. "The woman came in to freshen up and have a burger, not to carry on a conversation with you. And by the way, I'm shuttin' you off."

The bartender was a few drinks too late. The man's breath might just curl Lauren's locks—if it didn't set them ablaze first.

The man placed his hand on her shoulder.

The hair on the back of Lauren's neck bristled.

"Get your hands off her," Doug said.

"It's alright. I can handle this." Lauren clutched the man's wrist and removed it from her shoulder. Then she rose to her feet and faced him. "Jason, you've had a little too much to drink tonight. My friend and I are going to eat a burger, then leave. Do you have a problem with that?"

"No, ma'am. I ain't got no problem with that. I's just tryin' to be friendly."

She palmed her hip. "Well, if you don't mind, we'd appreciate a little privacy for our dinner."

Doug's eyes had popped wide open.

The din quieted. Everyone was watching her.

From the other side of the room, another man spoke. "You tell him, lady. It's about time someone put Ole Jason in his place. Ain't that right, Jason?"

Jason wobbled and looked at the man. "Whaddaya talkin' 'bout, P—Petey-Poo? If I had a dime every time you shot your big mouth off, I'd be rich."

The man—Pete—got up and walked over to the threesome. "You stay away from her, you understand?"

"I ain't a-scared o' you. Let's you and me settle this once and for all."

The bartender stopped his busy work behind the counter. "Simmer down, gents. If you have a problem with one another, I suggest you take it outside."

"Jason," Pete said, "why don't you go back there and sit down and let these two travelers have some peace and quiet."

Jason mumbled something, then staggered to the door and outside.

Lauren's back stiffened, her eyes darting left then right, her hearing shifting into a higher gear. *Oh no. Our belongings.*

The sound of a vehicle door slamming and an engine firing slowed her pulse.

Tires screeched as the vehicle drove away.

"There," Pete said. "He won't bother you guys anymore. Too bad. He's such a nice guy, but when he drinks too much, he's trouble."

"Thanks for helping out." Doug looked at the bartender while jerking a thumb toward Pete. "I'll pick up this kind gentleman's tab."

The bartender set burger plates in front of Doug and Lauren. Doug ordered a beer and Lauren a Coke. They ate quickly, visited the bathrooms, then left the bar. Doug paid for all three meals and dropped a generous tip.

# CHAPTER 4

With headlamps on bright they crossed the empty street. The hubbub from the bar diminished the farther from it they walked.

Lauren scanned the grounds and peeked inside her tent. Everything seemed to be as they'd left it. "Did you have unusual wallpaper in your bathroom?"

Doug laughed. "How'd ya know?"

"Just a wild guess. I owe you for dinner."

"Don't worry about it."

"I'm not worried about it. I just want to pay for my own meals. That was part of the deal, remember?"

"Yeah, you're right. Let's square up tomorrow." As Doug pivoted to duck into his tent, he stopped. "You sure put that troublemaker in his place. Where'd ya learn that technique?"

"When you're the only white woman living among African villagers, some of them pretty rough, you learn all sorts of interesting techniques or you don't get by."

Doug pooched his lips and nodded.

Lauren retrieved her violin case and dropped it inside her tent.

The two travelers said good night to one another and crawled into their tents for the evening.

Before turning off her headlamp Lauren grabbed her cell phone and opened her Bible app. However, the noise from the bar caused her mind to wander. *Jeffrey probably had another bimbo draped over his arm while I was practicing my survival skills across the street. He couldn't even return a phone call when the going got tough. At least my travel partner's willing to fight for me.*

Still, her heart yearned for more of Jeffrey. The more miles she cycled into remote areas, the deeper the longing. It seemed strange to her how that worked, like she had more of an addiction to him than a healthy attraction.

She navigated on her phone to a passage she had grown to know and love since childhood.

> Love suffers long and is kind; love does not envy; love does not parade itself, is not puffed up; does not behave rudely, does not seek its own, is not provoked, thinks no evil; does not rejoice in iniquity, but rejoices in the truth; bears all things, believes all things, hopes all things, endures all things. Love never fails.

She and Jeffrey had shared meaningful love as friends, but when they crossed the line to romance, something went wrong. She couldn't pinpoint the problem, but it was a constant source of internal strife, like the chafing on a cyclist's inner thighs with every pedal stroke. The rider knows it's there. It's not going to stop her routine, but without treatment, it will do her damage. She wanted balm for her heart.

The sound of snoring from the neighboring tent broke her train of thought. She'd felt strong on her first day back on the road, but it'd been a long day.

The ruckus across the street dwindled as doors slammed and vehicles rumbled away, so she turned off her headlamp and offered up a silent prayer.

*Dear Heavenly Father, I love You. Thank You for another day surrounded by the beauty of Your creation and safe travel. Thank You for a travel partner who wants to protect me. Continue healing the hurt in his heart from his losses. And bring physical healing to Freddie. Lord, I would love to hear from You about Jeffrey. My heart longs for him, but I'm not sure he's right for me. Help me to find my contentment only in You. Thank You for Your Word, which helps me know what true love looks like. And, oh, I almost forgot . . . help Jason with his drinking problem. Bring people into his life who can share Your love with him. May he find peace in You. And thank You for Pete coming to my defense. I pray for peaceful sleep tonight for Doug and me, and another exciting day tomorrow. Go before us, Lord. In the precious name of Jesus, amen.*

After breaking camp early the next morning, Doug and Lauren cycled down Main Street and discovered a family restaurant opening its doors. They walked in and ate a big breakfast. No amount of food seemed too much, given the calories Doug burned each day.

He was used to paying for meals in his former life in sales. And for almost anyone he liked. Lauren ranked high on that scale. Reluctantly, after she squared up with him on the prior evening's meal, he allowed her to pay for her own breakfast—at her insistence.

The cook offered advice on the route ahead, consistent with that of the state trooper the day before, but he also recommended a side trip to Philipsburg.

Twenty miles into a headwind neutralized the advantages of flat terrain and low traffic on Montana Route 1. Along the way, a few quirky exhibits presented irresistible photo opportunities, among them a museum of area creatures fabricated from unusual materials and many cattle skulls blanketing two trees beside the road.

In the distance, snowcapped mountains marked the Continental Divide. Lauren shouted from behind him, "Looks like climbing ahead. I can't wait."

Doug could. His heavy recumbent lagged on inclines. But he would get revenge on the other side of the mountain.

Cattle grazed in a fenced pasture against a splendid backdrop. Rugged, snow-covered mountains framed a stream in the foreground and empty roadways twisted around natural barriers, inviting adventurers to discover the wonders around the next bend. Quintessential Montana. A parallel rail line with grass sprouting in the middle pointed to trailblazers from yesteryear.

Finally the road to Philipsburg appeared. Doug turned left, Lauren close behind.

Within a mile they discovered a quaint town brimming with activity. The downtown looked like it had been plucked from the set of a Western movie. Two-story brick buildings trimmed with vibrant colors lined the street, with restaurants, bars, barbecue joints, a soda fountain shop, and even a motel or two.

Lauren spotted a candy store and bolted toward it. She leaned her bicycle against the side of the building, then darted inside. Doug caught up to her.

It was the "World's Greatest Candy Store," or so the owners thought. Nothing he saw contradicted their claim.

Smiling, Lauren flitted from counter to counter, her eyes apparently drawn to what her taste buds might remember from childhood.

The interior sparkled, cleaner than a water bottle scoured with soap and neater than an organized tool chest. Large, wood-trimmed glass counters sat atop an old-fashioned hardwood floor, both in mint condition, showcasing mounds of chocolate. On the wall, shelves held fishbowl-shaped glass jars with metallic covers seated at an angle. Inside the jars were every variety of hard candy customers could imagine, giving new meaning to the term "eye candy."

Excited children ran about gleefully before pleading with their parents for a delectable taste.

Lauren tipped her head at the sight of them, watching their every move.

Doug remembered those sounds well, like when he took Douglas Jr. and a few of his friends to the carnival. Those years were behind him, but the memories warmed his heart. Would he ever entertain another season of life like that? Maybe, if it involved a woman who knew how to love them well. He was looking at one.

Lauren crouched alongside a preschool girl and pointed to a display of colorful hard candy with animal faces inside the glass counter. "See the bear? . . . And the doggie?"

The toddler nodded.

Lauren got up and turned to a woman nearby. "She's absolutely adorable."

"Oh, thank you. She's a sweetie."

"I'll say."

Yes, Lauren would make a fantastic mother. So loving and with strong moral character.

But should he be entertaining these thoughts at sixty years of age? He wandered outside to check on their belongings.

Ah, the sound of children. Lauren missed the giggles, the exuberance, the inquisitiveness, even the infighting at the orphanage. Would she ever get to experience this firsthand? Time was shrinking.

She bent down again. "Look! A giraffe."

The little girl reached her arms toward Lauren, who looked up at the girl's mother.

She nodded. "It's okay."

Lauren hugged the little girl. "What's your name?"

"Jamie."

"That's a nice name, Jamie."

Jamie. Her brother's name. In a wheelchair for the rest of his life while she bicycled America and traveled the world.

Missing her brothers from afar eased the pain of facing the injustice head-on. A drunk driver had crippled them. But at least Jamie and Nick made it out alive. That's more than she could say for her parents.

She'd come to terms with that but preferred not to be reminded of it. Even forgave the man who did it—just a boy really. And now, amazingly, he was training to become a youth pastor.

Nick and Jamie knew something about her most people didn't. How could they not?

Would she ever have a family of her own? Maybe, if she found someone who understood her secret and could be trusted with it.

Would Jeffrey have understood? Sometimes she was convinced he would. Other times, no way. But she'd never tested him, despite being engaged to him. It'd been easier to indulge him in his interests rather than exposing her biggest vulnerabilities.

But she needn't dwell on that now. A new world was unfolding. And if God chose to answer her prayers in the affirmative, someone special could be around the next turn in the road.

Lauren could browse this store much longer, picking up gifts for people she held dear. However, such gifts would only weigh down her bicycle. And Doug was waiting outside.

Instead, and knowing chocolate would make a mess, she bought a pack of Necco wafers and a pound of jelly beans, then left. With climbing ahead those calories would soon vanish.

"Want a jelly bean?"

"Maybe later. I'm ready for lunch. You?"

"Yes."

"We have a big climb ahead of us. We best not linger here too long."

"This place is amazing. I could spend the entire afternoon here, let alone in that candy store."

They located a barbecue restaurant and feasted on pulled pork sandwiches.

After lunch Lauren browsed more shops for an hour while Doug studied a map. *Jeffrey would be climbing the walls if he were here with me now.*

They departed around one thirty.

# CHAPTER 5

Butterflies fluttered in Lauren's stomach. Perhaps her last trip through a pass gave her pause—when Freddie's life had changed forever. It could have been her. No wonder she'd treated herself at the candy store and been so reluctant to leave the adorable little town of Philipsburg.

Flint Creek Pass stood between the travelers and parts east.

Doug invited Lauren to lead the way, and she charged ahead of him on her Trek 520.

The climb, still west of the Continental Divide, was long and slow. The higher they ascended, the narrower the roadway became.

The road far ahead appeared chiseled out of the side of a mountain. Left of the road, the landscape transitioned from conifers to barren terrain to a buffed cliff where a sheen from the sun's rays glowed like molten copper. On the other side, a vast canyon splashed with evergreen trees offered spectacular views of rugged country as well as the road they'd just traveled, switchbacks snaking around the green hills.

A concrete barrier, about two feet thick at the base and three feet high, separated her from a treacherous fall into the splendid landscape. She was grateful for the barrier, but atop her bicycle, her torso rose above it.

Her heart fluttered. One moment of inattention, one bobble and . . .

This barrier would be much easier to fly over than the one when Lauren tried roller derby as a teen. And the landing would be . . . unthinkable. This was no time for weak knees as her muscles burned above and below them.

A lull in traffic allowed the two of them to ride in the travel lane and enjoy the views against the deep blue sky as they inched higher.

Another glance to her left and Lauren jerked her head toward the heavens. She squinted. *A white head and tail.* Warmth radiated through her chest. With only wind propelling its outstretched wings, the bird soared with majestic grace.

Suddenly another appeared, higher than the first.

They symbolized not only the country she loved but also promises from above. Lauren's eyes moistened before water trickled out the corners of them. She'd never seen bald eagles in their natural habitat, certainly not in Uganda where she enjoyed exotic sights on every safari. But no bald eagles. She'd never even seen them in captivity, only in videos.

She peeked in her rearview mirror. Doug had fallen back on his heavier recumbent. Regardless, creeping up the incline with no place to stop, this wasn't the time to point out her discovery.

As cars approached in either direction, she gathered herself and eased her bicycle to the narrow space between the white line and the immovable guardrail. It was as if she were skirting the banks atop Murchison Falls in Uganda, minus the thundering cataract. At least there, her feet were planted on solid ground.

Her heart thumped and her palms grew sweatier.

The climb steepened, slowing her pace and threatening her balance. As she crawled higher, the adjacent canyon encroached on her pathway inch by precious inch until it swallowed the road's shoulder, forcing her into the travel lane.

Why hadn't she checked her bungee cords? What if they let loose when she stood to pedal and jostled her load? Her violin would go flying and, if it tipped in the wrong direction, be devoured in the canyon below. Her parents had presented that to her on her thirteenth birthday.

Good thing motorists recognized the hazards. They provided plenty of clearance when passing. Finally the last of them drove by.

After riding low gear for over an hour around several switchbacks, a turnoff offered a reprieve. Lauren pulled to the right to catch her breath, and Doug eventually followed.

"Wow!" She stretched out her arms at chest height as if to encompass the 180-degree vista of the amazing canyon below.

Doug pointed across a ravine to their left at the face of a mountain. "Look!"

Lauren glanced over, then did a double take. "Awwww." A moment later a lump formed in her throat.

Apparently a chainsaw artist had hewn a large section out of a dense stand of conifers to leave a bare swath in the perfect shape of a heart. No jagged edges, but a masterpiece. Its diameter must have measured many yards across.

Doug's mouth hung open. "How did they do that?"

Lauren remained speechless. The striking image led her to one place and only one. Jeffrey would join them on the ride up the remainder of the pass. Doug wouldn't see him, but he'd be with Lauren nonetheless. Her heart raced.

"Is something wrong?"

Lauren shook her head. In slow motion. She'd come here not to remember and celebrate him but rather to start anew while worshipping her Creator. Jeffrey had no business becoming a phantom stowaway. If she'd been less prone to reason, it would have been easy to assume he'd commissioned the fabulous work. Why couldn't she get him out of her mind?

"Hello?" Doug said.

"I'm sorry. I just can't get over it."

"I know. It is pretty amazing, isn't it?"

"Yes, it is." Lauren gathered her thoughts. "When you look across at that, what do *you* see? What's it make you think of?"

"Well, if you're wondering whether it makes me think of Ruth, of course it does. But I can also admire it for what it is. It's big. And look at that incline. They needed heavy equipment. And safety gear. Impressive. What's it make *you* think of?"

Lauren gazed off into the canyon with queasiness clutching her stomach.

She hesitated, then responded. "Several things." She looked back at the heart and then at Doug. "Mostly, God's goodness. His blessings come to us in so many unpredictable ways." There. Lauren had avoided an awkward moment. "Tell me about Ruth."

"She was one of a kind. Sacrificial, loving, easy to get along with. Ruth was faithful to God. I couldn't believe how faithful, even when she suffered so much in the end."

"I'm sure you made things easier for her. You sacrificed too."

Doug looked away. When he didn't respond, Lauren added, "It takes a real man to take care of someone and let them die at home."

Doug remained silent, then lowered his head.

Finally he looked up. "I have a confession to make. When we met on the road in Oregon, I wasn't totally truthful with you. I—I wanted to care for Ruth at home, and intended to, but . . . I didn't."

"Oh?"

"There was so much going on, and she was getting such good care at the hospital. I'm sorry for misleading you."

Lauren cocked her head. "Thank you for telling me the truth. Any other confessions?"

"Not that come to mind."

"Have you told your sister yet what you're up to?"

Doug's head dropped again. Then he chuckled. "Carmen knows. Finally."

"Why all the secrecy?"

Doug looked away as he tugged on his earlobe. "When I was younger, before Ruth came into my life, I struggled with depression. One thing led to another, and I started having suicidal thoughts. When she came along, she rescued me from all that. But when she got sick, well . . . you know . . ."

"Got it."

"Yeah. Then I met you and Brother Jim."

"The Bible says, 'If any man be in Christ, he is a new creation. The old is gone. Behold all things are become new.'"

Lauren and Doug cruised downhill for miles, toward Anaconda, coasting many stretches and hammering others. The free fall, with a fresh breeze whooshing across her skin, exhilarated Lauren.

A lake at altitude changed the scenery. Nothing like the size of Lake Victoria but offering the same calming effect. Then several phenomenal views of the rugged mountains lining the Divide shot goosebumps down her arms and legs.

Thanks to the artwork atop Flint Creek Pass, thoughts of Jeffrey filled Lauren's ride. The gleam in his eye and the mellow tone of his voice chased her. Yet the faster she rode, the more distant they became. Though she hadn't been running from her problems like Doug had, the advantages of discovering new places in wide-open spaces soothed her heart.

Rather than wallowing in disappointment, she would choose to discover more of what life had to offer. Why look for sympathy or expect God to play Santa Claus and drop a dream man into her life? Jeffrey had his own set of issues better left to him. If she became saddled with them, she would never realize God's best for her life. She could make room if the right person came along, but single life had its rewards too.

They rolled into Anaconda. Rooms were sold out. She felt grimy, and Doug had a gamy odor from several feet away. Or maybe that was her. Regardless, they grabbed a quick supper at a local sandwich shop and cycled to the city park on the edge of town, where they set up camp in twilight.

After they pitched their tents, Doug yanked a pannier off his bicycle and began rearranging items, setting some of them on the picnic table. "I know we're close to town, but we still ought to hang a bear bag."

"You worry too much."

Doug's head snapped around, and he glared at Lauren, his brow furrowed. "Listen, you can either put your scented items in here and enjoy sleeping without critters sniffing around your tent or . . . you can go find another campground. I don't suppose our neighbors would appreciate our disregard for their safety."

"Maybe I will find somewhere else." Lauren jutted her chin out and avoided eye contact.

"Oh come on." He sighed. "I didn't mean to tell you what to do. I'm just looking out for you . . . and . . . trying to prepare for bed."

"Well, I can do just fine by myself. You would've never survived in Africa, that's for sure."

"I'm glad I never had to try."

She'd never heard Doug so blunt. Maybe her own curt responses were unwarranted, but it'd been a long day and she wanted to settle in for the night. Doug was always thinking about survival in the wild. Why didn't he simply let God take care of things? But he *was* looking out for her. "I'm sorry. I'm tired, and I just want to go to sleep."

Doug held out the open pannier. "Trick or treat!"

She tossed in some food and toiletries. Then she reached into the compartment of another pannier, pulled out a small jar of perfume, and placed it on top of the other items.

Doug looked in, then back at Lauren, shaking his head. After cinching the pannier shut, he looked toward a grove on the edge of the campground for a suitable tree. But another camper offered to store their bag in his car instead.

After they bedded down in their respective tents, Lauren pulled out her phone again to read her Bible app. A new text message appeared. It was from Jeffrey. She couldn't help but smile.

> After seeing you in Missoula, miss you all
> the more. Stay safe, Pumpkin Spice.

Connecting her favorite latte to the color of her hair, Jeffrey had coined "Pumpkin Spice" as an endearing term for her. The moniker had stuck and reappeared when he did—emotionally. But that was Jeffrey, dropping in and out of her life—and likely the lives of other women—when loneliness cropped up. Perhaps his latest female interest hadn't panned out.

Despite the pitter-patter of her heart, she thought better of responding. Why drag out the agony when God had something—or someone—better on the road ahead? She wasn't going to play the fool again, not with this splendid opportunity to heal from old wounds and embark on a new adventure. What better way to move on than to cycle through new places and be around people who didn't know her?

Lauren's pulse quickened. Her initial trip to the mission field fifteen years earlier couldn't match this.

She typed "new thing" into the search bar. Up came Isaiah 43:19.

> Behold, I will do a new thing,
> Now it shall spring forth;
> Shall you not know it?
> I will even make a road in the wilderness
> And rivers in the desert.

# CHAPTER 6

Lauren peered out her mesh tent door. Despite the chilling cries of wildlife late into the night, chirping birds and a glimmering sunrise announced the arrival of morning. The horizontal rays of the sun spotlighted a doe and her fawn nibbling on brush at campground's edge. She whispered, "Lord, I love You. You're amazing! Thank You for another beautiful day."

She wriggled out of her tent, the first to do so in the still campground. For ten minutes she stood in silence watching the deer until they looked her way and then bounded into a stand of trees. Not wanting to awaken other travelers, she crawled back into her warm tent to read Scripture.

Soon, however, noises emerged from other campers, including a loud one from Doug's tent.

Lauren chuckled to herself. Was that a buck snort?

She finished her reading, reviewed a map of southwest Montana on her phone, and rose to prepare breakfast.

Doug squirmed out of his tent. "How did you sleep last night?"

"Famously. You?"

Doug yawned. He stretched his arms over his head and then pressed his hands into his lower back. Again he yawned. "I slept well, but I don't feel rested. Maybe I just need a day off."

"I know we talked about avoiding Yellowstone, but I'm having second thoughts. I'm going to regret not seeing it."

Doug smirked. "Well, no one's stoppin' ya."

"It looks like we're off course. Any idea how we get back on it? The route I looked at earlier went straight through Yellowstone."

"Sure. I can help you with that." Doug grabbed a map from his pannier and began studying it.

*He's not going there. But he* has *been a good travel companion. Yes, we get on each other's nerves, but who wouldn't when traveling by bicycle?* "Are you saying that you won't go there with me?"

"You are perceptive. I wouldn't be caught there on a bicycle in a million years. You got any bear spray?"

"No, I don't. You think I'll need it?"

"Yeah, you'll need it. I mean, I hope you don't, but if you go to Yellowstone, you're cycling right into the teeth of grizzly beardom. I wouldn't go there without something to protect you. You're guaranteed to see bears, which means they're guaranteed to see you."

*Where's his sense of adventure?* "God protected me in Uganda."

Doug sighed. "Yeah, but He needs your cooperation. He's given us tools so we can take responsibility for our own care. In this case, they're called bear spray and guns."

"Alright, smarty-pants. I understand."

Doug recoiled. "Get up on the wrong side of the air mattress?"

"I'm sorry. I'll look for bear spray in town this morning. Why don't we make a deal? I'll make breakfast if you pick out a route or two that will get me to Yellowstone."

"Seriously? Lauren, come on. It's so much better traveling together. You don't really want to go there, do you?"

"I do."

Doug sighed. "Then you're on."

Lauren looked up from the map long enough to dish another spork full of diced ham and eggs from the food pouch to her mouth. She understood the routes Doug suggested would get her to Yellowstone, but she wasn't sure which to take.

I-15 seemed like a bad idea. It would require backtracking. Granted, interstates came with a wide shoulder, but Doug had sustained a flat tire on the last one because of debris. Another route would send her farther down I-90 than the third route.

Why would someone who wanted to experience all that nature had to offer choose to bicycle on an interstate with tractor trailers whizzing by at eighty miles per hour? She'd had her fill of that two days ago. "So if I go to Butte and then through Twin Bridges, are you saying there are no shoulders?"

"No, I'm saying I don't know. You can check out trucker videos on YouTube. But it might be hard to tell the road conditions on a phone. Maybe the Montana DOT has a traffic flow map on its website. You could always try reaching back out to Bicycle America for advice." Doug shoveled in another glob of oatmeal. "Even if those roads have no shoulders, could they be as bad as US Route 12 in Idaho?"

"Oh, I loved that road. It was so beautiful."

"Yeah, but you remember as well as I do what happened there."

Lauren's head dropped. "How could I ever forget?"

"If you ride the interstate, at least you'll have services. Looks like there are frontage roads, but hard to say what they're like without talking to someone who knows. Even then, locals don't do a good job translating the conditions to bicycle travel. And remember, we're riding along the Continental Divide. Who knows what climbs you'll be facing. Are you sure you want to do this?"

Lauren ingested her final bite of oatmeal. "I think I'll ride to Butte and take Montana Route 2. Then I'll head to Twin Bridges."

Doug looked at his map again, then at Lauren's. "Yeah, that gets you back on the Bicycle America route before West Yellowstone. Sounds like a good plan. This route we've been following takes me to Montana Route 2 via Butte as well. If you'd prefer, I can take my rest day after we part ways."

"You know, you really have a good heart. Thank you. Let me think about it."

"Okay." Doug finished his breakfast and crawled back into his tent.

Lauren didn't want to offend him and genuinely appreciated his help and company—at least when things were going smoothly. She weighed her options as she tore down camp and packed her bicycle.

After she changed into her biking shoes, she went over to his tent. He appeared to be sleeping. She could just leave, but that didn't seem right after what they'd shared together. "Doug?"

"Huh . . . oh . . . I dozed off. What'd you decide?"

"I'm all ready to go. Are you staying?"

"You need bear spray, remember? By the time you get it, I'll be ready."

"If you can tough it out, I'd welcome your company."

"I'll meet you at the sandwich shop."

"Sorry, ma'am. We're all out of bear spray, but I could sell you a firearm. They're much more effective. Just need a driver's license and a quick background check. Can I assume you're a resident?"

A gun seemed rather extreme. And she'd never fired one. They caused harm. "That's okay. I won't be needing a gun."

"Ma'am, you can check the local department store on the edge of town. Or pick some up in Butte if you're heading that way. Either way, I wouldn't suggest cycling anywhere near Yellowstone without some form of defense."

"Thank you for the reminder."

"Before you go, you should know a female cyclist was mauled last month when she got in between a mama and baby bear. Lucky for her, she survived, but she'll never look the same or walk the same. Something happens every year."

"Thank you again. I'm sorry for her accident. That's so sad. I hope that means this year's attack is behind us."

The man shook his head, and Lauren walked out.

Before mounting her bicycle she noticed Doug cycling toward her.

"Get it?"

"No. They're all out. But he said I could pick up a can on the way out of town or in Butte."

"Why don't you just get a gun? Everyone else around here carries one."

"I don't need a gun. Besides, I wouldn't know what to do with it."

"You'd figure that out quickly if you found yourself cornered by an angry bear."

Three youths Lauren had worked with years ago shot themselves to escape their pain. Only one survived, but with nightmarish repercussions. Maybe the other two would've found another way to end their lives had they not had access to firearms, but guns had been their first and last choice of destruction.

On the outskirts of town, they passed a shopping plaza.

"Wanna stop?" Doug said.

"Let's go to Butte. I'm just getting warmed up."

It'd been seven months since Doug had said goodbye to his beloved Ruth. Somehow it felt much longer than it had only a month ago. That's when Lauren dropped into his life, and the coincidence was not lost on him. He was enjoying his life now. The road ahead seemed brighter.

Montana Route 1 led to I-90, where the pair hopped on the interstate to squeeze through another mountain pass. The scenery from the open space of the interstate mirrored his new outlook. Balding mountains, covered with evergreens at their base and only a smattering at the top, surrounded them. Snow dusted the tops of a few mountains in the distance.

Lauren shouted from behind, and Doug slowed until she came abreast on the wide shoulder. "Wow! Can you believe how beautiful those mountains are?"

"You got that right."

But more than her observation, the enthusiasm and joy resounding from her voice made Doug feel like he was cycling on air. While traveling with someone had its moments, what a blessing it was to still have Lauren by his side.

A pair of tractor trailers roared by. Noxious diesel fumes tainted the pristine air.

*I hope pedaling up those beautiful mountains doesn't kill me.*

Once through the pass, they exited the interstate and followed frontage roads to a more tranquil setting.

# CHAPTER 7

Over two hours after leaving Anaconda, Lauren and Doug entered Butte.

They'd ridden more than twenty miles without stopping. Bathroom breaks in communities could be more awkward than in remote areas because not all establishments offered public facilities. Lauren couldn't drop her pants roadside here like she could where no one was around. The interstate had posed a similar dilemma.

Finally a small, rustic gathering spot on the outskirts of Butte appeared. It looked more like a barn than a bar, with its weathered wood turned gray and a few shingles askew on top. The muffled sound of a jukebox and the *Open* sign flashing neon orange lifted Lauren's spirits, despite the iron bars in the dark-tinted window. Judging from the line of bikes outside—the kind with tailpipes—it was a hangout for bikers. But there was no time to scope out the place. She needed a bathroom, and quick.

She scooted into the building to the sound of "Born to Be Wild" and glanced around for restrooms.

The bartender pointed to the far corner.

The backs of several men wearing leather vests with club logos disappeared as, one by one, the men swiveled around to see why the bartender pointed. Eleven o'clock in the morning seemed early for beer, but that wasn't stopping them.

Leers from two wild-whiskered men reminded Lauren that she was the only occupant wearing shorts, let alone spandex. A spike of adrenaline hit her, as did a chill. Ugandans used to look at her with curiosity, perhaps due to her fair complexion, so she'd become accustomed to attention from strangers. But this was different.

Even so, the mounting discomfort of the fluids she'd consumed the past two hours, the sight of a few leather-clad women, and the daylight streaming through the cracks in the door persuaded her to run to the bathroom rather than outside to her bicycle.

Mercifully the song ended.

She pivoted to the bathroom and nearly bumped into a biker coming in the other direction. As he passed her, she turned and noticed a patch across the back of his shoulders that read *Rattlers*.

He, too, turned around. "Watch where you're goin', toots."

After she exited the restroom, one of the women got up and intercepted her. "Whatcha doin', sistah?"

"Oh, I just had to use the restroom. I have a full day of cycling ahead of me."

"Cyclin'? As in, *bi*-cycling?"

"Yes. I'm riding across the country." Lauren's internal clock was approaching zero, and she needed to get out of here. She turned to leave when—

"Oooooo-weeee. Hey, everybody, this gal's bicycling across the country. No kiddin'. Would ya look at that? Won't that mess up your pretty hair and nails?"

*Pretty* must have been a relative term after two evenings with no shower. But when a few chairs scraped against the wood floor and burly men rose from them, a lump the size of a wad of energy bar formed in her throat. She gasped for a breath.

As others approached to join the banter, a man at the bar swiveled around, got off his stool, and walked toward Lauren and the woman. Tattoos covered his arms, each as thick as Lauren's thighs. Emblazoned on his right arm was a spotted snake curled around a set of handlebars, its fork-tongued face doubling as a headlight. The name *Charlie* arced beneath it. A bandanna covered the top of the brute's head, with a scruffy beard springing forth below it.

He stopped in front of Lauren and glared down at her. "Travelin' alone?" His eyes proceeded to undress her.

The smell of beer invaded her nostrils.

Revving engines silenced outside.

"Not exactly." Lauren's honesty had always been lauded as a worthy trait, but it might not play well in this setting.

Two other hooligans stepped forward.

Her chest squeezed as she sucked in air.

"What's that supposed to mean?" The man's lip curled. He'd apparently not showered in a month.

The door flung open. Doug walked in. "Lauren, let's go."

Another ruffian close to the door slammed it shut and returned to his seat.

"Not so fast, fancy-pants. We ain't done talkin'."

Again the door opened. In sauntered three giants, bigger than the one questioning Lauren. When one of them turned to close the door, a distinctive patch arced from shoulder to shoulder on the back of his leather vest. It read *Narrow Gate Bikers*. The red letters popped against their black background. When he turned back around, she noticed a white cross on the vest's front, splotches of red dripping from it.

Rather than sitting for refreshment, the trio lingered near the entryway, hands on hips, perhaps sensing they'd arrived in the midst of an unfinished discussion.

"Howdy," the first and largest of them said.

Lauren's inquisitor looked over at the intruder. "You again?"

"Yeah, headed to Sturgis, just like you. You ain't givin' this young lady a hard time, are ya?" The man stepped forward.

Doug grabbed Lauren's arm and pivoted to leave. "Let's go." As he led Lauren toward the door, he exchanged smiles with the friendly giant. "See you on the road."

"Sure thing. Y'all be safe out there now, ya hear?"

Once outside, Lauren muttered, "It felt so dark in there. Creeped me out."

Doug nodded. "We had all sorts of biker gangs around LA." He pointed at a logo on the rear fender of one of the parked motorcycles. "I didn't notice this until you were in there."

Lauren recognized the snake-infested emblem. *Rattlers MC* appeared in script above the sinister artwork. On the motorbike beside it, *Curl up with a Rattler* surrounded an adaptation of the same logo, with a dagger protruding from the snake's mouth in place of its tongue. A chill traversed her spine. On the other side of her, *1%er* appeared inside a diamond-shaped emblem.

Shouting emanated from the bar.

Doug pulled out his phone and snapped a few quick photos of the motorcycles, including the few misfits with crosses on them. "Let's get out of here."

Lauren started for her bicycle, then stopped. "What about the men who got us out of there? We can't just leave them."

"What can we do for them that they can't do for themselves?"

"Call the police?"

Doug cocked his head. "Okay. But not until we're a half mile down the road."

They hopped on their bicycles and departed with the urgency of children who'd escaped the clutches of a bully. After several hundred yards a gunshot rang out.

Their slow speed would be no match for motorcycles. Doug pushed harder. Unlike at the bar in Drummond two nights ago, these boys took tension to another level, apparently willing to shed blood over it.

He sped past Lauren, who'd squeezed her brakes. Still on the main road, she suddenly stopped.

So he did too. "What're ya doin'?"

"It's been more than a half mile. I'm calling the police."

"Wait! Let's get off this road."

Doug pointed at a road to the right, began cycling, and turned onto it. He cycled through tree cover that would mask them from the main drag. Lauren followed him.

He pulled off the road and waited for her under a canopy of trees. She rolled in.

"Okay, try your call now."

She dialed 911. "I'd like to report a disturbance. It happened at a bar on Rustlers Road." She looked up at Doug. "Where are we?"

A swarm of motorcycles rumbled on the main road.

"Outskirts of Butte, southwest side."

The sound got louder but soon faded as the bikers passed them, unaware of their presence.

"We're on the outskirts of Butte on the southwest side of town. We're on bicycles. We were in the bar to use the bathroom. I think a bunch of motorcycles just left the scene . . ." She looked at Doug. "Cattle Call?"

He nodded.

"Yes, that's the one. Some biker gangs were there. I saw a patch for the Rattlers. Then three men from Narrow Gate Bikers came in. We got out before the shouting began. Then we heard a gunshot as we left . . . Okay. Thank you." Lauren ended the call.

"What'd they say?"

"They said they'd come check it out. But they made it sound like a common occurrence."

Doug looked down at his map. A nauseated sensation washed over him. "I don't like this."

"Like what?"

"I *really* don't like this." He dug into his pannier and fished out his six-shooter, placing it in the makeshift holster of his belt bag.

Lauren frowned. "What are you doing?"

Doug looked at her. "Can you think of a better way to protect us?" He looked down at his map. "We should find somewhere to eat, but I'm not inclined to get back on that road just yet."

Lauren pointed to the grove of trees beside them. "Let's eat here."

"Good idea."

A half hour later, after firing up the Jetboil and consuming two pouches of freeze-dried food, Lauren and Doug resumed their ride. Despite the distant *vroom* of motorcycle engines, they assumed the coast was clear.

The duo headed toward the south end of Butte.

Lauren couldn't get that close encounter with the motorcycle gang out of her mind. *Doug will keep me safe, but if I go to Yellowstone without him, maybe I do need some form of protection.*

They stopped at a department store. She scurried to the sporting goods aisle while Doug guarded their bicycles outside.

A middle-aged man wearing a corporate vest met her from behind the counter. "Could I help you, ma'am?"

"Yes. I'm heading to Yellowstone. What can you tell me about bear defenses?"

"I have bear spray as well as firearms . . . ah"—he looked at her cycling shorts—"but not handguns. If it were me, I'd take both. And I'm not just trying to sell you something you don't need. I get paid by the hour. There's a good gun shop in town if you need a handgun. They may ask for proof of Montana residency. Are you traveling alone?"

Maybe she would be, but not now. So she said, "No." She looked to the side for a moment. The pit in her stomach deepened. "How prevalent are biker gangs in Montana?"

"What makes you ask?"

"We saw some bikers an hour ago at a bar on the southwest side of town. One of the patches said *Rattlers*. Kind of scary looking."

"Just so ya know, there's biker gangs everywhere. And, yeah, I've seen reports of gangs doing bad stuff around here. Meth labs in secluded places and a big presence on Indian reservations." The man looked at Lauren's helmet. "You cycling through?"

"Yes."

"In that case, you definitely need some protection, and for more than bears."

"Has there been a lot of violence in this area?"

The man smirked, then his expression softened. "The biggest issue around here seems to be suicide. Young people in particular. Five students in our school system took their lives last year."

"That's so sad. How big is Butte?"

"Thirty thousand."

Lauren stepped away from the counter as her mouth opened. She stared wide-eyed at the man. "You're kidding. That seems like a high suicide rate for such a small city."

"Suicide capital of the US."

She stepped closer to the counter to keep the conversation semi-private. "It's hard to imagine, given the beauty here."

"Well, come back in the winter, live here for a month or two, and see if you still think it's so beautiful."

She studied the man's face. His sarcasm seemed like a sincere attempt to get her to heed his advice. "I don't want a gun. But I will take you up on some bear spray."

"Whatever you say, ma'am." The clerk looked at her and pursed his lips. "Make sure you read the instructions *before* you need to use it."

Armed with two cans of bear spray, Lauren followed Doug as they turned onto Montana Route 2 toward Whitehall, reentering the forest on another sparsely traveled road.

A few miles later the grade steepened, slowing progress. The thunder of motorcycles approaching from behind raised goosebumps on the back of Lauren's neck. No one was around.

The rumble of Harleys echoed through the forest, coming in and out of earshot as Lauren and Doug twisted around switchbacks, creeping their heavy loads up the pass.

The roar increased. When she could no longer hear herself pant, she began trembling.

The motorbikes caught up and rushed by. The lead driver waved as he passed, saluting the pedal-bikers with a thumbs-up.

Lauren's chest loosened.

Smoke puffed out with the blat of accelerating engines. The motorcycles ascended the next incline and disappeared. Their pungent exhaust fumes dissipated as the wilderness suffocated the disruptive noise.

A hawk chattered from atop a tree to her right.

The climb intensified. Her legs burned. However, in her rear-view mirror, the road twisted to the size of a pin far below, the splendid vista competing for what little breath she had left. Hard to believe how far they'd risen.

Skinny and erect lodgepole pines lined either side of the road, extending to infinity around them. The travelers had become one with nature.

She pulled onto a scenic turnout, where she could appreciate the panorama without the stress of balancing her bicycle during their inch-by-inch ascent. Doug soon joined her.

Across the road a rock ledge narrowed to the apex of their surroundings, pointing heavenward.

Lauren scanned the forest. "Glorious, isn't it?"

"Sure is. I think we're at the Continental Divide." Doug looked down at his map. "Pipestone Pass."

"There's no one around. This is incredible. Did you see the views behind us coming up?"

"Fantastic. Must've been fifty or a hundred miles out."

Lauren checked the time. "The sun's getting lower. Any places to stay in Whitehall?"

Doug unfolded the map. "There's a bed-and-breakfast off Route 2. Do you have a signal?"

"Yes."

Lauren called and booked two rooms. "Look for a gravel road to the right in about five miles. There's a sign for *Wild Divide B&B*. They're a half mile off the main road."

The two took one last look to absorb the spectacular surroundings at Pipestone Pass.

Before long they crested the mountain and accelerated downhill. The wind against Lauren's face and the effortless free fall invited the illusion of weightlessness. Several miles later they sped by a road on the right.

Doug looped back to look for a sign. "This is it."

The rocky road beneath her narrow tires felt more like cycling an icy mountain-bike trail. They skidded left and right as they crawled along the treacherous lane.

Lauren squeezed her brakes but fell over before she could put her feet on solid ground, smacking against a rock. "Owww."

"You okay?"

Pain radiated from her elbow. She crawled out from under her bicycle. Rubbing her elbow, she stretched out her arm, then flexed it.

"Yes. I'm okay. Stupid me. I shouldn't have ridden that gravel."

She lifted her bicycle and began walking it.

Doug dismounted and walked his bicycle beside hers, struggling to push the loaded recumbent with its underseat steering.

Lauren's arm was throbbing. *What if I broke something? How will I ever get through Yellowstone, let alone get home? And what if I have a more serious mishap when I'm alone?*

"You're kinda quiet," Doug said. "You okay?"

"Yes, I'm okay."

# CHAPTER 8

With a few hours of sunlight to spare, Lauren and Doug rounded a curve and found a larger *Wild Divide B&B* sign than the one at the mouth of the road. A border collie barked as it approached them with its tail wagging, followed by a golden retriever, its sleek coat shimmering. Doug reached out his hand to pat the retriever while the collie circled Lauren.

She flexed her arm. The pain was subsiding.

A man atop a paint horse waved. He seemed busy with ranch chores but pointed them toward the large building a few hundred feet ahead. Several Black Angus were grazing in a fenced pasture.

Doug and Lauren rested their bicycles against the side of the ranch house. A kitten, white with black splotches, rubbed against Lauren's ankles, its soft fur caressing her skin.

Goosebumps climbed her leg.

She picked up the kitty and cuddled its soft fur close to her face. Its purring pulled her heartstrings. She stroked its coat, bringing forth a squeak from its tiny mouth.

As Doug reached for the doorbell, the door opened.

"Welcome!" A lady with long, graying hair set in a loose braid opened the door wider. "Come in."

Lauren set the kitten on the ground, then followed Doug inside.

"I'm Lucinda, one of your hosts for the evening. That's my husband, Jack, on Scout. We're glad you could make it. Did you have trouble finding us?"

"Not really," Doug said.

Lauren closed the door behind her. "I love your cat."

"Well, don't get too attached." Lucinda smiled. "We lose them faster than dollar bills at a casino."

"What do you mean?" Doug said.

"The predators around here outnumber the domestic stock. We're losing cattle left and right."

Lauren winced. "Oh, the poor thing. It's so precious."

The muffled sound of feet on crushed rock grew until the door swung open with a squeak. The man they'd seen on the horse walked in, a holstered gun slung on his hip.

"Hello, I'm her other half. You can call me Jack."

Doug and Jack shook hands.

Likely in their fifties or early sixties, Lucinda and Jack greeted one another with a kiss. She smiled as he wrapped his arm around her.

Then she looked at Lauren again. "We're not about to confine the cat to the house. We've used fences, cages, and other shelters with limited success."

"What sort of predators are you talking about?" Doug said.

Jack chuckled. "We have 'em all here. Wolves, cougars, bears, even eagles. Foxes too. The research geniuses thought it was a great idea to load up Yellowstone and the surrounding area with more bear and wolves. But they didn't give landowners a vote. Too many predators, too little food. It makes the predators wander farther from their habitat for food and attack animals they otherwise wouldn't. Then there's eagles—we can't shoot 'em. Another protected species. Yup, too many predators. But we're tryin' to change that." He grinned.

"Jack's a guide. We host a lot of hunters."

Judging from the head mounts in the open living quarters, that wasn't surprising.

"Did you shoot all these?" Lauren said.

Jack went around the room, pointing to each trophy mount, seven in total, including two bears, a cougar, an elk, a deer, a wolf, and a fox. "I bagged this one, my son this one, Lucinda shot this nasty guy from point-blank range, I got those two, Lucinda that one, and our other son the one over there."

"That 'nasty guy' looks like a grizzly bear," Doug said.

"Right you are. Scared the livin' daylights out of us. We'd been tracking a cougar. It snuck up behind us, then let out a growl. Never been so scared in all my life. Lucinda swiveled around in time to save the day. Never seen one that close. Alive, that is. And don't care to again."

Lucinda stepped forward. "Let me show you to your rooms."

The two followed her downstairs. In an open lounge area a large tapestry of a grizzly bear in a winter setting hung behind a timber-framed sofa. Issues of *Backwoodsman* and *Outdoor Life* sat on the glass coffee table. A shared bathroom stood between their rooms, which were appointed with professional photographs of Yellowstone and its inhabitants.

Lauren and Doug retrieved what gear they would need for the evening—plus all scented items—and locked their bicycles together outside. Other than wildlife that might chew through a pannier, their belongings were far removed from city pilferers under the open night sky in the wild recesses of Montana.

Breakfast the next morning was like no breakfast Lauren had ever had. She'd enjoyed wild game in Uganda, but never elk steak.

"We're taking different routes today," Doug said as the four of them sat at the table. "Do you know where Route 41 is?"

Jack looked at him with furrowed brow. "Why? It's always better to travel in pairs." He turned toward Lauren. "Especially when one of ya is female."

"Lauren wants to take in Yellowstone. I'd like to avoid it altogether."

"I can't say as I blame you. It's smothered with tourists this time of year." Lucinda got up and followed the scent of coffee cake into the kitchen.

Lauren remained content to enjoy another bite of her cinnamon toast with homemade strawberry preserves.

"Route 41 is just down the hill out here. About five miles. Turn right onto the main drag." Then Jack looked at Lauren. "But it does get quite hilly in places, especially if ya plan to go through Virginia City. There's some cool places over there—old mining towns. Nice scenery too. But it's a long way between services."

"That sounds so exciting!" Lauren caught Doug rolling his eyes.

"Some of the roads that way lack shoulders, but the traffic may be sparse enough to give you plenty of room—at least until ya get closer to the park. You're 140 miles, give or take, away from Yellowstone. What's that, two or three days on a bicycle? Maybe four with the hills."

"What about places to stay along the way?" Doug said.

"There's places to stay in Twin Bridges . . . Ennis . . . maybe even Virginia City, but I'd call ahead. Plenty of places in West Yellowstone, but they fill up fast this time of year and will run you some money."

"I can always stay at a campground," Lauren said.

Jack raised his eyebrows. "You could, but you may be competing for space with motorcyclists. Sturgis is coming up. We've already had several of them come through here."

She pivoted on her chair. "How bad are the biker gangs around here?"

"This time of year, there's plenty of 'em around. They won't bother most people as long as folks stay outta their way. They don't bother me, but I'm a man. Are you carryin'?"

"Carrying what?"

Jack looked at Doug, then back at Lauren. "A gun."

"No, just bear spray."

Lucinda returned from the kitchen with slices of fresh coffee cake. "My girlfriend cycles for exercise, and last year some bikers stopped when she flatted. Said they wanted to *help* her." She air-quoted the word *help*. "Made her super uncomfortable. Lucky for her, a sheriff rode by at just the right time. Then she called her husband and got off the road until they'd all gone to Sturgis a few weeks later."

"I'd recommend indoor accommodations for the next few weeks. Other than that, campgrounds with plenty of people around." Jack eyed Doug. "Where are you headed?"

"Frontage roads along I-90, then into Wyoming once I clear Yellowstone to the east."

"You'll have plenty of options on that route. And good scenery too."

*Maybe it isn't such a good idea to split ways with Doug around here. But do I want him to escort me all the way across the country? Besides, I can't imagine being this close to Yellowstone and not going there.*

"Thank you for the advice," Lauren said. "And for breakfast. So delicious."

With their gear packed the two travelers said goodbye to their gracious hosts. They walked their bicycles back to the main road, then coasted four miles downhill to Route 41. They stopped and unclipped their shoes. Straddling her bicycle, Lauren walked it alongside Doug's but at a comfortable distance.

Doug twisted around to speak, then discovered she was beside him. "You text me each night, you hear?"

*Awwwww!* Lauren smiled. "Only if you do the same for me."

Doug nodded. "Are you *sure* you wanna do this?"

"Yes, I'm sure. My parents always wanted to take us to Yellowstone but never got the chance. I can't pass this up."

He glanced skyward as he took a deep breath. "You know, you could always head east out of Yellowstone if you want a riding partner again."

"Maybe I will. I just need to do this. I'll see how it goes."

Wincing, he nodded. "Okay, if you insist. But, please, be safe."

"Could I pray for us before we part?"

Doug gazed at her.

She looked back, her cheeks rounding into a smile. She couldn't help it. Warmth filled her chest cavity. Something about him was so sweet. And they'd been through so much together since meeting only a few weeks ago. His glazed look was beyond interpretation, other than a connectedness they would always share from the experiences God had allowed them. Her head tipped to one side in curious anticipation.

"Sure." Doug cleared his throat. "Go ahead." He shut his eyes and bowed his head.

Lauren did likewise. After a moment of silence to still herself, she began. "Dear Heavenly Father, we ask that You keep us in Your care as we venture separately to parts unknown. Lord, thank You for connecting us and bringing us to this intersection safely. May our interactions with the people we meet honor You. Give Doug peace as he travels. Plant in his heart a strong desire to know You better. Thank You again for this opportunity to enjoy the wonderful world You created for us. In Jesus's name, amen."

"Thanks, Lauren." Doug leaned toward her with his arm outstretched. His bicycle began to fall, so he grabbed the under-seat handlebars and adjusted his stance. Then he rested his hand on Lauren's shoulder. "Be safe."

"I will. You too." She leaned down, cupped her hand on his arm, and pulled close to him, resting her neck against his. Her heart fluttered, so she backed away with a smile. "I should go now."

Doug nodded, his puppy-dog eyes tugging at Lauren's heart.

She mounted her bicycle. "Bye."

He remained silent, his blank stare saying what his lips couldn't, though it was a message she couldn't decode.

*What are these feelings inside?*

Yet the road drew her. She began cycling Route 41. She looked around to see Doug sitting on his bicycle watching her. Turning her head to watch where she was going, she waved her arm and gazed at him in her helmet-mounted rearview mirror, the image shrinking with each pedal stroke until it blurred. Water had formed in her eyes, though she knew not whether from the wind against her face or from leaving a special friend behind. He sat motionless on his bicycle. Then she rounded the bend and could no longer see him.

He shouldn't have let her go like that. A woman with Lauren's physical attributes would be a prime target for a sick man—or a healthy one looking for meaningful companionship. She'd departed defenseless, but for a couple cans of bear spray and prayers to the Almighty.

Doug stared down Route 41. *I could catch her.*

However, he knew better. A woman after freedom would find it one way or the other. Besides, the route she was traveling not only contradicted *his* better judgment but also the opinions of others who knew more about the area. Maybe she expected him to come after her. All the more reason to let her learn a lesson and stay clear of the consequences himself.

Ruth had made so many decisions like Lauren's. They exasperated Doug, when Ruth kicked logic aside in favor of unrestrained emotion. Too much heart with too little head often led to him helping her pick up the broken pieces of a disappointing escapade—or a shattered dream. *Women.*

However, something more troubling had frozen him in time and space. Yet again he'd been abandoned, left alone in his sorrow. Maybe that's why she'd asked God to give him peace. *Hmmmpf. She could've helped fulfill her own request if she weren't so blasted headstrong.*

Doug scanned the countryside. Indeed, nothing—and no one—was around, other than what God had put here, *plus* a few road signs that acknowledged impending decisions for travelers. His had already been made.

Logic aside, the pit of his stomach suggested he already missed Lauren. The sensation worked its way up to his face. When water formed around his eyes, he caught himself. *Don't be silly. She's too young for you anyway. I have her number, so maybe I'll see her again. But why did I let her go?*

Chirping birds interrupted his rumination, suggesting he was *not* alone. A gentle breeze caressed the whiskers on his cheeks and the hair on his arms and legs. *God, I know You're busy up there, but if You could help me and protect Lauren, I sure would appreciate it. And, I don't know, can You do something about this ache in my heart?* He grabbed the handlebars, clipped into the pedals, and cast off.

# CHAPTER 9

Route 41 had little traffic. When Lauren reached Silver Star, the road expanded with a rideable shoulder, and the surroundings didn't feel as remote. Roadside trees had all but disappeared in favor of grasslands. Mountains rose in the distance, right where they belonged for a cyclist who was more interested in logging miles than climbing. The water in the Jefferson River sparkled as it turned toward her before snaking its way north. Life was good.

*I wonder how Doug is.*

A sudden jolt shook Lauren. Then a loud ping rang out.

The rear end of the bike kicked left. A rock the size of a Ping-Pong ball flew into the grass. In a split second the vibration had worked its way from underneath the bike up her spine into her mouth, where her teeth clenched. She squeezed the handlebars as she pedaled on.

However, the ride felt different. A glance downward, and she gulped. Her rear tire was as flat as the valley around her. She slowed to a stop.

What would she do now? She hadn't had a flat tire since she left Portland nearly a month earlier. When she first met Doug, he'd just fixed a flat on his bike. He expressed shock and concern over her admission that she didn't know how to do the repair. She'd watched YouTube videos before embarking and packed a bike repair pamphlet. Thank goodness the bike shop had outfitted her with the necessary tools and supplies. But where had she put them?

As she wheeled her bicycle off the pavement, she checked for snakes, then rested it on the grass before removing the rear panniers. She pulled out a stuff sack labeled Spare Parts and rummaged around in it until she found a set of tire levers and a spare tube. The mechanic at the bike shop had demonstrated how to fix a flat tire, but she'd never done it herself.

Where to begin? She could call Doug, but they'd already gone in different directions. Besides, it would give him reason to say, "I told you so." But he knew what he was doing when it came to bicycle repairs. She didn't.

As she looked at the tools in her hand and the bicycle on the ground, the sound of a vehicle caught her attention. An old pickup truck with a rusty bumper approached, its body patched with multi-colored sheet metal. As it stopped, blue exhaust fumes passed over the firewood piled in the back and caught up in Lauren's throat.

A man with straggly gray hair, who mustn't have shaved or shampooed in at least a week, hopped out of the truck wearing grungy overalls, then limped toward her.

"What's a purdy girl like you doin' out here? Ya lost?"

Lauren looked up and down the empty road. "Just a flat tire, but I'm all set. I have what I need to fix it."

"Ya sure? Cuz we can load that thing in the back and take her to the nearest bike shop." The man flicked his head toward Route 41 North. "Up in Butte."

"But aren't you heading in the opposite direction?"

The man's eyes scanned her from head to toe, then toe to head—looks that Lauren's radar was accustomed to detecting.

Then he smiled. Her dentist back in Locust Grove would have a field day with this guy.

"Ma'am, for you, I'd make a special trip. Ain't got nuttin' goin' on today. Just headin' to Yellowstone to take care of a few loose ends, but it can wait."

"No, that won't be necessary. But thank you."

The man stepped closer. Lauren whiffed a nasty odor, then coughed. Apparently he'd not bathed in a week either.

Eyeing the tube and tire levers in Lauren's hand, the man reached out to receive them. "Lemme see if I can help."

*God, I just want him to go away. Help me please.*

"No, I appreciate the offer, but, really, I have everything under control."

The man scowled. "Are you sayin' get lost? Ain't I good enough for ya? Huh?"

Lauren studied the expression on his face. "I'm sorry. I didn't mean to be rude. It's just that—"

An object to the north caught her attention. A man was hammering the pedals of his loaded bicycle as it rocked side to side.

The old man looked around and saw the cyclist approaching. Then he spit into the grass. "Fine. Have it your way." He trudged to his truck, slammed the door shut, and sped off, granules from his spinning tires sprinkling her shins.

As the broad-shouldered cyclist approached, he shouted, "Have a problem?"

"I had two. But now I'm down to one."

The man, dressed in khaki cargo shorts with a loose-fitting, bright-orange top, squeezed his brakes. His mountain bike rolled to a stop three feet from Lauren's side.

When he removed his sunglasses, her heart skipped a beat. Eyes as blue as the Montana sky looked back at her. Wavy blond locks peeked out around his helmet. Thanks to the summer sun, he wore a raccoon's mask, the skin around his eyes much fairer than the golden tan on the rest of his face.

"Hey, I'm Lars. Did you break down?"

"Hey, Lars, I'm Lauren. Yes, I have a flat. You came in the nick of time."

"Who was that who sped away?"

"A stranger who wasn't helping me any."

"Guy seemed like he was in a hurry. I ate his exhaust a few miles back. I'd be glad to help you fix the flat."

Lars got off his bicycle and set it on the ground behind Lauren's. "That's not a violin, is it?"

"Yes, why?"

"I've never seen a violin on a touring bicycle. And I've seen a lot of touring bicycles around here." Lars stood well over six feet tall. When his ring-less hands reached for Lauren's tools, bulging biceps slid out of his sleeves.

Lauren dropped the tools into his hands. "How can I help you?"

"This'll just take a minute."

Within no time Lars had removed the rear wheel and replaced the damaged tube. "Here. I'll hold the tire while you pump it up. How's that?"

"That sounds fine."

"Where's your pump?"

Lauren looked below her bicycle frame's top tube, but the pump wasn't there. *Oh no.* Her breath caught in her throat. "Where's my pump? Never mind, I have CO2 cartridges."

"Oh, don't waste those." Lars set the tire on the ground and retrieved his pump. Then he attached it to the valve stem and looked up at Lauren, who stood ready to pump. "Mind if I do it for you?"

"It's alright. I can manage."

"Where you heading?"

"Yellowstone."

"Me too."

Lauren kept pumping despite the increasing resistance and an arm still aching from yesterday's fall. "I've always wanted to go there."

"I've been there many times."

"You from around here?"

"Yeah. Missoula."

"Do you know Pastor James Covington of New Hope Alliance?"

"Yeah, not real well though. Brother Jim knows lots of people."

Lauren stopped pumping and pinched the tire. "How's that?"

Lars looked at the recommended inflation on the wall of her tire, then at the gauge on the pump. "Just right. But it looks like you may have damaged your rim. You didn't ride it by any chance?"

Lauren grinned sheepishly.

"Let's hope it holds up. I can ride with you if you'd like."

"Thank you. That would be great."

Lars's strong draft pulled Lauren into Twin Bridges in no time.

A stilted water tower stood over the town it identified, its flat surroundings visible for miles. It looked like it had been there for decades, maybe even a century. No fancy lettering or pictures, only black letters on a riveted steel tank painted aluminum gray. A firehouse-red rice hat topped the conical sphere. The piers matched that of a radio tower, except for being fanned out and wider at the base. A few accoutrements could've rendered an artifice of a long-legged Mr. Tin Man.

A water tower in a mountainous region seemed out of place, but this area was as flat as a Midwestern wheat field, though mountains in the distance encased the grand valley.

Along Main Street, they stopped at the Beaverhead Grill. Lauren offered to buy lunch. It was the least she could do for him saving her day and rescuing her from a bad experience with . . . well . . . a dirty old man.

"So what are you doing with a violin on your bicycle?" Lars handed his menu to the departing server.

"It's part of who I am. I couldn't leave home without it."

"I see. And where's home?"

"Virginia now. But I lived in Africa for fifteen years."

"You're kidding."

"No, I'm not kidding. Actually Montana reminds me more of Uganda than Virginia. I love it out here. The views are amazing." Lauren admired his chiseled chin. "What's it like to live here?"

"The winters can be long and hard. Summers are nice but short. The population swells with tourists. But they help pay the bills."

"I'm glad we can help."

Lars chuckled.

"What keeps you here?"

Lars glanced out the window. "My kids."

"Oh, you have kids? How many?"

"Enough to keep me occupied."

"How old are they?"

"Twenty-four and twenty-two . . . and two . . . He lives with his mother."

"Do the others live with you?"

"They're pretty much on their own."

The server set their burgers on the table.

After chitchatting about Lauren's tour, Lars's bicycle rides in the area, and Yellowstone National Park, they finished eating.

"Could I treat you to an ice cream sundae for dessert?" he said.

"Ooool! I love ice cream."

With limited dessert options at the restaurant, Lauren paid the bill, and they rode down the street to a bar their server had recommended.

"We have the best ice cream in town. Come right in and have a seat," the bartender said.

The Watering Hole had five stools in front of its bar, but Lauren walked past an older couple eating sundaes at a table to her left to sit at the next table.

Lars followed her.

Light-quenching black curtains on two windows along the back wall—the only two in the establishment—were open enough for the afternoon sun to stream in and illuminate the dark-stained floor. A man with a ten-gallon hat drank from a beer mug at the far end of the bar.

Lauren ordered the classic hot fudge sundae.

"I'll have the same, but do you have amaretto?" Lars said.

"Sure do."

"I'd like a touch of that on mine. And a cherry on top if possible."

"Ma'am, would you care for any liqueur on yours?"

Lauren looked down, then shook her head. "No thank you."

As the bartender turned away, Lauren looked up at Lars, who grinned. His teeth were whiter than the snow atop those distant mountains, intensified by the dark tan on his cheeks. Dimples that would accept dimes deepened as his smile widened. A wash of emotion spiked in her chest.

She looked away just as he said, "Do you have kids too?"

"Just two brothers . . . No. No kids. Although I used to have hundreds."

Lars's forehead wrinkled.

"In Uganda." She hoped her trembling voice didn't show through. Maybe if she got him to talk more, she'd come to her senses. "Are you close to yours?"

The bartender brought their desserts to the table. "I understand you can build up quite an appetite on a bicycle. Are you two passing through on a trip?"

"Yes," Lars said.

"Did you know about the bike camp across from the fairgrounds, down by the old children's home?"

"Children's home?" Lauren said.

"It's closed now, but Twin Bridges had an orphanage for years. They came here from all over the state. After the gold boom went bust, hard times landed children at the home. I suppose their parents just couldn't afford to provide for them . . . or didn't want to."

"That's so sad," Lauren said. "Is there any way to tour it?"

"Tour it. Why, ma'am, there haven't been any kids there for decades. Although, rumor is they still haunt it . . . The property's just wasting away."

"I worked at an orphanage in Uganda. Orphans and places that took care of them are near to my heart."

"I must say, that's the first time anyone ever asked me for a tour of the old children's home. Let me make a call or two. I know the owner. He's been looking to unload that property for years, so maybe he'll show you around."

"Thanks. I appreciate your kindness."

"I knew there was a bike camp," Lars said, "but I've never used it. Do they take reservations?"

"First come, first serve. Lots of people traveling through here on bikes, so I'd stake your claim early. It's south on 41. You may need to share space with other cyclists. I'm not sure how it works, to tell you the truth. Some people got together several years ago and put up a small shelter with a shower. And it doesn't cost a cent. The Beaverhead River is right there too if you want to cool off."

Lars's eyebrows shot up.

"That sounds interesting," Lauren said.

The bartender left the table, and the two scooped spoons into their sundaes.

"Want to jump in the river after we get out of here?" Lars said.

"Maybe."

After they finished, the bartender returned with the check. "I just heard back from the owner of the orphanage. He gave me the caretaker's number. I wrote it on the check. He said to give her a call and she'll show you around."

# CHAPTER 10

The road came with little traffic and astonishing views. Buttes and barren escarpments created an obstacle course for Doug to cycle. A prominent opening to a hillside cavern piqued his curiosity. Rather than awakening den dwellers that might not welcome his intrusion, he pedaled on.

A deer jumped the wire fence on his left and darted across the road. Two others behind it saw Doug and veered to their left, bounding ahead of him in a race he would never win, their white tails flashing before the pair stopped while Doug passed.

A solitary rail line accompanied his journey through a valley covered with yellow-green grasslands. Lime-green brush or a smattering of trees popped up as he twisted through larger-than-life hills, overlaying one another as the road squeezed through. One hill was speckled with conifers. Beyond it a larger hill was shrouded with them, a dark-green contrast to the cyan sky. The sun played peekaboo with splotches of white clouds, their shadows adding another dimension to the panoramic hills. The closer he came to them, the larger they grew, the sharper the panoply of their green hues, and the more Doug trembled.

Monumental reminders, they were, of his minute space in the universe, declaring the royalty of their Creator. Ruth would have reminded him why, had she been here. But he was getting the picture. Nearby meandered the Jefferson River, assuring him safe passage through the labyrinth of hills while sparing his muscles for steeper climbs.

In Three Forks he united with the headwaters of the Missouri River. The width of Main Street and its Western facades looked like a movie set. Lunch consisted of Angus beef burgers and the fixings. Thereafter, ample farmland with majestic snowcapped mountains beyond them wowed him.

But there was no one to share it with.

*Wonder how Lauren's doing?* He considered texting her and sending pictures of the beauty around him but thought better of it. She was probably huffing and puffing to altitude right now. Or cruising through a mining ghost town. *I can't wait to hear about her adventure. If I ever will.*

With only twenty-eight miles on the day and plenty of daylight hours remaining, early afternoon didn't seem like the time to be calling it a day. However, free shelter and a tour of an orphanage from another era were more than Lauren could pass up. Plus Lars and a dip in the river.

The pair cycled to Jessen Park, where they discovered the bike camp.

Lauren rested her bicycle on the side of an unfinished plywood building, the lone structure there. An alcove beside the door housed a sink with running water and a mirror for revealing a rider's haggard appearance after a day in the saddle. Around the side of the building sat two picnic tables in a fenced bullpen with a bike stand for repairs and an outdoor grill in the corner. Two white doors were labeled *Shower* and *Toilet.*

"This has about everything a cyclist needs for an overnight stay." Lauren entered the building through the lock-less screen door.

Lars followed her, the door banging shut behind him.

"Oh, isn't this cute." She read notes from past visitors on the whiteboard. "'You made my day, Twin Bridges. Thank you so much' . . . 'Best overnight stay I've had yet' . . . 'Twin Bridges rocks' . . . 'The Atlantic Ocean or bust.'" And then the obligatory "Kilroy was here," complete with picture.

"A guest book." Lars opened it. "Anchorage, Alaska; Fairfax, Virginia; Trois-Rivieres, Quebec; Fulton, New York . . . Dunedin, New Zealand? . . . Wales, Scotland; Massachusetts." He flipped to the page with the last entry on it, entered his name, and handed the pen to Lauren.

"Lars Andersen. Let me guess. Swedish?"

"Very good." He looked over her shoulder as she wrote her name, her hand shaking. "German?"

"I haven't a clue. Just American, I guess."

Lars began studying notices on the walls, anything from local advertisements to route suggestions to rules of conduct.

Wooden benches and counters ran along the walls of the small, one-room structure. Light from ample windows cast a sheen on knots in the plywood floor, which seemed more inviting given that an overstuffed chair and couch had seen better days. Several power outlets would allow Lauren to recharge her phone and tablet.

Locals or other cyclists had left items in a basket on the floor. The sign read *Montana Mystery Grab Basket: Take or Give.* Among the hodgepodge were a few water bottles, spare spokes, a small journal, a bottle brush, a map of Montana, and an energy bar still in the wrapper. Someone had apparently sat on it in 90-degree weather.

A small tin canister with a slit in the top for donations hung on the wall.

Lars read from the rules of conduct. "It suggests pitching a tent outside."

"Oh look!" Lauren opened the glass door of a cabinet. Inside were maps and bicycling books. However, she pulled out *The Holy Bible*. "Wonderful. I need a break from my phone. Ever read this book?"

"It's been a while. Never all the way through though."

"You should try it sometime. It's a life-changing read."

Lars smiled. "Maybe I should . . . But right now, what do you say we get cooled off before showering?"

Lauren's cheeks lifted as she looked at Lars from the corner of her eye. "Last one in showers last." She ripped her phone from her back pocket and set it on the counter, then tossed her helmet in the chair and kicked off her cycling shoes.

Meanwhile, Lars prepared for the mad dash too.

Lauren was out the door first, but Lars overtook her at river's edge. She giggled.

Before stepping in, Lars yanked off his shirt.

Lauren did a double take. He hadn't a hair on his massive chest. His pecs bobbed as he swung his arms around six-pack abs. Then he dove in.

Her mouth hung open as she watched him resurface. He came out of the water and shook his head with such exuberance that drops of cold water freckled Lauren's arm.

She screeched. "That's cold!"

"You can say that again. But it feels good. Come on in."

Lauren stuck her toe in the water, then squealed and yanked it out.

"Come on."

"Okay, I can do this." She took one step into the stream. The water came halfway up her calf. Then she dropped her other foot onto the riverbed.

Goosebumps started up her exposed legs and made their way across her torso, then traveled onto her neck, arriving as two other strains reached the tips of her middle fingers. She went deeper. "I can't believe how cold this is." Her teeth chattered.

Lars held out his hand.

Lauren trudged toward it, the current enveloping her thighs.

He backed up a step, then another and another until he had coaxed her to the middle of the river in chest-high water.

Now within reach, her heart beating faster, she inched her shaky hand toward his. But something stopped her.

Beads of water dripped from Lars's matted golden locks onto his strong shoulders—like those of an Olympic weightlifter—and trickled back where they came from. "I see fear in those beautiful eyes of yours." He stretched his arm farther and leaned toward her, his hand beckoning her.

She lifted her hand out of the water and moved it closer to his, closer than before, closer than ever. Her heart pounded as she lost herself in the blue current of his eyes. He was like something she'd never seen before. So perfect. So pleasing to consider. Then—

*What am I doing?*

"I can't. I'm sorry." Her hand plunged into the crisp mountain waters as she turned away.

Lauren sat on a bench inside the camp building as water pulsated through the plumbing. Lars was showering last despite winning the race to the river.

She combed her wet hair, then noticed her phone lighting up.

I can't believe the beauty of this state.
Incredible! Where are you?

She typed a message back to Doug:

Twin Bridges and, yes, amazing! Where are you?

Lauren dialed the number of the caretaker of the orphanage, a Mrs. Junkins, and set up a tour in an hour. When she hung up, her phone vibrated. Another text:

> On my way to Bozeman. What's it like there?

> Beautiful. It's a tiny town, but people are friendly.

> Where are you staying?

> At a camp for cyclists. It's lovely.

> Are you okay?

> Yes. I'm good.

The roar of motorcycles filled the air, increasing in volume as they approached the building.

"Let's stay here tonight," one man shouted.

"Looks like some cyclists," another said.

"That don't matter," yet another said.

She crouched from view but peeked out the window. Five of them. Unkempt with leather vests and large, tattooed biceps. A lump rose in Lauren's throat as her phone vibrated in her hand.

> Glad to hear it. Have a great night.

It was good of Doug to check in. He didn't need to know about her flat tire . . . or about Lars . . . or about the most recent visitors to the campground. Good thing Lars was around.

The motorcyclists parked their bikes about fifty yards away. She replied to Doug:

> You too

Then Lauren finished her hair, careful to stay out of view.

*Ka-thump!* The rush of water through pipes ceased.

She dropped her phone into her handlebar bag.

A few minutes later the shower door slammed. Then the spring in the camp building's screen door flexed as the hinges squeaked. Lars entered, the door smacking its casing behind him.

Murmurs and hoots from the campground's newest guests competed for her attention as Lars said, "That felt great."

She nodded. "That it did."

"Have you thought about where you want to sleep tonight?"

"Some fellow campers just arrived."

Lars walked to the window. "Oh yes." His forefinger and thumb caressed his chin line as he studied the scene. "We could stay in here."

"Let's figure that out later. I arranged a tour of the orphanage in about forty-five minutes. Wanna go?"

Lars hesitated, flashed his pearly whites, then nodded.

# CHAPTER 11

Lauren led Lars to the gate and then dismounted her bicycle. The sign read *Montana Children's Center*. Among several brick buildings that had seen better days, an old Victorian house drew her attention. Her heart leaped.

She looked at the sign again. "I can't believe it. From 1894 to 1975."

A woman with straight hair pulled back into a tight bun approached, peering at them through round, wire-rimmed spectacles.

"Mrs. Junkins?"

"Yes." Mrs. Junkins opened the wrought-iron gate. "Welcome to the Montana Children's Home. Won't you please come in. We've been waiting for you." She let out an awkward laugh with what sounded like hiccups interrupting it.

Though more appropriate for the home ahead of them than the occasion, her dress caught Lauren's eye. A stiff collar acted as a vise, holding her head straight. Puffy sleeves adorned a white top that cinched to her bustline before giving way to shades of red on black panels widening toward a flared bottom.

"I love your dress," Lauren said.

Mrs. Junkins let out an abbreviated laugh as disjointed as the first. "It was my great-grandmother's. She wore it here years ago."

"It's beautiful."

Mrs. Junkins's stone face showed no cracks.

She closed the gate behind them and turned up the road into the facility, her long Victorian dress scraping the fractured pavement.

Lauren and Lars wheeled their bicycles past the *No Trespassing* signs and walked behind Mrs. Junkins until they reached one of the many brick buildings. They propped their bicycles against the building and followed her inside.

"This is the auditorium."

In the floor tile a pair of drama masks overlaying a lyre greeted visitors. A stage, encased with thick mahogany woodwork and floor-to-ceiling, wine-red curtains, took up much of the front wall. Rust-colored water stains streaked the side walls, and crumbles of plaster from the ceiling littered the floor. A set of four stairs on either side of the stage led through doorways. Steam radiators below double windows in front of the stairs and at other spots along the side walls once heated the space.

"I love this," Lauren said. "Is it okay if I take photos?"

"If you wish."

"I can picture kids in here laughing and playing. Even singing."

"Some people say they can still hear them." Then their tour guide offered a brief but nervous laugh.

Beady-eyed, Lars snapped his gaze from wall to ceiling to wall to floor to the stage.

"Is something wrong?" Lauren said.

He shook his head and continued to absorb the surroundings.

"Let me show you the living quarters."

As the trio walked to their next stop, Lauren pointed to a hole in the ground encased in tile, with rainwater gathered on one end. "What's that?"

"That was our indoor swimming pool—until the roof fell in." Again that laugh.

"No way," Lauren said. "For a place this old?"

"Most of these buildings were built in the early 1900s. The castle"—she pointed to the large Victorian centerpiece of the grounds—"dates back to 1894."

"How many kids stayed here?"

"Seven hundred at its height. Here's the girls' cottage."

"That must be more than live in the entire town," Lauren said.

"Twice as many."

Lauren followed Mrs. Junkins, who ducked into the doorway of another building. Lars trailed behind, looking around at the many buildings. Most were brick. Between two of them, a pair of half-moon basketball backboards faced one another, their white metal speckled with rust and grass sprouting through crevices in the paved court between them. The campus's water tower, aquamarine in color, stood on metal stilts in the distance.

Once they were in the building, the bright light of summer shone through curtainless windows, illuminating bright-orange walls.

"It was quite an operation in its day. Hospital, in-house dentist, shops, school, gymnasium, pool, twenty-five buildings in all."

Lauren's jaw dropped. "The fellow at the Watering Hole said the owner was trying to sell it."

The trio strolled through a Gothic archway and down a hall, glancing into rooms on either side, their footsteps echoing in unison.

"When he bought this property, all he could see were opportunities. A hunting-and-fishing resort, a rehab center, a retreat, a boarding school, maybe even a college. The beauty here and the lack of distractions make this a prime location for the right fit. But the people who look at it can't see what we see."

"I do." Lauren stopped and scanned the hallway.

"Well, the ones that can don't have the money." Mrs. Junkins took a step down the hall and let out a quirky laugh, which stopped as abruptly as it started. She turned around. "Or the gumption."

Lauren tilted her head and gave Mrs. Junkins a sad smile.

Lars had his head down, staring at the floor, nibbling on a cuticle.

They strolled through a back door.

"Most people want to see the castle, so let me take you there. Why so much interest? It looks like you two have better things to do than wander through a junk heap"—she hiccup-laughed again—"I mean old relic like this."

Lars held out his hand toward Lauren, inviting her to answer for the two of them.

"Oh, this isn't a junk heap. I worked at an orphanage. In Uganda. This is high-class compared to what we had."

The threesome walked toward the four-story Victorian building, which thirsted for a fresh coat of white paint.

With an octagonal wooden turret atop a brick underpinning on one of its corners, its architecture and natural setting drew Lauren into a bygone era. Once through the front door, a long wooden staircase, curved at the top, greeted them, as did a musty smell.

*How many small hands have grasped the ornamental ball at the end of that banister, especially if their little behinds slid to a stop in front of it?*

Suddenly Lars stopped and put his arm in front of Lauren. His head pivoted side to side, his wandering gazes flashed across the ceiling.

"What's wrong?" Lauren said.

"Did you hear that?" His face flushed. "Listen."

Mrs. Junkins smirked. "It's recess time." Then her laugh slipped out of her one-cheeked smile. "Come with me."

She led them up the creaky stairway, its steps worn hollow from the feet of thousands of stampeding youngsters.

They explored the building from top to bottom. Lauren peppered their host with questions, mostly about tending to the needs of orphans in yesteryear.

When they exited the building, Lars let out a huge sigh, perhaps to displace dank air with fresh. "Don't you think we should go now?"

Lauren looked at her phone. "Oh, I could stay here forever."

"I wouldn't recommend that," Mrs. Junkins said.

Lauren's brow furrowed.

"You don't want to be here after dark. Things change then."

"Thank you for your tour," Lars said. "We best be going now."

He led Lauren to the front gate, bicycles in tow. Mrs. Junkins followed.

Lauren craned her neck every several steps to capture final glimpses of the orphanage but had little time to do so to keep up with Lars.

He scooted ahead to open the gate, rested his bicycle on the sign outside, and came back to close the gate behind Lauren.

"I hope you enjoyed your visit to the Montana Children's Home. Do visit us again. And please let me know if you hear of anyone looking for a beautiful and unique place. Someone who could use a facility like this . . . with a little vision for what it could become and the patience to develop it." She let out one final awkward laugh. "We enjoyed having you."

"Thank you so much for showing us around," Lauren said.

Lars merely nodded to Mrs. Junkins as he mounted his bicycle.

# CHAPTER 12

Lars followed Lauren into the bike camp building, where they sat on wooden benches across from one another.

Lauren scratched her arm. "You hardly said a word at the children's home. Was something wrong?"

"No, nothing wrong. But I'm glad to be out of there."

"What do you mean?"

Lars sighed. "I've heard all sorts of stories about that place. Not many of them good. My grandfather lived there as a boy."

"Your grandfather was an orphan?"

"I guess in some ways. He was reunited with his parents in the late sixties. But the damage was done."

"Damage?"

Lars ran his hand through his bushy blond mane. "My uncle said Grandpa's stay there really messed him up. He was abusive to both my uncle and my father."

"I'm sorry to hear that. How did it affect your father?"

Lars looked out the window, gesturing at the motorcycles. "They're still here . . . Have you given any thought to where you want to stay?"

With their motors off, Lauren had all but forgotten about them. Smoke rose from a campfire with men talking and laughing around it, each holding a bottle. They seemed more docile than she expected. "I'm fine staying here."

"Here meaning *here*?" Lars pointed to the plywood floor.

"Oh no. Outside. In my tent. Like it says on the wall."

Doug wheeled his bicycle into the Gallatin Motel in Belgrade, the spring-loaded door slamming behind him. As he walked past the pine-scented bathroom with its sparkling chrome accessories, a laminated sheet of paper propped on a pillow stared at him.

He leaned his bike against the cedar paneling and picked up the typed note.

> Welcome! Your stay in our humble abode and our service to you are about more than what you paid for your room. Please make yourself at home and let us know how we can make your stay just right. We want you to be comfortable and ready for what lies ahead. We are grateful you are here. May God grant you peace and rest.
>
> We invite those you love into your thoughts and dreams. May your phone calls and messages be sprinkled with joy and your journey ahead be safe. May your days before you pass to the Other Side be pleasant and profitable as you serve and bring joy to others, including those you love most.
>
> —The Management

Warmth ran through his body. Despite countless motel stays while working in sales, Doug had never seen something like this.

*"Those you love."* Ruth and Carmen fit that category, but how could they love *him?* And how could he serve them, let alone bring them joy? His kid sister was thousands of miles away. And Ruth . . . *That's a little too heavy right now.*

Nonetheless, the note sure beat the musty room with grungy carpet that usually welcomed him. Here, drapes without holes covered the windows. And the overstuffed chair looked brand-new. Even the clerk was helpful, explaining how to avoid trouble on I-90 the next day.

He pulled out his phone and noticed a message from Brother Jim:

> Maggie and I have been praying for you and Lauren. Travel safely and please do think about that job offer we talked about. I'll be in touch.

That's another thing he'd never experienced before—people like Brother Jim and Maggie. As pastor of a church, Brother Jim had more important things to tend to than texting Doug. He sent back:

> I will. Thanks again for everything. You guys are the best.

After Lars prepared dinner, he and Lauren ate on the counter inside the bike camp building, then they pitched their tents as the sun dropped on the horizon. Lars retrieved two lawn chairs from inside, and the two sat at a 45-degree angle to one another and watched the half-moon ascend.

"My compliments to the chef."

"Hard to go wrong with freeze-dried food."

"Do you mean 'hard to go right'?"

Lars grinned, then winked at her.

Lauren's heart skipped a beat. A vision of Jeffrey darted through her mind, but she refused to indulge it.

She pressed her shaking lips together and looked at Lars from the corner of her eye, swallowing hard. A floodlight above the camp cast a glow on his sleek cheekbone. Raising her eyebrows, she adjusted her position and took a deep breath—never losing eye contact with him. "How is it that your significant other allows you to get away like this?"

Lars looked away, his Adam's apple bobbing as he swallowed. "Just lucky, I guess."

"So, what do you do for work, Mr. Lars Andersen?"

"I paint."

"No wonder you were speechless at the orphanage today."

"No, on canvas. I'm an artist."

"*Really?*" Lauren leaned toward him. "I've always wanted to paint."

"I'll bet you could. Anyone passionate enough about their music to carry a violin cross-country on a bicycle must have an artist buried inside."

"Oh, that—yes."

Lars lifted his chin. "Would you mind showing me your talent?" His Adam's apple caressed his neck with every syllable.

Lauren glanced over his shoulder at their neighbors, who were still laughing and drinking, lost in their own conversations. "I don't want to interrupt them. Seems like they're having such a good time."

"Let's hope they wear themselves out by bedtime."

"Yes. Let's hope." Lauren couldn't take her eyes off him.

He met her stare, then looked down.

"Tell me about your kids."

"Jake's the oldest. Fresh out of culinary school. He landed a job at a high-end restaurant in Denver. Josh still has another year at a trade school. He's studying for his master plumber's license. You should see his carpentry though. Highly skilled, with little training. Really proud of my kiddos."

"So, Jake as in Jacob? Josh as in Joshua?"

"Uh-huh."

"Those are biblical names."

"Yes. Yes, they are."

Lauren waited.

"My ex, she was kinda religious. I mean, I went to church and everything, believe in God, stuff like that. But she was . . . well, a little over the top."

Lauren merely stared at him while her heart beat faster.

"And then there's the pistol. Oliver, that is. Ollie is my two-year-old. Love that kid."

"And it sounded like you two aren't together now?"

Lars shook his head, then looked off in the distance, seemingly fighting his emotions.

Lauren placed her hand on top of his. It was an act of compassion—until her stomach fluttered and her heart thumped. She pulled her hand away and grasped the arm of her lawn chair. The cool air of nightfall coupled with underutilized emotions brought chills, causing her other hand to tremble.

Lars wiped his face with his other hand, then turned to Lauren, riveting her with those eyes of his. "It's okay." He placed his hand on top of hers.

They searched one another's eyes.

Lauren's heart pounded as Lars leaned closer.

Unsure what was happening, but unable to resist, she leaned closer too.

Suddenly her chair reached the precipice. It toppled into Lars, sending her flying. She bounced off his bicep.

Startled, Lars backed away, and his chair also tipped as Lauren face-planted onto the lawn. She turned over, and two of the motorcyclists were staring at them, shaking their heads. With Lars still on the ground, she giggled.

"Whoops," he said. "Sorry I dropped that pass." He smiled.

# CHAPTER 13

After the neighbors settled down and turned in, Lauren and Lars did likewise.

But Lauren could not sleep. She hadn't experienced these swirling emotions since high school. The impetus for them was lying in a tent a few short feet away.

Yards beyond, the flowing river offered its calming effect. An owl hooted after every other thought.

She checked her phone again. It was 10:30, and Maggie had sent a text message:

> Jim and I are praying for you and Doug.
> Safe travels. So glad we got to connect.

Before she could respond, Doug texted:

> Good night. Sleep tight. Don't let the
> bedbugs bite.

She texted back:

> gn

*Nothing from Jeffrey. But why should there be?*

She reached beside her air mattress, felt the can of bear spray, and then grabbed the Bible she'd found in the camp building. She knew the passage well but flipped to it anyway.

> Do not be anxious about anything, but in every situation, by prayer and petition, with thanksgiving, present your requests to God. And the peace of God, which transcends all understanding, will guard your hearts and your minds in Christ Jesus.

She closed the Bible and hugged it.

Peace? She wasn't feeling it. How could she?

*Father God, Thank You for safe passage to Twin Bridges. It's so beautiful around here. The tour of the orphanage was awesome. And thank You for bringing Lars along at just the right time. Help Mrs. Junkins find a buyer for the property. May those bikers next door know the power of Your resurrection in their lives. And give that old man—*

Across the way one of the bikers belched, interrupting nature's nighttime serenade. Lauren chuckled to herself.

*Give that old man in the rusty pickup something that makes him smile and convinces him that You love him.*

*Lord, I'm scared. Every time I look at Lars, I come unraveled. He makes me so nervous. You sure made a handsome man there. Help me, please. Calm me down.*

*I love You, Lord. And, oh—please keep Doug safe. And thank You for Brother Jim and Maggie. They sure are special people. In Jesus's name, amen.*

Then another passage came to mind: *"Above all else, guard your heart, for everything you do flows from it."*

Dawn broke to the sound of snoring next door.

A half hour later Lauren and Lars stole away from camp, anxious to cycle before vacationers might clog the roads to Yellowstone.

A distant, solitary mountain range, appearing as through a murky lens, suggested climbing ahead, despite the wide-open grasslands surrounding them. Trees and brush dotted the plain. With a generous shoulder, a warm tailwind, and Lars ahead of her, the ride south on Route 287 to Sheridan whizzed by.

A mile past Alder, Lars pointed. His finger drifted right as the two approached a handful of elk grazing. He rolled to a stop.

Lauren squeezed her brakes. "Oh, they're so precious."

Lars pulled his phone from a back pocket and snapped a few shots, the oblivious creatures chomping a few hundred feet away. He dismounted his bicycle and eased it onto the grass. "Why don't you come this way and I'll get you in the shot," he whispered.

Lauren hesitated, then rubbed her cheekbone. *Is this a good idea?*

Yet a few pictures here would capture a unique memory and the surrounding landscape. No part of this ride reminded her of either the Washington Beltway or Uganda. Rather than walk her bike forward, she got off and set it alongside Lars's. She pulled off her helmet, unfurled her hair, then smiled.

A few shots later Lars handed his phone to Lauren. "Would you mind? I need one for a friend."

She snapped shots of him in front of the elk. Then she took two pictures of him with her own phone, handed it to him, and swapped places.

Lars returned her phone and retrieved his. "Just a minute. I need to send this."

While Lars texted, Lauren sent Doug a photo of herself.

The duo followed the road east, beginning a gradual climb on the now shoulderless road. Gone was the flatland, as Highway 287 cut through rolling hills, their embankments pockmarked with scruffy brush and sporadic trees.

Soon they approached Nevada City. Lauren's odometer read twenty-seven miles. No wonder she was so hungry. "Do you want to eat?"

Lars nodded ahead of her. "Sure do."

To their left, old log structures lined the main drag, dark brown in color, with a few displaced rail cars across the street from them. One car read *Chicago, Milwaukee, St. Paul.* The car beyond it, *Great Northern.* They rested on tracks to nowhere.

Plenty of buildings—looking more like showpieces than businesses—but no apparent restaurant. Some of the people milling about sported vintage clothes. Everyone else gawked at the surrounding props.

A man with suspenders holding up his baggy brown trousers stood in front of the Museum and Music Hall. He was looking down at a chain-tethered pocket watch pulled from his vest.

With Lauren following, Lars crossed the road and rolled to a stop near him. "Hey. Any places to eat here?"

The man looked up and smiled. "Your best bet is Virginia City, two miles up the road. But would you like a tour first? Wouldn't want you backtracking on that bicycle of yours."

Lars looked around at Lauren.

"Tour? Of what, may I ask?"

"Ma'am, this here is a restored city from the Montana Gold Rush of the 1860s. This area was buzzing with activity back then. Over ten million dollars' worth of gold extracted from Alder Gulch. That would be billions today."

Lauren tilted her head. "What's the Music Hall?"

The man glanced at the violin case on Lauren's rear rack. "Yes, I can see you have an interest in music, ma'am. Why don't you come in and check it out. We have a music machine or two inside."

Lauren looked at Lars. "Can we?"

"Sure."

The two dismounted, leaned their bikes against the hitching post, and followed the man inside.

A woman sat behind a counter of what appeared to be a gift shop. Piano music from the Roaring '20s emanated from an open door beside her.

Lauren followed the sound to its source, ducking into a room filled with all manner of large musical relics. The yellowed ivory keys of a player piano moved up and down as a scroll of music rotated around a drum inside a glass cabinet. She turned around and faced a Wurlitzer horn organ. Carousel music began pouring out when a boy pushed a button on it.

When the tour guide caught up to Lauren, he explained the history of the two music machines and how they produced sound. Then he drew a semicircle with his outstretched hand. "We believe this to be the largest automated music machine collection in the world."

Meanwhile, Lars had drifted out a door in the back.

Lauren looked at a merry-go-round chariot and then a coin-operated piano, the more fascinating props among the eclectic set of musical paraphernalia.

She pivoted again, and her jaw dropped at the sight of a more conventional-looking organ. Between two sets of stops in the facing above the keyboard was the brand name *Vocalion*. *New York* and *Worcester* appeared underneath it.

The tour guide spoke from behind her. "That's not a mechanical organ."

"Can anyone here play it?"

The man sat and winked at her, placing his fingers on the keys.

When "Amazing Grace" came forth, Lauren's heart skipped a beat.

The man's head swayed as he caressed the keys. Upon finishing, he started to get up—

Lauren placed her hand on his shoulder. "Wait."

The man turned, wrinkles in his forehead.

"Do you think I could join you?"

"Oh. A duet."

The man slid to the right to make room for her, but she rushed outside instead and grabbed her violin case.

When she returned without her helmet, the man, who'd risen from the bench, looked up. "Ooooh." He sat again.

Lauren pulled out her violin and tuned it.

The tour guide grinned. "You'll be in much better tune than me."

"Okay, can we take it from the top?"

The man nodded. "A one, and a two, and . . ."

The two began playing.

A boy in the corner who'd been staring at a clown on one of the carousel machines looked up. Then he stepped toward them. The gift shop attendant appeared in the entryway, then walked in, her arms folded to her chest. From a side room, an older couple slid in, eyes peeled to the pair.

Lauren eased her bow across the strings while the organist's head swayed.

Another couple walked through behind the last one, nudging them closer to the musicians. Visitors from the front room strolled in.

When Lauren and the tour guide completed the first verse, they continued to the second, then the third as more music lovers stepped in.

When the sixth verse concluded, the boy, now beside Lauren, broke the momentary silence. "That was good."

The gift shop attendant clapped her hands once, paused, then again and again in more rapid succession until others joined in the applause.

As the clapping subsided, Lars entered from the back, his helmet visible above the heads. The crowd parted, and he stepped forward until he reached the duo.

"Do you know 'In the Sweet By and By'?" one woman said.

The guide sitting at the organ shook his head. No sooner had the words "Sorry, ma'am" come out of his mouth than Lauren nestled her violin underneath her chin and raised her bow.

As she began to play, she caught Lars's eyes, crystal blue like the waters of Lake Albert in Uganda. She wrestled to steady her bow as a flood of emotion washed through her. She looked away to gather herself.

When she began the chorus, the sound of a stout baritone sent shivers down her spine.

> "In the sweet by and by,
> We shall meet—"

She looked up to see Lars singing. A second wave pummeled her, stronger than the first. Her hands began shaking.

"—on that beautiful shore;
In the sweet by and by,
We shall meet—"

She lost it. Her bow clunked the strings as she dropped it to her side, her hand still trembling. An image from her past flashed through her mind.

He kept singing:

"—on that beautiful shore."

"Thank you so much." It was the woman who requested the song. "That was magnificent."

"Beautiful," the tour guide said.

Lauren ripped her eyes away from Lars. Blood rushed to her face. Why did he have to butt into her performance? If he only knew . . .

"Th—thank you." She located her violin case and stepped toward it.

"Do you know any others?" another man said.

"I—I'm sorry. We have to go now." Lauren put away her violin and left.

The blat of a Jake brake from I-90 awoke Doug.

He grabbed his cell phone and powered it up.

gn

At least he heard from her.

Good morning. Hope your day goes well. Safe travels.

With little reason to shower and shave, Doug donned his cycling apparel, grabbed his map, and headed for the continental breakfast. A waffle, oatmeal, and two bananas, including one for the road, would give him plenty of carbs.

His route planning presented him with either the interstate or a back road with an unspecified length of gravel. After cycling through the remote Clearwater National Forest in Idaho weeks earlier, hugging the interstate on a day like today would provide the comfort of fellow travelers and ample places to stop for food, a bathroom, and conversation. Maybe his Iowa farm roots had given way to the citified lifestyle he'd adopted in LA.

"Going for a bike ride today?" A stranger with a friendly smile and sunglasses hanging from his V-neck shirt stuffed his used paper plate into the trash.

Doug nodded. "Oh yeah. Beautiful state."

"If you're going to Yellowstone, you might want to reconsider. Bumper to bumper. I was there yesterday and couldn't believe how the traffic disregarded cyclists. I ride too, so I know a little bit about what you face. One RV forced a poor soul off the road right in front of me. Didn't have a clue."

"Urgh!"

"The guy toppled over once he left the pavement. He was okay though."

"I'm glad I decided not to go there."

"Safe travels." The man slapped Doug's shoulder before he put his arms around two kids and ushered them to the lobby.

After breakfast Doug wheeled his bicycle out of the motel room, checked out, and took a frontage road, landing him in Bozeman, where he cycled through downtown to change things up.

Road signs directed travelers to Yellowstone National Park, as they had the day before. *Maybe I can catch up to Lauren.* But he'd already decided not to go there for good reason. He had a better idea.

He stopped, swiped his phone, and wrote:

> A guy at breakfast said cyclists are getting run off the road in Yellowstone.

Before sending it he looked up. A nostalgic sign affixed to the top of a building with a grid of steel supports read *Hotel*

*Baxter.* She wasn't going to heed his advice if she didn't listen to the bed-and-breakfast hosts. It really was none of his business, though he somehow felt responsible for her.

He erased the message, then typed:

> Are you still planning to go through Yellowstone?

But that wouldn't work either. She had her mind set on seeing it. Once he shared the warning, she'd just blow it off. In her eyes it would only accentuate his cowardice, so he deleted that text too.

He soon turned onto the ramp to I-90 eastbound. In a car he would have accelerated up to speed. But on a bike, speed was a relative term.

Once on the highway, an eighteen-wheeler flew by at what had to be over eighty miles an hour. Another followed it. The strong draft propelled him with ease but also buffeted his contraption, making it harder to steer. He squeezed the handgrips tighter. High-speed big rigs became the norm, and he did his best to acclimate.

Eventually a sign to his right advertised grizzly bear sightings. *No thank you.* He examined the grounds anyway—as much to look for breaks in the fencing as to spot a bear. Despite the presence of neither, with open range around him, he pedaled harder.

The curvy interstate ahead disappeared around mountains that grew with each pedal stroke. Doug hadn't seen a freeway like this . . . well . . . ever.

As the climb toward Bozeman Pass steepened, the road narrowed. The shoulder beneath him took the brunt of the reduction.

An animal stood at the far end of an adjacent field filled with rolls of hay. Doug squinted, and the animal began to move. A big, dark one. Not just any animal though, but a moose, prominent rack included.

"Well look at that."

Doug stopped and took pictures.

A pack of a dozen Harleys rumbled past him, led by beards and flapping bandannas incapable of taming mops of greasy hair. Bulging biceps emerged from patched leather vests.

He sent a picture of the moose to Lauren. After a long drink from his CamelBak, he continued up the pass.

To his right, a westbound train met him. The engineer tooted twice and waved. Doug nodded while grunting along, paying closer attention to the ever-shrinking shoulder, the rumble strip beside it, and traffic in his rearview mirror.

As he pushed higher, the median disappeared, the east and westbound lanes clinging together like a pair of magnets separated only by a concrete barrier, the noise and fumes intensifying in the confined space.

Now climbing above the rail line and with mountains encroaching from the sides, a horn blared behind him.

Then another.

He glanced at his mirror.

Two tractor trailers loaded with lumber clogged both lanes, approaching at high speed.

Doug shook.

His recumbent wobbled before he gathered it.

The driver in the near lane was looking out his side window at the other driver when his tires smacked the rumble strip.

Adrenaline exploded inside Doug.

He veered to the right on what little shoulder remained, squeezed his brakes, and clunked against the guardrail, coming to an awkward stop, tipping onto his right side.

The driver had corrected at the last second, but a rush of air streamed across the goosebumps on Doug's left arm and whistled through the vent holes in his helmet.

Just beyond him the trucker tooted and let off the gas, allowing the other rig to pass.

Doug lay dormant. Pain coursed through his right arm, so he clenched his teeth.

After the pounding in his chest subsided, he pushed himself off the guardrail. His fiery red arm glistened in the sunlight. He grabbed a water bottle and squirted it to wash out the abrasion, bringing tears to his eyes.

So much for worrying about Lauren.

As he wound closer to the top, the shoulder vanished, as did the rumble strip. He could reach out and touch those giant tires beside him if they nudged closer.

*Help me, God.*

A steady stream of barreling tractor trailers buffeted his load. He avoided looking in his mirror, instead focusing on the three-foot path to safety.

Finally the grade moderated and the shoulder widened as he crested the summit.

He stopped and took a deep breath. He leaned his recumbent against a post and swiped his phone. Lauren had sent a picture. Her flowing strawberry-blond hair draped her shoulders, her teeth gleaming and cheeks beaming.

Doug smiled.

But soon it faded as his stomach clenched.

Lauren wasn't the type to take selfies and share them around. What's more, the image was a full-body shot in front of a herd of what looked like deer. *Who took this picture?*

# CHAPTER 14

A mile east of Nevada City on Route 287, a more conventional downtown with modern construction appeared. An opera house graced the end of a strip mall, with a covered boardwalk in front.

Lauren slowed her bicycle. "Let's eat."

"Good idea." Lars pointed to a restaurant in saloon motif across the street.

A familiar pickup truck was parked in front of it. There certainly couldn't be another one like it. No more firewood in the back though.

Lauren looked farther down the street. "Oh look! An ice cream shop. I wonder if they serve food."

"Let's check it out."

Once seated, Lars said, "Was something wrong at the Music Hall?"

Lauren glanced sideways. "Oh, it was nothing."

"You stopped playing."

She nodded and grabbed a menu propped between a napkin holder and a bottle of ketchup. "I'm hungry."

*Or maybe not.*

She couldn't shake the feeling in the pit of her stomach, like she'd eaten a bad slice of wild game. Nor could she chance a glimpse of that gorgeous face of his.

"Is everything alright?"

"Yes . . . It is."

After she'd all but memorized the menu, she finally looked at him. "Where are you cycling to?"

"I'm just cruising. To Yellowstone. No firm plans really. I hope you don't mind if I tag along."

Her stomach twisted tighter.

But it might help to have a man with her, especially with so much wildlife around. She could think of worse options for a traveling partner. Plus he knew the area.

She pulled out her phone to check the mileage to West Yellowstone. While looking at a picture of a moose from Doug, she said, "Where did you learn that song?"

"Gram. She used to sing it all the time."

"You have a magnificent voice, you know."

"I've been told that a time or two."

The server came to take their orders.

After she left, Lauren looked up. "You sound like you've been trained. Ever thought about singing professionally?"

He flashed his dimples at her. "You're the one who drew the crowd."

Lauren fidgeted. "For me it's a God thing."

Lars chuckled.

"Anyway, I'm planning to ride through Yellowstone. It's another eighty-six miles. So we'll need to stop."

"That thing probably doesn't tell you about the climb out of town, does it?" He smiled. "The good news is, once we make it to the lookout, it's all downhill. About nine miles to Ennis. It's a rush."

"I like the sound of that."

"There are places to stay in Ennis, but that's short mileage and they're probably booked already. Fly fishers and overflow of tourists from Yellowstone. Maybe a campground in Cameron? That's anywhere from thirty to fifty miles from here. Flat riding though."

That would give Lauren opportunity to learn more about this mystery man with the rich baritone voice who loved to bicycle. As long as thoughts of Jeffrey didn't join the ride.

A stiff climb pushed them to higher altitude east of Virginia City. Lauren had become accustomed to climbing with the weight on her bicycle, but it still slowed her to a crawl. Lars was way ahead of her.

Partway up the ascent, with cars and RVs passing her at high speed, a bird soared high in the sky ahead, its impressive wingspan miniaturizing its body. It swooped large arcs, as if tracing letters. The message was incoherent but for the majestic motions.

The bird's head was white. The land of the free. Home of the brave. *Wow! Another bald eagle.*

The adrenaline rush quickened her pace. She gazed up intermittently, watching the road enough to stay on it but out of the travel lane.

When the bald eagle glided directly overhead, she squeezed her brakes and clipped out of her pedals, rolling to a stop. Straddling her bicycle, she pulled out her phone and snapped a few photos. Another eagle soared into view, higher than the first. The message was becoming clearer, but it wasn't from those magnificent birds.

Isaiah 40:31 came to mind. She was already mounting up with wings like eagles. She could bicycle here forever without growing weary. This was incredible. She'd already been waiting on the Lord, but did Lars fit in?

When Lauren finally crested the hill, goosebumps freckled her arms—not because of the spectacular views but the cooler air.

Lars grinned. "What took ya?"

With her last few pedal strokes on the reduced grade, she coasted to a stop beside him and exhaled. "Made it." She dug into a pannier for her windbreaker. "Did you see those eagles?"

"No. I didn't even notice them. We see them here all the time."

Lauren scanned the panorama before them. "Wow! What a Creator."

"The Madison River Valley." Lars pointed. "That's the Madison Range beyond." Then he swept his arm to the right. "Yellowstone's over there."

"Is that snow?"

"Yup."

A vast plain stretched to the mountain range beyond, knolls in the foreground speckled with trees and brush, injecting green on the brown hues. The tiny road on which they would travel connected a few small structures before vanishing into the scene, streams distinguished only as crevices meandering through the valley. Wisps of clouds smudged the sky, diluting it into myriad shades of blue. Its enormity cradled the distant mountains from aloft.

The fresh breeze glanced off Lauren's cheeks. Only an occasional vehicle interrupted the serenity, the eastbound ones soon to blend into the masterpiece in front of her. She could savor this for hours. But it was time to become a part of the scene herself. "I guess we need to go."

"Don't worry. There's more pleasure ahead. How's a two-thousand-foot drop sound?"

The pair coasted downhill toward Ennis. Lauren's speedometer hit forty-three miles per hour. After eight miles, just outside town, the terrain leveled off. A right turn onto US Route 287 led them through a small, bustling downtown, then across the Madison River, where several men were fly-fishing, and onto a flat stretch for miles.

With a rumble strip separating the wide shoulder from speeding traffic, she relaxed. She could enjoy the scenery and push as hard or as little as she wanted. Her odometer read forty-five miles for the day.

They stopped in Cameron, where a store among a cluster of wooden structures marked the hub of the rural town.

Lauren removed her windbreaker, stowed it, and retrieved her phone. Three new voice messages. *Jeffrey Maddox.* Her heart thumped.

Lars was scanning his phone too.

Reaching for the voicemail icon, she hesitated. No. Not here with him.

Lars pocketed his phone. "How are you feeling?"

"Great, actually. I could cycle this road forever."

"It gets harder. But if you have another twenty miles in you, we can make it to the Madison River Campground. They won't turn us away. And it's right by the river. Meanwhile, I need to go talk to a man about a horse."

Lars walked into the store.

Lauren pulled out her phone and listened to the first message. "Hi. It's me. Hope you're doing well. Just checking in."

The sound of his voice sent tremors through her soul.

The second message was left a minute after the first. "And I . . . I miss you."

Lauren turned away from the storefront and gazed at the beautiful countryside, heart in her throat. But what was the big idea, him calling her like this? It was thoughtful of him to check in. Or maybe it was something more. But if it rocked her world every time he messaged, perhaps she shouldn't respond.

She listened to the third message. From Doug. "Hi, Lauren. I just wanted to make sure you're doing okay. I hope the scenery down by you is as beautiful as it is here. Please let me know how you're doing. Stay safe. Goodbye."

That was sweet of him. Doug really was a good guy. After what they'd shared together in the past few weeks, she wouldn't forget about him anytime soon. She wondered—

"Ready?" Lars hopped on his bicycle.

Lauren pocketed her phone. "Yes. I am. After I go to the bathroom too."

Soon the pair had added more miles in the flat valley. The Madison River came back into view, with anglers whipping their fly rods or casting from the riverbanks. The surrounding mountains and the sky encompassing the adjacent grasslands kept the aesthetics first-rate, despite the frequent car or RV speeding by. The sun kissed Lauren's right cheek on the southward trek, while the anticipation of Yellowstone spurred her robust cadence.

Lars coasted until she caught up. "You fish?"

"I tried it in Uganda, but I prefer catching them at the market or in a restaurant."

Lars laughed. "Me too."

A pack of motorcycles rumbled by. Chunky men sat atop most of them, bandannas flapping on their heads, sunglasses shrouding their faces. Bulky arms sprouted out of each side of similarly patched leather vests as they cruised down Route 287.

*Lord, please protect them.*

After a few more pedal strokes Lars said, "There's another campground that'll be less crowded than Madison River. It's only a few more miles. Wanna stop there?"

Maybe it'd be better if they did stay at a crowded campground. She might not get lost in those eyes of his. But maybe this was God's way of moving her on. Besides, anyone who could sing a hymn like he could was worth getting to know better. She looked down at her odometer. Seventy-one miles. "Sure."

In a couple of miles they turned right and crossed a bridge over the river. The sign read *Campground* with an arrow pointing left, but Lars went straight instead, onto a dirt road, standing to maintain a brisk pace.

Lauren followed, checking the mileage on her odometer.

The road narrowed as the forest enveloped it, the late-afternoon sun shrouded from view.

A mile passed.

"Where are we going?"

"Up ahead."

Her question seemed fairer than the response, but Lars knew where he was going.

In another half mile they turned left onto an even narrower road. A few yards in, a stream appeared. An outhouse flanked the small parcel. A crude firepit with two charred logs sat alongside the water. No one was around. A solitary picnic table, once green and flat, had served up lunch for one too many insects. A short signpost with two sets of bolts stood beside the firepit. The upper set had nothing attached to it. A sign on the lower set read *At Your Own Risk*.

Lauren's stomach churned. "I don't know about this."

"It'll be fine. I've stayed here a time or two." Lars leaned his bicycle against the table and pulled his tent from his bicycle. "It's quiet. The rushing water will lull you to sleep."

Slowly Lauren wheeled her bike to the other end of the table and removed the bungee cord securing her violin and tent.

"Don't worry. I have bear spray and a gun." He winked at her. Then he set his phone on the table.

As he turned away and unpacked his tent, she couldn't help but notice. *"Robin"?*

Can't wait to see you. You heartthrob,
you! Only . . .

Her stomach fluttered. *Just who is Robin?*

The remainder of the message was masked.

It was none of her business anyway. Served her right for reading his message. Besides, why did she care?

Lars glanced up, and she looked back at her violin. He pocketed his phone.

She pulled her tent off the rear rack and turned to consider where to pitch it.

Meanwhile, Lars had pulled his tent from its sack, along with poles, stakes, and fly, and placed them on a flat piece of ground next to the stream.

He looked up. "Want some help?"

Lauren examined the campground's small footprint. She would have separate quarters from Lars, but not much space between them. Of course, that might be a good thing.

She dropped her tent on the opposite side of the picnic table. "Sure, thank you."

"Wanna take a dip before it cools off?"

Her breath caught in her throat. Before thinking, she said, "Sure."

*Uh-oh, what am I doing?*

The memory of their dip the day before flashed through her mind.

Lars removed his helmet and ripped off his cycling jersey, flashing her a side glance and a dimple before he strode into the stream. "Phew, that's cold!"

"Really? I'm coming in too." Lauren tossed her helmet near her tent and placed the contents of her pockets on the table. As she waded into the stream, goosebumps covered her skin. When the water reached her knees, she stopped.

Lars, submerged from the waist down, splashed his chest and wiped down his arms and face. "Oh is that ever refreshing."

A few body lengths away, Lauren stood with her mouth open and watched him. Rays from the late-afternoon sun seared through a stand of trees and shimmered atop the water flowing alongside him. Each of his pecs squeezed to his chest, one by one, as he reached his thick arms around his back to wash it.

When he noticed her stare, he swung his powerful forearm across the water with his hand cupped.

A deluge smacked her torso, the cold water sending a shiver through her body. She wobbled before catching her balance.

"Look, you!" She splashed back. The fresh mountain water slapped his face. She giggled.

He smiled. And whacked back with both arms, sending a torrent knocking her in the head, his biceps flexing as he shielded his face from her next assault.

Doubling down, she flailed her arms with whatever force she could muster, stepping toward him to increase the odds of a direct hit, laughing along the way.

He did the same—

Until she stopped. Those magical eyes of his pierced her as beads of water glimmered on his golden eyebrows. A quivering sensation rippled through her chest.

A vehicle roared past the campsite.

*What am I doing?*

He ducked into the water and swam toward her.

She backed away. "I—I'm freezing." She turned and dashed out of the stream, leaving him in the middle, arms floating atop the current.

# CHAPTER 15

Doug stepped out of the shower in his motel room in Livingston and brushed his teeth. He still couldn't believe he was the man staring back from the mirror. Not the same guy who'd embarked on this adventure over two months ago. He stretched his arms and legs, then flexed his muscles. Very little soreness or fatigue. And even more definition. Granted it was a short day of cycling. He'd stopped when another sign to Yellowstone appeared. Besides, Bozeman Pass had delivered enough thrills for one day.

But how much better would it have been had he shared it with someone? The thought echoed in the silent room.

Lauren hadn't returned his phone message. Not that she should. She'd been so wonderful to him after life as he'd known it had come to an abrupt end, leaving him wondering if he would too. Lauren was kindness personified. And the troubles they'd encountered together just a couple of weeks earlier . . . she had dropped into his life at the perfect time.

But then he let her go.

*What kinda fool am I?*

Brother Jim said it was no accident Doug and Lauren met when they did. Maybe, just maybe. But, no. Impossible. She was much too young. She needed a vibrant man—he looked in the mirror again—well, a more vibrant man . . . to raise a family with. Someone as strong in faith as she was.

But then again he wasn't born yesterday, and who knew?

He envisioned her shapely body atop her bicycle, those ginger locks of hers flowing in the breeze. And the curl of her lips when she smiled. Those hazel eyes.

Doug dressed and lay down on the bed. After propping himself up with pillows, he reached for his cell phone on the nightstand.

Still no message.

He scanned his photos, selected one, but before sending it, shook his head. No, she didn't want to hear from him, or she'd have returned his call. Or at least texted.

Doug set the phone down and opened the nightstand drawer. A Gideons Bible. Did that ever bring back memories. He pulled it out, nestled it underneath his chin for a moment, then opened it and scanned the topical references inside the front cover. *Loneliness.*

He flipped to Genesis 2:18.

> And the LORD God said, "It is not good that man should
> be alone; I will make him a helper comparable to him."

Yeah, that was a problem. "Comparable to him." What women were like Doug—or would want to be? But maybe. How many women would venture across America on a bicycle by themselves?

As he removed his right hand to scratch behind his ear, the Bible flopped open to another chapter, nearer the back. He grabbed the book and noticed a twenty-dollar bill inserted there. He pulled it out and noticed verse 10 underlined in ink.

> For we are His workmanship, created in Christ Jesus for good works, which God prepared beforehand that we should walk in them.

If that were true, what was he doing on an open-ended bicycle trip? Sure, he could do good things out here, but this joyride was so much about him. What good works had God prepared for him to do?

Then he remembered Brother Jim's suggestion. Doug knew all about the sales process—following up with people, showing how his products could help them, then urging them to give what he was selling a try. But pitching a nonprofit cause? Sales were hard enough. How could he motivate people to part with their money when they received only a thank-you in return?

Working with Brother Jim, though, would offer him the opportunity to learn so much more from one of the wisest people he'd ever met. And these Montanans and their beautiful state—that wouldn't be too hard to get used to.

Still, an anvil had lodged in the bottom of his gut. Why couldn't this opportunity have come along while Ruth was around?

No. He wasn't ready. The hole was still there. And there was more to discover.

Doug reached for his belt bag and placed the twenty into it. But when he grabbed the zipper, he stopped.

He pulled the twenty back out and returned it to where he'd found it. Then he dropped one of his own in Genesis chapter 2. Using the motel's pen, he scrawled a star beside verse 18. Surely it would mean something to someone else. And maybe that wanderer would be cycling through here alone and could use the money for a meal.

The sun was setting, and the cool of the evening fell. Lars had gone into the woods to change his clothes, which gave Lauren the chance to change inside her tent.

Her phone vibrated, so she pulled it from the pouch atop the door. *Maggie Covington.*

"Maggie! It's so good to hear from you."

"Jim and I have been thinking about you, so I thought I would call to see how you're doing."

"We're just outside of Yellowstone. Should be there tomorrow."

"I'm glad to hear you're still traveling together. How is Doug?"

"I'm not with Doug."

"Oh?"

Lauren swallowed. "We parted ways a few days ago, in Whitehall. Then I met a man named Lars who helped me fix a flat tire." She lowered her voice. "He's so handsome."

That was far enough. She needn't know the effect he had on her heart.

"Be careful, Lauren. You've just come off a big disappointment."

"That's good advice. Thank you."

"Are you familiar with Proverbs 4:23?"

"Is that the verse about guarding your heart?"

"Yes."

"Thank you for the reminder."

They chatted a few minutes about Virginia City and what was ahead in Yellowstone.

"It sounds like Lars is back."

"I should let you go. Jim and I will be praying for you."

When Lauren exited the tent, Lars was building a fire.

"Is that legal?"

He placed another log on the fire. "It is if they don't catch me." He looked up at her and grinned.

Lauren's chest tightened.

"Here. Help me."

The two cleared their items from the picnic table and moved it in front of the fire, where the warmth soothed her tired muscles.

Lars fished in his pannier and pulled out a cup of Ramen noodles. "Want some?"

"Sure. Why not."

He grabbed another one, heated water in a portable boiler, and poured the water into the two cups. "I've been wondering. Why are you out here all by yourself? A beautiful woman like you could be a target."

Blood rushed to Lauren's face. "It's a long story."

"We have all night."

"Let me see if I can condense it for you. This trip is a gift from my late grandfather. Before I settle down. Only it looks like I won't be settling down anytime soon."

"Okay. Maybe you could uncondense it enough for me to understand."

"The trip's my bachelorette party. Only now I'm not getting married."

Lars's brow jumped. "I see. Is this a good thing?"

Lauren stared into the fire. "I don't know." She got up and reached into her pannier. "Would you like a bagel with peanut butter?"

"That sounds great. Please."

As they ate, they conversed about eagles, the climb out of Virginia City, and the long, flat stretch through the valley.

After finishing up, Lars cleared his throat. "You seemed a bit skittish at lunch when I asked you about what happened at the Music Hall."

Lauren sucked in a nervous breath.

"Why did you stop playing?"

She gazed into the surrounding forest, now lit only by the glow of their campfire. "You have my father's voice."

"I do? Well, tell him I'll return it for the chance to spend more time with his lovely daughter."

"I—I can't."

"What do you mean?"

"He's not with us anymore."

Lars tilted his head, studying her eyes.

Lauren took another deep breath. "My folks were killed by a drunk driver when I was in college. We used to play music together, as a family."

"I'm sorry."

"I'm okay with it now." She shooed a mosquito from her leg. "God redeemed it."

When she looked up, he was staring into the fire with two vertical creases separating his eyebrows.

"And you at the orphanage. Your mind was miles away. Were you thinking about your grandfather?"

"Never heard anything good come out of that place."

"What happened?"

"Abuse. The worst kind. With repercussions down through the generations."

Lauren placed her hand on his arm.

He looked at it, then raised his chin until he was staring into her eyes.

The moments leading up to her first kiss from Jeffrey rushed in. Lauren yanked her hand from his arm. "I—I'm sorry. I can't . . ." She looked away.

The chirping of tree crickets filled the space between them.

When she ventured another look at him, his face wore a sideways smirk, one prominent dimple suggesting this conversation could be continued at another time.

The two cleaned up the campsite and placed their food items in a large stuff sack Lars had pulled out of a pannier, along with rope. He knotted the rope around the neck of the bag. "I'll go find a place to hang this."

After he left, Lauren grabbed her phone. She could call Jeffrey, but what would she say? Certainly not, "I miss you. Could we get back together?" Besides, Lars would return soon.

Instead she opened the text thread with Jeffrey and wrote:

> Got your message. Thanks. Doing well. What a beautiful state! Saw an eagle today.

She paused. *No. Too much detail.* She changed it to:

> Got your message. Thanks. Doing well. Hope your work is going well.

Before she could push send, a holler echoed through the woods. Her hands shook. It sounded farther away than Lars could have walked.

She listened.

Branches crackled to her right. She snapped her head that way. No sight or sound from there. But something was in those woods.

She ingested a faltering breath. Then another.

A pine scent drifted by. The river whooshed behind her.

Stars filled the sky. She scanned the dotted panorama until—

Another shout from the same direction as the first, but louder, sending chills down her arms.

Then more crackling to her right.

It sounded like a critter.

"Lars?"

The snapping of wood broke the silence. A chill traversed her spine.

She pulled a can of bear spray out of her pannier and scanned the campsite and its surrounding woods. Nothing!

She reread her text message to Jeffrey, then pushed send.

Where was Lars? How long did it take to hang a bear bag?

She listened to Doug's message again. Truth be told, she'd have been more comfortable at this campsite with him than Lars. Not that his looks were any match to Lars's, but . . . something about Doug calmed her, like an old friend who understood her without an explanation. And . . . well . . . maybe he needed her after what he'd been through.

No.

For heaven's sake, he was old enough to be her father. Still, she missed him. She really did. He was also old enough to know a woman's feelings lived in a straw hut rather than a brick building. At least that's what her daddy tried to tell her oh so many years ago.

She could call Doug back, but would someone hear her? They probably shouldn't be at this campsite. And Lars could return anytime. She typed:

> It is so beautiful here. Saw an eagle today! Wish you were here.

Lauren sent it.

Soon the faint sound of scuffing grew louder. Her pulse quickened. The shadow of a man entered the campsite, a beam of light bouncing with his steps.

"Sorry. Had to talk to a man about a horse."

Lauren let out a big sigh. "Did you find a place?"

"Yeah, but it took a while."

After he sat at the picnic table, she reached for her violin.

Lars jerked his head toward the campsite entrance, then looked back at Lauren. "Ah . . . I would love to hear you play again, but . . . maybe it's time to get some rest." He painted on a smile. "Besides, we don't want to wake the neighbors."

# CHAPTER 16

The constant flow of water alongside Lauren's tent should have made rest after a seventy-mile day even easier. But first came her devotional time. And then a trip to the outhouse before closing her eyes.

She'd heard Lars unzip his tent, zip it back up, and wish her "Good night," but the sounds afoot hadn't stopped. Or was it an extra strong babble every now and then from the river? Or a dying ember murmuring in the firepit? She pawed around beside her mattress and found the bear spray, then put it beside her makeshift pillow, where it would be accessible should the need arise.

An owl hooted.

She adjusted her head on the stuff sack of clothes. Then she navigated to the book of Matthew and the Sermon on the Mount.

But she thought of Genesis and "It is not good for man to be alone."

Lauren had always cherished her independence, but was this too much of it? Since leaving Uganda, there'd been a dearth of young people around her. The ride had been wonderful, but she missed the exuberance of kids. Would she ever have her own? Not if she kept pushing away every man who showed an interest in her. Or got close enough to make her heart flutter.

Still, she wasn't about to mortgage her future with a man who didn't understand the meaning of commitment. *But did she?* The company of a good man was delightful, but being under the thumb of one?

Which was worse, being alone or tied down? Or heartbroken? Right now it was being alone. Her heart had been a yo-yo with Jeffrey. Sometimes it was safer to keep guys at a distance.

*Lord, I don't like this. Maybe I* am *afraid. And all I hear is time ticking away.*

Suddenly a distant cry echoed, like someone in distress.

*Lord, help whoever it is.*

When it sounded again, she started, then froze to listen.

She slumped back on the mattress, pulling her sleeping bag tighter around her shoulders.

Another hoot.

She started reading the Sermon on the Mount.

Soon the sound of snoring joined the crickets outside.

A few minutes later the murmur of motorcycle engines pierced the dark, increasing in volume as Lauren's heart rate accelerated. She stopped reading and listened.

The rumble grew. Maybe just a few bikes, but louder still. Then it swelled, echoing in the surrounding forest.

Her brow dampened.

She'd left most of her belongings outside. They wouldn't fit in the tent anyway. She pulled her arm out of her sleeping bag and groped for her violin case. There. Then she leaned forward, snatched her zip pouch from the pocket above the doorway, and slid it into her sleeping bag.

The motorcycle engines burbled as whoever was driving them let off the gas. Just outside the entrance to the campsite, she guessed. She shielded her phone's screen, powered down the device, and shoved it into her sleeping bag.

Someone yelled over the noise, then the throttles were reengaged and the rumble became much louder. Light flashed against her tent.

Lauren gulped. She'd set her peach-colored top on the picnic table to dry.

"Someone's here already!"

The motor noise approached her tent so fast it might strike her any second.

"That ain't stoppin' me!"

Then the loudest motor shut off. "My bladder's 'bout to s'plode." A squeak rang out as if the bike was propped onto its stand.

"Hurry it up, would you." Someone goosed an engine. It sounded like the only one running.

"I don' feel s'good."

Feet shuffled.

"It's no wonder."

*Thump!* Something hit the tent.

Lauren froze.

"Oops." Out came a burp. And the strong smell of alcohol. In Uganda nothing good came from that scent.

She drew in a breath, then another.

"Anybody home?"

Where was Lars? He couldn't sleep through this.

"We don't have all night."

The feet shuffled away. Then a spring twanged and the outhouse door slammed shut. Which reminded her . . .

Then, muffled behind the door, he retched. On and on the agony went.

Her stomach roiled.

"Disgusting." The motor revved. Twice.

After the outhouse door smacked again, feet shuffled nearer.

"Bro, these people deaf . . . Or these belongings all ours?" He belched.

"Would you come on. We don't have no time for petty larceny. They're waitin' for us."

Stench filtered through the tent and hung up in her throat.

After a *squeak* and a *ka-thump*, kickstarting the engine failed. The man muttered an expletive. "Shupid bike."

"Just use the electric start, fool. Are you gonna be able to balance that thing?"

With another kickstart the motor fired. "What're ya talkin' 'bout?"

The engine accelerated into gear, the noise leaving the campsite.

Lauren exhaled.

As the roar faded into the distance, she took several more deep breaths. Maybe a gun wasn't such a bad idea after all.

"Lauren?"

Heart still racing, she wasn't ready to respond.

Lars unzipped his tent and trudged out.

"Are you okay?"

"Yes," she managed. "You?"

"I am. I wasn't expecting the neighbors to show up so late tonight."

He walked away, then the outhouse door sprung open before smacking shut. He soon walked past her tent and wished her another "Good night."

After a couple of minutes wide-eyed, she unzipped her sleeping bag and moved toward the tent door.

Water whooshed as a chorus of crickets chirped.

She donned her headlamp and crawled out of her tent, clutching the can of bear spray. The stillness of the night gripped her.

Lars's tent on the other side of the picnic table appeared dark and dormant. She sniffed the air. The nasty odor lingered.

She slipped on her flip-flops and stepped toward the outhouse, careful to shine her headlamp where her feet would land. Her time had definitely arrived.

As the distance closed, the foul smell assaulted her nostrils. The door, with its pitch-black, crescent-moon cutout, hung ajar, sagging in its warped frame. It might stink to high heaven, but it would beat the woods. Especially with what she'd heard from them earlier.

She slowed and dropped the can of bear spray, raising her hand to her face to cup her nose and mouth. As she stretched her other hand toward the door—

"Need to talk to a man about a horse?"

She gasped and turned.

It was Lars, his blue eyes hidden in the shadow, moonlight casting the outline of his chiseled chin. "Oh. You scared me."

"Sorry. I didn't mean to. I wouldn't go in if I were you."

"Wh—why not?" She turned and reached for the door.

"Don't do it."

The gravity of his tone stopped her, but she couldn't wait any longer. As she grasped the door, her hand slipped on something wet. "Ewwww."

The smell of bile and beer nearly gagged her, but she stepped in anyway—until her foot skidded, nearly losing her balance. Goo slid between her toes, oozing onto the top of her foot.

Her headlamp shone across the toilet seat, then the floor, both covered with chunks and fluid. "Gross!" Another wave of stench drenched her nostrils.

She huffed, then ran toward the sound of the rushing water, smearing her headlamp as she redirected it to see where she was going. When she reached the riverbank, she kicked off her flip-flops but couldn't find a place to get in. So she sat and reached her legs for the water.

Lars approached from behind. "I'm sorry, but I tried to warn you."

"Lord, help me." She stretched down farther. Just a little more—she began to slip. She screeched.

Lars's firm hands swept beneath her armpits. "Shhhh."

She exhaled as he pulled her up. "Wait, I need to get that stuff off."

"I can drop you down, but I don't know how deep it is."

"Can . . . can you just hold me . . . until I say stop?"

Lars inched her down.

"Don't let go."

"I won't."

The current began to guzzle her feet. "Okay, that's good." She swished around her yucky foot.

Lars lifted her from the abyss and sat her on the riverbank. Then he knelt behind her and wrapped his arms around her. "You're okay," he whispered. "Everything's going to be just fine."

His embrace felt surprisingly comforting. She took a few deep breaths to quench the frenetic pace of her heart as his biceps squeezed against her arms, his pecs against her back.

"You can trust me."

She rested her hand—the clean one—on his powerful forearm, first squeezing it, then resisting the urge to caress it.

"You're right. I do need to go see a man about a horse. And fast."

"Do you want me to go with you?"

She hesitated. "And if I said 'Yes'?"

"I'd escort you to a secluded spot in the woods where no one would see you. Of course, that would be about anywhere right now." He chuckled. "Then I would turn my head and walk several feet in the opposite direction, then ask you if that was far enough."

"Okay."

The two rose. Lars pulled a water bottle from the picnic table and squirted Lauren's flip-flops to remove the vomit. Then he doused her hands. He put his arm around her and held her close as they walked toward the woods, passing the outhouse.

"My bear spray." She picked it up. "Ew, that smell."

"Hopefully it doesn't attract hungry critters, but at least they'll have something to feast on besides us. It's not like we can relocate now."

They kept walking.

"Who were they?"

"The neighbors."

"Okay. This should be good."

Lars released her.

"Thank you."

He turned and took a few steps toward the campsite. "Is this far enough?"

"As long as you look the other way, yes."

As she turned, a dark plastic jug caught her attention. She aimed her headlamp at it. *360 Twin Primary Chaincase Oil.* A few feet to the right, along with empty beer cans, a shiny piece of metal, holes on the top and bottom, lay on the grass. She stepped that way and flipped it over.

*US Forest Service. Day Use Only.*

Lauren stowed her headlamp in the pouch above the tent door and slithered into her sleeping bag. Heart pounding, she opened her Bible app to Psalm 23:

> The LORD is my shepherd;
> I shall not want.
> He makes me to lie down in green pastures;
> He leads me beside the still waters.
> He restores my soul;
> He leads me in the paths of righteousness
> For His name's sake.
> Yea, though I walk through the valley of the shadow of
> death,
> I will fear no evil;
> For You are with me;
> Your rod and Your staff, they comfort me.

Yes, it was comforting to have a man around, especially in times like these. The Ugandans had always looked after her. God provided comfort when needed the most.

Lars was there for her. What would've happened had she been alone?

The purr of an engine increased to a frisky growl as it approached. Lauren squeezed her phone. The vehicle rumbled closer, crunching rocks and pinging pebbles until it vanished in the opposite direction.

She exhaled.

# CHAPTER 17

The sun coaxed the early-morning chill heavenward until it vanished into the beautiful Montana skyscape. Doug glanced at his phone, which was vibrating within its mount. *Jeffrey Maddox.*

Why was *he* calling?

That fella wasn't too bright for a well-educated, city-slickin' lawyer. Who in his right mind would let Lauren slip through his hands?

Three eighteen-wheelers sped by, rocking his recumbent as he crept up a knoll on the shoulder of I-90. Even if he wanted to field that phone call, he wouldn't hear a word of it.

*"Wish you were here"* drifted through his thoughts.

With traffic buffeting his load and a longing tugging his heart, *he* wasn't in his right mind either.

A horn blared from a passing car. The driver waved in his rearview mirror. Then a band of Harleys roared past. Roughly twenty of them.

Riding this road again wasn't really his idea, but frontage roads didn't always go from point A to point B. Sometimes the only way there was to hop on the interstate through another mountain pass. Besides, who wanted to wind around hills or climb them? Interstates could be hair-raising, but they were usually straight and steady, a welcome break from the type of climbing recumbents didn't do well. Or at least those who propelled them.

Fifteen minutes later a sign read *Bridge Closed, Crossover Ahead.*

An exit ahead offered hope for a better route. Plus a chance to see if Jeffrey had left a message. So he rolled down the ramp and into an abandoned lot.

He listened to Jeffrey's message:

"Hi, Doug. I'm at the courthouse on a break. Just checking in to see how you guys are doing. Please give me a call. Safe travels, my friend."

Poor Jeffrey. He must be having second thoughts. Who wouldn't?

Doug glanced at the clock on his phone. Jeffrey was probably still in session.

Reaching into his pannier, Doug fished out an energy bar. He placed his phone back into its mount and grabbed a water bottle. After he bit into the bar, a small Toyota pickup with a cap pulled up.

A man opened the door and placed one foot on the ground. "You ridin' the interstate?"

"I was." Doug gestured to the road beside them. "Does this road go to Columbus?"

"Not really. It's the long way around. And not a great road. Listen, why I stopped"—he pointed toward the interstate—"the eastbound lane is closed over the Yellowstone River. Repair work. They're diverting traffic onto the westbound lane."

"Can a bicycle get across the closed highway? Maybe if I walk it?"

"Not unless you can balance it on a steel girder."

Doug sighed.

"There's a traffic light, but I reckon you're not fast enough to get across before it changes . . . Look, I can provide you cover."

"That's mighty kind of you. Right now?"

"Yeah, I need to be in Billings in an hour."

"In that case, let's go." Doug wrapped up the energy bar, dropped it into his pocket, and snapped in his cleats. "I'll see you up there."

Once back onto the highway, a large, orange construction sign pointed left, across the median, now paved as a crossover. A traffic light hung from a cord suspended over the entrance to the westbound road, with a few eastbound cars and trucks waiting for it to turn green. Brake lights shone red as more vehicles passed him. A Jake brake bellowed behind him.

Doug looked in his rearview mirror. With his blinkers flashing, the man in the pickup pulled onto the road behind Doug, then waved out the window for him to go.

Did this guy realize Doug rode only ten to twelve miles per hour on a flat stretch? Regardless, any cover was better than no cover, even if it irritated a few motorists behind them. Maybe he should wait for the light to cycle through once, find out how much time it allowed him, and catch his breath to bolt across the bridge when the light turned green. But that would only delay the inevitable and possibly make the man late.

With westbound traffic trickling across the bridge, he decided to go for it in anticipation of the light turning green soon. He crossed the median on the temporary roadway and began passing the cars with idling motors choking his supply of fresh air, leaving his Good Samaritan stuck behind several vehicles. Staying to the right, Doug rolled onto the skimpy left-hand shoulder of the westbound roadway. The bridge appeared a quarter mile ahead. The closer he pedaled to it, the longer the bridge grew.

The torque of a diesel engine blatted behind him. He glanced in his rearview mirror, then swiveled his head. He hadn't even made it to the bridge and the light had turned. Cars were approaching fast.

He squeezed the brakes and stopped. Cars accelerated on by. With no guardrail to block him, he wheeled his bicycle off the pavement.

A few big rigs roared past him, followed by his Good Samaritan. With nowhere to stop, he waved as he, too, went by. Then he turned off his flashers.

*Oh no! Why didn't I ask him to load my recumbent into his truck? But it probably wouldn't have fit anyway.*

Using both lanes, more eastbound traffic followed until vehicles queued up again behind the stop light.

Maybe it was better to travel into traffic anyway. Or turn around. But that didn't seem like such a great idea either. Where would he go if he exited the interstate?

If he crossed over to the wider right-hand shoulder, on his left, how would he get back across once over the bridge? Assuming he made it over the bridge.

Instead he stayed right and cycled on.

When he mounted the bridge, what little shoulder he had left shrank to about three feet, smooshing him between the white line to his left and a railing to his right. He could easily look over the railing at the river but fixed his eyes on the narrow path in front of him instead. A chill ran through him, but not because of the cool breeze from the water below.

Traffic began filling the road ahead, roaring closer as he glimpsed water through the railing. A tractor trailer entered the passing lane and headed straight toward him. His sweaty palms clutched the handgrips.

The trucker laid on his horn as the eighteen-wheeler with a box trailer in tow barreled toward him.

Doug's breath caught in his throat. His hands shook as he squeezed the handgrips, thrusting his legs forward to keep his jalopy as straight as possible while preparing for the onslaught of the truck's draft. *Lord, protect me.*

The rig flew by, the hurricane-force wind knocking his helmet sideways, obscuring his view of the road ahead. The blare faded until the trucker laid off the horn.

Another blast sounded ahead of him.

His heart pounded.

Doug jiggled his head in a futile attempt to right his helmet and regain his vision. *Why didn't I tighten it?*

The sound grew louder. This wasn't just an automobile or a pickup.

He let go of the right handgrip, grabbed his helmet, and straightened it.

The bridge railing appeared farther away than before. Ahead, the grill of another eighteen-wheeler barreled toward him, its horn blaring louder by the second.

The truck drifted toward the other lane to avoid him.

A motorist in that lane jerked toward the other shoulder and laid on his horn.

The trucker corrected, veering toward Doug.

Doug swung to the right, toward the white line, the scant shoulder, the low railing, and the Yellowstone River.

A rock bounced off his helmet as the rig rushed past him, its wheels clearing him by a mere two feet. The gust pushed him farther to the right until he knocked against the railing, his head tilting over the edge until it snapped back.

Nervous inhalation filled Doug's lungs with needed oxygen.

Ahead, westbound vehicles began queuing behind a traffic light suspended well past the end of the bridge. A crossover a quarter mile in the distance might just deliver him to safe passage. If he could make it.

He glanced in his rearview mirror. A black plume poured from a smokestack on another tractor trailer. Vehicles clogged both lanes, racing toward him from behind.

He pushed the pedals harder. There was nowhere to stop and no time to do it.

A siren wailed, increasing in volume.

He looked behind.

A Montana state trooper approached, blue lights flashing. The rush of vehicles slowed as the police car pulled in front of the big rig in the near lane.

Doug sighed. The pounding in his chest eased.

The cruiser escorted him until he reached the shoulder on the eastbound roadway. Much like a NASCAR pace car, the trooper pulled off to the shoulder, which allowed the vehicles behind him to jockey for position on the open track and resume their race.

The trooper exited his vehicle. "Out for a joyride on the interstate, are we?"

"Hi, Officer." Doug leaned back on his recumbent as the trooper walked in front of him.

"We received complaints about a cyclist on the interstate. Thought you might need help." The trooper grinned beneath his opaque sunglasses. "We don't design these crossovers with cyclists in mind."

"Thank you." Doug shook his head. "I thought I was a goner."

"Well, it could be worse. Just be glad you're not over in Yellowstone."

Lars and Lauren had cycled eight miles in the Madison River Valley, veering eastward with the river on the south side of US Route 287. The shoulder narrowed as the climb began, evergreen trees encroaching on the surrounding hillsides, a guardrail separating the two of them from the Madison River.

Lars twisted his head around. "Up ahead is Quake Lake. A big earthquake in 1959. Seven point three. Giant landslide. Killed some people. Grandpa always talked about it."

Cycling with a tour guide familiar with the surroundings had its advantages, especially one who'd cooked breakfast. She'd woken up in a fog after dreaming of cycling in a wedding gown. With alterations, of course. Maybe little ones weren't as far away as she'd wondered. But, like her other dreams, it had no groom.

Lauren pushed harder as her bicycle slowed on the uphill grade. An RV cruised by, hugging the shoulder. Her heart quickened while her breath hung up.

A mile later, when she rounded a bend, a brown mass without vegetation appeared.

Lars pointed straight ahead. "That's it."

After more exertion they curled higher until the river was no more. A *National Forest Geologic Area* sign pointed left for the visitor center.

"Wanna go up?"

Lauren glanced left at the large barren mound and sucked in air. "I would rather go down. But, yes, it sounds interesting."

After exiting I-90, Doug stopped roadside and pulled out his phone. No messages other than the text he'd received from Lauren the night before. He reread it. Her wish for him to be with her had warmed his heart. But wishing it didn't make it true. That's where he wanted to be too, just not in Yellowstone.

He called Jeffrey. "Hi, what's up?"

"Hey, Doug. I just wanted to see how you guys are doing."

"Well, I can update you on me if you're interested."

"Where's Lauren?"

"I haven't heard from her today, but I'm guessing she's fast approaching Yellowstone National Park. I just hope she remembers her bear spray."

"What do you mean?"

"Think about it. It's not like she can hide in the cab of a vehicle should she cross paths with a wild animal."

Silence.

"You there, Jeffrey?"

"Yeah. How come you're not with her?"

"I like bears, but only when they're in captivity and I'm not. Plus vehicles. From what I understand, they could be worse."

A crisp breath filled Doug's ear.

"So you're nowhere near her?"

"We might still be in the same state, but we've gone in different directions. So, no."

Jeffrey said nothing.

"Sounds like you're worried about Lauren."

"You could say that."

"I just about . . ."—no, he doesn't need to hear that—"She's a big girl. She can handle herself."

"I don't like this."

"Forgive me for stating the obvious, but there's not much you can do about it. Especially from where you are."

"Do you know if she's with anyone?"

Doug scratched his jaw. *Good question.* "I don't."

"Okay, thanks for the update. Are you doing okay?"

"I am now."

"What do you mean?"

"I just had the adventure of a lifetime on I-90."

"What were you doing out there?"

"It's a long story."

"You guys are crazy. I'm glad you're okay. Be careful, would you? I'm going to check in with Lauren."

*I should've gone with her. I don't like this either.*

After reading about the tragic earthquake, viewing the natural beauty amid the unnatural rock formations, and eating an energy bar, Lauren followed Lars down from the visitor center, coasting until they turned back onto US 287 eastbound. Dead trees poked through stagnant water as they wound their way around Quake Lake to their right.

In the distance mountain ridges added texture to God's handiwork. The road weaved around hills and water, a moving canvas of artistic landscapes snapshotting itself at every turn. The splendid scenery brought tears to Lauren's eyes, but the thought of the people who'd lost their lives at Quake Lake dampened the awe.

Her phone vibrated in the back pocket of her jersey.

They twisted past the Refuge Point turnoff. When a large body of water appeared, the grade leveled and the horizon flattened into the distance. The breeze dancing across Hebgen Lake cooled Lauren's overheating body. The wide-open space energized her soul.

They stopped roadside at a turnoff.

"Wow! I can't believe these views."

"Nice, aren't they."

"Oh they're much more than nice. Can you believe how God thought this stuff up?"

Lars smiled at her. But it soon faded.

"Did I say something wrong?"

"I guess it's easy to take these views for granted. Not sure why God chose to bury those poor people in an avalanche of rocks though."

Lauren's stomach knotted, and she looked away.

"Give me a few minutes." Lars leaned his bicycle against a tree and scooted down a path, phone in hand.

Lauren pulled out her phone. Jeffrey had called and left a message.

"Hey, Pumpkin Spice. I hope you're safe down there in Yellowstone. I called Doug, and he said you had parted ways. I'll check in later. Feel free to call if you get bored or need anything. Miss you."

Her heart thumped. Between him and Lars, it was getting a workout. Being on her bicycle in the open air trumped either of those options for now. But she couldn't bicycle at night when loneliness cuddled her to sleep.

How should she respond? Or *should* she respond?

A few Canada geese squawked as they zoomed in formation across the rippling waters.

Lars strode up the path. "I'm hungry. Why don't we find a place to eat in West Yellowstone."

Fifteen relatively flat miles later traffic increased as they approached West Yellowstone. A familiar, rusty pickup chugged past them, filled with firewood. It backfired, a cloud of black smoke billowing from its exhaust pipe. Lars coughed while Lauren held her breath.

Once in town, they stopped at Jennifer's Deli, where they planned their entry into Wyoming and Yellowstone National Park.

# CHAPTER 18

Lars walked across the street to Park Quick Stop to pick up packaged food for both of them. Lauren sat outside Madison Valley Bike Shop, where a mechanic was working on her bicycle. She checked her phone. Jeffrey had left another message. A tremor flashed through her hand before she pushed play.

"Hi. It's me. Hope you're doing well. Please call when you get a chance."

Did she owe him a return call? If it was anybody else, of course. Why did she hesitate with him?

Sweat formed on her brow. She took a deep breath and pushed the call icon.

"Hi . . . Lauren? . . . Is that you?"

"Hello, Jeffrey. I'm returning your call."

"I just wanted to make sure you're doing okay."

After a moment of silence he added, "Are you?"

"Yes, I'm okay."

"Where are you?"

"West Yellowstone. Just outside the park."

"Do you have bear spray?"

"Yes, I have bear spray."

After another silence Jeffrey said, "I miss you."

Her heart rate picked up. Why was this so hard?

It's not like he didn't ask for this distance between them. What did he expect when he took interest in another woman besides his fiancée? Ex-fiancée, that was. She needed to end this call before Lars interrupted it.

"Look, Jeffrey, I need to go. Thank you for checking up on me, but I'm really okay."

"Well, it's good to hear your voice again."

Lauren took in a breath and waited.

"I . . . I love you."

She'd heard those words from him so many times, and she knew he meant it. But he was only adding more complexity to an already complicated set of emotions.

"I need to go. Goodbye, Jeffrey."

Her heart banged. She pictured him singing as part of the congregation at church, reading briefs on his computer, hiking with her in the Blue Ridge Mountains, and sweeping her into his arms.

But those were only memories now. She needed to move on.

As she walked into the store, the mechanic released the bike-stand clamp and lifted her loaded bicycle before easing it to the floor. "This should be good to go. The chain was a little thirsty, but other than that, things look pretty good."

"Did you check the rim?"

"Yes. It's fine. I trued the rear wheel just a bit. And we got you a new pump."

"Thank you. And thanks for bumping me to the head of the line."

"That's quite alright. We always give priority to long-distance cyclists." He looked at the violin case strapped on back. "Must be a challenge with all that weight on it."

"It's not too bad."

"Do you have bear spray?"

"Yes." The thought of last night's riders rumbled to her consciousness. "Say, is there a gun shop in this town?"

The man studied her. "You're not a Montana resident, are you?"

"No."

"Then you'd have trouble purchasing one. Besides, it's a felony to discharge a firearm in Yellowstone no matter what you're shooting at."

"Oh! I didn't know that. Thank you for the info."

Lauren paid at the register and wheeled her bicycle out of the shop, where Lars stood holding the bag of bagels she'd added to his list.

They bicycled US Route 20 East, with heavy traffic in both directions. In less than a mile, a large *Yellowstone National Park* sign appeared, painted brown to match the decor. Lauren's heart leaped.

Motorists in three lanes of a dozen cars each waited at the gatehouses to pay the park fee.

A forest ranger waved the two of them to the front of the line, then collected twenty dollars from Lauren. "Do you have bear spray?"

"Yes."

Lars, who had a pass, nodded.

"I suggest you put it where you can deploy it quickly. Like in a pocket or a holster. It's not like you can jump in your car to protect yourself."

Lauren took a deep breath. "What kinds of wildlife should we expect?"

"Bear, wolves, bison, elk, deer, moose. The bison may seem docile, but they can be aggressive. Make sure you stay at least a hundred yards from all wildlife at all times. If you find yourself in close proximity to a bear, back away slowly. You can't outrun it on those things."

"We will," Lauren said.

"And don't be afraid to use your spray. Just don't do it until the bear is within sixty feet of you, particularly if it's charging you. Factor in the wind direction too, so it doesn't drift off before the bear sniffs it."

Lauren nodded.

The attendant handed her a map. "Where are you staying tonight?"

"Madison," Lars said as he lifted a hand to decline the map. "Already got one."

"Lucky you're on bicycles. The campground is full, but they'll find a place for you."

Lars nodded.

"Any questions?"

"Are we in Wyoming now?"

"Just about." The attendant smiled.

"Thank you for the advice. I can't wait to see what's here."

The man smirked. "Well, be careful. A cyclist tenting near Madison got mauled last week. Lucky for him he survived with only a few stitches. Your pass is good for seven days. Enjoy your visit and stay safe."

As they cycled away from the gatehouse, Lars twisted his head around. "They always overdo it. I've stayed over here plenty of times and never had an incident."

Warmth washed through Lauren. An ample, paved shoulder allayed concerns she'd had about narrow roads in Yellowstone.

As heavy as traffic was entering the park, it was worse leaving it. Cars, RVs, and pickups pulling boat trailers clogged the westbound lane.

Several miles east the Madison River joined them on the north side of the road. Then eastbound traffic stopped. Lauren and Lars, however, continued, passing vehicle after vehicle until a hulking furry head popped up beyond the car roofs.

A buffalo—or, according to the park attendant, a bison—was lingering in the middle of the road. Not like the ones on her

African safaris, but furrier, with a shaggy face and without the handlebar-mustache horns.

People who'd exited vehicles were pointing cell phones at it, narrating videos. Others sat out their windows.

Lauren slowed to a stop, but Lars kept going.

Many motors were off, leaving only the voices of excited children and the revving engines of impatient motorcyclists to fill the afternoon breeze.

Lars reached the first car in line, stopped, then waved her forward. It sure didn't look like a hundred-yard buffer. He waved more emphatically nonetheless.

She fished out the bear spray from a pouch on the outside of her pannier and wedged it into a pocket on the back of her cycling jersey. She mounted her bicycle and crept forward.

Two motorcycles pulled out in front of her and sped to the front of the line. After pausing, the riders gunned their engines and blasted past the hulking animal, startling it, the roar fading into the distance.

The bison lowered its head and started toward Lars, but knocked into the grill of a Toyota Camry instead, rocking it.

Several women and girls close to the front screamed. Along with them, a few men scurried to their vehicles. Those perched on vehicle windowsills or rooftops vanished inside.

Lars turned his bicycle around and pedaled toward Lauren several car lengths back.

The bison grunted, then snorted.

Lauren's phone vibrated in her back pocket.

A car horn up front blared.

The bison dealt the Camry another headbutt, then another. It growled and smacked the pavement with its hoof.

Frozen with her hair standing on the back of her neck, Lauren glimpsed Lars pulling up beside her, her eyes darting between him and the bison.

Someone nearby called out, "Hey, you two wanna get in?"

Lars kept a vigilant eye ahead of them. "If we need to."

But Lauren dismounted her bicycle, yanked the violin case from it, and put the bike on the ground. "I'm getting in." She flung open the door and jumped into the pickup, violin first.

Lars waited outside.

Lauren situated the violin case on her lap, then looked over at the driver. Her heart sank. She peered over her shoulder. Sure enough, firewood obstructed her view out the back window.

How could it be? But with so many people around and Lars on the other side of the door, did it matter?

The man grinned, revealing a few missing teeth and a silver cap, the pockmarks above his beard stretching. "Where ya heading?"

"To a campground."

"Which one?"

A dank smell permeated the cab. Near the bottom of his scruffy beard, remnants from his last meal—or one a couple days ago—matted the whiskers.

Lauren hesitated. "M—Madison."

"Fancy that. Me too."

"How long do these delays last?"

"Five minutes to an hour or two. Ya never know."

The man stared out the windshield.

Lauren did the same. "Aren't you . . ."

"Yup. That's me."

She swallowed the lump in her throat and looked out the side window at Lars, then at the man. "Well . . . thank you."

"Couldn't let a purdy thing like you stay out there with that nasty critter."

The bison let out another groan. Up ahead muffled shrieks and giggles escaped open windows.

Lauren stuck her head out the window. Lars was gawking at the scene in front of them. *Is he just going to stay out here?*

Another snort filled the air, as did laughter from children popping out of car windows like jack-in-the-boxes. Lars smirked but didn't budge.

"Is that there a fiddle?"

Lauren pulled her head back into the cab. "It's a violin."

"Same difference. Kinda awkward for a bicycle, ain't it?"

The bison bellowed. With one more headbutt jostling the Camry, it turned and sauntered across the road several feet in front of Lars.

Lars leaned closer to the pickup until the beast roamed across an open meadow and began munching on a shrub.

"Thank you again. It was kind of you to invite us in."

As the vehicles ahead began to move, the man looked toward the river on his left. "Stay safe."

Lars and Lauren cycled through stands of ramrod-straight pine trees on either side of the road, sparse in places, some without bark, and damaged in other spots from fire or pestilence. A mountain range stood to the north, visible through gaps in the roadside trees. Oncoming vehicles with visors down and drivers' palms blocking the sunlight increased as the number of cars overtaking the duo diminished.

Where had the long, gorgeous views that accompanied them here gone? Nothing but bland green trees ahead. And the traffic? This wasn't what she'd signed up for. But when they crossed a bridge over the Madison River, hope for more beauty ahead beckoned. Chartreuse grassland lined the river as it snaked through the valley on the right side of the road, rock- and pine-covered hills draped behind it.

A large animal dipped its snout into the river. The presence of antlers suggested it was a male elk. *This is more like it. Maybe this is what draws an artist like Lars. Or what an artist like Lars draws.*

The river zigzagged alongside them before hugging the road, boulders dividing the current on its way to Montana. The pair cycled on as the sun lowered behind them.

They reached Madison Campground before sunset. Dense groves of pine trees offered unlimited hiding places for skinny kids while branches twenty feet off the ground brought ample shade to the camp lots ahead.

A pair of yammering teenage boys walked by. "Would you cut it out," one of them said.

The other one backhanded the bill of his companion's baseball cap, knocking it to the ground. He laughed and galloped into a sprint before his cohort retrieved his cap and chased him.

Lars shook his head as he and Lauren leaned their bicycles against the side of the check-in building and waited for a couple requesting change at the window.

When they left, Lars stepped forward. "Any room for us?"

The clerk's untamed eyebrows flared as he squinted. Strands of white hair flopped every which way on his balding head and shimmered under the overhead light. "We're full. But"—he glanced at their helmets—"we'll make room. How's that?"

Lauren's heartbeat slowed.

"It'll be ten dollars each for you and the missus."

Lauren peeked closer to the window. "Does that include two tents?"

"There's only room for one. I was gonna put ya behind the office, right by the restrooms. It has a canopy."

"We're—"

"We'll figure it out," Lars said.

Lauren's chest tightened.

"Check with your neighbors to see if you can fit your food into their bear box. If not, come back and see me."

Lauren nodded.

The clerk pointed around his shoulder. "It's right behind me. Can't miss it." He handed Lars a pamphlet. "There's a ranger talk at the amphitheater tonight at nine."

"Sir?" Lauren said.

"Ma'am?"

"We're not married."

The attendant chuckled. "That doesn't seem to stop people these days. But if you need a lot for two tents, I can put you on the fringe of the tents-only area. Go to the last loop, down by the river. There's a restroom right there too. Across from lot 289. But it might be more restful up here."

"What do you mean?"

"Wildlife."

Lauren tucked in her bottom lip.

"Ma'am, make sure you leave your food in a bear box. That goes for anywhere in the park."

The man unfolded a map and showed them the lot.

The two retrieved their bicycles and wheeled them away.

Lars grabbed his phone and pulled a stuff sack out of a pannier. "I'm gonna go stretch my legs."

"You don't want to miss the presentation, do you?"

"I'll take a rain check. I've seen that presentation so many times I could give it . . . in my sleep." Lars grinned. He poked the screen on his phone, smirked, then frowned and pocketed his phone. "I've got an extra double-fudge energy bar in my handlebar bag if you'd like one. Help yourself. It's just extra weight at this point—I need to start going back to my chocoholics meetings."

"Thanks, but I'm going for a healthier meal tonight." Maybe she should have taken him up on it just to see what he had in his handlebar bag. Maybe learn more about Robin.

As he walked back toward the camp store, Lauren checked her phone. No indication who had called and no coverage. Zero bars.

Who knew when she would get a signal.

At nine o'clock the sun—and the temperature—had dropped enough to require a base layer and tights. Cloud cover shrouded any moonlight, providing ample darkness for the ranger's short video on park safety and his upcoming presentation, "Animals of Yellowstone."

As the video's music faded to silence, a couple with four restless children plopped onto the wooden bench in front of Lauren. The calming ripple of the nearby Madison River disappeared downstream.

"Welcome, everyone. I'm Ranger Ferguson. Tonight we're going to explore animals you'll see in Yellowstone National Park."

For thirty minutes Ranger Ferguson covered interesting facts and behaviors of deer, elk, wolves, bear, bison, and raccoons and how to deal with close encounters with them. He assured his audience they would see some of these fascinating animals, perhaps closer than they would choose.

# CHAPTER 19

Lauren exited the women's facilities, cupped her hand over her eyes to ward off rain sprinkles, and returned to their makeshift lot.

That familiar rusty pickup was parked across the way, in lot 282. The truck's bed was empty. The old man sat at his firepit, his hand clutching the bill of his baseball cap as he swatted the air. He looked up.

Lauren offered a sheepish wave as she placed her violin, case and all, into a plastic bag.

He nodded, then stared into his smoky pit.

Lars pushed a tent stake into the ground and wrapped a guyline around it. When Lauren approached, he said, "I was going to set yours up, but I couldn't find the poles. Where'd you put them?"

"In the bag with the tent, fly, and stakes. I always put them there."

"They're not there. Check for yourself."

"What do you mean? I used them last night." Lauren swiped the opened bag from the ground. She squeezed it and then fished her hand into it. *Did I leave them at the campground last night?* "I couldn't've," she muttered. Her fingertips touched her forehead.

"Are they in your panniers?"

Lauren checked each pannier faster than the one before it, then unbuckled her violin case before returning it to the plastic bag. Not there.

She froze, then pressed her fist against her lips, her eyes glazing over.

More sprinkles soaked into the arms of her base layer until they morphed into light rain.

"Come on. Get in here with me. There's room." Lars crawled into his small tent, onto his inflated air mattress, and scooted to the side.

Lauren swallowed.

Three campers ran for cover in the lot across from them as the rain increased. A spring-loaded door smacked a few lots down. Then a few kids ran past while the adults with them strode up from the river.

"It's a lot drier in here."

She grabbed her air mattress, sleeping bag, and violin, closed her panniers, and ducked into Lars's tent, rubbing against his rock-hard quad as she slid forward.

A few more camper doors slammed shut.

"Welcome to my humble abode."

Lars had apparently had enough time to clean himself, though the campground had no shower. She, on the other hand, smelled like the orphanage's hamper on laundry day.

"Thank you."

"Don't mention it. Figured you might need the rest after all those miles the last few days."

Sleep? With him by her side?

The insides of the tent were tighter than full capacity at the orphanage bunkhouse with scarcely more air space than a compressed stuff sack. Her inflated mattress would eat up three-quarters of the floor space at her disposal, leaving inches between the hunk of a man beside her and whatever critters might be sniffing her from the other side of the nylon. Or insects buzzing close by in search of a midnight snack.

Lars reached forward and zipped up the inner mesh.

She'd not been in such tight quarters with a man since she'd walked away from Jeffrey. Maybe that's why her breathing hadn't settled down.

She had more productive things to do than risk looking at Lars or thinking about Jeffrey.

Darkness descended with each passing minute.

She nestled her violin case in the corner by her feet, unfurled her air mattress, and began blowing it up, keeping her eyes focused where they should be, on the expanding vinyl tubes.

"Need help?"

She shook her head as she took in another deep breath, lips pinched against the valve. Then she heard a snap.

Lauren looked sideways, eyes widening, pulse accelerating.

Lars had unbuttoned his pants.

He reached his thumbs under the waistband and began to work them down as he wriggled on the mattress.

What kind of PJ party was this going to be?

She pinched the air valve and removed her mouth from it. "What are you doing?"

"I've got shorts on. You don't expect me to sleep with my pants on, do you?"

Maybe she could give him that, but she wasn't about to remove hers.

Once Lauren's mattress was inflated, she pulled her sleeping bag from its stuff sack and laid it over herself and the mattress. She found the opening and brought her knee to her face to thread her foot into the bag. She missed it.

On the next try she leaned sideways to get more leverage but lost her balance. She rolled on the mattress until she whammed into Lars's side. "Oops—sorry!" She rocked back but lost her balance again, her head knocking against his chest this time.

Lars laughed. Then he put his arms around her.

Lauren's breath hung up.

Rain began pelting the tent.

His bulging bicep pressed against her shoulder.

She cleared her throat. "Ah . . . excuse me."

"Need some help?" Lars set her upright on her air mattress, then reached down and opened her sleeping bag.

She stuck her feet in and slid the bag up to her neck, clutching it with both hands beneath her chin.

Then she chanced a look at him.

The restroom floodlight filtering through the inner mesh cast a sheen on his blond, curly hair, his eyes sparkling like sapphires, his teeth gleaming like ivory on a keyboard. The slope of his nose drew her gaze to his sturdy chin. She wanted to reach out and touch it, then trace that masculine jawline as if she were gliding her bow across her violin strings, elongating the last note of an entrancing lullaby.

But here? And now?

She loosened her grip.

He raised his hand and inched it toward her, as if cycling a steep hill that would never end.

Her heart pounded.

His iridescent eyes would not let her go.

His hand drew closer to her face.

Her eyelids swept moisture from below them, bringing better focus to the stirring image before her.

Ever so gently he touched the hollow of her cheek with his finger, then stroked the bone above it once, then again.

She blinked, trying to mask the quivering inside, powerless to stop him—or not wanting to.

His fingers combed her hair ever so slowly, her heart racing faster with each stroke, until his hand was engulfed. He took a deep breath, eyes locked on hers.

Who was this man? Did it matter? This was a feeling she'd never experienced. Ever.

One of her hands let go of the sleeping bag. She shouldn't do it. But why not?

She reached.

And touched. That chin. The bristles of that beard beckoning for more of her.

Her heart fluttered. Then skipped a beat as his hand caressed her neck.

She dabbed at his chin again, then trickled her finger along his jawbone, grazing its stubble, as brisk and unmovable as his musculature. And equally as inviting. She drew in a deep breath and eased it out, her eyes staying on his.

The more she touched, the more she wanted.

He edged closer. As did she.

Shorter, faster breaths.

She couldn't stop this.

They moved closer still.

He cupped a hand alongside her cheek. "You are beautiful."

It wasn't his voice, at least not the one she'd been hearing for two days.

"Absolutely stunning."

She'd never heard that before. Not about her. She closed her eyes. This couldn't be happening. Who was this man?

His lips touched hers.

She shook, her lips locked in place.

He pressed in.

Fear gripped her.

She opened her eyes and pushed him away. "No. This isn't right," she whispered.

"What do you mean 'This isn't right'? Haven't you ever been kissed before?"

"It's not right. I'm sorry if I led you on."

"Oh come on. We're adults."

The two bantered in heightened whispers, mindful of sleeping neighbors. Lauren dared not trumpet an embarrassing misunderstanding throughout the campground.

"I need to go."

"Where? It's raining outside."

"I don't care. I'm leaving."

"Suit yourself."

Lauren wrestled with her sleeping bag to extricate herself, knocking heads with Lars in the process. Finally she untangled herself, pulled her gear out of the tent, and scurried to the restroom with it. The rain hadn't let up.

The sound of water running in the men's room stopped.

Lauren grabbed her gear and peeked out the door.

A man cleared his throat, then footsteps clomped until the door opened.

"Excuse me," she said before realizing the mystery man was no mystery at all. Not Lars, but the next worst thing. Well, that wasn't totally true. He did try to help her earlier.

"Evenin'." The old, bearded man tipped his cap.

"Good evening," she whispered.

He squinted. "Whatcha doin' with a sleeping bag in the restroom?"

"Oh, that." She looked at it then smiled at him. "I was looking for a little shelter and a place to sleep for the night."

"In the can?"

"Well, no. You see, I lost my tent poles, and . . . it's raining."

"Yeah, I can see that . . . And your fiddle?"

"It's not a fiddle. You don't happen to know where I can get some cover?"

The man yanked on his beard, then scratched his chin. A moment later he nodded. "Come on." The man turned, waved her on, and walked toward his campsite.

*Oh no.*

But she had no other options.

He stopped and turned around. "You comin'?"

Lauren balled up her sleeping bag around the violin, put them under her arm, placed the inflated air mattress over her head, then stepped into the rainy night.

They reached the man's lot and walked underneath the canopy in front of his tent.

"The way I see it, ya have three choices. In there"—he pointed inside the tent—"out here or"—he pointed at his truck—"in there."

At least she had options. But inside his tent wasn't one, not after what just happened. The last one might otherwise have been an option, but that smell.

"If you want the tent, I'll sleep in the truck," the man said.

"No, I couldn't ask you to do that."

"Ya didn't."

She wasn't about to return to Lars's tent. And could she sleep outside, with people walking to the restroom or who knows what else might be sniffing around? Plus how wet it was? "Can I lock your truck?"

"You could if the lock weren't broke."

"I guess that'll have to do."

"You guess? Miss, no one's makin' ya."

"I'm sorry. I would be . . . g-glad to use your truck. I appreciate your kindness."

"Something go wrong with your biker friend?"

Lauren ran her toe across the ground.

"Anything you wanna talk about?"

Shaking her head, she walked toward the pickup. Once she reached it, she turned around. "Thank you. I really do appreciate this."

Maybe she would get used to that odor. She took another whiff. Not likely. It was a cross between stale body odor and stinky feet.

Then again she had her own smell to contend with.

She'd made a trip outside to retrieve her handlebar bag and her cosmetics stuff sack. The tiny bottle of perfume wouldn't touch this challenge. She had bug spray, but that would surely lead to asphyxiation. Rolling down the windows would only invite mosquitoes and moisture from the rainy night.

She looked at her phone. The charge was down to 8 percent. She might need that if she ever got a signal back. An electrical outlet might be around, but in the tents-only area? It wasn't worth scouting out, and besides, the phone would get wet or stolen.

Before turning it off she looked at the clock. Ten forty-five.

Then she remembered. *Oh no.*

She'd forgotten to put her food in a bear box. Who knew where the nearest one was? And with rain bouncing off the hood of the truck, they could have it.

She scrunched down on the bench seat, balled up what portion of her sleeping bag wasn't covering her body, and tucked it under her head, then closed her eyes.

*Lord, I don't know. Maybe this wasn't such a good idea. I love the scenery here, but it's just hard. Maybe I should've listened to Doug.*

*I wish I had someone to share life with, Lord. It just seems to never work out. I'm not sure it ever will. And to be honest, I get scared when a guy shows interest in me. Is that a sin, Lord? I do trust You. Help me, please.*

*And please help Lars. I don't think he had bad intentions. But I do know myself, and I don't think it was a healthy situation. But maybe You're trying to answer my prayers and I won't let You. I don't know. I'm just . . . well . . . When I get right down to it, Lord, I'm lonely.*

And on it went. Minute after minute, hour after hour. Replaying her fun times with Jeffrey, the anticipation of marriage to him, then the breakup. The excitement she'd felt with Lars. And what she'd experienced with Doug—not just on the road, but back at the Covingtons'.

Rain continued to plunk on the truck's roof.

The restroom door slammed several times before, finally, she fell asleep.

A tap at the window woke Lauren from a deep sleep. It was light out. And her rescuer was peering in through cupped hands, beard kinks flattened against the glass, sunshine illuminating his graying eyebrows.

"Are you gonna sleep all day? It's nine o'clock. I gotta get me on the road."

Lauren blinked and worked her head in a circle, stretching her stiff neck. "Sorry. I'll get up." But her head dropped on her makeshift pillow, and she dozed off.

When the driver's door opened, she awoke with a start.

The old man had a plate of bacon and eggs in his extended hand. "Made ya some breakfast. You're gonna need it if you're ridin' today."

Lauren shook out the cobwebs again, then sat up. The smell of bacon overtook the dank cab.

"Thank you. That's so thoughtful of you." She accepted the plate. "Sorry, I didn't get much sleep last night."

She rolled down the passenger-side window. A bird was chirping in the adjacent pine tree amid the chatter of children playing.

"I'll git ya some coffee?"

She could see his breath when he spoke. "That's quite alri—"

But he was already out of earshot.

Lauren stuck her head out the window. The fresh morning air drew water to her eyes. Lars was gone. Her stomach sank. But if he knew what she knew about herself . . . it was just as well.

Twenty minutes later Lauren had vacated her overnight cocoon while the bearded man cleaned up his campsite.

"Thank you again. I owe you an apology. Mr. . . ."

"Name's Hank. And you don't owe me nothin'."

"No, Hank, I . . . I was wrong about you. I'm sorry."

"Well, I git that all the time."

"I noticed on the map there's a choice up ahead. I'm planning to go south through the Grand Tetons, then into Colorado. Is that a good idea?"

Hank tugged his beard. "Where you endin' up?"

"Virginia."

Hank shook his head. "Norris Junction to Canyon Village would be a lot safer on a bicycle. Better views too. Then head south to Fishing Bridge and you'll hit Route 14 East to Cody. Just turn left when you come to the stop sign out at the loop road. And bang a right at Norris. Be careful from Canyon Village to Fishing Bridge. Can be dicey."

"Dicey?"

"Yeah. Lots of bison holdups over in Hayden Valley. And no shoulders."

"How far is it?"

"'Bout thirty miles to Canyon Village. Another fifteen to Fishing Bridge. Campgrounds at both of 'em."

"Will I go by Old Faithful?"

"No, that's the other road. Too much traffic. Way too much."

"Will that route take me to the Tetons?"

Hank chuckled. "I wouldn't go there on a bicycle. Road construction south of the park."

Maybe she could avoid more climbing if she headed east through Wyoming. And perhaps reconnect with Doug? After last night that didn't seem like such a bad idea.

"Do you know where the closest camping store is?"

"Canyon Village. Right on your way. You watch out for yourself. Ya hear me?"

Lauren smiled.

As Hank's pickup rolled out, she waved.

*Lord, thank You for the kindness of this misunderstood man named Hank. Please forgive me for judging him. I ask that You prosper him and put a smile on that weathered face of his. And maybe clean him up a little too if You have time. I love You. Amen.*

Lauren picked up her gear and walked toward her bicycle, dodging puddles along the way. When she looked up, her packs appeared unharmed. *Phew!*

A set of tent poles leaned against her bicycle, not a drop of water on the clear plastic bag they were in. A scribbled note stuffed inside the bag read *Need these?* The letters *e* and *s* were both inverted, perhaps a bored young camper with too much time on his hands feigning a bison learning to write.

# CHAPTER 20

Lauren cycled north along the Gibbon River, grateful she'd added another layer of clothing. Lighter traffic that honored the forty-five-miles-per-hour speed limit and a shoulder with ample width allowed her mind to wander.

What happened to those tent poles? Was a bored teenager playing tricks on her? Had she dropped them somewhere and Lars discovered them before he set out in the morning? Or had he snitched them to lure her into his tent?

She didn't want to believe that. He'd made her feel alive. She'd enjoyed his company. *Why do the good ones always seem to fly away?*

Maybe she should have stayed in his tent last night. But Mom or Dad wouldn't have approved. Nor would Father God. And if Lars lacked self-control, could she have stopped him? No, it was best to get out of there. But did it cost her an opportunity? Maybe Lars was offended. Or embarrassed? Was she thwarting God's attempts to answer her prayers?

She climbed to an overlook of Gibbon Falls and read its placards. She'd never heard of a caldera, but she was climbing out of one. Uganda had volcanoes, but nothing like this. The caldera sprawled thirty miles wide and forty-five miles long where the volcano last erupted oh so many years ago.

But did the scientists really think the earth existed in its present form 640,000 years ago? That seemed like a bunch of malarkey. Hadn't they read the Bible?

The falls whitewashed the jagged rocks as their powerful *whoosh* plunged eighty-four feet to the bottom of the Gibbon River, so the sign said.

Lodgepole pines formed tufts atop cliffs that funneled water on either side of the falls into a lush green valley below, breathtaking from her perch, a just reward for the exertion to get there.

As she resumed her ride, evidence of a not-so-dormant volcano bubbled, smoldered, and spewed from the ground, steam or spray drawing attention to multicolored rocks, soil, and pools of acidic water from nature's chemistry lab. A pungent odor lingered.

Beyond the rising steam an animal pranced, then stopped and looked her way, its ears pointed skyward, its dark snout aimed at her. It looked like a dog with long legs. *A wolf!* Its thick, light-gray coat shimmered in the sunshine. She reached for her phone, but it wouldn't power up. The beautiful creature lost interest and resumed course.

She arrived at Norris Geyser Basin and leaned her bicycle against a tree near the parking lot, entrusting it and her belongings to the distracted tourists of Yellowstone. She strode the trail boardwalk for the full panoply of thermal features. The sign warned spectators to stay on the wooden walkway, not only to protect the prized natural features but to avoid a fatal catastrophe. The park ranger the night before spoke of a couple who'd wandered off the boardwalk and been swallowed up by the fragile crust, with one body unrecoverable as high temperatures plus acid cooked it.

Amid hissing, gurgling, rumbling, and the smell of food gone bad, one geyser sported a pool of burnt orange, another pale turquoise, while yet another shot spray into the sky before fizzling. Mind-boggling.

Children giggled behind her, then shouted with glee as steam puffed out of the ground. She missed those sounds. Would she ever hear them from her own children?

She'd had chances to adopt orphans in Uganda but felt ill-suited to raise them by herself. Granted her best friend in high school grew up in a single-parent home and turned out fine, but Lauren would prefer a child have the advantages of what both a mother and a father offered. That's why the orphanage staffed at least one man and one woman. It's also why so many children lived there.

She understood orphanhood all too well, though she was in college when her parents died. Still, it left a deficit she'd been struggling to fill for over two decades. Surely by now she was equipped for motherhood. Would she ever find a man willing to give enough of himself to help raise well-adjusted kids? And take joy in doing it?

Maybe God had something else for her. The thought echoed in her hollow heart.

No shortage of attractions filled Norris Basin, but more miles awaited. As she turned to leave, a steam vent to her right spouted a cloud of heat particles, which soon dispersed aloft.

When would the whole area blow its top again? The park ranger said there would be signs, but would it catch everyone off guard like Mount St. Helens had, as unexpected as a thief in the night?

Cycling toward Wyoming reinvigorated Doug. The scenery remained spectacular. Huge rolls of hay dotted hillside fields. In the southwest a chain of snowcapped mountains rose into the sky, their exposed faces sporting a deeper blue through the distant haze. Heavy trucks still passed him, but with less frequency and greater respect for his safety than on the interstate.

Which one of those distant hills was Lauren cycling behind? A dull ache in his gut persisted as he thought about where she was now—and where he wasn't.

He didn't worry about her so much as he missed her. Cycling the rolling hills in this majestic setting, with sunshine warming his arms and legs, brought tranquility and ample mind space for an avid daydreamer's worst nightmare.

His travels through Oregon and Idaho had offered similar retreats, and he needed the isolation then. Ruth would've rejoiced in this setting. He'd come to fully appreciate her too late to relish what she had to offer. Yet a healing he never thought possible had transformed his sorrow to gratitude. So many fond memories, but what could have been. Furthermore, where would he be without her prayers? He'd discovered a new mindset, one that preferred another person to share thoughts with—and not just any person.

If only he'd gone with Lauren, maybe she could have used him around, particularly in Yellowstone. Her faith embodied everything Ruth stood for. The lead weight sunk heavier in his stomach. He might never see Lauren again. She'd made such a difference in his life. Why did it take losing someone to find out how much they meant to you?

Maybe he should contact Brother Jim about his ministry right here, right now, and talk about his job prospects. Or perhaps his kid sis, Carmen, would join him for a few miles. But that wouldn't happen for someone with a desk job who'd used up her vacation time, let alone someone over two thousand miles away.

He entered the small town of Joliet. The map showed an unpaved shortcut, knocking off seven miles from his ride to US Route 310. When he arrived at the turn, however, the gravel looked worse than he'd hoped for, with larger rocks that would make his ride rough.

He checked his phone. No new messages.

Doug began cycling the gravel road to test the travel conditions. He could always turn around and go the long way. After an initial rise the roadway improved. However, after another mile, it became more challenging. He crawled on, careful to avoid a fall, certain he'd rather not cycle another mile and a half back to Joliet and then all the way around to Fromberg.

The straw fields on either side of him and the rolling hills speckled with evergreens and brush in the distance urged him forward. A gentle breeze whispered peace.

The balancing act was tricky. Time and again his rear wheel slew and spun on the slippery rocks before finding traction. When he sped up, his balance waned, so he traveled slower to avoid a hard fall. No one was around to rescue him.

As he crept over another rise, a deer sprang over the thin barbed-wire fence and darted across the road. Some sort of canine pursued it.

Doug's heartbeat accelerated. He unclipped from his pedals and squeezed his brakes. He snapped a few pictures as the deer bounded across the open field, its pursuer losing ground. They vanished into a depression.

For the next half hour Doug fishtailed his recumbent bicycle across the remaining miles of that gravel road. Finally telephone poles cropped up, and he soon found solid ground and increasing speed on the paved shoulder of US Route 310.

South of Fromberg his phone display lit up. He stopped to answer. "What's up, Jeffrey?"

"I haven't heard a thing from Lauren."

"Did you expect to?"

"I've left several messages."

What part of breaking up did Jeffrey not understand? It wasn't like Lauren owed him anything. Yes, they were friends, but, well, there must be a lot of wide-open space in Yellowstone and plenty of things to do, let alone hills to climb and miles to travel.

But then again Lauren hadn't returned Doug's call either. "I wonder if she's lost cell coverage."

"Seriously? It's a national park, for crying out loud."

Doug glanced to the west, beyond a vast landscape with nary a human soul or man-made structure, the panorama screaming wilderness. A guy who wore a suit and fancy shoes every day could never relate to this.

"If I booked a flight out there, any idea where I would land? And what direction she's heading?"

"I can only guess. There are only so many roads in and out of that place. But do you realize how many miles you would need to travel to find her? Even then, you could be disrupting her plans."

Jeffrey remained silent.

Maybe that wasn't the best way to put things. Jeffrey knew her better than Doug did. "Well, you know what I mean."

"No, I don't."

"I can only speak as a fellow bicycle traveler, but when you're on an adventure like this, it's hard to deviate from your goal. She was adamant about visiting Yellowstone and I wanted nothing to do with it."

"Yeah, I thought more about your reasons why. It has me worried."

*Hmmm. Lauren handled the encounter at the bar in Drummond perfectly.* "Lauren knows what she's doing." *Unless her bicycle breaks down.* "As long as her bike holds up, she'll be fine." *Or she surprises a hungry bear or an angry man.* Maybe there was good reason to be concerned.

"Please let me know if you hear anything at all from her," Jeffrey said.

"I will. And please let me know as well."

"Deal."

# CHAPTER 21

En route to Canyon Village, trees wrapped around both sides of the road. Then a meadow popped into view with a herd of bison grazing.

Lauren squinted.

Another creature was wandering in the background, in front of a wooded area. *A bear!* And big enough to be a grizzly.

A low dose of adrenaline kicked in.

Several feet behind the bear, a cub bounded. Two more hippity-hopped after them.

*So cute!*

Mama stopped so her little ones could catch up, then ducked into the woods. The sight brought a smile to Lauren's face before a pang needled her like a sharp straw from a barren nest.

In the clearing across the road, a bull elk stood, its full rack sweeping the air as it reached its snout to the ground.

*God's creation sure is magnificent. And complex. Doug would be kicking himself if he knew what he was missing.*

*How many people live a mundane existence and never encounter such grandeur?* It was a privilege to be here. But it couldn't quench the longing inside. How much more would she have enjoyed this adventure with someone special by her side? She knew a man couldn't meet her deepest needs—that role was reserved for God alone. But having Him in her life didn't remove the desire to share it with someone else.

A few miles later Lauren wheeled into Canyon Village just before two o'clock. She had plenty of time to fit in a meal, see the Grand Canyon of the Yellowstone, and cycle another fifteen miles before dark.

Rather than another energy bar, a banana, or a peanut butter-slathered rice cake, a fresh meal might better propel her to Yellowstone Lake. Maybe the establishment would allow her to charge her phone.

She pulled into a parking lot, then spotted a building with a sign for groceries and souvenirs. She rested her bicycle against a post in the shade, grabbed her water bottles, then walked the short distance across the parking lot and went in.

It felt like a return to civilization, certainly the commercial aspect of it. A stuffed, life-sized "Billy the Bison" drew her, along with a few other curious people, but the appeal soon faded. She checked her phone. Deadsville. She refilled her water bottles and used the ladies' room, where she removed her extra base layer.

When she came out, the back of a head of blond hair in the far-off soda fountain area caught her attention.

*Lars?*

Another man walked with him and—

She gasped for air and squeezed her eyes shut, then opened them wide. *No . . . No, no, no, no.*

Their hands were stitched together.

When the blond-haired man pivoted to sit down, sure enough, it was Lars.

Lauren cupped her hand over her mouth, then turned away to avoid eye contact, her heart pounding.

She sneaked another glance.

Lars's friend sported a dark, well-trimmed beard. Hand and arm gestures animated their conversation as if between long-lost friends getting reacquainted.

Wow, were his wires ever crossed. With three kids. And two ex-wives with broken hearts left to fend for themselves. And putting the moves on her last night. What happened?

Lauren slinked across the lobby and slipped out the door. Lars's bicycle appeared beside it. Apparently he'd not seen hers. Or maybe he had.

She gazed into distant trees, shaking her head. Then it hit her.

*"Abuse . . . With repercussions down through the generations."*

She could go back in and confront him. She could simply leave. Or she could wait.

*Lord, help me. I don't know what to do. He's such a good guy. And to be honest, it's a little heartbreaking.*

An eatery across the parking lot caught her attention. She wheeled her bicycle to the entrance and leaned it against the building.

Halfway through lunch she looked up. Lars stood in the entry-way. Her pulse accelerated even as her stomach sank.

He stepped her way.

Her stomach churned.

"I saw your bicycle outside and figured you might be eating lunch."

She glanced at him. "Oh, hi."

"Look, about last night. I—I'm sorry if I came on too strong. It's just that . . ."

"Just that what?"

"I dunno. I just lost myself in those hazel eyes of yours."

He wasn't playing fair now. But what did she expect?

"You're a beautiful woman, Lauren."

She twirled her fork in her salad. "Where's your friend?"

"What friend?"

She stopped rearranging her salad and looked up, careful to avoid those spellbinding blue eyes of his. "The one you were holding hands with at the soda fountain."

Lars hung his head. "So I guess you know."

"Robin?"

"Yeah."

"Where is he?"

"He works over in the lodge. He was on break."

"Is he why you came to Yellowstone?"

"I come here often. It helps me get away."

*Oh brother.* "From what?"

"Myself, I guess."

"But when you arrive, here you are."

"Yeah."

She massaged her salad with her fork again. "What kind of a stunt was that with the tent poles?"

"What do you mean?"

"Don't give me 'What do you mean?'"

"Did you find them?"

"You know I found them. Right where you put them. I guess I should thank you for at least having enough decency to return them."

Lars shifted his stance. "I didn't take them."

Did he really expect her to believe that? "If *you* didn't, then who did?"

He looked her straight in the eyes. "I don't know. All I know is I didn't take them. Why would I do something like that?"

Now that was a good question, especially if he was more interested in men than women. But he sure did seem sincere. She pierced him with a glare.

Then his eyes spoke to her even as he said, "Look, I'm sorry if you think I betrayed your trust, but I didn't."

"Oh? Under the circumstances, why would you lead me on? Doesn't that seem wrong to you?"

Lars hung his head again, then shook it. "Yeah, I can see where you're coming from. I—I just . . . It's so confusing."

"I'll say."

"I—I just bailed out this morning because I thought you were upset with me."

"That would be correct. Although *disappointed* might be a better word."

"And I wasn't trying to lead you on."

Lauren took another bite of her meal, but it too was hard to swallow. She washed down the salad parts with a swig of water. "Why don't you fill me in. What's going on with you?"

"I would if I knew."

"You can do better than that."

"You sound like my counselor."

Lauren flashed a half grin, then took another bite.

"I'm sorry, I—I can't."

He turned and left.

She wanted to say—yell—"Wait," but something inside overruled her. Maybe it was a good thing she'd never see him again, even though her heart ached over it. A good cry might help if she wasn't so numb. But this was neither the time nor the place.

The park map showed two roads to view the Grand Canyon of the Yellowstone. The North Rim Road was longer, one-way, and would circle her back to Canyon Village. She'd had enough of Canyon Village.

She cycled a couple of miles south on the Grand Loop Road and, following the sign to the South Rim Road, turned left and crossed a bridge over the Yellowstone River.

The sound of the rushing water and the sight of white rapids quelled her restlessness. It was time to put the drama behind her, and this was an ideal setting to do it. The fresh scent of the pine and fir trees coaxed another deep breath from her. A stiff, cool breeze caressed her cheeks.

She pushed on to the end of the road. The sign read *Artist Point*. She leaned her bicycle against a tree.

As Lauren walked toward the lookout, the roar of water in the distance grew.

A couple with two preschoolers stepped off the cement platform. "That was so beautiful," the woman said to her mate.

Lauren stepped up and walked to the edge. As she grabbed the railing and looked out, she gasped.

The river she'd crossed minutes earlier had become a gushing waterfall a mile or so in the distance, rugged escarpments framing it on either side before it dropped and then wandered hundreds of feet below. The Master Artist had painted the jagged canyon walls brown, rust, orange, yellow, white, and gray. The kaleidoscope of colors danced in rhythm to the water, the sun and its shadows, and the watchful eyes that flashed across them. The Craftsman had yanked apart the cliffs as if by a giant earthquake, using time and distance to delight onlookers.

"Mommy! Look!" A boy with a woman Lauren's age pointed across the canyon, his mouth wide open. The cliff, wearing an evergreen flattop, had been whitewashed with volcanic ash, and globs of orange, red, and pink drizzled from halfway down before disappearing behind trees poking out from the near rim.

*Lord, You're amazing!*

After lunch at a bar in Bridger, Doug had followed Route 310 South toward the Wyoming border, where the landscape became flatter and more barren. A train on the east side of the road accompanied him.

He crossed the border and rolled into the hamlet of Frannie. With a population of 157, the sign declared it the *Biggest Little Town in Wyoming*. A bar on Main Street awaited the work crew from a nearby lime plant and any lonely travelers who might be passing through. Doug stopped for a soda and water for the road.

When he checked his phone, it still had no new messages. What was going on with Lauren? Why did he leave her?

Multicolored, barren hills with a few oil rigs enveloped the road as he rode to Lovell, where he stopped. Despite ample daylight remaining, another eighty-mile day had spent his weary body. He wheeled his bicycle into the motel room and looked at his phone again. Nothing.

It was beginning to feel like he wouldn't be able to reconnect with Lauren. Despite no such plans, he desperately wanted to see her. And ride with her. This cycling alone didn't cut it. But as she would say, "God has a plan." He'd ventured forth to discover more of the world around him before settling back down, and he would continue until the Almighty dropped His pinkie out of heaven—or a lightning bolt—and stopped him.

A shorter, more forgiving trek on flat terrain would do him well tomorrow. From the looks of the map, Someone had stuck mountains east of him. The Bighorn Range. He hadn't planned on that. Thought he was home free when he left Montana. But what did he know? He'd never been here.

The elevations looked higher than he'd ever climbed before. Downright nasty. Two options seemed apparent. Due east immediately over the range, or head south, then east the next day through Powder River Pass.

He reviewed online cycling journals, which suggested the southern route might be better. Worland was only seventy-one miles away with little elevation gain. Just what he needed.

There might be another benefit to the southern option. If Lauren had broken free from either the allure or the clutches of Yellowstone National Park and headed east—as he'd suggested to Jeffrey—perhaps they could meet up in Greybull or Worland before he turned east and lost touch with her for good. But that meant she'd need to return his messages. He wasn't holding his breath.

He put away his iPad and checked his phone for messages again. Brother Jim had texted him:

Doug, Maggie and I are praying for you. Feel free to call and update us when you can.

Doug sighed. Maybe talking to Brother Jim was what he needed. He poked the call icon.

"Thanks for your text, Brother Jim. I appreciate your prayers."

"That's quite alright, Doug. How's it going? Where are you?"

"I made it into Wyoming today."

"Have you heard anything from Lauren?"

Doug paused. This was precisely what he needed. "No. No, I haven't. I . . ."

"I'm sorry to hear that, Doug."

Was his tone that obvious?

"Yeah, I miss her."

"Are you alone, Doug?"

"Yeah."

"That must be tough after all you've been through."

"Got that right. Brother Jim, could I ask you a question?"

"Sure."

"I've only known Lauren for a few weeks. And she's quite a bit younger than I am. But, man, I miss her. Is that normal?"

"You two shared some powerful things together in these few weeks. And God has a way of bringing people together at the right time."

Doug cupped his forehead.

"I don't know why He brought you two together, but it's clear He did. So, naturally, it would make sense that you'd both feel a strong sense of loss when parting ways. Do you follow me?"

"Yeah. Yeah, I do follow you." Doug took a deep breath. "Brother Jim, do you think a sixty-year-old guy should be pursuing a forty-two-year-old woman?"

"A good friendship is a gift. Maybe it's no more than that. But to answer your question, at your ages, I really don't think age is the most important factor. It's more about God's leading, what He is doing in each of your lives and whether, together, you would be better able to fulfill His calling for both of you.

"With that said, age may be a factor from Lauren's perspective. I can't speak for her.

"She's also been single all her life, so she would be giving up some freedom if she married."

"All I know is, it's lonely out here. And I miss her."

"Being alone isn't easy. But God can make a provision."

Doug's eyes began watering.

"Maggie and I are praying for you. And now that you've shared this, we'll know better how to pray."

"I appreciate it, Brother Jim. Please say hi to Maggie for me."

"I will, Doug. I will.

"And maybe my timing isn't the greatest, but we're moving forward with our youth suicide prevention ministry. Doug, we think you could make a real difference for us. I hope you keep us in mind."

"I will, Brother Jim. Thank you. It's so good to hear your voice."

"Be safe, and please keep us posted."

"Okay."

Doug disconnected the call.

As he looked across the small room at the mirror, a bedraggled face peered back. He backhanded his fist into the pillow beside him. Then he released a few pent-up tears.

# CHAPTER 22

Traffic stood still. A herd of bison moving at glacial speed had hijacked the Grand Loop Road north of Hayden Valley. The friskier in the group moseyed across the pavement at an angle that suggested they'd be joining the motorized vehicles—or vice versa—on the trip to Yellowstone Lake. Others were simply camping out, reminding the humans either why they came to Yellowstone or who was in charge here.

Amateur photographers stood next to open car doors and in the beds of pickup trucks capturing videos and pictures.

A ranger approached Lauren. "Make sure you stay well away from them. They may look docile, but they're capable of sending you and your bicycle on a ride with one flick of a horn."

Lauren nodded. She'd seen the sign somewhere. They'd killed people. And despite their lethargy they knew you were there and would spring into action when they felt threatened. They could jump fences and run thirty-five miles an hour. She couldn't outpace them.

It seemed the hundred-odd bison blocking the road would be there until sunset. That would pose another problem. She was at least an hour away from Fishing Bridge, where she planned to stay for the night.

Behind her, cars, pickups, and RVs lined up. And a cyclist straddled his bicycle, dressed in the same-color shirt Lars wore at the eatery. As she walked her bicycle in front of an RV to hide herself from view, it was too late.

Lars mounted his bicycle and wobbled it along the narrow shoulder until reaching her. "Hey. I was hoping I would catch you."

"Why?"

He looked ahead at the lingering herd of bison. "I'm ready to talk."

His tone bled blue, his eyes hollow. No pretense. No joy. But was this a good idea? Regardless, he'd cornered her.

"You awakened something in me." He cleared his throat. "I want to find out what it is."

Lauren looked around. This wasn't a place for a private conversation. She wheeled her bicycle off the pavement and rested it on the ground.

Lars did the same.

They sat side by side in the grass, facing the herd of bison up ahead.

"What happened? What happened to your marriages, and why did I just see you holding another man's hand?"

Lars dropped his forehead into his hand. Then he took an elongated breath and exhaled. "Jennie . . . we were both so young. We grew apart . . . or never grew together. We stuck it out for six years, then decided it just wasn't working."

"You said she was religious."

"Oh yeah. That's an understatement. Big-time rule-follower. Drove me crazy."

"Did you guys try counseling?"

Lars chuckled. "I've been in and out of counseling most of my life. Jennie? I'm not sure she needed it, but she gave it a go anyway." He pulled up some grass and sifted it through his fingers. "It wasn't a good experience. The counselor just didn't get us. But she's better off now. Married a guy who shares her religious beliefs."

"Has counseling helped you?"

He looked toward the western horizon, the sun gleaming in his face. "I dunno. It seems like I never measured up to my parents' expectations . . . Dad's in particular. He was a tough hombre."

Lauren watched the bison amble along but kept listening.

"And then there's . . ." He yanked another clump of grass and began picking at it. "Have you ever known a person who is attracted to someone of the same sex?"

"Not personally . . . Not that I know of."

Lars cleared his throat. "The conflict I feel . . . in my sexuality, I mean . . . it's brought on things like anxiety and depression. At least in my case. Sometimes I'd just like to get off this train."

"Help me understand. You're obviously attracted to women. How can you also be attracted to men?"

"You know how, when you see a guy you're attracted to, there's a pull inside. Maybe your heart rate increases or you feel extra vulnerable or nervous around him. Butterflies maybe. There's something physiological happening inside. Then there's the longing to be close to someone. Does that make sense? It's almost like a rush."

"Kind of." Blood surged to her head. She was feeling those things right now. "But isn't there a mental filter . . . for me it includes the spiritual . . . that says pursuing this is good and right?"

"That's an interesting question."

"Just because I'm attracted to a guy doesn't mean I should entertain intimacy with him. There are so many factors that go into relationships."

He nodded. "I'm with you."

"I know you said earlier that you believed in God. Have you ever given Him a chance?"

"Oh yeah. I went to church with Jennie and the kids all the time. I just felt so out of place there, like I could never measure up."

"None of us measure up."

Lars hesitated. "What do you mean?"

"Well . . . we all have our sins."

He laughed. "I've not spent much time with you, but I'm guessing there's not much sin in your life. And if there is any, it's nothing compared to mine."

Lauren's stomach clenched. "It's not a contest."

"I know, but what have you done wrong?"

*He doesn't know . . . But what if he did?* "The standard is perfection. None of us hit it. That's why Jesus had to come to earth to die on the cross." She looked at him. "Do you believe that?"

"I'm not sure what I believe."

"What about your second wife?"

Lars raised his eyebrows. "There was none." His Adam's apple bobbed. "Ollie came about on a fling."

"I take it she has custody."

"We share it."

"God wants to set you free, Lars."

"You *are* like a counselor. But a better one than I have."

She smiled. "Not so fast. You get what you pay for."

Lars laughed, returning her smile. A gust of wind fluffed his thick blond hair.

"God just needs your cooperation."

"Ha-ha. Good luck with that. I'm not the best when it comes to rules."

"It's not about rules. It's about a change of heart."

The traffic ahead was beginning to work its way past the bison. Most of the herd had crossed, but some were still on the road walking south. Northbound vehicles began streaming through on the left side of the road.

Lauren got up and dusted off her backside. "Looks like our time has come."

"From the looks of the western sky, just in time. Are you heading to Bridge Bay?"

"Fishing Bridge."

"There's no tent camping there. Too many bears."

A chill tickled Lauren's spine. "Are you serious?"

"Four miles past Fishing Bridge will land you lakeside."

That put even more urgency into resuming her ride. But how was she going to pass through this herd of bison? "Going back to see Robin after work gets out?"

"Maybe when I go back through. Mind if I ride with you?"

She cocked her head. *He needs this. And there's something about him . . . .* "If you want to."

Lars got up and stuck his head through the open window of a pickup crawling on the road beside them. "You wouldn't give us a lift past these bison, would you?"

"Glad to."

A mile later Lars unloaded their bicycles, panniers and all, and the two resumed cycling.

Hayden Valley offered splendid views of the Yellowstone River and the wildlife that lived there. Bison, bears, and elk appeared in various spots, none of them interested in mixing things up with gawking tourists.

Lars suggested a quick stop at Mud Volcano. Despite a heavy sun preparing for its evening rest, Lauren agreed.

They stepped onto the boardwalk. Steam rose as they approached the main attraction. The smell of sulfur reminded Lauren of Norris Geyser Basin. Dark-gray sludge rippled, swirled, and whooshed incessantly.

A group of tourists had gathered at Dragon's Mouth Spring, where steam puffed out of a cave. A spectrum of yellow hues glistened on the wet rocks as a rumble emanated from the opening.

As Lars and Lauren pivoted to leave, two women in their twenties, waiting their turn in the front row, were staring at Lars.

He seemed oblivious to it.

Heat rushed to Lauren's face. She led Lars back to the parking lot and climbed onto her bicycle.

He flashed his dimples at her. "Was it worth the stop?"

"Yes, I'm glad we did. But—" She pointed toward the sun. "I'd like to be at the campground by dark."

"Me too. Let's go."

When Lauren accelerated through the parking lot, her bicycle wobbled. She looked down and stopped. Her stomach sank.

Lars, meanwhile, had flown onto the main road.

"Lars!" she shouted.

When traffic cleared, he circled back. "What's wrong?"

"Look." She pointed at her flat rear tire.

"I can fix that in no time." But when Lars looked further at Lauren's flat tire, he grimaced. "Uh-oh. Do you have any enemies?"

"What do you mean?"

"That flat is . . ." He reached down and pressed his thumb against the tire, revealing a slit about an inch-and-a-half long. He felt the other side. "It looks like someone poked a knife through your tire. And I promise it wasn't me."

Lauren closed her eyes, dropped her head in her hands, and let out a deep sigh. "Didn't know I had enemies like this. Can it be repaired?"

"It's random. Stuff like this happens." He stroked his chin. "I can build a reinforcement . . . a boot . . . But you ought to get the tire replaced as soon as possible. Are you heading to Cody?"

"Yes, but isn't that like a hundred miles away?"

"About that. We could have one drop-shipped, but who knows how long that'll take. And we'd need a ship-to address . . . And a cell signal."

Lars unloaded Lauren's panniers. He removed the wheel, then the tire and tube. From the used tube, he cut out two pieces and glued them onto the inside of the tire, covering the gashes. Then he added four more, pressing his thumb against them until the glue dried. He installed Lauren's replacement tube, mounted the repaired tire, and put the wheels back on the frame. When they pumped up the tire, the air held. The whole job took a half hour.

"Wow! You're good. And I learned a lot watching you. Thank you."

"I wouldn't put any more than sixty to seventy pounds of pressure in it until you get a new tire."

With daylight waning Lars pulled out a flashing red light and affixed it to Lauren's rear rack. Then he placed a flashing white light on his handlebar. "I'll lead the way."

The two cycled toward Fishing Bridge in heavy traffic. Drivers were courteous except for the inattentive ones scoping for wildlife. And as dusk approached, the animals would be moving. Another bison jam would ensure a ride to the campground in darkness.

Lauren stopped momentarily to don another layer.

The darker it got, the tighter she clenched her handlebars—and the more she checked behind herself for vehicles.

*You will keep in perfect peace whose mind is stayed on You. I trust You, Lord. Help me not to doubt. And please deliver us safely to the campground.*

As they rolled past the sign pointing them to Bridge Bay, Lauren glimpsed yet another RV approaching in her rearview mirror. The driver was staring across the road at something in the trees, and the RV drifted right.

"Watch out!" she yelled to Lars. Then she rolled off the pavement and stopped, as did he. The driver corrected just in time.

Lars shouted at the driver, gesturing for added emphasis. Then he said, "Watch where you're going, buddy."

Lauren agreed with his sentiment but would have chosen a different way to express it. "That was scary."

"Thanks for the heads-up."

"Have you ever been hit over here?"

"A sideview mirror glanced me one time, but the vehicle was just crawling. A lot of close calls though."

A mosquito buzzed around Lauren's ear. She shooed it away, then whacked one on her leg. She opened her handlebar bag and began digging. "Want some bug spray?"

"No, I'm good."

She applied the repellent, then the two resumed pedaling. The headlights from the vehicles shone on Lars's rear reflector, which became a beacon for Lauren as she pushed her pedals harder than she had all day.

By the time they arrived at the Bridge Bay Campground, it was pitch-black. But the light still shone in the office.

Lars sprang to the counter inside ahead of Lauren. He looked across at a middle-aged woman with dark-rimmed glasses resting on a prominent nose. "Do you have a space for two bicyclists?"

"Sure. We always accommodate cyclists. Twenty dollars is all I need for two people."

"We have separate tents, so two spaces would be good . . . if you have them," Lauren added.

"I can put you over on Loop J—440 and 441. By the restroom. It's quiet over there. Right in the woods, so the wind isn't too bad."

Lars dropped a twenty on the counter, but Lauren insisted she pay her own.

"Make sure you place your food in the bear boxes. They understand we don't want them here, but it doesn't take much to lure one in."

Lauren swallowed a lump.

"You'll be okay. Just be sure to use the box." The attendant showed them a map of the campground and how to access the site. "Where are you heading?"

Curious about his itinerary, Lauren remained silent, but Lars said nothing.

"Cody," she finally said. "Do you know where the closest bike shop is?"

"You might find some supplies up at Canyon Village. We have a store here too. But if you need service, we're talking West Yellowstone. You can reach it in a day. I believe Cody has several bike shops too. It's just a longer trip, but you might get there in a day. It's eighty miles or so. Pretty drive."

Lauren rubbed her clammy arm. "Do you have showers?"

"The RV park in Fishing Bridge. Four miles up the road toward Canyon Village. They're closed now, but they open at seven in the morning."

After the two exited, Lars said, "Not that I want to see you go, but Cody is doable. It's downhill."

*He's not going with me.* With the effects of their tent encounter the night before still coursing through her veins, the next hour or two might determine whether parting ways was good or bad.

"If you choose to backtrack, I'll ride with you to make sure you're okay."

Her stomach fluttered, but she merely nodded. "That's very kind of you."

If she headed back to West Yellowstone, she might never get through the park. And the traffic on that last stretch of road would make anyone head in the opposite direction. Where was Doug? Could they reconnect?

# CHAPTER 23

Lauren went to the ladies' room and plugged in her phone to charge.

After setting up their tents and depositing their food and other scented items into a bear box, Lauren and Lars sat side by side at a picnic table in near darkness, the floodlight from atop the far end of the restroom casting a dim light. Trees separated them from adjoining campsites. A few campers wearing headlamps passed by on their way to the bathroom before retiring for the evening.

"Do you really think there are bears around here?"

Lars nodded. "For sure. I've seen bison in here too. But we've taken the right precautions. And bring your bear spray to bed with you."

After a moment of silence he said, "Do you think it's wrong to be gay?"

"By gay, do you mean same-sex attraction or acting out on it?"

"Both." He slapped his forearm and whisked away a dead mosquito.

"Let's deal with the back half. If Jesus were in our midst . . . I mean physically right here right now . . . would you ask Him that question?"

"Sure, why not?"

"I mean, would you really need to ask Him that question?"

Lars paused. "It might embarrass me."

"Uh-huh."

"I think I follow you."

"Are you looking for permission to do something your conscience is telling you is wrong?"

Lars cleared his throat. "I've never thought of it that way."

"I can tell you what the Bible says about it if you're interested."

"I think I already know. I've heard the word *abomination* tossed around. Is that right?"

Lauren nodded.

Lars leaned back against the table. "What about the first part of my question?"

"If you really want to know what I think, I think you're asking the wrong questions."

"How so?"

"I'm sure it must be hard when your wiring doesn't work the way most people's does. So I want to be respectful. But to me, someone's struggle with homosexuality could be a symptom of a deeper issue. Because, Lars, we all have issues. We really do."

"But mine is a big one."

If he only knew about hers. But she wasn't ready to share it.

She shooed a horde of mosquitoes from around her head. "I'm not so sure it's any bigger than anyone else's. Yes, sexual sin comes with high stakes because the Bible says our bodies are the temple of the Holy Spirit. But in the end, the questions you ought to be wrestling with are 'Is the Bible reliable?', 'Is Jesus who He said He was?', 'What is His good plan for me?'"

"Interesting. What makes you say that?"

"Because anything else is just a distraction from what's most important. When you make Jesus your Lord and Savior and submit to God's authority, the Holy Spirit will live inside you and help answer those questions. You'll be better equipped to face your temptations."

"What are *your* temptations?"

That was easy to answer. But should she, with him sitting right beside her on a dark night, heavy tree cover shrouding them before she entered her overnight cocoon next to his? Honesty was one thing. Wisdom was quite another.

So she said, "I'm tempted to take things into my own hands. To get ahead of God. I need to wait patiently for Him to meet my needs."

"And what needs are you waiting for Him to meet?"

"Well, other than a new tire . . ."

The two laughed before Lauren placed her index finger on her lips. "Shhhh. We don't want to bother the neighbors," she whispered.

Lars chuckled.

She repositioned on the bench to coax more blood into the overtaxed tissues of her sore hind end. "Relationship issues have been a challenge for me."

Lars slid closer. His arm plopped onto the top of the picnic table behind her.

Lauren squirmed, then shivered. "I had a fiancé until recently. And now"—she hugged her arms to her body—"I'm wondering . . . It's complicated."

"Always. I agree. Relationships are the hardest."

"I don't know about you, but I'm getting eaten alive out here. And freezing."

"Let's get under cover. My tent is bug-proof."

"So is mine."

"Okay."

That wasn't what she meant, but how could she say no? He might be seeking a deeper spiritual dive, and who was she to stand in the way of that? Was she just going to shoo him away with the mosquitoes?

Another part of her wanted him in her tent. The comfort of a man when animals were prowling, a good mechanic who had her back, a compatible travel partner, and . . . the intimacy of a near kiss the night before.

She retrieved her phone from the restroom, unzipped her tent, and crawled in, leaving the mesh open for him to follow.

When he slid in, the scent of his body overpowered her. Yes, he'd cycled over fifty miles, but he also smelled like a man. "Can I ask that we keep our distance this time?"

"You can always ask. But you gotta admit, it's a little cramped in here, so you'll forgive me if I accidentally brush up against Your Highness."

"Funny." She zipped up the mesh, then swatted at a mosquito that had made it in uninvited. Another buzzed by her ear.

He leaned on his side, facing her. "There. Is that enough room for you?"

Her mind's eye connected his deep voice with those rich blue irises of his. Her heart thumped. "Yes. Thank you." Her voice quavered. *You keep in perfect peace she whose mind is stayed on You.* She would try to convince herself of that. She pictured Jesus on the cross.

She took a more relaxed breath. "You said you went to church with your ex all the time. Why?"

"It seemed like the right thing to do. The kids needed to learn right from wrong. And be able to decide for themselves."

"You mean about Jesus?"

"Yeah. I think we all need to work through that."

"I agree." Lauren scratched her cheek. "And what did *you* decide about Jesus?"

Lars sighed. "I'm not sure. I still have questions."

His response lingered in the dark silence.

"I went to church with Gram as a teen. She was a strong believer. No one doubted where she stood."

"It sounds like that spoke to you."

"Yeah."

He cleared his throat. "Like, how was it that you decided, with your parents getting killed and all?"

She knew from youth group long ago that dating evangelism was a no-win situation. And she counseled young people in Uganda to avoid it. But here she was.

"I saw the difference Jesus made in their lives. I see it more and more in others the older I get." She swatted at the buzzing near her ear. "Did you ever make a profession of faith?"

"What do you mean?"

"You know, did you ever repent and ask Jesus into your life?"

"Oh that. No. No, I never did do that."

"Is it something you've thought about doing?"

"Not really. Those years are so far away now. And . . . well . . . I'm still wandering through life, trying to figure things out and find happiness."

"Do you think you're going to find it"—maybe she shouldn't go here, but it was already halfway out her mouth—"in a relationship with another man?"

Lars took a deep breath. "I don't know. It's something I've always suppressed before now. And wondered about. So many people are trying it. Why not?"

"Because God says not to?"

"He says not to do a lot of things."

"That's because He loves us and wants to keep us from harm."

"You should know something."

"Oh, what's that?"

"The pull is different. Like, with you, I mean. Much different. And I think in a good way."

What was that supposed to mean? Maybe she should just get out of this conversation, with him lying here right beside her. What if he reacted negatively? But a decision for Christ would change his life. What if this opportunity slipped by and he never made that decision?

"Lars, there's only one relationship that is not going to let you down."

"You sound quite sure of yourself."

"I've lived it."

"And here you are, alone. Has God really come through for you?"

"It's not about Him coming through for me."

"Look, if I decided to give God a chance . . ."

"What? Is it Robin?"

"I don't know. It's just that, well, you know, the Bible is quite harsh in its treatment of gay people. That just doesn't seem right."

"It's also hard on adulterers. But some of the strongest believers once committed it. Not to mention liars, cheats, drunks, and thieves. That's according to the Bible, not me. Who are we to determine the standards? None of us are perfect. But God offers a better way. And if you would give Him a chance, He might just deliver you from the temptation." *And then could something become of us?*

A mosquito hovered between them.

Lars backhanded it, then looked away. "I need to get some rest. I've got a showing this weekend, and I need to get back. I wish I could ride with you to Cody, but I really shouldn't. I hadn't planned on coming this far, and it's a long way back."

"No, that's okay. I understand."

"Just so you know, I chose you over Robin."

Warmth flushed through her body. She'd never competed with a man before. But it seemed to be a compliment nonetheless. "Thank you. I'd have been lost without you."

"Do you mind if I sleep here?"

Part of her wanted him to stay, but not under these circumstances. Thank goodness she smelled like a garbage dump. "No, I'm sorry. I can't. But I'm flattered."

Early the next morning Lauren awakened to the sound of Lars's voice. "Got some breakfast for you."

She rolled forward and unzipped her tent. Steam was rising from a bowl of oatmeal. "Is that cinnamon I smell?"

"Yeah, I loaded it up for you."

Daylight illuminated the morning chill when Lars breathed. "Figured you would need an early start to make it to Cody. You have a long day ahead of you. As I do."

"What time is it?"

"Six thirty. Sun's been up twenty minutes."

He was right. Especially if she hoped to get in a shower.

"Once you make it through Sylvan Pass, it's all downhill. Don't let the lake fool you. We're already at high altitude. So not much climbing. When you crawl out of the caldera, you're home free. It's an ear-popping drop. Several thousand feet."

Two nights in Yellowstone had given Lauren all she'd hoped for. Maybe more than she needed, but she would never forget it. To reach Cody would require more cycling in one day than she'd ever done, roughly eighty miles on Route 14 East.

She pulled the plug on her air mattress and scrambled out of her tent.

After she threw on additional layers, they ate breakfast. Then they packed up, loaded their bicycles, swapped contact information, and hugged one another goodbye.

Lars checked her rear tire. "It's holding up well. You should be fine."

Lauren smiled. "Thank you again. And remember, God loves you and has a plan."

He nodded, his dimples exploding below his gleaming eyes, their color reminding Lauren of geyser pools she'd witnessed the prior day.

They cycled back to the intersection near Fishing Bridge, then she slowed as he cycled north toward Canyon Village. A lump formed in her throat. Another one gone. When would it end?

*Lord, help him to surrender. And help me to carry on alone.*

Where Yellowstone Lake fed the Yellowstone River, she crossed over churning current that had begun its own long, downhill journey to the ocean. Crystal-clear water magnified sage-green lichen teeming on riverbed rocks.

A few boaters and kayakers had also gotten an early start to the day. A boy and a girl on the bank of the river took turns casting a fly rod while a man who seemed to be their dad instructed them. Lauren's vision blurred as her eyes moistened. *Dad would have loved Yellowstone.* She bit her lip, then squeezed her eyes shut a few times to whisk away the tears.

She stopped at the Fishing Bridge RV Park and treated herself to a shower, laundering her dirty clothes at the same time. She donned clean shorts and a top, then added two more layers. To dry her wet clothes, she attached them inside-out to her panniers.

Apparently the bears were still sleeping.

# CHAPTER 24

Doug's early-morning departure wasn't happening. His body ached. He rolled over and went back to sleep.

A half hour later he arose, groggy. He blinked hard and snatched his phone from the nightstand. No messages.

If he departed as planned, he might never see Lauren again. He'd logged lots of miles, and Yellowstone was a circuitous route. If Lauren was traveling east through Wyoming, he might whiz past her. And if he heard from her, he could even travel southwest and join her on the southward trek to Colorado.

No, he couldn't leave yet. Not until he heard from her.

Besides, he was still exhausted and needed more sleep. He lumbered to the motel office and extended his stay for another night.

Upon returning, he checked the internet. Cell coverage was spotty in Yellowstone. Maybe that explained her silence. Maybe not.

This could be his last chance for a rendezvous and reuniting with the best travel companion he could ever find. He didn't want to bother her, but . . .

He grabbed his phone before he could change his mind. When she didn't pick up, he left a message.

He crawled back into bed and fell fast asleep.

Waves lapped Yellowstone Lake's shoreline to Lauren's right. On it went for the next ten miles with the sun glistening across its rippling waters. With ample shoulder, gawking RV drivers—the few who were up—posed minimal concern. She did her own share of rubbernecking at the panoramic vistas to the southwest.

The lake wore an evergreen-trimmed skirt, snowcapped mountains admiring her trappings from a distance. She paled in size compared to Lake Victoria, but dwarfed other bodies of water Lauren had seen in the States.

Despite the altitude, the road climbed ever so gently. From Lauren's ethereal perch with its splendid views and with her now on autopilot, she was basking on a tramway but a few feet from heaven.

As she rode, however, the ravages of a forest fire unfolded to haunt the landscape. Charred trees stripped by howling winds and bone-chilling winters pierced the blue sky. Others had toppled from the abuse, littering the sparse vegetation like an abandoned game of Pickup Sticks.

In a few miles the coniferous wasteland cleared, as a double-humped mountain grew ahead of her, gray and rugged, a green beard on its cheeks and chin. After another twist in the road, the spectacle morphed into the shape of an Egyptian pyramid.

Lauren must have climbed out of the caldera, its spewing geysers, steaming hot springs, bubbling mud pots, and fascinating colored turf now mere memories.

Thinner air at altitude was sapping her. She pulled onto a turnout to yet another breathtaker—mountain peaks and valleys dressed in natural hues, a three-dimensional living and breathing Van Gogh. A stiff, forest breeze without a hint of air pollution flowed through vent holes in her helmet, quelling the blood pulsating under her locks.

Emerald evergreens had smothered their charred predecessors, revitalizing the setting and privileged onlookers like Lauren. A few puffy white clouds cast shadows on the multilayered hills, sunlight accenting a larger mountain in the background. The sensory stimuli triggered a hit of adrenaline.

*Absolutely amazing! God is so good. So mighty. So majestic.*

The rumble of motorcycles heading east interrupted her reverie. After the noise yielded to serenity again, she offered a prayer of thanks for the beauty and her safety, asked a blessing on Lars and the motorcyclists who'd passed by, then resumed her ride.

As Lauren ascended, a turnout appeared alongside a lake. She pulled off and rested her bicycle against a picnic table. The sign read *Sylvan Lake*.

A solitary Subaru hatchback sat along the fringe of the parking area, a bicycle handlebar and a backpack visible through the back window.

A bird chirped. Others answered it.

She followed a path through some brush for several feet, leading her to the shoreline. The cool breeze brushed her face as if from a low-speed oscillating fan. The temperature had dropped as the climb had risen—not surprising with snow covering the mountain to her left. Nor was it a problem given the blood coursing through her body on its endless mission to nurture well-used muscles. She would need to don warmer clothes before resuming her ride.

As she leaned over the water, an image of herself flexed in rhythm to an undulating mirror. Farther ahead it reflected the sky above, then upside-down mountains and inverted trees. Blue, gray, white, and myriad shades of green, the image reversed itself as she scanned the far shore and looked up into the heavens.

The solitude was God's megaphone to her soul, His voice loud and clear. The sun cast shadows in the crannies of the snow-drizzled mountain peaks, which nested in the evergreen tapestry beneath them. The cerulean trim with white wisps above and rippling below garnished the multi-seasonal master-piece. How could anyone experience this and not discover a Creator beyond human comprehension?

Despite the breathtaking grandeur the pit of her stomach echoed. She hadn't talked to anyone for hours. Was this the cost of doing things on her own terms? The traffic had thinned with each mile. Most of the cars were entering the park instead of leaving it. And rather in a hurry to do so.

Jeffrey. If she could've coaxed him out of that stuffy world of his, what enjoyment they could have shared here together.

Maybe her loneliness was her own doing. Was she too independent for her own good?

Doug surely would have appreciated this. He'd seen more of life and wasn't face-planted in work anymore. Plus he understood adventure. And a bit more about wom—

The wind stilled.

And the chirping quieted.

Lauren's heart rate slowed with her breathing. Though her head froze with the rest of her body, her eyes scanned left, then right.

A noise breached the silence. From behind her.

A branch crackled.

Then a sound, like scratching on pavement.

Her heart paused, then increased its cadence.

A moan pierced the solitude. From the depths of Hades.

Lauren's legs went limp. She shifted her feet for balance and sucked in air.

Slowly she swiveled her head. Then her torso.

A guttural rumble shook her like a cacophony of aftershocks from a seven-point earthquake.

She reached into her back pocket for the bear spray, but all she felt was her zip pouch. *Stupid!*

Another crackle.

She peered through the brush toward her bicycle—and she saw it.

And it saw her. And huffed.

The ranger's presentation at Madison Campground suggested she speak in a calm voice. Talk, yes, but calm? A scream seemed more fitting, could she have mustered it. Backing away wasn't an option with a lake behind her . . . and with rigor mortis setting in.

The massive brown ball of fur stood on its hind legs and stared at Lauren, its round ears erect.

"Easy, boy."

Her words were met with panting sounds, then woofing.

"I'm not here to"—her voice cracked—"to hurt you." She drew in a shaky breath.

Maybe it would find a snack in one of her panniers. If it got distracted there, would swimming toward the other shore be of any use? No, didn't the ranger say to stay put until it wandered off? She was a good swimmer but no match for a carnivorous appetite his size. Or back away slowly? Or drop and cover up? No, that was when things went from bad to worse.

Her bicycle was visible from the road, as was the beast. But she wasn't. Where were all those vehicles from yesterday?

The bear's head dropped from view, but it moaned like something she'd never heard before. Deep. Restless. Grating. Menacing.

She sucked in more air.

Another branch snapped.

Lauren peered through the brush again. A snout pointed back at her, closer than before, with curled lips exposing deadly incisors, a hump rising behind its ears.

Her breathing increased.

It huffed, then its gray face wrinkled as two fangs on either side of its mouth dropped into view against a backdrop of pink, slimy gums and a tongue, the growl sending chills from Lauren's head to her toes.

Her mind whirled. *Think, Lauren. Think.* "Lord Jesus, help me." But she had not even a slingshot. If only she'd brought the bear spray.

More huffing. The hump on its back rising higher.

"I—I'm not—I'm not going to hurt you."

The faint sound of engines crescendoed as motorcycles approached from the west.

The furry mass turned its head toward the sound and grunted.

The group of motorcyclists eased off the gas, then rumbled into the parking lot.

"Hey, I wonder where the cyclist is," one of them shouted over the racket.

"I'm here. Help! Help!"

"I gotta take a leak, but I'll do it at the top," another shouted.

The bear looked toward the sound of the voices from the other side of the brush and dropped to all fours.

"Help!"

Another bike arrived and backfired.

The bear sprang toward her, huffing.

She screamed.

The bear brushed Lauren's side, knocking her to the ground. Adrenaline spewed through her body.

Water splashed behind her, so she turned. The bear was swimming toward the other side.

"Help!"

The motors revved as the bikers pulled away and hammered east, the blat of their engines fading with each shift of their gears.

Lauren swiveled around.

Fifty yards from the shore the bear had reversed course and was approaching fast, water splashing around it.

She scrambled to her feet and dashed toward the thicket. But she tripped on a root and fell, skinning her knee.

She looked back.

Only twenty yards away.

Shaking, she sprang to her feet and shot through the bushes, her stiff cycling shoes clopping onto the pavement.

*The Subaru.* She sprinted to it, lifted the passenger's side door handle, but it was locked. Same with the back seat door. She vaulted to the other side. Both doors locked.

Branches started snapping.

*The bear spray.* She ran around the back of the Subaru, stopping momentarily to check the hatch. Locked.

Arriving at her bike, she fumbled with the pannier latch and looked up.

The bear's snout poked through the bushes, its massive body emerging. Growling, its claws scraped against the pavement as it bounded toward her.

The latch finally opened. She dug inside, pawing around for the canister. Wrong pannier.

She opened the one across from it and snatched the bear spray.

Forty feet away the bear huffed and charged.

She aimed and pushed down on the orange piece of plastic, but nothing came out.

She screamed. Twenty feet away.

*The safety.* She pushed the tab forward, then sideways, but it didn't come off. She gulped. It was too close now.

When she pressed back with her thumb, the safety came off. She pressed the trigger.

Right at the bear's snout.

It stopped. Then backed away.

Quivering, she kept spraying until it sprayed no more.

The grizzly turned to look at her, then swiped a paw against its nose. It wheezed. Slowly it walked in the other direction.

She tossed the empty can of bear spray into her pannier, closed both panniers, and jumped on her bicycle. Frantic, she tried to clip into her pedal, but her foot slipped, and her knee banged against the frame. Undeterred, she pushed down on the pedal again and heard the click. No sooner had she wobbled onto the roadway than a handful of vehicles passed her. She closed her eyes for a moment and drew in a deep breath, her hands trembling as she struggled to get up to speed. She looked in her rearview mirror. The bear was nowhere in sight.

A mile later, still moving slower than she wanted to, Lauren passed a smaller lake and crested Sylvan Pass. The sign read *8,530 feet*, her highest altitude yet. No wonder it was so cool.

Both sides of the roadway had morphed into nothing but sand and rocks. No hiding places for animals here. She stopped and donned another layer. Still no signal on her cell phone. Then she pushed off toward the east gate and Cody, tremors flushing through her body as she clutched the handlebars.

# CHAPTER 25

The descent from Sylvan Pass exceeded Lauren's expectations. Separated by robust guardrails in random assortments of metal, stone, and wood, a ravine plummeted on the right side of the road while rock-hewn cliffs rose above her on the opposite side. A couple at one turnout shared a pair of binoculars to feast on the scenic buffet.

The spectacular views of the hills in front of Lauren captivated her, and she ignored the encroaching guardrails, the adjacent ravine, and the soft rear tire. She was flying and couldn't be bothered. Traffic was light.

Gentle curve followed gentle curve, the fresh mountain air brushing her cheeks. She swayed from one side to the other with the slightest of leans. With little reason to pedal, she kept her hands on the brake levers, applying mild pressure whenever her speedometer topped forty or a sharper curve appeared.

She couldn't get far enough away from Sylvan Lake. The allure of the majestic hills and valleys quieted the echoes of huffing, moaning, and growling, quelled the shaking in her chest, arms, and legs.

A group of motorbikes filled her rearview mirror, the sound increasing with their size. With no oncoming traffic, they whizzed past in the westbound lane, two by two, a dozen or so in total. A few of them raised fists in the air.

On it went as she descended from the heavens, breathtaking sights visible for miles. Her speed alone brought comfort, because it might discourage a bear without the willpower to chase her. A meal or bathroom break could wait for indoor accommodations. She swallowed to relieve the pressure in her ears.

Route 14 reminded her of US Route 12 through the Clearwater National Forest in Idaho. Rugged, untapped wilderness with beautiful evergreens blanketing the hills. But this topped her ride in Idaho because the longer vistas and extended free fall were so pleasurable.

A mountain stream joined her at lower altitude before she passed through the east gate and out of the park. With the ear-popping drop of the last several miles, Lars was right. She hoped for more coasting ahead.

A couple of miles past the gatehouse, a large wooden structure with a green, corrugated-metal, steeply pitched roof was her first hint of civilization since Fishing Bridge. The sign said *Pahaska Tepee*. Old Glory rose high above the complex. Surely there would be a restroom and food here.

After ordering lunch and using the restroom, Lauren checked her phone. She had three voice messages and three texts.

The first voice message was from Jeffrey:

"Hey. I'm checking in to see how you're doing. I hope you're not mad at me. Please return my call when you can."

The second was also from Jeffrey:

"I haven't heard back from you, so I'm kind of concerned. Are you alright? Call me. Please."

Doug had left her a message too:

"Hi, Lauren. I've heard some concerning reports about Yellowstone and cyclists. I hope you're safe. Please call if I can help in any way. I'm loving the scenery up here. Met some good people too. Sure wish we were riding together."

One of the text messages was spam. Another was from Jeffrey:

> Hey! You okay? I'm getting concerned.
> Maybe you lost your phone or something.
> Hope you're well. Miss you.

The other was from Maggie:

> Hi Lauren. It's Maggie. Just wanted you
> to know that Jim and I are praying for
> you. So glad we got to meet you. Would
> love to hear from you when you're able to
> reach out. Blessings.

Lauren texted back:

> Just able to pick up your message. It's
> good to hear from you. I'm so grateful
> for your kindness. I loved spending time
> with you. Thank you for remembering me.
> Your prayers have been working!

She would finish her ride into Cody before responding to the men.

A healthy meal, a break, and engaging conversation with fellow tourists—though none traveling by bicycle—lifted Lauren's spirits and her energy.

She continued east to a widening landscape until encountering rugged escarpments on the left side of the road, red in color, barren and jagged, reaching high above her. A wider shoulder and gentler decline translated to more pedaling and a speed in the high teens for miles. A tailwind swept in more joy.

Eventually a prairie unfolded with horses and cattle grazing.

To her right the river grew until it became the Buffalo Bill Reservoir, with innumerable gallons of aquamarine water. Saw-toothed mountains stood in the background, facing the early-evening sun, which cast glitter across the sparkling water.

With the entrance to a tunnel just ahead, she turned into the pullout to capture more photos.

A Ford F-150 pulled in, its passenger-side window lowering. "Which way are you heading?" the burly driver shouted.

"To Cody."

He nodded toward the road. "Those tunnels aren't safe on a bicycle. I can give you a lift."

Lauren approached the vehicle. The man, probably in his forties, wore a dark, untrimmed beard and an unlabeled, black baseball cap. His potbelly sprawled around the bottom of the steering wheel. "Thank you for letting me know. Is there an alternate route?"

"Yeah, in the back of my pickup." He appeared to have chewing tobacco in his mouth.

"No, I mean that I could cycle."

"Not unless you want to do some climbing and add more miles. You'll enjoy the views, but you may run out of daylight before you get anywhere. And you might see a critter or two."

Lauren's stomach tightened. "I've stopped for a break. But thank you for the offer."

"I'll wait as long as it's not . . . like, an hour."

"No, but thank you anyway. It was kind of you to stop, and thanks for letting me know."

The pickup peeled out and sped away, the sound of its motor muffled as it disappeared into the tunnel.

She breathed a sigh of relief.

But why hadn't she asked how long the tunnel was? She could ride through with her lights on or try to land a less intimidating offer to transport her to the other side. Who knew how wide the shoulders were.

A large RV whizzed by heading for the tunnel.

Fifteen minutes later, as the sun descended the western sky, no one else in a pickup with an empty bed had stopped. Lauren dug out her flashing lights and put them on her bicycle. The only thing worse than riding through that tunnel would be finishing the ride to Cody in the dark.

Off she went.

Before entering the tunnel she stopped so several cars would go in first. With no more eastbound cars in sight, she cycled into it.

The temperature plummeted. A dank smell infiltrated her nostrils before settling in the back of her throat.

A continuous bank of lights overhead dispelled total darkness but did little to help her see. As her eyes adjusted, no headlights shone from the east. It was quiet other than the trickle of water.

"Yippee!"

The echo verified the tight confines. She pedaled harder to speed her passage.

Headlights shone in the distance, and the rumble of a tractor trailer grew in volume until it shook her. The noise became deafening. She stopped and clasped her hands to her ears as it flew by.

Then lights appeared in her rearview mirror. She swallowed and eyed what little shoulder remained before walking her bicycle as far to the right as possible. Her heart thumped, but this journey had only begun.

An RV overtook her, its breeze rocking her toward the tunnel wall. A moment later an oncoming tractor trailer whizzed by—much faster than the posted thirty-five-mile-an-hour speed limit. A gust of diesel fumes smacked her face, choking her next breath. Two more cars from the east passed by.

*Did that guy say "tunnels," as in more than one?*

She climbed back on and bicycled until the small square of light from each end matched one another.

A car behind honked.

She started. If ever there was an appropriate time for foul language, this was it.

The vehicle overtook her with a teenage boy hanging out the front passenger's side window. "Get off the road!"

This was also no time to rebuke them. Instead she concentrated on the narrow shoulder and watched for vehicles approaching from behind. She would deal with her emotions when—and if—she made it through.

She looked down at the tire Lars had rebuilt but couldn't see it well. It still felt soft, but she was glad he'd been there for her and warned against overinflating it. What would happen if that thing gave out in here?

Finally the light shining through the east opening grew more rapidly in size. After a few hundred feet she thrust herself into the light, pulled to the side, and grabbed a water bottle, shielding her eyes from the brightness. After several deep breaths she chugged water while wondering what kind of person honked at a cyclist and screamed in her ear inside a long tunnel. If people only understood what they were doing. But then again this was her idea.

With tunnel hazing under her belt, she cleared two smaller ones with ease. It was all downhill from there with likely enough daylight to reach Cody.

When businesses appeared, she breathed relief even while pedaling harder. With the sun perched on the ridgeline behind her, traffic picked up alongside the Cody Rodeo grounds.

An emotional free-for-all tugged inside her. She'd experienced her best cycling day ever, escaped a harrowing wildlife encounter, squeezed through dark tunnels filled with RVs and big rigs, and been sent off by a man who could have fit into her dreams. And two more wonderful men, concerned for her well-being, awaited word from her.

Had she reached the pinnacle of her life, and it was all downhill from here? What would she tell Jeffrey and Doug?

# CHAPTER 26

When Lauren walked out of the motel bathroom refreshed from her shower, her phone, face down on the nightstand, was vibrating. Her knee stung, but at least she'd cleaned it up.

She rearranged the towel around her, lay down on the bed, and grabbed the phone. It was Jeffrey.

She sucked in a quick breath. He was concerned, so she answered the call.

"Hi, Jeffrey."

"Where are you? Are you okay?"

"Yes, I'm fine. I had a great day of cycling. I've never cycled so many miles in one day. Eighty-five! Can you believe it?"

"I'm relieved. Did you get my messages?"

"Yes, I—I had no cell coverage."

"For three days?"

*He misses me.* "Coverage is spotty in Yellowstone . . . and . . . my battery died."

"I'm just glad you're okay. Where are you?"

"Cody, Wyoming."

"You're kidding. Where in Cody?"

"I'm at the Grizzly Inn. Why . . . why do you ask?"

"Because I'm at the Cody airport."

Her arms tingled. "Really?" After a long day alone, seeing Jeffrey would be a welcome diversion. But what was he doing here?

"I just rented a car, and I'll be right over. Have you eaten yet?"

"I just showered. I need a little time to get ready."

"I'll be over at eight, and we'll find a special place to eat."

After hanging up, she dug into her toiletries bag. Her pill bottle was missing. She clawed through the pannier, then squeezed the pockets of her cycling jersey. Nothing. Maybe she'd left it somewhere? No worries. She hadn't needed it in months anyway.

More importantly Jeffrey was in Cody. And she would see him within the next hour.

A knock sounded on Lauren's door.

A shot of adrenaline kicked in.

He was fifteen minutes early, and she wasn't ready. It's not that she had much makeup with her or any fancy clothing, but . . . well, she did want to look her best. It'd been well over a week and several hundred miles since she last saw Jeffrey.

She walked out of the bathroom and looked through the peephole. It was a man she didn't recognize. "Yes? Who is it?"

"It's Greg from the front desk. Someone brought these in for you."

She didn't recognize him from the check-in counter, but maybe there'd been a shift change. "Could you please hold them up so I can see what you have?" It was a bouquet of red roses.

Lauren opened the door.

"He said take all the time you need. He's waiting in the lobby."

"Okay. Tell him I'll be out in ten minutes."

"Yes, ma'am." He handed Lauren the vase and walked away.

"Thank you." She closed the door.

She set the flowers on the desk. They were beautiful. She stooped to nestle her nose in one of the blossoms and took a deep breath. Lovely.

But Jeffrey wasn't typically a flowers kind of guy.

A text message popped into her inbox. *Lars Andersen:*

> Would love to FaceTime with you. Been
> thinking . . . Miss you.

A warm rush surged within her. I wonder how he is. And if he considered our talk.

When she returned to the bathroom and looked in the mirror, her stomach flip-flopped. Should she really accept those flowers? It's not like she could take them with her anyway.

But she didn't want to insult a man she'd wanted to marry and who had flown out to Cody to see her.

Would she be able to get any food down feeling like this? But spending time with Jeffrey was a special treat after days on the road and now holed up in a motel in Wyoming. She couldn't say no.

She combed her hair one last time. Her shorts and top would have to do. They were the best clothes she had to offer him.

After another deep breath she dropped her motel room key into her pocket and walked down to the motel lobby.

Jeffrey smiled and stood in his lawyer-best suit. His brown eyes twinkled as he spread his arms wide.

She walked into them.

"I've missed you," he said.

She'd not forgotten the comfort of being in his arms, but doing it for real rather than in her dreams accelerated her pulse. "I . . . I've missed you too." It was true, but not in the same way she used to feel it. "How did you know I would be in Cody?"

"Lucky guess. With a little help from Doug's intuition. I rented a car to drive to Yellowstone, but you saved me the trip. Come on, let's go. We can talk over dinner . . . What happened to your leg?"

"Clumsy me. Skinned my knee."

His hand rubbed against her wrist as they walked out. She thought better than to grab it despite the urge.

Jeffrey drove them to a steak house. "They say this is the best meal in town."

Seeing him again restored her appetite. And this would be a short rendezvous. It was time to relax and enjoy his company. "It smells good already. I could eat half a steer right now."

Six motorcyclists rolled in and cut their engines.

Jeffrey and Lauren entered the restaurant and sat at a round booth in the corner.

She asked about his latest legal cases in support of defendants who were mistreated because of their Christian beliefs.

He summarized them in five minutes, more concise than usual. "Thanks for asking about my work, but that's not why I'm here."

"The flowers are beautiful, Jeffrey. Thank you." It was the least she could do to thank him.

"I'm glad you like them. Tell me about your adventure through Yellowstone."

"Oh, you wouldn't believe that place. To be honest, it's a bit scary on a bicycle, with the wildlife, traffic, climbing, and all, but the scenery is both wonderful and mysterious. Did you know Yellowstone is an active volcano? Well, not really, but it has evidence of being one. Geysers, hot springs, fumaroles, and mud pots. They produce all sorts of colors due to how the minerals interact with the hot acids.

"And you should see Yellowstone's Grand Canyon. It tugged at my heart. God painted so much beauty there."

Jeffrey smiled. "It sounds like quite a trip. I can't believe you did that without cell coverage. Or a travel companion."

"Actually I did have a travel companion."

"Oh?"

She'd taken a picture of Lars back in Montana, but did she want to share that with Jeffrey? "His name is Lars."

"Is?"

"Yeah, as far as I know, he's not dead yet."

Jeffrey chuckled. "Where is he now?"

"He went back to Montana. That's where I met him. He helped me fix a flat tire. No, two. Which reminds me I need to buy a new tire. Someone ran a knife through my old one."

"What? I was concerned about a lot of things involving your safety, but that wasn't one of them." His eyes seemed to search for what was in her heart. "It's so good to see you."

She scratched her leg, smiled at him, then noticed the bikers sitting a few tables away. The vest on the largest man read *Rattlers*.

"Any run-ins with wildlife?"

Lauren hesitated. Did he need to know this? "We . . . we had to wait over an hour for a herd of bison to clear the road. Then I saw . . ."—she glanced sideways, then leaned forward and lowered her voice—"I saw a bear."

"How close?"

She sighed. "Closer than I would've liked. But it all worked out."

Jeffrey's head drew back. "Do you really think this cycling adventure is worth continuing?"

"Most definitely. I can't believe what a beautiful country we live in. And there's so much more of it to see."

Wrinkles formed in Jeffrey's forehead. "Lauren, I've been thinking."

She watched as the wrinkles grew deeper.

"I don't know what I'd do if something happened to you. And . . . well . . . ever since you've been gone, I've—I've missed you. I mean, really missed you."

Lauren tilted her head but said nothing.

"Have you . . . have you missed me?"

Her stomach roiled. "Well, yes, of course I've missed you. We know each other well, share a common faith, and have spent very meaningful time together. I'll always think highly of you."

"I'm just wondering . . ."

Jeffrey sometimes found it difficult to express his feelings. His pinched eyebrows and drooping shoulders belied his usual confident self. But maybe he was sensing she wasn't ready for what he had to say. "Are you okay, Jeffrey?"

Her phone vibrated. "Ooooh, it's Doug." A twinge in her chest alleviated her tension. "He's such a nice guy."

"Yes, he is."

She wasn't about to pick up the call even though she wanted to. But there was no escaping whatever was on Jeffrey's mind, plus the flowers . . . and reliving past pain.

The server came with their order. Just in time.

As they ate, Lauren described more of what she'd seen in the past week. Then she said, "What has God been teaching you since we last saw each other?"

Jeffrey grabbed his knife and trimmed fat from his T-bone steak. "That His love for us is immeasurable. That He makes all things new in their time. And . . ."—he stopped slicing his steak and looked up, knife in hand—"we need other people in our lives. And we're not guaranteed tomorrow."

"I see." She took another bite of steak.

"What has He been teaching you?"

She took a drink of water to wash down the swollen blob of food in her throat. "That He loves us extravagantly, His hand of protection is on us, and He hasn't forgotten about me. He's showing me a big world with lots of possibilities. And fellow travelers who need one another."

Jeffrey looked at her and nodded. "Right."

Lauren shoveled in a forkful of sweet potato. Then she looked over at the motorcyclists.

One of them was leering at her.

Jeffrey set his knife and fork down, grabbed the corners of the table, and shook his head. "I think about you all the time."

She could relate, but . . . "How's your new friend?"

His brow furrowed. "What friend?"

"You know, the one you told me about in Missoula."

"She's fine, I guess . . . Look, I didn't pursue her. My heart belongs to someone else."

Her chest tightened. Why did he have to say that? "We're traveling different roads, Jeffrey."

"That can change in an instant."

He didn't understand. "Maybe so."

"We can arrange to ship your bicycle back to Virginia and fly home tomorrow."

She set her utensils on the tablecloth and searched his eyes. "Jeffrey, I don't want to end this journey."

He broke eye contact, hung his head, and sucked in a breath.

"I'm sorry." Her heart twisted like a pretzel. This had to be harder for her than him. "Look. You're a good man. Don't ever doubt that."

"I—I love you. I don't want to lose you."

She swallowed. "Love isn't enough. You have so many possibilities in DC, Jeffrey. Why did you jump on a plane and show up here? And sending me flowers?"

"Because I love you."

Her chest tightened even more. Just two weeks ago he was having doubts. And now this? But, a few hours ago, she had narrowly escaped with her life. Maybe this was God's provision for her. Jeffrey had everything to offer—a deep, sincere faith, a difference-making job, an intelligent mind, and a strong and healthy body—so what did she have to lose? Furthermore, he was drop-dead gorgeous. Before going on her bicycle trip, she'd been looking forward to marrying him. Maybe she was just afraid of being tied down or making a commitment. But there was something else. Deep down he really didn't know who she was.

The freedom of the open road seemed a more compelling suitor. It didn't try to control her life. It spawned dreams rather than squelching them. It offered discovery instead of routine. But it couldn't give her children. Nor could it wrap its arms around her.

"Look, would you at least think about it overnight and let me know in the morning?"

How could she with the secret she'd never told him?

"What would I go back to, Jeffrey? No, don't answer that question. I know where I want to be for now, and it's on my bicycle. I hope you can understand that."

He tucked in his lips and nodded. "Yes. I understand."

# CHAPTER 27

Doug awakened to sunlight streaming in the window and immediately checked messages. His heart sank.

Maybe this was the end. What a difference Lauren had made in his life. But he'd let her roll out of it.

No sense pining away though. He had a wonderful opportunity nonetheless and would make the best of it.

He bicycled south on 310 all the way to what looked like the lunar surface. Wyoming's reds, tans, and sages had replaced the palette of Montana, with its greens, blues, and browns. A ridge of hills to the east rose from a barren plain, streaks of terracotta, rust, and tan brimming with rich minerals destined to become dollar bills. Steeper mountains rose miles beyond, dark blue in the distant haze, reflecting the cerulean sky above them while daring eastbound two-wheeled travelers to take up the challenge and indulge the senses with a closer view. Doug was tasting the bait but not swallowing it.

The view in front of him was captivating enough, otherworldly and majestic in its rugged, lifeless appearance. A few rattlers might live there, maybe a roaming deer or antelope, but what else could survive without greenery? How could bland look so marvelous?

Ahead, roadside hills rippled like choppy ocean waters. With the road empty and a wide expanse in front of him, he could drink in these sights for miles, never tiring of them.

Lauren's eyes popped open, but the rest of her lay dormant. Her knee pulsated, her forearms burned, and as she reached for the phone, which was vibrating on the nightstand, her wrist felt stiff. *Jeffrey Maddox.* "Hello?"

"Hi. It's me. I hope I didn't wake you up."

"Oh, it's alright."

"I have about a half hour free before my flight. Could I come see you?"

"I—I don't know . . . I have things I need to take care of before I go." She looked at the rear tire of her bicycle.

"I'll make it quick."

She'd dreamed about him last night. His coarse, five o'clock shadow against her cheek, his firm embrace . . . and wedding plans. Of course those never panned out.

Lauren couldn't see him like this. She needed time to freshen her appearance, and that wasn't necessary for another day on the road.

But he had gone out of his way to see her. And she'd bruised his ego last night.

She scratched her head. Seeing him to say goodbye seemed like the least she could do. And maybe if she took a quick shower and left it at that, he'd see that she wasn't all he was looking for in a woman.

"Okay. I'll be in the lobby eating breakfast in, say, fifteen?"

"Great. I'll see you then."

Was this going to lead to another heart-wrenching rejection? Of either one of them?

She showered, pulled on her clean set of bike clothes, and scurried to the lobby.

He'd already arrived, clad in law-office attire, his hair debonair. Absolutely stunning.

"Good morning," he said.

She smiled while admiring the man she'd had the good sense to marry—until he expressed doubts about their relationship . . . and mentioned another woman. Which reminded her that other women couldn't keep their eyes off him.

Breakfast would need to wait.

They sat and chatted for a few minutes about their day's agendas.

Then Jeffrey stood. "I don't want to keep you."

Lauren rose to her feet, her arms crossed in front of her.

He reached his hand out as he pivoted to exit the lobby.

Without thinking, she grabbed it and followed him outside. His touch formed a lump in her throat.

The sun sparkled as a businessman peeled out of the parking lot. Lauren squinted, raised her free arm to shield her eyes, and faced Jeffrey. "Thanks for coming."

He cupped her shoulders.

Her heart thumped.

His Adam's apple bobbed as he peered into her soul.

Then he took her in his arms.

And didn't let her go.

Instead he drew her closer.

And held her tighter.

"Jeffrey . . ." She whispered it with what breath she had left.

His grip remained firm, like a child who'd been wandering in the mall looking for Mommy. Or a lover who couldn't get enough.

But it was just her.

She squeezed back for a beat. It only seemed right, like he needed it.

His aftershave—gentler than she'd remembered—sent her mind adrift, wondering where Prince Charming was, if he'd ever show up. Even though his image stood in front of her.

"I've missed you so much." His breath touched her ear.

Her own breath caught in her throat.

She relaxed her muscles, but his swelled.

She couldn't let him do this to her again.

"I—I need to go."

"Yeah." He loosened his grip.

She took in more air.

Deep within, her heart yearned for a longer embrace, but not here, not now. And . . . not him?

The mechanic at Cody Bicycle Shop took one look at her loaded bicycle. "We'll get you right in."

"Thank you. That's so kind of you."

It was another privilege of long-distance bicycle travel. Attentive bike shops that went out of their way to get cyclists like her back on the road as soon as possible. They understood. Which was more than she could say about Jeffrey.

But his affections toyed with her mind. She'd already kicked his tires and been more than willing to marry him. That was then. She had other interests now. And he'd broken her heart.

She went outside and found a chair. It was in a public setting but, with no one around, would offer privacy. She texted Lars.

He responded immediately with a FaceTime invitation. Up popped his blue eyes and curly blond hair. "Hey, Lauren."

"Hello! How are you?"

"I'm fine. Where are you?"

She lowered the volume. "I'm at the Cody Bicycle Shop. I think you know why."

"I'm glad it held. How long do you have?"

"They took it right in, so ten or fifteen minutes."

"Thanks for accepting my call."

She asked about his return trip and upcoming showing, then updated him on her ride to Cody, glossing over the details of her grizzly bear sighting.

Then he said, "I've thought quite a bit about what you shared with me . . . about my—my lifestyle. What God thinks of it."

She turned down the volume further. "I'm glad to hear that."

"I told Robin I need a break."

Lauren's pulse skipped a beat. "And how do you feel about that decision?

"I'm not sure. It seems like if two people love one another, they should be free to express it."

"So why did you ask for a break?"

"I need better clarity on it . . . the lifestyle. I'm just wondering why there were no warning bells, if you know what I mean."

"The peal of a bell is only audible to those within earshot."

"That . . . that's deep . . ."

The bike shop attendant walked out.

"Just a second, Lars."

"Your bicycle is ready."

"Okay, thank you. I'll be right in."

"Wow, that was fast. Anyway, I was gonna say it didn't seem wrong. It felt like self-discovery."

"You might want to read the last half of Romans 1. Do you have a Bible?"

"Yes." Lars glanced sideways. "Romans 1. Okay, I'll do that."

"Well, time to pay up and get on the road."

"Before you go, I'm wondering if I might be able to come see you in a few days. I miss you."

Lauren couldn't help but smile. He needn't know about her elevated heart rate. "It's hard to know where I'll be."

"Do you mind if I stay in touch with you?"

"Not at all. I'd like that. And please let me know what you think about Romans 1."

"Romans 1. I will."

"Thanks for the FaceTime, Lars."

"Goodbye."

She sat motionless. The call was a shot of encouragement, but her thoughts returned to Jeffrey. So many confusing feelings.

Doug's phone vibrated. *Lauren Baumgartner* popped up on the display.

He clamped on his brakes as he steered to the side of the shoulder. Then he ripped the phone out of its caddy. "Is this my long-lost friend?"

"Yes, it's me," she said flatly.

Something wasn't right. "Where are you?"

"Cody."

West of him. "Are you okay?"

She didn't answer him.

Doug's stomach knotted. "Hello? You there?"

"I'm sorry. I'm here. Where are *you?*"

"I'm heading south on 310 toward Greybull."

"That's where I'm going. Route 14 East."

"It's been a pretty flat ride today, but I—I'm taking my time."

"Can I . . . ride with you?"

"Sure. I'd like that." Doug heart rate quickened. "You don't sound like yourself. Is something wrong?"

"I'll tell you about it when we meet."

"Fair enough. I'm going to eat lunch in Greybull. I'll text you when I'm settled. Have you checked your mileage?"

"Yes, but I'm not on the road yet. They just finished putting a new rear tire on my bike. I should get there in four hours if all goes well. Probably sooner. They say it's downhill."

"I'm a couple hours away. Do you want me to wait for you to eat?"

"No, go ahead. I'll munch on the road. But thank you for asking."

Doug rolled to a stop where US Route 310 met US Route 14. Lauren was somewhere on the east-west road in front of him. He could turn right and meet her, or he could cycle five miles to Greybull for lunch, like he said he would. Despite an empty stomach he pulled an energy bar from his pocket and turned right. Maybe he should text her, but wouldn't a surprise be better?

His snack and the thought of seeing Lauren helped him overpower a stiff breeze. Eighty-degree weather relaxed his muscles.

An hour later a cyclist approached, jackhammering the pedals on the opposite side of the road. Strawberry-blond hair flowed behind her, above a violin case bobbing from side to side in perfect cadence with the rotations of her bike's crank arms. Warmth flooded his chest.

He stopped and waved until her head turned his way.

She waved back, her teeth flashing white in the bright sunlight.

His heart thumped.

Her bicycle came to an abrupt halt. She dismounted, nearly tripping as her foot caught on the crossbar. After dropping her bicycle against roadside brush, she glanced to make sure the road was clear, then began running across the road.

Doug straddled his recumbent, dumbfounded, his heartbeat accelerating with each stride that brought Lauren closer. His chest might burst open any second. Without thinking, he stretched his arms her way, as much to absorb the impact of her charge than to embrace her.

The closer she got, the broader her cheeks stretched . . . and the wider his arms spread. She slowed before impact and wrapped her arms around him. And squeezed. Hard.

After a few seconds she let go. "Oh, am I ever glad to see you. But what are you doing here?"

"I thought you might want someone to ride with. Things didn't seem quite right on the phone earlier."

She sobered. "That obvious, huh?"

He smiled, reached out his hand, and rested it on her arm. "What did you do to your arm?"

"That's what happens when a tractor trailer puts you in a vise and squeezes."

"Ooowwww." She tilted her head from one side to the other, eyes twinkling despite a somber expression.

Doug glanced down. "And your leg?"

"It's a long story." Then she started. "Let's go. We can talk about everything later. You don't know how good it is to see you."

# CHAPTER 28

Lauren trailed Doug as the two continued on Route 14 East toward Greybull. The gradual decline coupled with the tailwind lightened the load and cooled her body from the warm sun overhead. Her speedometer registered more than sixteen miles per hour, as it had for miles, much faster than normal. The farther she cycled from Yellowstone, the more anxiety faded into the distance.

Doug's presence brought such comfort. Why would anyone want to cycle this rugged, isolated terrain alone—unless of course one was stuck with the wrong person. She hoped Doug hadn't misunderstood her exuberance to see him.

The rugged, rust-colored hills gave way to a fertile valley, with its assortment of soybean, hay, and wheat fields among barren plains. The wide-open space miniaturized the travelers and the cares of the world. This was communion with God. The longer the expanse, the deeper the connection.

Doug pointed to the right. A herd of pronghorn eyed the pair, perhaps as fascinated with them as *they* were with the tan animal's white underbelly and its distinctive dark snout and eyes. Lauren had never seen anything like them, not even in Uganda. White stripes corrugated their necks. Each pronghorn stood at attention, peering at them, ready to spring into action.

She was so glad not to be traveling alone anymore. Doug gave her the security of togetherness but also the space to continue wrestling with what she'd told Jeffrey. He understood she had thoughts she wasn't ready to share. She'd never had a friend quite like Doug. Jeffrey could take a lesson or two from him.

They arrived in Greybull just after two. Doug scanned the businesses en route before rolling up to the Greybull Family Restaurant. The hostess seated them at a booth.

After the server took their orders, Lauren sighed, then shook her head, staring at him. "Thank you."

Doug nodded. "A hard few days?"

With lips sealed, she inflated her cheeks and shook her head. "Have you ever said something just because you had to and then questioned it later?"

"Yeah, I suppose I have. It's commonplace in sales."

"Jeffrey showed up."

Doug's eyes widened. "Really!" He knew Jeffrey had been worried about her but couldn't imagine he would try to find her without more specifics on her location. And he hadn't let Doug know, despite their deal. How did he find her so quickly?

"He came to my motel last night. In Cody. He was concerned because I hadn't responded to his messages."

"I can kinda relate to that."

"I'm sorry. I had no cell coverage in the park. And then when he came . . . it threw me."

"I thought coverage might be an issue. Are you glad you went?"

Lauren smirked. "Good question. I saw sights and experienced things I'll never forget. So, yes, I think it was worth it. But I know now why you traveled another route. I'm not about to turn around and go back."

"What was it like?"

Lauren described the thermal features, the altitude, the road conditions, and the wildlife. She'd apparently made it through with no close encounters.

"Sounds fantastic!"

"It was. And can you believe there's a Big Boy server west of Cody, standing on a stone pedestal, waiting for customers out in the middle of a field?"

"What?"

Lauren giggled. "He's a statue." Then she cocked her head. "I suppose, as time goes by, I'll remember the high points and lose sight of the traffic and other hazards. After seeing Jeffrey last night, that process has already begun. I was both elated and put out with him."

"Put out. Why?"

"I'm not sure. I've gotten so many mixed signals from him."

"He must care a lot about you to fly out and see you."

"I think he does. But I felt so awkward. He had flowers delivered to my room before we went out to eat."

Doug raised his eyebrows.

"I felt . . . pressure. That's what it was. He just swooped in and expected me to respond to him as if nothing happened since we got engaged. I do have feelings for him, but . . . I don't know. Jeffrey's life is so much more structured than life on the road."

"What life isn't?"

She grinned. "You do have a point."

"Maybe he's carrying too much weight."

"He's not on a bicycle."

They chuckled.

The server set their meals on the table before dashing off for the next order.

Doug grabbed his fork. "I mean he's gotta have lots of responsibilities as a trial lawyer. He's not detached from ordinary life like us."

Lauren nodded. "I felt bad because . . . well . . . I feel like he pushed me into a corner, and I had to be abrupt to get out of it."

The odor of onion rings wafted from Lauren's plate. She noticed Doug eyeing them. "Want one?"

"Sure."

"Enough about me. Tell me about your ride."

Between bites of an onion ring, Doug explained where he'd been and what he'd seen. Then he said, "I've missed riding with you."

"I've missed you too."

After lunch the pair cycled south toward Worland, where they hoped to stay at a motel before heading east across the Bighorn Mountains.

Doug couldn't help but ponder her words for miles. *"I've missed you too."*

Jeffrey was crazy to pressure Lauren. That would only push her away, especially after a bike ride through a pristine wilderness that millions of people spent thousands of dollars to visit every year. But Jeffrey was too buried in his own world to understand that.

They stopped alongside the road for a rest break. While Lauren sought cover to relieve herself, Doug pulled out his phone. Jeffrey had sent a text message.

> Hey. Sorry about not getting back to you sooner. Lauren is fine. We had supper last night in Cody. Where are you?

Well, Jeffrey showed some interest in what Doug was doing. Good for him.

Should he tell Jeffrey he was being too forward with Lauren? That his antics were creating space between them? Maybe they *needed* more space between them. So Lauren could consider other options.

He started typing:

> We met up near Greybull. Ate lunch there. She's doing well, but glad to be out of Yellowstone. I think—

Lauren popped up from behind a distant knoll and began walking back to the road.

Doug deleted everything he'd written and instead sent:

> Heading toward the Bighorn Range.

He swallowed, then put his phone back into its cradle on his bike's boom.

Maybe he would say more later. Maybe not.

With less than ten miles to Worland, Doug pedaled steadily despite the wind whipping across him from the west. Lauren was ahead of him, setting a reasonable pace after what must have been nearly eighty miles on the day.

Suddenly her legs slowed to a stop. Her bike wobbled. Then down she went, flopping toward the adjacent plain.

"Lauren!"

She lay in an awkward position, jerking and twitching.

Doug yelled her name again.

He caught up, jammed on his brakes, and scrambled off the bike.

She still hadn't answered him.

Her eyes were rolled up, showing only white as her body convulsed.

He dashed behind her, lifted her torso over his, leaned her on her side, and cradled her. If she banged against anything, it would be his soft body.

He thought better of removing her helmet until she regained her faculties but kept her head against his shoulder to stabilize it. "You're going to be okay," he whispered. He'd seen this sort of thing a few times with a college friend. "Everything's going to be just fine."

He reached down and twisted her foot until it snapped out of her pedal. The other one was already free. Then he pulled her away from the bicycle.

A minute later she stopped trembling and the cobwebs lifted. Then she started and looked at him. "Oh no. I didn't."

"Just sit for a minute. You're going to be fine."

"Thank you. How long was I out for?"

"Just a few minutes. Is anything sore? You took quite a fall."

"My shoulder." She rotated it and grimaced.

"You okay?"

"Yes, I think so. It hurts, but it's not sharp."

"Your panniers cushioned you from a harder fall."

Lauren lay on her bed at the Sleep-O-Rama Motel in Worland, Wyoming, staring into the mirror on the opposite wall.

Doug now knew.

But he'd handled it so well. Holding her, easing her to her feet, and omitting any inquisition or embarrassing comments. Even offered a comforting hug until she pulled herself together, then adjusted the brake lever on her bicycle. What would she have done if she'd been alone? Or with someone else? He even picked up a sandwich for her while she got ready for bed. He knew she needed the rest without her telling him.

But could she trust him with what haunted her most?

The pharmacies in town were closed for the evening. Small pharmacies didn't carry her medication anyway. Nonetheless, she messaged her doctor to request a prescription. Rapid City looked big enough, even though it was several days away. In the meantime she hoped she wouldn't put Doug in another awkward position.

Before saying "Good night" and heading to his motel room, Doug had agreed to meet Lauren at McDonald's by six in the morning for what appeared to be a challenging day of cycling, up and over the Bighorn Range to Buffalo, with few places to eat or stay in between. He'd suggested a rest day, but Lauren wanted none of it.

She hadn't offered much of an explanation for what happened. But she was entitled to share as much or as little as she wanted. It must have been frightening to lose control like that, particularly on a bicycle.

As Doug finished his meatball sub, it seemed insufficient to replace the calories he'd burned but would have to do. He needed to relax, then sleep.

He leaned back on the pillow, grabbed his phone, and eyed its screen.

Call me when you free up.

He punched the call icon beside Jeffrey's name.

"Hey. Thanks for returning my call. I'm sorry I didn't get back to you sooner about Lauren. She's fine."

"Yeah, that's what you said in your text."

"I guess I did . . . She seemed a little standoffish. Any idea what's going on with her?"

"Well, as I understand it, you guys broke up, and now she's continuing on this grand adventure. She probably didn't expect you to drop in like you did."

Doug could have added that he and Lauren had reunited, but it would probably come up anyway. Jeffrey didn't need to hear about Lauren's seizure.

"I . . . I just miss her."

Any guy who'd spent any time with Lauren would miss her. And Jeffrey's revelation came in a tone of voice atypical for the self-assured lawyer. Doug detected pain. It was easy to spot. He had enough of it himself.

"How did you leave things with her?"

"We'll always be friends. Of that I'm sure. But I'm wondering if that's enough."

Doug wasn't sure what to say.

"Are you guys planning to reconnect and travel together again?"

"We . . . we actually joined up today. And, yes, we'll be traveling together for now."

Jeffrey cleared his throat. "Well, could you take good care of her?"

"As much as she'll let me." He didn't need any encouragement to do that.

"And let me know how things are going."

Doug popped his eyes open wider and shook his head. Maybe he should suggest Jeffrey buy himself a bicycle and meet them in Buffalo on the other side of Powder River Pass. But that wasn't going to happen—at least he hoped not.

"You take care, Jeffrey. Nice talking to you."

# CHAPTER 29

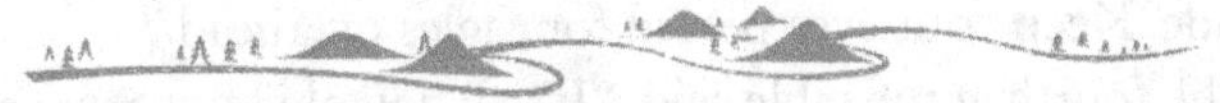

When Lauren rolled into McDonald's just before six, Doug had a hot coffee waiting for her. Each of them ordered the Big Breakfast with Hotcakes.

A group of elderly men shared war stories across from them. One looked at Doug. "Those your bicycles out there?"

Doug nodded while chewing on a pancake.

"Where ya headed today?"

"Buffalo."

"That's a long poke on a bicycle. Did you know you're going through Powder River Pass? It's nearly ten thousand feet. It snows up there just about any time of year."

Lauren smiled as she spread jelly on a biscuit. This was going to be another adventure. However, the wrinkles on the bridge of Doug's nose deepened.

"It's relatively flat to Ten Sleep, then you'll begin a long climb. Almost six thousand feet. Up."

Doug glanced sideways. "That's higher than Yellowstone, is it not?"

"Yup. Most people don't realize what they're in for. I hope ya avoid the storm on top. He-he."

Another codger chimed in. "They'll be okay, Max. From the looks of those rigs out there, this ain't their first rodeo."

A man across from them who'd been looking out the window turned his head. "Weather forecast sounds just fine."

Lauren glanced at her phone's clock. They would have about fourteen hours of daylight. "Are there places to camp along the way?"

"None I'd recommend," Max said. "And not many at all. Unless of course ya do your own thing."

Doug looked at the man. "What's up there for wildlife?"

"Nothing that'll bother ya too much. Black bear in the forest. You'll hear coyote. Mostly pronghorn and bighorn sheep at higher altitude. Keep your eyes peeled for eagles overhead."

The fourth at the table said, "It's all downhill once you reach the top."

*Forest?* She hadn't been in one of those since Sylvan Lake.

On US Route 16 to Ten Sleep, the terrain mirrored what they'd enjoyed the day before. But Lauren couldn't wait to see what lay ahead. Multihued strata embossed the cliff faces of the barren, rust-colored hills while scrubby vegetation dotted the surroundings. A herd of pronghorn, standing as pillars of salt, stared at them from atop one of those hills.

Thirty miles in, after cycling through Ten Sleep, they began climbing. A sign announced their entry into the Bighorn National Forest, where more trees sprouted with each passing mile. Clouds formed on the horizon.

They cycled through a canyon, switchbacks snaking them onward and upward. Occasional motorists gave them plenty of berth at low speeds.

Doug pulled into a turnoff overlooking the canyon. "I don't like the looks of that sky."

Lauren scanned the surroundings. Still no buildings. "We'll be okay. Don't worry. God has our back."

They continued their ascent. Soon trees blanketed the hills around them, swaying in the breeze. How trees had materialized after passing through barren countryside the past two days was beyond her, but they added vitality and beauty, as well as additional green hues to the Wyoming color grid.

Wind whistled through Lauren's helmet and made progress more difficult. The higher they climbed, the stiffer the wind—and the darker the sky.

A lake appeared alongside the road, leaves on aspens shimmering. Nothing like they'd seen earlier in the day.

Doug pointed to the heavens and shouted, "I don't like this!"

"It's alright. We must be near the top."

"Is that a good place to be?"

They donned rain jackets. Lauren covered her violin with a plastic bag, and they cycled on.

Soon granular pellets pinged Lauren's helmet. First they were light, then hit with more force.

"Hail!" Doug shouted. "Good thing we have helmets. Let's get under cover."

Great idea, but other than a large tree, where would they find it?

They pulled off the road.

"What about under those trees?" Lauren said.

Doug led them as they wheeled beneath a gigantic fir tree, no darker than under the blackened sky. "Let's hope this storm doesn't come with lightning."

Hail descended in angular sheets, bouncing on the pavement before rolling downwind. The wind chilled Lauren's overheated body as it stuffed her nostrils with evergreen fragrances.

A crack sounded in the distance. From which direction was unclear.

Then the sky lit up. A deafening clap of thunder followed. Tingles flashed through Lauren's body.

Doug shook his head.

"What should we do?" Lauren said.

"I dunno." Doug raised his hands and splayed his fingers. "Pray?"

"That's alway—"

Another rumble of thunder shook her. She shivered.

A bolt of lightning struck so close she heard the sizzle right before its thunder detonated.

What had they gotten themselves into?

When another loud clap of thunder shook the ground, Lauren dropped her bicycle and shot toward Doug. He raised an arm, and she nestled under it.

What would she have done without him here? And who could comfort her like this after the adventure was over?

A half hour later the hail, driving rain, and electrical storm subsided. The sun came out. Lauren's grip on Doug's side eased. He'd discovered a delightful benefit to inclement weather, but time was now working against them. They wheeled out from under the giant fir.

His odometer showed forty-six miles. They were only halfway to Buffalo.

"We need to get moving. It's almost three o'clock, and we haven't even reached the top yet. Once we do, it should be clear sailing . . . at least that's what the guy at McDonald's said."

Less than a mile from where they'd taken refuge, they entered a small, lakeside store and replenished their fluids.

Ninety minutes later, with the sun warming the cool breeze at altitude, the duo crawled to the summit of Powder River Pass. Doug wheeled up to a sign that read *Elev. 9,666 ft.* On the opposite side of the road, a jagged pyramid of rock formed the peak.

Lauren leaned her bike against the signpost and grabbed a water bottle. "Wow! We did it. That was *so* hard."

Doug took a deep breath and leaned back in his seat.

"Must be nice."

He furrowed his brow. "What?"

"To be able to sit in a recliner all day, even when you're not pedaling."

He chuckled, then tipped his head back and shut his eyes.

He heard Lauren rummaging through her load but kept his eyes shut and relaxed. They still had over thirty miles to go, and if God stuck any hills between them and Buffalo . . . he needed the rest. They would soon be racing the setting sun.

The breeze glanced off his face. As his legs surrendered to the fatigue, his load began to tip. He caught it before pancaking.

Then the silence broke.

Doug opened his eyes, and there was Lauren, eyes closed, bow caressing the strings of her violin. Her lips cinched on each corner of her mouth, cheeks full of joy. Her bow reversed course.

The tune sounded familiar, but its tempo did not. He wouldn't interrupt to ask. They needed to get while the getting was good, but . . .

Her bow and the fingers of her left hand moved faster, as did the music. Doug's head caught the rhythm, nodding to the beat. Now he recognized it, and he smiled.

Lauren opened her eyes, locked them on to Doug's, and picked up the pace even more.

Their heads danced together, Lauren's bound to her violin.

Another verse, faster than the previous one. Doug's head could no longer keep up, but Lauren could. Her fingers became pistons, up and down to capture each note in the nick of time as her bow became a crosscut saw ready to fell a tree.

She slowed the pace for the finale, adding a stinger for good measure.

Doug grinned. "'Go Tell It on the Mountain.'"

"I'm so glad you recognized it. Do you know the lyrics?"

"'Go tell it on the mountain, over the hills and everywhere' . . . That's about all I know."

"It goes like this:

> "While shepherds kept their watching
> O'er silent flocks by night,
> Behold, throughout the heavens
> There shone a holy light.
> Go tell it on the mountain . . .

"And so forth. It's an African American spiritual. I just couldn't resist in this setting."

Doug gazed at the surrounding landscape. "It's not what I expected, but it's still marvelous."

"God's creation is so amazing."

Doug looked her in the eye. His heart skipped a beat. "You're amazing." The words slipped out before he could filter them.

She dropped her head and looked away. "Do you really think so?"

"You're one of a kind, Lauren. Look at you out here. We've cycled fifty-five miles and climbed five thousand feet, and you still have it in you to play such an apropos song with such talent and flair. Not many people could do that."

She returned his look. "Thank you."

The downhill ride from Powder River Pass did not come as advertised. Instead they discovered one hill after another. The descents were grand but not continuous. Lauren's legs ached.

According to Doug it was thirty-five miles to Buffalo. The sun was setting behind the hills in her rearview mirror.

At the apex of another roller, Lauren added a heavy base layer beneath her jacket. Doug did likewise.

She wasn't used to this type of solitude. Life in Uganda was filled with hubbub. Kids, kids, and more kids. Plus staff members who shared life together. Nevertheless, the change energized her. It was so easy to speak to God out here . . . and hear back from Him.

Doug was also great company. He filled something inside her that'd been missing for a long time. Without him it would be so . . .

Lonely.

That's what her life could become now that Jeffrey was out of the picture. Solitude like that would make a grown woman cry. *No thank you.* She needed someone, and she needed the sound of children in her life.

But what exactly did Doug mean by *"You're amazing"*?

Was he admiring her musical talent, her fitness level, or was it something more? Had she given him the wrong idea? Or was that what he had done to her?

As dusk darkened they picked up speed on a sharp decline.

Up ahead Doug whooped. Coasting at breakneck speed or pedaling with ease was great. But she'd enjoy it better if she could see where she was going and avoid objects on the shoulder before hitting them.

*God, please keep us safe. And thank You for Doug. Lord, I want a special companion to share life with. And children. Would that be okay with You?*

# CHAPTER 30

The campsite in Buffalo was plugged full of motorcycles and mostly men wearing leather and sporting facial hair. It didn't help that Doug and Lauren had arrived at nine o'clock. His spent muscles yearned for a mattress, but his stomach rumbled.

The attendant tapped a pencil on her cheek. "Not much room tonight."

Doug looked at the upside-down campground map on the counter. "Can you squeeze us in somewhere?"

She pointed to the far corner of the map. "I can put you beside the restroom."

*Not again.*

Doug looked at Lauren, who nodded. "We'll take it. Any food here?"

"Sorry, everything shuts down early in this town. You might find something you like in the vending machine though. It's right outside the door."

With the vending machine's offerings unable to match what Doug had inside his pannier—which wasn't saying much—Doug and Lauren weaved in and around parked motorbikes and wandered to the back of the small campground. They arrived in the middle of a party.

The two found a small plot of grass outside the latrine, where they pitched their tents.

"Could I make you a Fig Newton peanut butter sandwich?" Lauren said.

She was reading his mind. "That would be great. I can't wait to get some sleep."

As Lauren reached into her pannier, a heavyset man staggered toward them, an open bottle of beer in his hand. "You guys wanna drink?"

"Oh, no thank you," she said.

Doug shook his head.

"Where ya been?"

"Powder River Pass," Doug said.

"Get caught in the storm?"

"Uh-huh."

"Man, I thought it was bad on a Harley. Wouldn't wanna have been ya."

Lauren dipped a plastic knife into the jar of peanut butter. "It wasn't so bad. It's an adventure."

The man looked at her, apparently trying to focus, then let out a burp. "'Scuse me, ma'am." Then he tripped on one of Doug's tent stakes, lost his balance, and crashed into Lauren's tent.

A man in the lot across from them said, "Charlie, what are you doing over there?"

The others in the group laughed.

One of them said, "Would you look at the hottie? Ooooo-weee!"

Lauren glanced at the group, then at the man who'd fallen into her tent. He was still trying to extricate himself.

"Are you alright?" she said. "Did you hurt yourself?"

The man grunted as he rolled to his side, steadied himself, and tried to get up.

Doug had seen—and heard—enough. He helped steady the man so he could rise to his feet. The strong scent of alcohol told all.

Meanwhile, the catcaller ambled toward their lot. Another biker with chains dangling from his vest followed him.

"You guys going to Sturgis?" the trailing man said.

"Where's that?" Doug said.

"The question's not *where* but *what*. Haven't you ever heard of Sturgis?"

In fact, Doug had heard of it . . . during his youth in Iowa.

"Gonna be a million there. One big biker party. We's gettin' started early." His grin revealed a chipped front tooth in the glimmer of the floodlight on the latrine.

The catcaller grabbed Lauren's shoulder. "Ain't you a pretty thing." Then he glanced at Doug. "You too, with those skinny-legged shorts on that fat rear end of yours."

"Get your paws off her, bud."

"Who you callin' *bud*?"

Doug reached for the belt bag around his waist, where his gun and other valuables were stored. But it wouldn't be easy to fish out his six-shooter here without making a scene. Besides, he and Lauren were outnumbered. No doubt, these ruffians were armed. "Leave her alone. Please."

"Get back here, you guys," came a voice from the group at their campsite. "Got another cold one waitin' for ya."

"Come on, Charlie. Let's leave the spandex king and his mistress alone."

After the three moseyed back to their site, Doug inspected Lauren's tent. One of the poles had snapped. The tent's roof hung low, and the entire left side had collapsed.

"Let's get outta here."

She searched his eyes. "Where will we go? You heard them at check-in. All the motels are booked. It's also pitch-black out."

"I don't trust these drunks." He looked around, spying several parties in adjoining lots. He grabbed his phone. "Wasn't there a church on the way into town?"

"Yes, I believe there was. First Trinity. What about the city park?"

Doug found the church's website and examined a picture of the grounds. "The park's probably as overrun by scoundrels as this place. I don't trust them. Time for a little stealth camping. You up for that?"

Lauren's eyes sparkled in the scant light. "I sure am. I could sleep well at the foot of a cross. And we'll be right on time for church in the morning."

"Is it Saturday?"

"Actually, I've lost track. The days all run together."

In his past Doug would've beat feet in the other direction anytime church doors swung open. Not now . . . and not anymore.

Hordes of motorcycles flew past Lauren and Doug on I-90 East toward Gillette, Wyoming, chaps flapping in the wind. She had googled Sturgis before Doug got up. The guy the prior night hadn't exaggerated much. They might see upwards of a half million people. Poker tournaments, a Jack Daniels tasting, a Harley-Davidson show, and contests for beards, mustaches, and tattoos. Maybe she could calm things down with a few tunes. Lodging options would be scarce, even if they knew ahead of time where they would stop for the evening in that part of South Dakota.

The sign back at the on-ramp read *No Services 66 Miles*. That was okay, because the wide-open terrain had become more forgiving, though uninspiring compared with the last several days.

She stopped to use the bathroom behind a gigantic roll of hay in a roadside field. While Doug rested on the shoulder, she checked her phone. Two missed calls, an hour apart. From Jeffrey. But no voicemail.

He'd sent a text message after the last call:

I miss you! Stay safe.

Usually he was so preoccupied with work he didn't have time for her.

When she came out from around the bale, Doug was walking his recumbent along the shoulder.

"What are you doing?"

"Did you notice the poor critters?" He gestured to the flattened balls of tan-and-white fuzz peppering the highway.

"I was wondering what those were."

"Bunnies. Stuck there with their last meal."

"Ewww."

Doug stopped, leaned to his right, and picked up an empty plastic bottle. Then he pointed it at her. "This is just what we need for a more permanent fix for that tent pole of yours. Along with a little duct tape. Although you're still welcome to swap tents with me."

*So sweet!*

After another overnight stay on a church's grounds in Gillette, Doug convinced Lauren they should leave the interstate at Moorcroft, opting for the route through Newcastle to Custer, South Dakota, to avoid the town of Sturgis. He wanted to keep her away from as many drunken eyes as possible. They spent an evening at a strip motel in Newcastle before a handful of pronghorn chased them out of Wyoming under threatening skies. The route no doubt avoided several thousand motorcyclists, but plenty still accompanied them, zipping past oil operations and crawling through the Black Hills National Forest.

By the time they reached Custer, motorbikes clogged the downtown streets, parked in rows like dominoes, but who would dare nudge them? The duo decided to avoid the congestion and find a place to eat lunch in a quieter setting.

Five miles later they found it beneath a tree beside the parking lot at the Crazy Horse Memorial, as yet a work in process from the looks of the scaffolding. But the high forehead and the prominent hook nose clarified whose land they were cycling through.

As Doug and Lauren munched on peanut butter-covered rice cakes, a dark-skinned man wearing a beaded headband and blue jeans got out of his old Dodge Ram pickup with a boy about the age of six. The man wrapped his arm around the lad, then pointed at the monument as they walked toward it.

Doug chuckled. "Makes me think of the time I took my son to see the Wigwam Motel in San Bernadino."

"How so?"

"Maybe just the way he's pointing. Each room was shaped like a standalone tepee. He loved it."

"Air-conditioned, I assume."

"I'm sure . . . I can't imagine living in one of those without walls, a door, and a lock."

The man and the boy passed under the entryway arch that read *Never Forget Your Dreams*.

"Well, imagine no insulation or heat and no indoor plumbing with cold air coming down from Canada in January."

They finished lunch and cycled sixteen miles to Mount Rushmore. It might've been Native American turf, but four presidents watched over the land, leaving no doubt who was in charge.

While Lauren went to the restroom, Doug texted photos of Crazy Horse and Mount Rushmore to his half-sister Carmen.

> What!? On a bicycle? You must be kidding.
> I'm jealous.

Carmen would really be jealous if she knew what an adventure he was experiencing. Having Lauren with him made it even better. How would returning to everyday life ever compare to this?

When he looked up, the same man and boy they'd seen at the Crazy Horse Memorial walked up and stood a few feet away from him.

"Who are they?" the boy said.

"Presidents of the United States. You see that guy on the left?"

The boy nodded. "I've seen him before."

"That's George Washington. He's one of the men they call the Founding Fathers. The one beside him is another Founding Father, Thomas Jefferson."

"Why do they call them Founding Fathers?"

"They led the move to gain independence from the British and helped set up the US government."

The boy looked up at him. "Is that our government?"

"No, we have our own. We were here first though. But we still have to obey theirs too."

The boy squinted at the man.

"It's complicated, son." He pointed to the mountain. "The next one, Teddy Roosevelt, was not a good man."

"How come?"

"It's a long story, but he didn't treat our people well."

"Who's the other man?"

"Abe Lincoln. Many people think he saved America. When the Northern and Southern States were fighting one another."

"Is there room for you to put another one here?"

"There's room, but they haven't worked here for years. I'm only working at Crazy Horse."

"Excuse me," Doug said. "Are you a sculptor?"

"Yes."

"We saw you down at Crazy Horse. Impressive work."

"Thank you. We have a whole team." The man eyed Doug's recumbent. "Where are you heading?"

"East. Across America."

"Whoa!" the boy said.

"When will Crazy Horse be completed?"

"Not in my lifetime. Private funding is hard to come by."

The boy tugged on his father's sleeve. "Who will they put here next?"

Doug froze. He looked up at the courage in that chiseled chin of Washington and the depth of character in Lincoln's sunken eyes. Then he shook his head.

The next morning at a campground in Keystone, Doug awoke to the smell of coffee and cinnamon. Lauren had prepared a bowl of oatmeal for him.

After eating they cycled toward Rapid City. Dark clouds gathered, rumbling louder than the Harleys flying by, as Doug and Lauren descended.

Before those thunderheads could bang together and spill their ire, the two rode to a restaurant in Rapid City. After lunch they would pick up Lauren's prescription at the pharmacy, stop at a camping supply store for a new tent pole, and leave behind the biggest city they'd see for weeks.

A server with copper skin came to their table with her ticket pad. Her jet-black hair was pinned in a bun with what looked like a bone. Doug recognized an AA tattoo on her wrist, a triangle inside a circle.

Before the server left, Doug said, "Quite a raft of bikers on the roads."

"I take it you're not from around here."

"That be true."

"They drop in early each August and leave a week later in a cloud of blue smoke. Other than that, ain't much goin' on around here. You two bikers?"

Doug nodded.

Lauren smiled at the woman. "We provide our own power."

"Where you from?"

"LA," Doug said, then gestured toward Lauren. "And Virginia."

The server stiffened and frowned. "What are ya doin' *here*?"

"We just dropped in for a bite to eat."

"What's it like here?" Lauren said.

The server grimaced. "If you want the truth, it's depressing. I'd rather be back on the rez, but that's no picnic either. Lots of suicide around here."

Lauren's bright countenance imploded. "I'm sorry."

The woman slipped away as if she'd seen a ghost.

"That's so sad."

Doug sighed. "I hope I didn't say the wrong thing."

"Have you given any more thought to Brother Jim's job offer?"

"Yeah, actually I have. I just don't feel the timing is right. There's too much out here . . . and in here"—he pointed to his chest—"to learn about."

"As you can see, there's no shortage of need."

Doug nodded. "So where to next?"

"I looked at the map last night. I'd like to travel to an Indian reservation."

Doug scowled. "Whatever for?"

"I want to see the living conditions for myself. Get a better sense of the need."

"It's not like we'll see tepees. I know a thing or two from growing up in Iowa. It's not the kind of place I'd choose to visit. More the opposite."

"Jeffrey's told me all about how Native Americans wandered North America . . . before European explorers came and staked claims. The white man had more sophisticated weapons. We squeezed them onto small footprints of land. Broke promises."

The server returned, took their orders, and left.

"Jeffrey compared the plight of Native Americans to sardines. They once swam vast waterways, but then we stuffed them into a can and shoved them into a cupboard for our own convenience. I think it's tragic."

That fancy-pants lawyer would never bicycle onto Indian land. It was easy to talk a big game from a posh office in the city. "I'm not sure I wanna go there."

"I feel for them. Don't you want to see what their life is like? . . . You missed out on Yellowstone."

Doug cocked his head. "Did I?"

"We may never have a chance like this again."

No doubt she'd do it all by herself again. He'd missed her so much when she went to Yellowstone. Maybe this was another chance to get it right.

# CHAPTER 31

Lauren glanced down at her phone. Another missed call from Jeffrey. The text he'd sent her the prior evening in Rapid City made it sound like he still wanted to be with her. It's not like she didn't share some of those feelings, but he was the most insecure man brimming with confidence that she'd ever known. Maybe she brought out the worst in him.

But she, too, had felt insecure every day she was with him. That wasn't totally Jeffrey's fault. He hadn't slammed into her parents' car at seventy miles an hour, drunk. Why did life deal such blows when you least expected them?

Deep down, getting close to someone—really close . . . just the thought of it tossed her stomach. Only God was fully trustworthy of being there for her. But was He asking her to make room for someone else? Trusting them not to crush her again when she least expected it?

And then there was the risk of sharing her secret. Doug had handled her seizure better than she would have expected. Perfectly.

But as for secrets, he only knew the half of it.

Maybe a close relationship wasn't worth the agony. Her life had been full as a missionary. Heart connections with fellow believers loving and serving underprivileged children together made up for her lack of intimacy. What could top that? Except now, they were gone.

And she was alone.

She slid the toilet paper back into her trash baggie and climbed the embankment.

Doug was staring at the surroundings. "I can't believe it. Look!"

"Uganda had nothing like this. It looks like sand."

The grasslands with their rolls of hay were morphing into random piles of pumice. They formed elongated peaks, from two sides rather than four, striated in tones of brown, beige, and tan, as if gigantic dump trucks had dispensed them to solidify over the ages. Mesas appeared as flat-top haircuts, exclusionary lookouts over the prairie they'd sprouted from, their veins capable of whisking away torrential rainfall or ushering windblown dust atop themselves.

As they pedaled on, a familiar seal—the one Lauren had seen in Yellowstone—appeared on a large sign. *Badlands National Park.* Larger rock formations now lined the road, more in clusters and ranges than pop-up wonders.

Doug investigated. "Coarser than 24-grit sandpaper." Then he pointed to the southwest, where dark clouds were gathering.

The duo continued, no shelter in sight. Cattle and horses grazed in an adjacent field.

In the early afternoon they stopped roadside to eat. Lauren dug out her peanut butter and rice cakes and offered one to Doug. He contributed a banana and energy bar.

A pickup approached. The driver pulled off the road, and a middle-aged couple climbed out.

"How's the riding?" the man said.

"Great!" Doug said.

Lauren swallowed a bite of banana. "This landscape takes my breath away."

"Hi, I'm Donna," the woman said to Lauren. "Where are you guys staying tonight?"

That was a good question.

"We've stayed at a few churches and campgrounds," Doug said. "Any of those around here?"

"A few, but you need to be careful," the man said.

Doug furrowed his brow.

"Youth gangs," Donna said.

"Urgh. We had those in Uganda. Losing a boy to a gang was our worst nightmare."

"You worked in Uganda? How cool is that? My name's Rick, by the way." The man extended his hand to Doug. Then he shook hands with Lauren.

Doug raised his hand to the back of his helmet. "Youth gangs?"

"You're approaching the rez. I'd be careful. Donna and I ride in this area, but we try to be home well before dark."

"Thank you for warning us," Lauren said.

"We'd invite you to stay with us," Donna said, "but it looks like you're traveling in the opposite direction. We live in Rapid City."

A conversation ensued about bicycling in South Dakota. After several minutes they exchanged contact information, and the pickup drove away.

After resuming their ride the flatlands finally rose, bringing them to an overlook of all that was good in the badlands. Awesome in their peculiarity, magnificent in their expanse, the gray-frosted landscape belonged on another planet.

Lauren pulled her phone from her back jersey pocket. Another text from Jeffrey. Probably another flip-flop of confused emotions. She had enough of those herself. She would read it later.

Doug, on the other hand, was drinking in the otherworldly view unencumbered.

The tourists in the few cars parked there only spent minutes taking in the view before getting back in their cars. They would fly past what she and Doug had savored for hours, unable to see, smell, hear, feel, and touch the way bicycle travelers did. Those who took the fast, easy way were like people so obsessed with their jobs they'd trade these opportunities for meetings, cubicles, and appointment calendars. That was Jeffrey.

Would he ever discover the life he was missing? Could she ever experience it with him?

She walked up behind Doug. "Thank you."

He started, then turned around. "For what?"

"For sharing this adventure with me."

"Glad to. Sure beats doing it alone."

Lauren awoke with the sun.

They'd found a church off the reservation that agreed to let them sleep out back, hidden from the road. Bedding down early had minimized the attention they might draw after sunset. Other than the roar of an intermittent motorcycle, few travelers had passed by.

She powered up her phone. Then she reread Jeffrey's text message from the day before:

> I miss you soooo much. I need to see you
> again.

Her heart bled. *Oh Jeffrey.* It's not like she didn't miss him too. How could she respond to that? Maybe no response would be best.

It was hard to imagine what life would be like on the reservation. Its residents were displaced from lands their ancestors had inhabited for centuries. *It would breed anger and contempt. How will the cycle ever be broken?*

She opened the Bible app. Searching for "oppressed people," up came Isaiah 14:2.

> Then people will take them and bring them to their place, and the house of Israel will possess them for servants and maids in the land of the LORD; they will take them captive whose captives they were, and rule over their oppressors.

That verse pertained to the Israelites, God's chosen people, but what about the Native Americans? Would they ever mete out retribution for what had befallen them?

The landscapes she'd cycled through were magnificent. However, it was August. The weather would be harsh in winter. And a sign she'd read explained how the white man had slaughtered thousands of buffalo in the 1800s, crippling an important food source of the Native Americans.

It was so unfair.

Yet people used the word *unfair* when they thought they hadn't gotten what they deserved, which suggested God had let them down. What happened to Freddie, a fellow cyclist in Idaho, wasn't fair, landing in the hospital the way he did. He'd gone out of his way to help, and it cost him dearly. Regardless, God could still use it to accomplish His purposes. And she would never forget Freddie.

Usually Lauren rose before Doug, so he walked over to her tent and said, "Are you up yet?"

"Yes, I was just waiting for you."

"You're probably reading that Bible of yours again."

Lauren laughed. "What about you? Have you been reading it too?"

"Not so much. It's hard to fit a Bible on a bicycle. Too heavy."

Lauren crawled out of her tent. "Why not use an app on your phone?"

"That's not a bad idea."

Lauren showed Doug her app. "The Gospel of John is a great read. If you want to read the first chapter, I'll heat water for oatmeal. How's that sound?"

"Fair enough."

Lauren fixed breakfast while Doug read. The text was more interesting than he remembered. He liked the part about those receiving the Light becoming God's children.

"Do you like kids?"

He looked up. "Yeah, I like kids. Why do you ask?"

She smiled and tilted her head. "Just wondering."

"I assume you do since you worked with them so many years."

"Yes. I miss them."

Doug resumed reading.

"Do you wish you'd had more?"

He glanced sideways. "It wasn't going to happen."

"Go ahead. I'm sorry for interrupting."

After he finished reading, she said, "Have you thought about where we might stay tonight?"

"Not yet. I'm still recovering from yesterday." Doug pulled out his map.

"You heard Donna and Rick. Maybe we should book rooms."

"Assuming they have them. The map lists two motels in Crow's Foot. I'll give them a call." Doug grabbed his phone, then smirked. "Could I use yours?"

Lauren stirred the oatmeal. "Go ahead. It's early, but maybe they'll answer."

He plugged his phone into a charge stick and picked up Lauren's phone. When he navigated from the Bible app, there was Jeffrey's text message. He sure was persistent. Poor guy.

Doug called the higher-rated motel and booked two rooms.

"Wow. Last two rooms. When I told her we were on bicycles, she said, 'You're lucky to get a room. Make sure you get here before dark. Middle of the afternoon would be best. We'll be watching for you.'"

A few minutes later Lauren said, "Breakfast is ready."

Just before eight they began cycling into the sun. Maybe the glare would wake Doug up.

*"Do you like kids?" . . . Interesting question.* And she'd thanked him for cycling with her. She must be enjoying his company.

According to an account he'd read online after meeting Rick, Crow's Foot was the epicenter of the Golden Prairie Indian Reservation, known for drunkenness, brawling, domestic abuse, and squalor. That description had spawned research for another route east. However, the alternatives were longer and came with other challenges. And Lauren would never have foregone a trip through the heart of the reservation.

It had about fifteen thousand inhabitants, with a thousand living in Crow's Foot. A casino was the economic hub. Passing through the reservation would take at least two days.

The wheat and corn in the gargantuan fields swayed in the stiff breeze. With the sun beaming at an angle, it reinforced the name of the reservation ahead. A variety of yellow hues accented the agricultural cornucopia around them. In the next mile a field brimmed with sunflowers in full bloom.

"That's so beautiful," Lauren said.

The bright, colorful hues drifted atop green stalks. Millions of flowers floated to and fro, pointing sunward, faces gleaming with a mahogany center before fanning out to orange, then yellow at petals' edges.

Wind gusted in the pair's faces, slowing them to a crawl despite the flat terrain. At six miles an hour, seventy miles with stops could take all day. Nevertheless, the ride ahead delighted Doug, with the perfect traveling partner, nary a cloud in the sky nor a car on the road, only vast fields with a few farms dotted among the crisscrossing roads.

As the sun climbed overhead, Lauren's stomach began to growl. She went to the bathroom roadside and caught back up to Doug, who'd stopped to review his map.

"There's a convenience store with a restaurant about a mile off route." He pointed to an intersection about a hundred yards away. "Let's go grab something to eat. I'm hungry." He clipped his shoe into the pedal.

Lauren stopped behind him. "Do you think that's a good idea?"

Doug turned around. "What do you mean? Aren't you tired of energy bars and peanut butter? We haven't stocked up in a while. I'd like fresh food."

"We've only gone thirty miles. I thought you said it was seventy to Crow's Foot."

"I did, but we have all day. What's another mile or two when you're going seventy? Besides, we already have reservations. On the reservation. Get it?" Doug smiled.

Lauren didn't appreciate the humor. "I don't want to get there after dark."

"The sun won't go down till eight thirty or so. We've got plenty of time."

*Did he forget what the motel clerk said?* "You go ahead. I'm moving so slow today you'll catch up to me anyway. How much farther before we turn?"

Doug looked at his map. "Oh, maybe twenty miles. Then we take a right on 301st Avenue. Can you believe it? This is just like LA—numbered streets."

"What do you want to do?"

"I wanna eat. Tell you what. I'll order takeout. I'll even deliver it. What would you like?"

"Chicken, fish, or a burger, but nothing deep-fried. Bread and veggies. Could you also get bananas for the road?"

"Anything else?"

"Yes." Lauren smiled. "How about a hot fudge sundae for dessert?"

"Funny. Will you be okay?"

"Oh sure. No one's around anyway. Let me check my phone first." Lauren looked down at her phone. It had ample power and signal. "Do you have a signal?"

Doug glanced down at his phone. "I sure do. It's almost noontime. If my math's right, I should see you in another ten miles. That could be a little after 1:00 if all goes well. See you then."

"Okay. Goodbye."

Doug twisted his body around and hammered on the pedals. Lauren clipped in and trailed him in increasing length until he turned left. Then she went on alone.

# CHAPTER 32

The road sign read *Welcome to Golden Prairie Indian Reservation*. The land on either side of Lauren was exploding with lush, iridescent wheat fields reflecting the brilliant sunshine, thriving in their peaceful environs. But at second glance the sign had bullet holes in it.

Five miles later a few vehicles passed her in either direction. And they were speeding. The bumper on the last one was held up with baling wire. A sticker on it had a bright-red null sign canceling the word *Freedom*, which was shaded with the stars and stripes of the American flag in a thick, balloon-shaped font.

Another car approached. A starburst crack in its windshield glinted the sun's rays. The young driver goosed the accelerator, causing the engine to backfire and cough out dark smoke.

With no paint covering its fender repair, a chattering econobox flew by. Another vehicle, with its rusty fenders and muffler riddled with holes, must have come from a junkyard.

Lauren's empty stomach knotted. These jalopies reflected anything but the robust fields surrounding them. Regardless, she carried on.

Her odometer reminded her of Doug's math. It was half past.

A silver Buick LaCrosse—more well-kept than the other cars—slowed as it approached.

Focusing straight ahead, Lauren pretended not to notice, pedaling as steadily against the wind as she had earlier while making as little progress.

As the vehicle met her, the driver's side window rolled down. An older woman looked her way. The car slowed to a stop.

So did Lauren.

"Where are you going?" The woman's tone of voice suggested Lauren needed permission to be traveling in this direction.

"Crow's Foot."

The woman looked in her rearview mirror and up ahead. "That's not a good idea," she said without a tinge of belligerence, only compassion and concern.

The well-groomed woman wore a dignified look, with dark hair, olive skin, and high cheekbones beneath her wire-rimmed glasses.

Lauren glimpsed lush wheat bending in the breeze on the other side of the road. "Oh?"

The woman scanned the surroundings. "Youth gangs. Crazy kids. You ought to choose another route while you can." The wrinkles above the bridge of her nose shouted concern.

"My friend took a side trip for food. He should be back in a half hour. We've booked rooms in Crow's Foot, so we should be okay."

"Which motel?"

"I'm not sure. My friend booked the rooms."

The woman took in a deep breath. Her face looked like that of a mother whose teenager was lobbying for a later curfew. A vehicle appeared on the horizon, about a half mile behind her. "I'll turn around and come back." Then she drove away.

Lauren resumed cycling.

A rattletrap pickup with three youths sitting abreast approached. Muffled hoots and hollers—and probably catcalls, were they more audible—increased and then diminished in volume as the vehicle flew by. Flailing arms and pointing fingers brought goosebumps to Lauren's bare arms despite temperatures in the 80s.

She pedaled harder, glancing in her rearview mirror after every few pedal strokes.

Ahead of her to the right, a farm road appeared on the edge of a massive cornfield. She turned onto it, dismounted her bicycle, and scooted it into a row of cornstalks, where she could monitor traffic undetected. Her cell phone clock read *12:45*.

Soon what looked like the silver LaCrosse approached from the west. Sure enough, it was the woman Lauren had chatted with minutes ago.

She dashed out from her secluded perch, leaving her bicycle hidden in the cornfield. With one wave of her arm, the Buick pulled onto the shoulder.

The passenger-side window lowered. "Why don't you get in, and we can talk."

Lauren hopped into the car and closed the door. "Thanks for coming back."

"Quite alright. I like to keep an eye out for cyclists. We've had so many problems on this reservation in recent years. I want to make sure our visitors are safe. A woman traveling alone through here is taking her life in her hands . . . Where's your bike?"

Lauren pointed to the field. "Over there." The dashboard clock read *12:56*. "Doug should be coming along anytime."

The woman's face had a weathered look, like it had stood tests of time and whatever else had come its way. "Is Doug your boyfriend?"

"No. Just a friend." Lauren shifted position on the seat.

The woman looked beyond her, peering into the distance.

Lauren turned to see what had distracted the woman. A ramshackle pickup left a wake of dust as it sped down the farm road toward them. The woman backed up the car to allow the truck to enter the main road.

As it approached, a lone male driver tipped a bottle to his mouth, then dropped it out of view.

"Oh dear." The woman forced a smile and waved as the pickup truck squealed onto the pavement and headed east.

Lauren waved too.

"We have so much of that." She pointed. "That road leads down to the river. Lots of indigent single men camp there. Some live there all the time. Others come and go. It's early yet, but he'll be smashed out of his mind by the end of the day."

"That's so sad. I take it they don't have work."

"No. Many of them live on government assistance. Some get help from family. Most of them are a menace to innocent people on the highway. Last week a cyclist was killed by a drunk driver. Another lost much of his gear while camping. Some kids got in there after he bedded down and went through his belongings. I suspect he was too scared, lying in that tent of his, to stop them. Even if he'd had a gun, he was way outnumbered."

Lauren absorbed the information but didn't react to it. Compassion was wrestling with concern for her own safety. And Doug's.

She pulled out her phone. "Oh, I don't have a signal anymore."

"Good luck with that. Cell service isn't very reliable here."

"Would you be open to driving down the road to make sure Doug is okay? I'm Lauren, by the way. Lauren Baumgartner."

"That's a good idea." She shifted into drive and used the entire width of the vacant road to turn around. "I'm Emma."

"He's on a recumbent bicycle." Lauren eyed the speedometer as the car accelerated. The last two digits of the odometer read *34.*

"I take it, Lauren, you've never been on an Indian reservation. The residents here are dropping like flies. Gangs have infested our young people. Drugs, drugs, and more drugs. That's on top of the alcohol. The suicide rate here is triple the national average . . . How old are you?"

"Forty-two."

"As a woman you'd have ten years left. It's much shorter for men."

"That's tragic. I used to work in Africa . . . Uganda. The numbers here are worse. I feel for your people."

After several minutes of conversation while scanning the countryside, Lauren looked over at the odometer again. *37*. No trace of Doug. Blood drained from her face.

A few miles later Lauren pointed. "That's the road he took."

"It's only a mile to the restaurant. Let's go check it out."

Lauren nodded.

"You may get a cell signal at the store. It's close to the interstate."

They drove to the restaurant and swung into the parking lot.

"I'd like to check with the employees," Lauren said.

Emma parked the car, and both of them went into the store.

"Have any of you seen a man in his sixties come in here within the past hour or so? In cycling attire?"

The few customers in the store either ignored Lauren's question or shook their heads.

The man behind the register, however, cocked his head and gazed at the ceiling. "Yeah. There was a guy in here. Ordered two hot meals to go and asked if we had any bananas. Once the meals came off the grill, he split. Friendly guy but seemed like he was in a hurry." He looked over at Emma and nodded. "Emma."

"Did you see which direction he headed?" Emma said.

As the clerk began to ring up a customer, his sideways-pointing thumb suggested Doug had indeed begun to retrace his steps. The two women thanked him and returned to the vehicle.

Emma checked her phone, then shook her head. "Any signal now?"

Lauren glanced at her phone. Her lips pressed into a grimace. "No."

Emma started the Buick. "How well do you know this friend of yours?"

"Well, if you're wondering if he took off on me, that's not Doug. He's very conscientious. There's no way he would've abandoned me."

"Hmmm . . . sounds like a good man to have."

Emma backed out of the gravel lot and headed back to where they'd come from. When she reached the main road, she turned east toward the cornfield with Lauren's bicycle in it.

A tear formed in the corner of Lauren's eye.

Emma looked over, then rested her hand on Lauren's shoulder. "We'll find him. He must have stopped for a break just off the road and we missed him. Keep your eyes peeled."

Several miles down the road they spotted a pickup truck on the shoulder. Two long, messy heads of hair appeared in the back window, but the driver was missing.

"These kids passed me after I passed you," Emma said. "They're *always* up to no good."

"Yes, I thought I recognized the vehicle."

Emma pulled up behind the pickup and shut the motor. Much to Lauren's amazement, Emma got out of the car and strode to the open window on the driver's side of the pickup.

Lauren rolled down her window and listened.

"Where's Red Feather?"

The mouth of the young man sitting in the middle was moving, but Lauren couldn't hear what he was saying. He wagged a finger to the right.

"Have you two seen a man riding a recumbent bicycle?"

The head on the passenger's side shook.

Emma glared in, then raised her voice. "Are you two telling me the truth?"

Muffled responses emanated from the cab, without animated gestures.

The profile of Emma's long face gave no hint of a smile. "You better be."

She walked back to the car and got in. "They haven't seen him. The driver's using the bathroom."

"Do you believe them?"

"Oh yes. They wouldn't *dare* cross me." Before starting the car she looked in her rearview mirror. "Looks like your friend may have caught up with us."

Lauren swiveled around and then breathed a huge sigh of relief. "Yes, that's him."

The two got out of the car and waited for Doug.

Meanwhile, the pickup in front of them sped away.

As Doug approached, he shouted, "Where's your bike?"

"I traded it in." Lauren beamed from ear to ear.

Doug stopped behind the car, where the two women joined him. "Traded it in? How are you getting home?"

"Well, just temporarily. Doug, this is Emma."

"I'm Emma Red Cloud."

"Oh, what a beautiful name." Lauren stretched her arm toward Doug. "This is Doug Zimmer."

"Emma." Doug nodded. "So glad to meet you."

"Doug."

"I'm so pleased to have met you, and thank you so much for your concern. And for helping me find my friend." Lauren furrowed her brow at Doug. "Where *were* you? We went all the way back to the store looking for you."

Doug handed Lauren a white Styrofoam container. "I downed a burger and took a shortcut on my way back. A customer outside the store showed me a farm road around some large fields. Absolutely beautiful setting, but a bumpy ride. The guy told me it would shave a mile or two. You could've called or texted."

"No signal. Hey, this smells good. What is it?" Lauren opened the container. "Wow! Look at the size of that burger."

"Sorry, it came with fries. I'll eat them if you don't want them. They didn't have bananas, so I bought apples instead. And I picked up different kinds of energy bars and a fresh jug of water. Emma, thanks for taking care of Lauren. Do you want an energy bar?"

"No thanks."

"Oh—and Lauren—I have something else. And you should eat it first." Doug reached into his side pannier and handed Lauren another bag. "It's double-wrapped."

She peeked into the bag and was met with cooler air. "Is this what I think it is?" She pulled out a white wrapper covering something on a popsicle stick, unwrapped it, and licked the drips from it. "Oh, how sweet. An ice cream bar. It's a little soft, but thank you, Doug." She tilted her head at him.

Despite the lighthearted exchange Emma's serious look hadn't faded. "It doesn't get any easier for you if you're heading to Crow's Foot. Lauren told me you booked two rooms. I'd suggest you get there as soon as you can, and definitely before dark. Where are you staying?"

"We're pretty slow." Doug checked his phone. "That's a tall order. May not happen, but it'll be close." He pulled out his map and flipped it over. "Lonesome Traveler Inn."

"That's on the main drag. You should go directly to it—no more shortcuts. I'd give you a ride if I could fit your bicycles and gear aboard, but that's obviously not going to work. You'll be okay once you get there. But whatever you do, don't go down by the river."

Lauren looked at Doug. "My bicycle is up ahead, hidden in a cornfield."

"A cornfield? What—"

"I'll explain later. Emma, would you mind giving me a lift back to my bicycle?"

"Of course not. Hop in. I'll wait with you until Doug catches up."

Doug began pedaling, passing the LaCrosse even before the women had gotten into it. "Last one there is a rotten egg!"

Lauren finished her ice cream bar before ducking into the car, her main course in hand. "Do you mind if I eat in your car?"

"Not at all."

A few miles later Lauren pointed. "That's the field . . . I think."

"Yeah, that's the road Tokala came out." Emma pulled the LaCrosse to the shoulder.

A pickup truck sat between the farm road and a stand of trees several hundred feet from the highway.

"Oh that little . . ." Emma muttered.

Lauren jumped out and ran to the cornfield, to the row where she thought she'd left her bicycle. Her heart skipped a beat. It was gone.

She checked the next two rows, then the previous two.

*Oh no!*

She raced back to Emma's car. "It's gone! What am I going to do?"

"Hop in. Do you have a signal?"

"No." Lauren closed the door as her breathing accelerated.

Emma put her hand on Lauren's shoulder. "Now now, everything's going to be alright. Let's wait for Doug, then I can take you down by the river. Somebody there probably knows something. Not much happens around here without someone else knowing about it. Then there's that pickup over there. It's owned by a couple I know and often used by their son. He's a bit slow. Probably hunting, but who knows what he's doing here.

"Are you *sure* you checked in the right place? Why don't we go back and look again."

The two walked to the field and canvassed a dozen rows either side of where Lauren thought she'd left the bicycle. When all seemed lost, they started back to the car.

Suddenly a loud hoot came from down the road. "Emma Red Cloud, look at me!"

A cyclist with no helmet was riding up the farm road, his arm swinging around like that of a rodeo cowboy about to lasso a bull, only this horse had a violin case strapped on back.

The closer it came, the longer her breaths. But . . . *Is it in the same condition I left it? And is anything missing?*

The bicycle rolled to a stop.

"Little Savage, what do you think you're doing? Gone for a joyride, have you?" A hint of a smile invaded the corners of Emma's mouth.

"Not much joy with these silly pedals. He-he-he. Not with mah boots. He-he. But she rides nice."

Little Savage wasn't little. He had the lean, muscular build and the garb of the rodeo competitors Lauren had seen as a child at the Pennsylvania Farm Show. They could fell a calf and tie its legs up in no time flat, but he lacked the proper gear . . . and, judging from his naivety, most likely the intuition.

"This yours?" he said to Lauren.

"Yes."

"I didn't mean to do it no harm. Just havin' some fun. He-he. Found it here in the cornfield and thought someone had abandoned it."

Emma preempted Lauren's response. "Little Savage, how many bicycle tourists do you know of who abandoned their bicycles and gear on this reservation?"

"I dunno. No one was 'round. I didn't take nothing but a spin. He-he." He got off Lauren's bicycle and held on to the end of the handlebar with his left hand while stepping away from the bike. "Here ya go."

"Thatta boy," Emma said.

When Lauren walked over to reclaim her bicycle, Little Savage stepped aside and let go of it, staring at Lauren's face with his mouth open.

She grabbed the bicycle before it crashed to the ground, then turned around to face him. "Thank you."

"Thank *you*, purdy girl."

Lauren checked over the bicycle and looked into her handlebar bag. Little Savage had done only what he said.

She wheeled her bicycle toward the road.

Emma followed her. "Say hello to your momma, Little Savage. You be good now."

"Okay, Emma Red Cloud."

The two women walked back to the car and spotted Doug on the western horizon. They exchanged phone numbers, and Lauren finished her burger while waiting for him.

"Call me if you need anything."

Lauren tilted her head. "I'm so glad we met. Thank you for caring."

# CHAPTER 33

For two hours disheveled vehicles whizzed by in either direction, increasing in number until three thirty when Lauren and Doug reached 301st Avenue. The captivating landscape surrounding them and the glorious sunshine belied the churning in Lauren's gut, which had increased with the frequency of the speeding rattletraps.

What would her heart rate be if Doug weren't here? *Two are better.* Yet they were no match for a gang of angry youth—or inebriated ones.

Once they turned onto 301st Avenue, however, her heart did accelerate. This could be Uganda or another third-world country, where poverty dwelt in rundown huts. Graffiti splashed in red paint on a boarded-up church building read *Not Home*, a cross in place of the letter *t*. To its left someone had jotted *Get high* with the letter *e* inverted. Above those were obscenities in yellow on a background splashed brown, perhaps masking earlier attempts to foment anger.

Missing roof shingles and others askew gave way to tar paper. Behind the church a handful of stones jutted out of the ground like crooked teeth, a picket fence thirsting for paint around them. Beyond the cemetery amber waves of grain glistened while swaying in the wind.

Across the road a rusty Chevy Vega with a smooshed nose sat on a support column high aloft the prairie. The large sign below it read *Don't put drinking on a pedestal.* A smaller sign beside it read *You could be next.*

They cycled past a burnt-out shack and then another.

Several more miles down the road, another billboard read *Meth with meth and it'll meth you up.*

Greedy villains were snatching money, giving only misery in exchange. None of their profits were reinvested here.

An advertisement for the reservation's gambling casino popped up, another effort of the rich to pluck money from those with none to spare.

Yet the natural beauty beyond the squalor quickened Lauren's heartbeat. The vast grasslands extended to the horizon, a sky as big as the one in Montana covering them. Large white clouds took turns shielding portions of the blue sky overhead. With kisses from the sun and caresses from the breeze, the boundless plain offered a spirit of freedom.

The irony, however, dropped a bittersweet weight in the pit of Lauren's stomach. Sin always messed things up. But whose sin was foiling the magnificence of the Golden Prairie Indian Reservation?

Fifty-five miles into the day, the sun was racing faster toward the horizon than they were toward Crow's Foot. Doug checked the time. He could kick himself for dilly-dallying earlier, chasing after a hot meal.

The headwind had slowed Lauren's pace. Even though the wind was abating, no way would they make it to the motel before dark.

"I'm hungry," Lauren said.

Doug was too. He'd been burning calories faster than he'd ingested them, but stopping would mean more miles in the dark. "Don't you have food in your handlebar bag?"

"I need more than another energy bar."

"Sorry." He kept pedaling.

With each inch of the sun's descent, the knot in his stomach tightened more. He was responsible for this. And for her safety. The bull's-eye on their back was growing by the second.

Several minutes later Lauren shouted, "Let's put on flashers before it gets any darker."

"We do that now, and it'll be dark. Let's squeeze out a few more miles first. Can you push any harder?"

"I'm stopping. You go ahead."

Doug checked his rearview mirror. Lauren was slowing, so he slammed on his brakes.

"Thanks," she said. "I appreciate it."

"Don't mention it."

While Lauren located her lights quickly, Doug couldn't find his.

She retrieved an apple from her pannier, took a bite, and grinned. "Want one?" Then she stared at the peach-colored sky in the west. Clouds overhead and to the east had taken on a similar hue.

"We don't have time for that." Doug pawed through his panniers a second time as Lauren strapped on her headlight.

She took another bite of her apple. "Are you stalling?"

Doug stopped rummaging long enough to look up at Lauren and sigh. As she placed a red flashing light on her back rack, he resumed his search.

"I just need to find my lights," he mumbled, glancing at her.

Lauren stood gazing at the long sunset, ready for nighttime riding, with neon reflective cuffs secured to her ankles.

Doug huffed, rechecking his rear pannier.

"Stop and think. When did you last use them?"

He paused to consider Lauren's idea. "I know where they are."

Moments later he snatched a ziplock bag from the interior pouch of a rear pannier. He slapped on a rear flasher and a headlamp, and the two resumed cycling.

Doug glanced in his rearview mirror a few times, glimpsing the sunset while the colors faded away.

As the dusk darkened, they would be doing exactly what Lauren had told Doug she didn't want to do—riding into Crow's Foot after dark. No sense fussing about it now though. She had more important things to tend to, such as staying clear of any cars that couldn't see them and getting to the motel as soon as possible.

Lauren could set up a tent, go to the bathroom, even play her violin wearing the puny light strapped to her helmet, but it was ill-suited for night riding. It was becoming pitch-black. With no streetlights in sight.

The fatigue in her legs reminded her how many times—infinite times—she'd spun these pedals around. The day's journey had to be reaching an end. But no end could she see.

If she could only feel Jeffrey's strong embrace now. With enough focus she could feel deep within her soul the definition in his lats and the squeeze of his powerful biceps next to hers. But that also brought pain, because his arms would no longer encompass her. He was probably up late reading a case brief, preparing arguments for tomorrow, or catching up on developments. He'd have no time for her anyway.

Lars's blue eyes accelerated her heartbeat. What would he be doing now? She imagined his curly blond hair and stout chest compressing into hers, his soft fingers caressing her face.

But Doug was here and now. The faint outline of his shoulders protruded from his seat back, his strong arms clutching his underseat handlebars. He was a good man. Reliable. Easy to be with. Time-tested. Safe.

*. . . if any man can be.*

Suddenly a chill passed down the back of her neck. The sound was unmistakable. A growl. Deep, guttural . . . dark.

And more real than imagined.

She looked around but saw nothing. Not even Doug. Where was he? Had she only imagined seeing him moments ago? Her voice frozen, the chill had gripped her legs now, but they kept whirling, her feet pounding the pedals with renewed vigor.

Another growl.

And claws scraping pavement behind her, like fingernails on a chalkboard but in rhythm to a horse's hooves.

Adrenaline spiked. She rode faster. The growl grew closer.

She screamed.

The growls coalesced with the sound of panting, so close its breath sent more tingles throughout her body.

A wheeze interrupted the ominous sounds as her predator ingested more air to catch her.

She pushed harder. And went faster.

The cacophony of pursuit grew louder behind her.

And impossibly closer.

Her heart pounded.

She glanced downward, careful to avoid the ragged edge of the pavement, but saw nothing.

It couldn't be a cougar—it would've caught her by now.

She glimpsed Doug ahead, closing ground on him. Faint headlights appeared in the distance, growing larger and brighter by the second.

A horn honked once, then again.

A menacing series of growls beat against Lauren's eardrums, interrupted only by the sound of propulsive huffs, right on her back wheel.

Goosebumps prickled her arms.

Adrenaline surged through her bloodstream.

The oncoming vehicle blared its horn and swerved toward Doug. The driver stuck his head out the window and yelled an obscenity as his pickup whizzed by.

Laughter trailed into the night as an empty beer can clinked onto the pavement once, then again and again until it rolled away.

And then silence. No horns, no laughter, no growls.

Her body shaking, Lauren finally caught up to where Doug had stopped. She unclipped one of her shoes and dropped it to the ground as she squeezed her brakes. A dark vacant road surrounded them. She could only pant.

Sitting on his recumbent bike seat, he tossed his head to the side, his light illumining heads of wheat across the road. "What a jerk!"

"Did you hear a scream behind you?"

"Punks."

"I—I just wanna get there," she managed.

"What's wrong?"

"Didn't you hear it?"

"How could I not? I thought he was going to hit me."

Lauren sighed. "Never mind."

Doug went on about "the disrespect of young people these days" while Lauren waited for her legs to stop trembling.

When her heart rate slowed, she clipped in. "Let's go." Then she pedaled past Doug into the darkness.

Traffic increased, signaling their approach to ground zero. This wasn't city, suburban, or even rural traffic. It traveled sporadically and fast, with more malfunctioning mufflers than not. The darker the night, the louder the noise echoing across the prairie.

Another vehicle equipped with mouthy passengers passed, then another approached. Screaming, hooting, and hollering raised suspicion about what fueled their ride. The driver jammed on the brakes, sending a screech into the night. The vehicle slowed.

Behind Lauren, Doug mumbled an expletive.

"Need a ride?" shouted the driver. Then he punched the accelerator, sending a much longer tire screech into the empty surroundings. An earthshaking backfire boomed.

It reverberated in Lauren's chest. Her hand slipped off the handlebar for a second before she righted the bike.

A girl seated next to the driver laughed uncontrollably. The scent of alcohol wafted out the open window. Then noxious exhaust fumes and the smell of burning rubber smothered it as the hooligans sped away. One lone taillight faded into the distance.

Lauren nearly choked before holding her breath. The fog cleared.

Before sundown the sight of graffiti had spelled anger, with charred buildings revealing a combustible setting and messy yards screaming for attention. Now not even the dark of night could hide the wretched disorder around them.

For an hour they cycled into the black of night. Yelling and screaming echoed from the distance. With siren blaring and lights flashing, a police cruiser sped past them in the opposite direction.

Finally dim light softened the darkness ahead.

A few miles later hope increased with the size and intensity of streetlights. They'd entered another town.

Ahead of them Lauren read the sign. *Lonesome Traveler Inn.* She eased up on her pedals. Below the motel sign hung a smaller one. *No vacancy.* "I'm so glad you reserved the rooms."

They rolled into the dark lot and leaned their bicycles next to the office door. It was locked.

The interior lights were off. Doug pushed an illuminated button next to the door, and a buzzer sounded.

Soon a heavyset woman came to the door as two kids ran circles around her. She flipped on the light and peered through the door's window. "I'm sorry, but we have no rooms."

A lump began to form in Lauren's throat.

"We called earlier and reserved two rooms," Doug said.

"I'm sorry. We're full."

"I gave you my credit card!" Doug shouted. "Don't tell me you sold our rooms to someone else."

"Mister, I told you to get here by mid-afternoon. If people come lookin' for a room in early evening, I can't turn 'em away. I'm sorry."

Doug's jaw muscle flexed. His head swung around as he processed what to do next. With gritted teeth he glanced back toward the woman. "I'm calling the police."

"Good luck with that. Police around here have their hands full with life-and-death issues. If you have tents, you'll find plenty of space to set up camp. Most tenters go down by the river. If you follow the road to your right, then after a mile take a left, you'll find a campground. That's the best I can do for you. Good night."

The light went out, then the woman turned and walked away. The two children remained, looking through the window.

"You can't do this!" Doug shouted.

The woman called for the children. All three vanished into another room.

"She probably didn't even credit the charge back to my card."

"No use getting excited about it. Look at the bright side. Camping will save us money."

"Save money. How about saving our scalps?"

"That's awful. These people can't help it if they've been stuffed onto a small parcel of prairie. Have a little compassion."

"Look, have you seen any signs of people willing to work since we landed on this reservation? Yeah, maybe the feds just sent them here to rot away, but from what I can see, they're all lazy. Nothing but waitin' for the next handout of taxpayer dollars. You and I are paying for that, ya know."

Lauren shook her head, muttered, and began cycling toward the road the woman had pointed out.

Doug followed.

Then she stopped and pulled out her phone to see if Emma had tried to contact her. "Emma texted! I don't have a signal. Do you?"

"What are the chances?" He checked his phone anyway. "Nada."

Lauren read Emma's message aloud:

> "If you get this, call or text. If the rooms fall through, I can put you up. It's small and crowded but safe. Five miles from the motel. Let me know."

Doug laughed. "Five miles in the dark will take us at least a half hour. And how will we ever know when we're there? We have to camp."

"I—I'm afraid you're right. But she told us not to go down by the river."

"You have another option? Can't see us cycling in the dark with no place to go."

"I think her words were 'Whatever you do, *don't* go down by the river . . .' I'm going to text her. Maybe the signal will come back."

> Just picked this up. Thank you. Motel fell through. Going to camp by the river.

She pressed the send button.

> Unable to send. Retry?

She selected *Yes*.

> Unable to send. Retry every 30 seconds?

Again she selected *Yes* and then put her phone away. "Urgh! It didn't go through." Lauren mounted her bicycle and pushed off. "Let's go."

# CHAPTER 34

A quarter mile from the main road, they'd lost all light but that from the slice of moon. They slowed to better navigate the rough and twisty road.

Lauren's front tire hit a pothole, a jolt ramming her arms and shoulders.

As difficult as it was to see, would other travelers see *them?* Sure, they had lights, but could someone barreling down a familiar road in the dark while impaired by drugs or alcohol avoid hitting them?

Lauren hugged the edge of the jagged pavement, peering for potholes. A vehicle rumbled behind them. She and Doug rode into the adjacent grassland until it passed them.

At least no bears roamed the prairie. The wildest of animals were likely steering vehicles or—God forbid—fellow campers who'd had too much to drink.

After they'd meandered for fifteen minutes, a sign for the river pointed left to a dirt road. The faint sound of revelry sent a chill down her spine. The noise grew as they turned onto the road.

Doug stopped.

Lauren followed suit.

He shone his headlamp on a *No Littering* sign. Glass from broken beer bottles lay beneath it. Another sign showed the image of a bottle of booze with a null sign over it. Fat chance tonight's campers were heeding it.

Lauren looked down at her cell phone for a signal. Nothing.

Doug stood and began lifting the back end of his recumbent to turn it around. "Let's go back to the main road and keep going. Surely we can find a better place to camp than this."

Of the voices she could hear coming from the river, none sounded female. "Okay. I don't think we have a choice."

No sooner had they turned their bicycles around than a pickup truck came barreling around the corner, its tires squealing. As it turned toward the dirt river road, the driver slammed on the brakes to avoid hitting the two of them. The truck skidded into brush. The engine revved as it backed up.

The driver laid on the horn and shouted out the window. "Hey, you guys. We got us some party guests." The strong smell of alcohol drifted into Lauren's nostrils.

"Let's get outta here." Doug's recumbent vaulted, and it hit the pavement with a jolt as Lauren's foot probed for her pedal.

Her head snapped back. Someone was tugging on her hair.

"Not so fast." The man pulled hard enough that she couldn't turn to see him.

She submitted, placing both feet on the ground. The heavy odor of beer made her stomach turn, as did the clammy hand clenching her arm.

"Leave me alone. Please. I've done you no harm."

Though Doug kept at a distance in the darkness, his silhouette dismounted his bicycle and began rifling through his pannier.

"Wasicu!" the assailant shouted. "A she-wasicu."

Another man in the cab of the pickup said, "No harm? Hmph. Wasicu have done great harm."

Then he exited the cab and walked in front of Lauren. "Oh, what do we have here? Pretty, pretty."

She couldn't believe her eyes. Fifteen or sixteen years old. She assumed the same about his drunken partner.

"Doug, help me."

His bicycle was lying on the side of the road now, and she could no longer see him. Then she heard a click.

The assailant wrapped his arms around her, jerked her up and off her bicycle, and squeezed her.

"No, don't!" she screamed. "I want to help you. I know the white man has taken advantage of you, but that wasn't me. I'm on your side." She began crying.

"Wasicu is sad. Oh, poor wasicu." The man lifted her and spun her 360 degrees before setting her feet back on the ground.

"Let her go."

It was Doug, somewhere in the darkness. She'd never heard him speak with such authority.

The two hooligans laughed.

"I said, let her go."

The one holding Lauren squeezed his arm around her neck harder. "Is that you, Dougy?" Then he laughed. "Make me."

*Bang!*

The gunshot rang in Lauren's ears. Where it came from, she didn't know, but she felt no pain.

The man holding her squeezed harder. He dragged her in front of the pickup truck, its lights blinding her as he yanked her hair repeatedly.

She shrieked. "Pl—please. D—don't."

The other ruffian joined them in front of the pickup. He flipped open a switchblade and held it to Lauren's neck. "Don't do anything stupid," he shouted into the night with a quivering voice.

Lauren finally glimpsed the one holding her. He was also a juvenile, his eyes bulging, his arms shaking.

"I said—Let. Her. Go."

Lauren sucked in a breath, then eyed the knife in the boy's unsteady hand, its blade shimmering in the headlight beam.

As he wrestled with his drunken tremors, his knife nicked her throat. Then it scraped her skin like a razor blade against glass.

She gasped, drew her head back away from the knife, and began hyperventilating. "No, Doug. They've got a knife. And they're young."

Sirens sounded miles in the distance.

Suddenly a car revved its motor from down the road, approached rapidly, and screeched to a halt at the entrance to the river road, its lights illuminating Doug. His gun pointed to the heavens.

The car door flew open. "Tatanka, is that you?"

Lauren's heart leaped. It was Emma.

The boy holding Lauren responded, "It's Daniel. Tatanka is down at the campsite."

"Daniel, these two people are friends of mine. Are you causing them trouble?"

The boy with the knife pulled it away from her skin.

"No, we were just havin' some fun when we heard a gunshot." Daniel released Lauren.

She ran to Doug and put her arms around him, sobbing.

Another vehicle stopped behind Emma's, a pickup truck with two men in it.

Emma waved to them.

The driver rolled down his window and stuck out his head. "Can we help?"

"Yes. Help them load their bicycles and gear into your truck. They're coming back to my place for the night."

Doug and Lauren climbed into the LaCrosse, each carrying a bag. Doug still had his pistol in hand.

"You can put that away now," Emma said. "They won't bother you."

Doug put the gun into his pannier, then wiped his clammy hand on his shorts. He looked into the front seat at Lauren. "Lemme see your neck. You've got blood on your shirt."

Meanwhile, Emma turned the car around and drove back toward town, the pickup truck with Doug and Lauren's gear close behind. They zoomed past the river road, where the youths were still talking outside their pickup. Several others had joined them.

Still visibly shaking, Lauren twisted around so Doug could look at her wound.

With his headlamp on, he cradled her neck with his hands and placed his thumbs on either side of the cut. Her skin was so soft.

His heart went *ka-thump*, but the sight of blood reminded him what he was there for. "It's just a surface wound."

He reached into his pannier and pulled out a handkerchief. Then he wiped her skin and dabbed the wound to clean it. "Press this on it for a while." He thought it more respectful to delegate the task, though he'd gladly have done it himself. "And take a few deep breaths. You're okay."

"Thank you." Lauren turned back around. After a few moments she looked at Emma. "I don't understand it. You have incredible power over the young people around here. Why?"

"I served as tribal governor for twenty years. Then I became an advocate for my people at the state and federal levels. They know I fight for their rights. I've earned their respect."

"I'll say," Doug said.

"They're so young," Lauren said.

"Daniel's father died two years ago. Addicted to heroin, started dealing, then crossed his supplier. Daniel's older brother committed suicide a few days later. Both boys have been into meth. It's epidemic here. Kids like Daniel grow up around drugs and violence. They know no other way."

*I would've plugged the loser full of lead if Emma hadn't arrived when she did. Can't believe how close a call it was for Lauren.* "Why don't they ban alcohol around here?"

"We have. It's illegal to sell or consume alcohol on the reservation."

"Then why is so much of it around?"

"They bring it in from across the border in Nebraska. A town of only a dozen residents but four businesses that sell liquor."

"Isn't there any law enforcement around here?"

"The funding is inadequate. You have to appreciate there's little economy on the reservation. Unemployment runs around 90 percent. We're so dependent on the United States government."

"Ninety percent?" Doug shook his head.

"Suicide rates here are three times the national average. If you lived here as a Native American man, your life expectancy would be forty-eight."

"Wow! I still don't understand why they can't crack down on the crime and clean things up."

"The federal money covers twenty-two police officers. With the challenges we have here, how can only twenty-two officers service fifteen thousand people living on the edge? They have more ground to cover than a few states do."

"Can't the feds shut down the Nebraska operation?"

"The feds don't want to be involved, and frankly the residents don't want them to be either. They're the face of the Lakota's problems. Local officials tried blockading the border. It failed. Not enough manpower.

"There's no simple solution to our problems. They're deep-seated. Our people are bitter. It goes back to the broken promises of the United States government in the 1800s. The people here have lost so much of their dignity and sense of purpose. Even their will to live."

"Could Daniel get arrested for assault?" Lauren said.

"No. It's not serious enough. The officers can't handle the workload they already have. They see danger like you just saw every day. And many of them do it without a partner to cover them. Always outnumbered. Putting their lives on the line every single day they put that uniform on. The rez is a dangerous place to live and work."

Doug's eye twitched. *Maybe I was a little too judgmental about them earlier.*

"Wasicu," Lauren said. "That's what they called me."

"The one who takes the fat. It refers to the white man, who invaded our territory many years ago, plundered our food sources, and forced us to live on a very small portion of the land we used to inhabit. It's a derogatory term."

"Why are you going out of your way to help us?" Doug said.

"Because you're innocent. And it's the right thing to do. Maybe these youngsters will figure that out."

"How did you know we were in trouble?" Lauren said.

"I called the motel at dusk to see if you'd arrived. She told me you hadn't and they were full. It happens frequently. That's when I texted you. When I didn't get a text back for hours, I thought your cell service might not be working. Then I got your message." She sighed. "I warned you not to go down to the river for good reason. I knew there would be trouble. I came as fast as I could."

"We're so grateful you did." Lauren said. "Thank you. I owe you my life. How can I repay you?"

"I'll think about that. Most of my people don't understand the value of connecting with other peoples. They forget that the real oppressors have been dead and gone for over a century. We still have greedy people and corrupt politicians today, but lots of good people out there understand that Native Americans have a hard life. The more people you connect with, the more likely you'll receive the help you need. That's what I believe. I'm an exception though, because I was educated at a government-run university and lived off the reservation for years. I missed my people, so I came back."

Emma turned on her blinker and pulled into a driveway. The mailbox read *Red Cloud*. "We're here."

She drove a few hundred feet to the house. The pickup followed. The outside light came on, illuminating the wagging tail of a German shepherd. He woofed a few times.

"Oh, Wolf, be quiet."

Doug turned to see the two men get out of the pickup and begin unloading his and Lauren's gear. "Who are they?"

"The fathers of the two families living with me right now. Both very good men."

"Do you have a family?" Lauren said.

Emma paused. "Well, I did. You see, that boy I asked about down at the river—Tatanka? He's my son's nephew. My son died of a drug overdose five years ago. And my husband died of natural causes last year."

Lauren touched Emma's shoulder. "I'm so sorry."

"He was much older than me. My family now consists of my people. There's no shortage of community here. It's not unusual for a dozen people to live together. When the sun comes up tomorrow, you'll see how small the houses are. As for my home, I have plenty of people living here, coming and going. I take in families who I know will work to get back on their feet. You two have air mattresses, I assume."

Doug nodded.

"Oh yes," Lauren said.

"You'll be in a room with three girls. They'll love to hear stories from your travels. It will be good education for them." Then Emma looked in the rearview mirror at Doug. "You'll be sleeping with four boys. Don't snore too loud." She grinned at him.

Doug chuckled.

"They're good boys. None of them are into drugs. But they're still young. I only ask that you leave your firearm in the shed along with your bicycles and whatever gear you won't be needing. It's padlocked."

Doug nodded again.

"It'll be a bit crowded, but we'll manage. I've put up twenty-one people in this house before."

As they entered Emma's house, about a dozen people with darker skin tones stared at Lauren. They stood in two groups, which she assumed to be by family. "Hey, everyone!"

"Hi," Doug said.

Other than a few giggles from the younger children, the rest of the people were quiet.

"I met these travelers earlier and invited them over for the night. I think you'll find what they have to share quite interesting so don't be bashful."

A few of the adults nodded their heads toward Lauren and Doug.

Then Doug extended a hand to one of the men.

The man grasped it. "Welcome."

"Thank you."

Others in that group said hello to Doug while the other family greeted Lauren. The woman she assumed to be the mother smiled and identified herself as Tashina, then introduced her husband and children.

Doug and Lauren swapped groups and greeted the others.

With the features of a model, Tashina's face glowed. She'd pulled back her long, dark hair into a braid. Snow-white teeth drew attention to her soft-spoken words of praise for each of her five children, three boys and two girls between the ages of five and thirteen.

Her husband, Elan, worked part-time at the casino and had for several years. The more she and Lauren conversed, the more the children talked and moved about. Most of them hung on to Tashina when not darting back and forth in the open living space.

The other man, Chaska, had just landed a job for a contractor off the reservation. His wife, Waniya, looked after their two tweens, a boy and a girl, while making quilts for a shop outside Rapid City.

The one-and-a-half-story house was neat despite so many occupants. How twenty-one people could fit inside was left to the imagination. Stairs led to a loft where the kids—and the travelers—would be sleeping. The boys' and girls' rooms each came with two sets of bunk beds that slept three children each.

Presumably, Doug would have floor space in one of the rooms. "He's a good man," Lauren had whispered to the mothers. "You can trust him."

Emma would sleep in her room off the kitchen area, while the couples slept in two larger rooms in the back of the loft. Wolf had his own house outside.

Lauren swathed her fingers across the cut in her neck and found more blood. "Do you mind if I clean up?"

Emma showed her the bathroom.

As Lauren nursed the wound on her neck, she caught her own eye in the mirror, rimmed red, her skin surrounding it not as taut as it once was. Today's twilight could have been her last sunset. So close. And the bear back at Sylvan Lake . . .

She'd chosen to cycle America to experience adventure, but this was too much.

Maybe she shouldn't have been so quick to judge Lars and flee his affections. Loving him was there for the taking, falling into her lap like manna from heaven. If only she'd recognized it.

And Jeffrey, he was likely recovering from another hard day in court, miles away in both distance and relationship. Oh, he'd always love her—and she, him—but she'd pushed him away. Why? He was sacrificing time and money to fight for righteous causes. He had so much going for him. And it could have been for them. What part of God-loving, successful, and handsome were not good enough for her?

And Doug. He had her back. And understood her. Maybe she should be more open to loving him on a deeper level. Was he who God had for her?

Any of these men could father her children. But they couldn't do it without her cooperation. *What is wrong with me? Maybe Maggie was right. Or is God about to take me Home?*

If Dad and Mom could see her now. But the safety of their love had faded as a distant memory.

# CHAPTER 35

"Would you tell us a bedtime story?"

The request came from one of the top bunks as Lauren nestled her tired body into her sleeping bag on the floor of the girls' room.

"Sure, as long as you tell me one too."

"Okay."

"A few years ago, in a distant land, a brave warrior named Ugula went hunting for an elephant."

"An elephant? Where did he go, the zoo?"

Giggles filled the room, including from Lauren.

"No, the elephants roamed wild in this faraway land. Ugula had killed one the prior year, and it fed his parents and siblings for six months. They also shared meat with the villagers and sold the tusks for cash. So out he went.

"It was hot. I mean *really* hot. As he wandered through the countryside, he came to a small farm. In the distance a woman was drawing water from a well. This wasn't just any young lady though. As Ugula approached her, he could see she was very beautiful. And he was so thirsty."

Each bunk bed had a face hanging out of it, two with hands propping up chins and the other hanging sideways.

"'Do you want a drink?' the fair maiden asked him.

"'Oh, yes. I would love a drink.'

"She smiled and pulled up a fresh bucket of well water, ladled some into a cup, and handed it to him. Ugula tipped the glass back and drank the whole thing.

"'I'll give you another drink if you solve a riddle.'

"He found her coy look inviting, so he said, 'Okay. What's the riddle?'

"'What is taller than you but only comes to your chest?'

"'Ah . . . I give up. What?'

"'You give up too easily,' she said. 'It's right in front of you.'

"She was the fairest young lady he'd ever set eyes on. 'I don't give up easily when I really want something. Could I come visit you again sometime?'

"'Only if you answer the riddle correctly.'

"The young man looked around and gazed in front of him. Then it dawned on him. 'The shaft of this well?'"

"What's a shaft?" the girl in the top bunk said.

"Oh, sorry, it's the inside walls of the well. Back to the story . . .

"The young lady's eyes popped open. 'That's right!' So Ugula stretched out his hand with the glass, and she poured him another cup.

"'When can I come back?' he said.

"'I'm here every day around this time. Shall I see you tomorrow?'

"For the next several weeks Ugula came to the well for a drink every single day. Then one day the beautiful princess was not there. He didn't know where she was, and it made him so sad.

"For the next week he came every day. But when he arrived, he was the only one at the well. Finally, on the eighth day, he came back for a drink. As he dipped the bucket into the well, a voice behind him said, 'Hi. I missed you.'

"'I missed you too.' But when Ugula turned around to look at the beautiful woman, instead he saw a plain, ordinary one. 'Is that you?' he asked. Her voice, though, was unmistakable. He'd heard it a thousand times before, even in his dreams.

"'Yes, it's me.'

"'Where have you been? I thought I would never see you again.'

"'I wasn't sure you would like me if you knew what I really looked like. But I couldn't keep up the charade. So I put my plain clothes on and didn't wear any makeup today.'

"The young warrior thought for a moment. 'Well, I have to admit that I couldn't stop looking at you at first. But after a while I was more interested in what you had to say and spending time with you. It may take a little getting used to, but as long as you're the same person, I would always want to see you.'"

Lauren paused. "Do any of you know the moral of the story?"

"I do," the girl in the bottom bunk said. "You shouldn't judge a book by its cover."

Lauren chuckled. "Well, that's true. But more than that, the true worth of a person, their character, comes from inside them. If you want good relationships, you'll connect with a person deep within their soul. It's not a natural thing for us. The Bible—"

A siren blared outside. After the wail faded, Lauren continued. "The Bible says that 'man looks at the outward appearance, but God sees the heart.' We want to be able to have the mind of Christ, to see others as He sees them."

A girl from the lower bunk said, "We learned about Christ at Catholic school. He died for our sins."

Lauren nodded. "That's right. He came and died so that we might have abundant life."

"Abundant life? What's that?"

"Well, it isn't tied to things like toys, clothes, or houses. It has more to do with feeling a deep joy inside no matter your circumstances. We find that joy when we make Jesus the Lord of our life. Have any of you ever done that before?"

The room was silent.

"That's okay." Lauren smiled. "He's right there waiting for you when you're ready to make that decision. He loves you with an everlasting love. You can't earn His love. He just gives it to you because it's who He is and what He does."

"My father says that white people call the Great Spirit 'Jesus Christ.' He said they're one and the same."

"Maybe so," Lauren said. "Maybe so. I've never thought of it that way, but you might have a point. You can read about Jesus in the Bible. Do you girls have Bibles?"

"Yeah. We got them from the parish."

"Well, I told my story, so what about yours?"

The girl who had requested the story, named Anpo, spoke up. "Okay. Here's mine. Many years ago there was a great warrior who went out on the Great Plains to hunt for a buffalo with five other warriors. He was the strongest man in the tribe. They rode their horses as fast as they could to the best place they knew about to hunt. When they got there, white men were busy dragging the . . . um . . . What do you call a dead buffalo?"

"A carcass?"

"Yeah, that's it. So the white men were dragging the carcasses of five buffalos to the train station. When the white men saw the great warrior coming with his friends, they raised their guns toward the clouds and fired several shots, scaring the horses and causing the great warrior to stop. He looked to one of his friends and said, 'White man taking more than he needs. Must stop.'

"The group of six hunters galloped toward the white men. One of the white men shot at them and knocked one of the warriors off his horse.

"'Whoa,' the great warrior said to his horse.

"The others stopped to help the warrior who was shot. Then the white men came over and told them to leave. 'Why don't you go hunt somewhere else. We've cleaned this area up,' one of them said.

"The great warrior was not happy. 'You take more than you need. You kill too many buffalos. Not good.'

"The white man looked at him and laughed. The warriors turned around and took the warrior who was shot back to their camp.

"These trips went on for years. Sometimes the white men would attack the warriors. The warriors began fighting back. They killed many of the greedy white men until the leaders of the white men signed an agreement. It made my people happy that we could finally live in peace, but eventually the white man broke his promise. They found gold in the Black Hills and stole the land back from us. They still haven't given it back.

"Do you know what the story means?" Anpo said.

Water seeped to the corner of Lauren's eye. "Never trust a white man?"

"Yeah. That's a story that my father always tells us."

"I'm white. Do you trust me?"

The room remained silent. The girl on the top bunk rolled over. The girl in the bunk below her looked away.

A lump formed in Lauren's throat. "I understand. But I want you to know that I do care about you. Have a good night. I'll see you in the morning."

The peacefulness Lauren had experienced when sleeping under the stars eluded her as she lay on her air mattress surrounded by children whose innocence was being sucked out of them. What would her life have been like were she unable to trust others?

Finally her tired muscles subdued her thoughts.

She awoke in darkness to the sound of glass smashing on pavement outside the home. An open window near the top of the loft let in the nasty scent of booze.

If it weren't for alcohol, Lauren's parents might still be with her. That drunk driver had also maimed her two brothers. She'd come to forgive the perpetrator and see God miraculously turn around his life to help other people. But she wanted nothing to do with booze. It had no redeeming qualities.

A mumbling male voice and shuffling feet followed the clamor outside. He sounded intoxicated. A siren blared in the distance. Lauren sat up and listened.

The noise had awakened one of the girls too. She sat up in her bed at the top of the bunk to gather herself for a moment, reached over, and quietly slid the window shut. Then she locked it and settled back into her bed without a word.

Lauren checked her phone. It was almost two o'clock. She fell back to sleep.

At two thirty the blasting of horns and the hollering of young men whooping it up awakened her. The pitter-patter of feet outside their room suggested a boy from the other bunk room was heading to the bathroom. That sounded like a good idea. She waited until the pitter-patter reversed direction, then crawled out of her sleeping bag and slipped into the hallway.

On her return trip she met Doug.

"I can't sleep," he whispered. "It's like a war zone outside."

"Yes. I'm glad we're in here and not out there."

"Good point. We need to get outta here tomorrow."

Doug walked to the bathroom while Lauren returned to the girls' room.

The next thing she knew, light was streaming through the window. Then the girls began stirring. Her evening's sleep was over. It was just before 6:00 a.m.

A cupboard door bonked in the kitchen.

Lauren walked downstairs.

Emma was making coffee. "Good morning. Did you sleep well?"

"The room was great, thanks. Those girls are adorable. I got in a few hours. Did you hear the ruckus outside?"

"Oh. That. It's so commonplace I block it out."

"I had a fun story time with the girls."

"Kids. They do love their stories."

"I know you said you had a son. Did you have any other children?"

"No. We had a late start. But I've taken in a few. Have a seat."

The two sat at the kitchen table while the coffee percolated.

"I can relate. I'm forty-two and never married. No kids. I can see, hear, and feel the clock ticking. B—but I had loads of them at an orphanage in Uganda."

"I was so busy getting an education and a career started that the idea of a family fell to the back burner. I woke up one day and realized I needed to get at it, but I was still too distracted . . . maybe even too picky for anything meaningful to develop. Wilhelm was already on the reservation when I returned. I missed my people. And he was one of them, so we married.

"What are you looking for in a man?"

Lauren lacked a ready answer, but offered, "Well . . . someone who is kind . . . knows who he is . . . has balance in his life, and . . . who . . . who loves the Lord."

"I see you're religious."

"I think a relationship with God is important. I couldn't marry a man who didn't have one. I do need to be picky there."

"Some of those requirements you listed may need your help."

Lauren furrowed her brow. "What do you mean?"

Emma eyed her, then smiled. "Let me give you an example. Wilhelm didn't have a lot of patience until he lived with me for several years."

Lauren grinned while holding back a laugh.

"And, to be perfectly honest, I was lacking a few things too. Things I really couldn't learn without a man in my life."

"Interesting. So I may end up getting what I pray for by"—she air-quoted—"earning it myself. And pay my husband back in ways I don't realize today."

Emma nodded. "You got it. Could I get you some coffee?"

"Yes, please."

Emma got up and poured Lauren a cup and one for herself. When she sat, she lowered her voice. "What about . . ."—she pointed upstairs—"Does he have qualities you're looking for?"

"He is kind, has balance, and loves the Lord. But I don't know. We just met a few weeks back on the road. Been through some profound things together. Parts of me really like him, but I just don't know. He's a bit older."

"That has its advantages."

Lauren looked through her. "We had some conflict before I went through Yellowstone. Stupid, petty things. Just kinda getting on each other's nerves. But I was so glad to reconnect with him in Wyoming."

"The small things can be important. But they also could come from someone who has never married and who, you know, may be getting more resistant to change." Emma raised her eyebrows.

"Stuck in my ways, you mean."

"At your age, are you afraid of commitment, a bad decision, or maybe just losing your freedom? I know they were real points of contention for me. I had to work through some things. Marriage is vastly different from being single. I had to learn to make sacrifices and be willing to surrender certain privileges. The way I see it, for marriage to work, you have to be all-in and leave the single life behind."

"That gives me a lot to think about. Thank you."

"Any other romantic interests?"

Lauren tilted her head. "Yes. I was actually engaged until recently. To a lawyer back in Virginia where I'm from. And then I met a guy in Montana who—I'm a bit embarrassed to admit this, but he about swept me off my feet. He's so handsome. And, well, probably more accessible than Jeffrey—the lawyer."

"You do have a lot to think about."

The door upstairs twanged on its hinges, and Doug emerged. Blood rushed to Lauren's face.

# CHAPTER 36

Sunshine illuminated the surrounding wheat fields as Lauren dipped and crested the rolling hills. The modest grades provided little resistance. Instead the curvy aesthetics urged her forward. A trailing wind provided smooth sailing and promised many miles through the undisturbed countryside.

Doug was up ahead, apparently eager to leave the reservation after passing through a handful of settlements that didn't measure up to the natural beauty and bounty surrounding them.

Daylight unveiled what the travelers had not seen on their dark ride into Crow's Foot. Graffiti was scrawled on many structures, even where people still lived.

Doug looked around and slowed. "Did you see the paint jobs back there? Or lack thereof."

"They reminded me of Uganda. But worse."

"How so?"

Lauren took in more breath and pushed harder to catch up to Doug. "In Africa the people's hope rose above their living conditions. The people here seem hopeless."

"Not all of them."

"Oh, I know. Could you believe those kids at Emma's? So sweet. Even though they're being robbed of their innocence."

Doug shook his head. "I can't imagine living here."

"Doesn't it make you want to help?"

"I wouldn't know where to begin."

Lauren had a few ideas. Reaching people in need of hope started with loving them. And being willing to get involved. "I think God gives us a well of love. We just need to be willing to let others draw hope from it."

A dingy pickup sped by, dust trailing in its wake. The young driver allowed the pair ample berth, but their presence hadn't slowed his pace. Most of the vehicles they'd seen young people driving came with at least three passengers, lively conversation, and tomfoolery in the wind. But this solitary soul drove with purpose.

As the truck crested the next hill, one brake light shone before he took a hard right-hand turn, kicking up more dust on an unpaved road. The beater halted on the top of a hill overlooking a great expanse. The door slammed as Lauren and Doug pedaled closer.

Would the two of them be a target of bad intentions? But with only one young soul aboard, that seemed unlikely.

Ahead of her Doug slowed to a stop. He reached into his pannier and pulled out his belt bag.

Lauren stopped behind him. "What are you doing?"

"Did you see how that kid flew past us? Like we weren't even here."

"He seemed uninterested in us."

"I don't trust him." Doug unzipped the belt bag and reached for his pistol.

"Why don't you put your gun away? He got out of his pickup."

"Yeah, that's what bothers me."

"We'll be okay."

Doug made eye contact with Lauren, then looked back toward the empty pickup, about a quarter mile ahead of them. He pulled out the gun and laid it on top of the pannier's contents, covering the bag but not snapping it shut. "Okay. Let's go. We're gettin' outta here before dark today. Fifty miles to sanity."

As the two climbed the next hill, they spotted the young man, who was looking in the opposite direction, toward the vast plain. When they reached the top—

"No—don't!" Lauren shouted as the boy inserted the barrel of a handgun into his mouth.

Startled, the boy turned around.

Lauren picked up her pace and turned off the pavement onto the dirt-covered overlook. "Stop!" She hammered the pedals as Doug trailed her.

The boy pulled the gun from his mouth and then backed up as the two approached. His tattered clothes provided only partial coverage for his bronze skin.

"Don't come any closer or—or I'll have to shoot *you*." The youth, no more than a middle teenager, waved the gun toward them.

Doug's brakes squeaked.

Lauren glanced in her rearview mirror.

Stopped with his feet on the ground, Doug was reaching into his pannier.

"Don't you dare," she whispered. "The boy's scared enough. See how skittish he is?"

She coasted toward the boy until he waved the gun at her.

"Don't come no closer!"

"We won't hurt you." Now only twenty feet from him, Lauren stopped and set her bicycle on the ground.

Acne and pockmarks covered his face. A skull-and-dagger tattoo on his right shoulder and burn scars on his arms belied the fright dripping from his brown saucer eyes.

She stepped toward him. "We want to help you."

"Lady . . . if you know what's good for you, you won't come no closer." The boy's hand shook as much as his voice did.

Lauren stopped but maintained eye contact with the youth. "Easy." She took another step.

The youth grabbed the butt end of the pistol with both hands, cocked the hammer, and extended his arms, lowering the gun toward Lauren. It shook in his hands.

Her heart hammered.

Noise from behind startled her. She turned to see Doug flipping open his pannier.

He grabbed his pistol but couldn't point it at the youth without putting Lauren in harm's way.

"No. Put it away."

Reluctantly Doug placed the gun back into his pannier, but his hand stayed there too.

Lauren faced the youth. "Why don't you put your gun down so we can talk."

He backed up and drew the revolver to his temple. "You . . . you . . . get away! I don't wanna live no more."

"You can't see it right now because you're so depressed, but God has a bright future for you. Don't cut it short. He loves you and has a plan for your life."

"Some plan *He* has. They found Papa's head busted open with a sledgehammer, and you're sayin' God has a plan?"

"She's right!" Doug shouted. "There's a better way."

The boy began sobbing. He dropped the firearm to his side.

Lauren advanced two more steps until the boy gathered himself, raised the gun overhead, and fired it into the air.

She stopped a few feet away from him and extended her arms toward him. "I'm so sorry for what happened to your papa. And God's as unhappy about what happened to him as we are. He's on your side. Don't listen to the voice that only wants to destroy you."

The boy's bulbous eyes searched Lauren's white face for hope.

"Drop the gun, son," Doug said. "Let us help you."

The youth's head dropped as his chest buckled in a spasm of emotion. The gun fell onto the patch of dirt beneath him.

Lauren stepped forward with her arms reaching for him.

He fell into them, heaving sorrow onto her shoulders. He grasped the back of her cycling jersey and held on for dear life as his grief sprang from the depth of his broken spirit.

Doug stowed his gun, stepped toward them, and put his hands on the boy's shoulders. Then he put his arm around his neck and embraced the two of them.

The group hug persisted for a few minutes while the youth purged emotion. Finally he paused to catch his breath.

Lauren's heart rate slowed. "Let's go sit in your truck and talk."

The boy nodded.

She led him to the cab while Doug picked up the boy's gun and dropped it into his pannier.

Lauren slid into the passenger's side first. Doug followed her. The boy plunked onto the driver's seat.

"Where's your mama?" Lauren said.

"I don't have one no more."

It'd been years since Doug offered wisdom to a youth struggling to find his way. This boy's circumstances would trump any situation he'd ever discussed with Douglas Jr. Nevertheless, disarming the boy brought relief, and with it, hope.

The boy hung his head, palming the hair on top, his troubled soul juxtaposed against the glorious setting, with golden wheat gleaming in the sunshine.

Doug leaned forward and looked at him. Burn marks covered the boy's arm. "What's your name, son?"

"Koda."

Lauren laid her hand on Koda's forearm. "What brings you here, Koda?"

The boy looked out the cracked windshield of the old Ford pickup. He opened his mouth, but no words came out.

"That's okay." Lauren squeezed his forearm. "Take your time. We have all day. And we care about you."

Doug cleared his throat. "Son, do you have any family left?"

The boy nodded and then shook his head.

They waited.

After several minutes the boy tried again. "I . . . I live with my aunt now."

"Is that your papa's sister?" Doug said.

"Yeah."

"How long has your daddy been gone?" Doug said.

"Two weeks."

Lauren groaned. "Can you tell us what happened?"

Koda drew in a deep breath and stared at the floorboard. "The drug lord came to settle up, and Papa had no money. He spent it on food for us."

A surge of emotion struck, and the boy doubled over, his head resting against the steering wheel.

Lauren rubbed his back.

He gathered himself and sat up. "They rolled in on Harleys. The man wasn't happy. One of his men grabbed Papa and took him outside. Papa cried out in pain, but the other bikers wouldn't let us help him."

"I'm so sorry," Lauren said. "How long has your mama been gone?"

"Last year they came to collect again. When Papa couldn't pay, they told him they'd take it another way. That's the last time I saw Maw alive. They had their way with her, but she fought them."

The youth's words hovered.

Finally Lauren broke the silence. "You've been through so much."

Doug reached his arm around her and gripped the boy's shoulder. "Son, I'm sorry."

"Do you have siblings?" Lauren said.

"Yeah. I have an older brother and a younger sister. The older brother left the rez a year ago. He's studying at the University of Sioux Falls to become a social worker. My sister lives with a gang. She's in a baaaad place. It's not safe."

"Where'd you get the gun, son?" Doug said.

"It was Papa's. He hid it from the drug lord because he thought we would need it someday." Koda looked up at Lauren. "That day was today until you came along."

"God knew you needed help."

Doug squeezed Koda's shoulder. "How old are you?"

"Sixteen."

"How can we best help you?" Lauren said.

"Well, you can't bring my parents back to life." The boy sobbed. "Or keep my sister safe."

"I'm glad you have your aunt, Koda," Doug said.

"Yeah, I suppose. She wants me to get back into school and go to college, but what's the use? I can't imagine leaving the rez like my brother did. But I also fear for my life every single day."

"Do you know Emma Red Cloud?" Lauren said.

"Yeah. We stayed with her just after my father was killed."

"She's pretty wise. Did she give you any advice?"

"Yeah. She wants me to stay in school and go off to college. She said I have what it takes to better myself and then give back to my people."

Lauren smiled. "I think she's right. But that won't happen if you end your life."

Doug squeezed Koda's shoulder again. "You can make your parents proud if you do what Emma says."

"Koda," Lauren said, "there's a Father in heaven who wants to parent you in their absence. He can make a way when there seems to be no way. He's the Master of the universe and He loves you for who He made you to be. Has anyone ever told you that before?"

"Yeah. Pretty much. We have a Catholic school on the rez. They teach us the white man's religion. We believe in spirits too, but I only heard about Jesus Christ since attending that school."

"Well, Jesus loves you so much that He came to earth to die on the cross for your sins. He wants you to have peace in your soul and be able to share joy with your people. Did they explain to you how to make peace with God?"

"I—I don't know."

"Would you like to know?"

"Sure."

"Doug, would you like to tell Koda how to find peace?"

Doug's leg began jiggling up and down. "Okay." *She would do a better job at this, but maybe she thinks he'll respond more favorably hearing it from a man.* How could he say no?

"Koda, God loves you. He—Well, He wants you to experience His love . . . personally. And He wants—He wants to help you. You see, we all have this problem called sin. We screw up. No one has to explain how, we just do it. Rebel, I mean. Against God. We choose to do wrong rather than right. Do you follow me?"

"Yeah."

"Our sin separates us from God and His love for us. Because He's perfectly holy, and we're far from it. That's why Jesus came to earth. He never did anything wrong, yet we crucified Him on a cross."

Lauren nodded.

Doug's leg relaxed. "The blood that He shed when He died on the cross became the sacrifice for our sins—all of them—past, present, and future. Jesus defeated the devil and rose from the dead. He pleads our case for us because we can't save ourselves.

"But not everyone gets into heaven. Only those of us who repent of what we've done wrong and ask Jesus to save us. It's the decision to submit to God's authority that gives us peace with Him. God then sends His Holy Spirit to live inside of us, to comfort us, and to guide us. The Holy Spirit will give you the power to face life with confidence. His supernatural power has turned around many lives that were headed in the wrong direction.

"Trust me"—Doug's voice shook—"it works. You see, I, too, didn't want to go on living. I was looking to escape, just like you. But I'm so glad I didn't. God got ahold of me and changed my life. He can change yours too."

Lauren's head turned, her lips curled into a smile, her hazel eyes glimmering.

Doug looked back at Koda. "God loves you and wants to be the Lord of your life. What's it going to be for you, Koda? More tragedy and heartache? Or a fresh start?"

"I dunno. I mean, it sounds good and everything, but I just dunno."

Doug's finger tapped his leg.

"A missionary came through last summer. Several of my friends made that decision . . . the one you're asking me to make. Two of them were shot dead in the past year. The other is wilder than—"

Tires screeched on the pavement. A pickup speeding by had slammed on its brakes. It backed up and entered the turnout.

# CHAPTER 37

Two young men exited the cab of the pickup. One of them brandished a rifle, the other a knife.

Doug gulped.

Koda fidgeted as if needing to act quickly but not knowing what to do.

Lauren jerked her head around.

Doug's heart pounded. "Who are they?"

The man with the rifle pointed it at the cab as the duo walked toward the truck. "Koda, get outta there!" the man shouted.

Koda started the pickup. "Get down!"

Lauren and Doug ducked, as did Koda.

Koda pulled a u-ie, spewing dust about. Gunfire sounded from outside the cab. A bullet pinged. The pickup sped past the men as another shot struck metal. The truck bounced onto the pavement and sped east. Another round shattered the rear window and smacked the windshield, leaving a nick and small crack there. Shards of glass sprinkled the passengers.

Doug pressed his hand down on the top of Lauren's helmet.

She leaned into him and grabbed his knee.

The Ford picked up speed as a squeal sounded behind them.

"Where are we going?" Doug said. "And who are they?"

"The gang must've sent 'em after me." Koda peered through the steering wheel and out the windshield.

Another shot rang out, then another.

Soon they were no longer rolling smoothly at high speed, but instead with the resistance of deflating tires. The truck swerved, approaching a ditch on one side of the road before Koda over-corrected and headed toward the other ditch, then steered back toward the middle of the road, slowing the vehicle to regain control of it. The bumpy ride on flat tires jostled the passengers before he stopped in the middle of the road.

Behind them the other pickup jammed on its brakes and screeched to a stop. The creaking of hinges and thudding of slammed doors kicked up Doug's pulse.

Koda reached under his seat, and as he pulled out a crowbar, his window shattered, glass peppering the three of them.

The gunman shoved the barrel of his rifle into Koda's neck. "Goin' somewhere?"

"Please . . . leave me alone. I didn't do you no harm."

"No one walks away from Blood Warriors."

The man's arm had the same branding as Koda's. The gunman's top lip curled alongside paint smeared down both cheeks of his unshaven face. His stringy mop of black hair dusted the top of his leather vest with every jerk of his head. "Get out."

Koda sat motionless.

"Get out!" the man screamed.

Koda's grip loosened, and the crowbar pinged on the floor of the pickup. He twisted his body to exit the vehicle.

The man slammed the door behind Koda. "Unless you two want to go up in a ball of flames, you can get out now too."

Doug opened the door and stumbled out. Then he grabbed Lauren's forearm and pulled her out. They ran a few feet into the adjacent field, hit the ground, and turned to see what was happening.

The other gang member tied Koda's hands behind his back.

As the young man with the rifle escorted Koda to the pickup behind them, the other ruffian stuffed rags into the opened gas tank of Koda's pickup. He looked up at Doug and Lauren. "Just in case you get some stupid ideas . . ." He lit the end of the rag, ran to the waiting pickup, and jumped in.

The pickup sped off, heading back to town, leaving Doug and Lauren alone.

The flame on the rag accelerated in seconds as it rushed toward the tank hatch.

Doug grabbed Lauren's arm again. "Come on." He pulled her farther from the road and the two ran.

Seconds later an explosion rocked the peaceful prairie. The torrent of air from the blast felled both of them. Pieces of glass and other objects splashed round about them. Doug shielded Lauren's body.

He turned to see Koda's pickup in the middle of the road, fifty yards away, engulfed in flames. Black smoke billowed toward the heavens.

Lauren shook her head. "We have to find Koda." She reached into her back pocket and pulled out her phone.

"And how do you propose we do that?"

"Urgh. No signal. Let's go get our bicycles." She scrambled to her feet.

About a mile west of the burnt-out vehicle, Lauren led them to the turnout where they'd left their bicycles. Not a vehicle had passed them.

Panting, Doug stopped jogging, his head hung low. "Gotta catch my breath."

"Come on." Lauren didn't stop. "There's no time."

Doug flipped open his pannier and pulled out his phone. "No signal. What about yours?"

"None. But I'm going to text Emma anyway. Perhaps it'll send when I get coverage."

> Ran into trouble on 289th. Returning to Crow's Foot. A 16-yo named Koda's in trouble. Gang members have him.

"Are you sure ya wanna backtrack?" Doug studied his map. "Why don't we go forward and find the closest law enforcement?"

"How far away is it?"

Doug looked to the east at the black smoke billowing skyward. "Who knows? We may find as little of it east as we did west. Maybe Emma *is* our best shot. But I'd feel a lot safer leaving the chaos behind."

As the couple retraced their wheel tracks, gray clouds gathered southwest of them. The more they pedaled, the closer and darker the clouds. Soon the ominous sky roiled ahead as if dropping jet-black sheets to the horizon, extinguishing more and more of the light of day. A bolt of lightning flashed to the ground. Then another.

Doug pointed. "Just what we need."

After another mile or so, he scanned the obsidian sky. "I don't like this. Did your text go through?"

They stopped while Lauren checked her phone. "Yes, but no signal now. And here's one in return:

> "Koda just lost his father. Do you know where he is?"

Lauren responded:

> He was taken hostage by two youths in the gang he's trying to leave. They traveled west by pickup about a half hour ago. We're heading toward you and the electrical storm. Still on 289th.

Thunder rumbled in the distance.

Twenty minutes later a car approached.

Lauren pointed. "It's Emma!"

The pair pulled off the road.

Emma waved and rolled down her window. "Got your text and called the police, but the on-duty officers were all dispatched on other matters. Hide your bikes and hop in."

Lauren noticed the billboard they'd passed a quarter mile back. "If we park them by the billboard, they'll be easier to find."

Thunder rumbled. Doug looked at the sky. "Let's hide them here. I'll put a strip of duct tape on the road. Come on."

Doug and Lauren wheeled their bicycles through the grass, farther from the road. They laid them in a depression.

Lauren pulled her violin case from her bicycle and strapped it around her shoulder. They rummaged through their bags for items they might need. Before returning to the road, Lauren pulled off her handlebar bag, and Doug grabbed a pannier.

Then Doug placed a strip of duct tape on the edge of the pavement. They looked over toward their bicycles but couldn't see them.

Meanwhile, Emma had turned the car around. "Hop in."

The southwestern sky flashed before a crack of thunder.

They jumped into the car, and Emma tromped on the gas pedal.

"Where do we start?" Lauren said.

"Down at the river. It's where they hang out."

"We just happened to come upon Koda as he was about to kill himself," Lauren said. "He had a gun in his mouth."

"Oh dear. He's a very special boy. And he's been through so much. We can't afford to lose him." She pressed harder on the accelerator.

The darkness overhead grew.

Fifteen minutes later a sign appeared on the horizon. *Entering Crow's Foot.*

A bolt of lightning snapped, a clap of thunder close behind. Hail began falling from the heavens, pinging onto Emma's car until stopping moments later.

She drove past the motel that had turned away Lauren and Doug the night before and headed to the river access road. Memories of that switchblade against her neck flashed into Lauren's mind. Emma turned onto the dirt road.

Tall grass swept the undercarriage as she navigated the rocky, narrow road through thicket, the car bobbing and weaving. Its springs creaked until it reached an opening where Emma stopped and opened her window, tilting her head toward the open air.

Lauren listened. Nothing but the flow of the river. The smell of a campfire wafted through the air.

Several tepees dotted the river's shoreline. To the right, smoke rose behind a tepee with a pickup parked alongside.

Emma turned off the car. She opened the door and stepped out. The others followed.

Lauren clutched her violin case, still slung over her shoulder.

Around his neck Doug draped a strap attached to his pannier.

Emma clenched his arm. "You got a gun in there?"

"Yup."

"Throw it back in the car. I'm sorry, but we're trying to curb violence here, not increase it."

Doug eased his gun from the bag and ducked into the car for a moment. When he returned, the bag still hung from his neck. "Okay. Let's go."

Emma looked at him, her eyes narrowing.

The three walked to the right, toward the smoke, the ominous sky threatening more mischief.

When they were almost there, a voice spoke from inside the tepee. "Who's there?"

"It's Emma. We're looking for Koda."

"He ain't here."

Emma shook her head ever so slightly. "Who am I talking to? Come out, young man, and identify yourself. Only a coward speaks behind a mask."

The tepee's heavy buffalo skin flopped open. Out walked a young man.

Lauren's heart skipped a beat. His dark-brown eyes looked familiar, though when she last saw them, the whites bled streaks of red. She backed up.

"Daniel, where is Koda?" A cord on the right side of Emma's neck jutted out.

Lauren got a better look at her assailant from the prior evening. Gone were his shakes, the fire in his belly, and even the smell of alcohol on his breath. The odor that replaced it suggested he'd gone days without bathing. He wore tattered rags that she'd never have allowed on the kids in the orphanage. Greasy hair dangled over his face, a porous curtain for his bulbous eyes, which unveiled the mystery of a lost soul. His missing teeth reminded her of a meth addict she'd met in Virginia.

Daniel looked down as Emma's eyes pierced him. "I dunno."

Emma smacked her hands together. "You look at me." She stomped her foot.

Lauren took another step backward while Doug stood in place, his jaw taut.

Something clicked inside the tepee. Daniel looked away.

"Who's in there?" Emma snapped. "Come out, you hear me!"

Doug reached to open his pannier.

Daniel glared at him. "I wouldn't if I were you. No strangers are allowed in this camp without clearance. We have what it takes to get rid of unwanted guests, especially if they misbehave."

Lauren caught Doug's eye and nodded toward the side of the tepee. A protrusion from inside the canvas pointed Doug's way. He froze, though it could have been a finger rather than the barrel of a gun.

"Who's in there?" Emma repeated several decibels higher.

Daniel finally responded, "We ain't lettin' 'im go."

"Just like your daddy. It didn't do *him* any good. If he could only see you now."

Daniel's cheek twitched. Then his head drooped.

Thunder rumbled in the distance.

Emma stepped forward. "There's a better way. Enough of this violence. It only leads to heartache . . . destruction . . . death." The amplitude of her voice increased with each word. "Why are you holding your own brother hostage? He's one of us, and he's done nothing to you."

"He broke the pact. Blood for blood. No one runs from Blood Warriors."

He had a point. Only blood would cover blood. But whose blood was up for grabs? These boys had wandered far from the right path. They were still young enough to be shown the way to it. Lauren had been down this path before, in Uganda. "Emma's right. You should be your brother's keeper rather than his enemy. Why don't you let him go?"

"We can't just let him go. Where would the justice be in that? But"—he peered at Lauren—"we can trade him."

Lauren took a deep breath. *This must be why my love interests have never worked out, why I survived the bear attack.* She stepped forward.

Doug huffed. "Lauren, what are you doing?"

Lauren's gaze remained bolted to Daniel's eyes. "It's okay."

"No, it isn't," Doug said. "It's not okay at all."

Her gaze still riveted to Daniel's, Lauren said, "Koda has his whole life in front of him. I've lived a rewarding life."

Another familiar youth emerged from the tepee—the one who'd set Koda's truck on fire. He had a rifle trained on Koda, whose hands were tied and mouth gagged as he stood in front of him.

"Tatanka, you put that gun down," Emma said.

"Make me." He waved the rifle at Lauren as if to pull her toward him, his skull-and-dagger tattoo prominent on his bicep.

She took another step forward.

"No." Doug slid his hand into the pannier.

"I wouldn't if I were you." Tatanka pointed the gun at Doug, who backed up and raised his hands in the air.

Lauren swallowed hard. "Me for him. Just don't hurt him."

"Okay, Miss Goodie Wasicu, if you insist." He untied the red paisley bandanna and ripped it away from Koda's mouth. Then Daniel flipped open his switchblade and cut the cords binding Koda's hands behind his back.

Koda's face was drawn. The boy had been through so much.

"It's time for you two to leave," Tatanka said. "Mato!"

Out came a boy who looked younger than the others. He pointed a pistol at Emma and Doug.

"You'll pay for this," Emma said.

She and Doug returned to the LaCrosse.

Meanwhile, Lauren's stomach churned.

Tatanka slung Koda up against the pickup. "What am I gonna do with you, boy? Do we need to go over what it means to be a Blood Warrior again? Huh?"

Koda was shaking. "I tell you, I didn't do it."

"Then who did?"

"I don't know. But I didn't."

"I believe him," Daniel said. "We got the wrong guy. Besides"—he looked at Lauren—"she's worth more."

Tatanka jammed his forearm up against Koda's chin, then got in his face. "If I ever hear anything about you stealing our drugs, I'll kill you. You understand?"

Koda half-nodded as he gasped for air.

Tatanka released his grip, grinned, and then put his arm around Koda. "Welcome back, bro."

Daniel advanced toward Lauren with rope in his hand.

"There's no need to tie me."

Tatanka snatched the rope. "Gimme that. We ain't takin' no chances. He slapped the bandanna around her face and cinched it tight across her mouth and cheeks, then knotted it at the nape of her neck. Then he tied her hands behind her back.

# CHAPTER 38

As Emma backed her car out, it jostled. "What was the big idea taking a gun in there?"

Doug gulped. He placed the extra gun back into his pannier and glimpsed his phone. "No signal."

"Check mine." She handed him her phone.

"Nope."

"They'll pay for this . . . And don't you ever try something like that again."

The car rocked its way to the main road.

*I can't leave Lauren like this.* Blood rushed to Doug's head. Then he knew. He did love her.

"Let me out. Please. Right now!"

Lauren had much more life ahead of her than he did, with so many people to help. And a family to raise. If it couldn't be with him, then maybe Jeffrey.

Emma jammed on the brakes. "Just what are you thinking?"

"I need to go back."

Before she could object, Doug flung open the door and bolted, pannier in hand.

Her door opened. "No, don't! You can't—"

But it was too late.

He stalked toward the encampment, then ducked behind some bushes when Tatanka approached Lauren. Doug peered through an opening between two branches.

She was sitting on the wet ground, blindfolded, her hands propping her from behind. Her violin case lay open beside her. With two other youth standing around a fire, Doug was outnumbered, but at least he was armed.

Tires screeched on the road outside.

Lauren's captors glanced at the roadway to Doug's right. His breath caught in his throat as he leaned his body behind thicker brush.

A moment later Doug chanced another glimpse.

Daniel was untying her hands.

Tatanka stood over Lauren. "Play something . . . now!" he shouted, then reached into the case, snatched the violin's neck, and thrust her precious instrument in her face, nudging her cheek with it. "Here!"

She fumbled the violin until she found its neck, then pawed the ground for the bow.

Tatanka yanked the bow from the case and ripped the blindfold off Lauren's face.

Doug frowned. That long, beautiful hair of hers had been chopped off.

Her squinting eyes drilled her captor's, her pale cheeks hollowed into the apparition of a servile peasant girl awaiting her master's next command.

"I said play it. Are you deaf?"

She stretched for the bow and took it from him, then slid a leg behind herself to stand up.

Tatanka shoved her back. "I didn't say get up. Just play it."

Lauren glared straight through him, then glided the bow across the strings with one long note, seemingly to tune the instrument or orient herself. It came out shaky and more melancholy than anything Doug had ever heard her play.

"Is that it? You can do better." He shoved her again.

Doug needed to do something. The next move that loser might make could hurt Lauren.

She straightened herself and began "The Blue Danube," competing only with an occasional crackle of the fire and the faint sound of motorcycles in the distance. Doug couldn't believe how lifeless the song sounded, nothing like the spellbinding performance around the campfire in Idaho when Freddie was with them.

Doug's stomach dropped. He pulled two wet branches apart to get a better look at her face as she played.

Then she saw him. And struck a sour note.

Tatanka swung around, his eyes aflame, as Lauren tried to rectify her mistake and continue the song.

Doug stood in full view.

Tatanka grabbed the violin from her and smacked it onto the grass. Out came a death twang. He looked toward Doug and yelled, "What are you doing here? Get!"

"Let her go."

Tatanka laughed. "You don't seem to understand. She's ours now"—he pulled a large knife from the sheath on his belt—"unless you want a haircut too."

Another youngster exited the tepee with strands of rope in his hands. Daniel grabbed one and retied Lauren's hands behind her back, then flung her on her side, what hair she had left swooshing over her face.

Doug walked closer. "Me for her."

Tatanka raised the dagger. "Not a chance." His voice cracked.

Doug reached for the top of his pannier with his off hand.

"I wouldn't if I were you."

The voice came from another youth who was brandishing a rifle. He pointed it at Doug. The pannier dropped to the ground as Doug raised his arms. "Me for her."

"Tie him up too," Tatanka said. "For now, at least. He's just excess baggage."

"You can't possibly think you can get away with this," Lauren said. "Emma will have the police here in no time."

Tatanka smiled. "What police? Or are you talking about my brother, the chief deputy? We have a mutual understanding. He has his turf. I have mine. We stay out of one another's business."

The roar of motorcycles increased. Tatanka waved off Daniel. "They're almost here. Don't bother tying him up."

Doug swallowed hard.

The bike motors waned, then burbled as four of them rocked into the encampment. The riders wore vests with multiple patches on front, assorted colors—mostly red and black—but similar. The hefty man on the left, with the longest beard and largest biceps, had a patch that read *Bruiser*. The ringleader, the cleanest shaven of the bunch, pulled forward, a *1%er* decal prominent on his fork. They killed their engines.

"You owe us money," the leader said. "And get that thing out of our faces if you know what's good for you."

The youth dropped the rifle to his side.

"We have something better, Big Dog." Tatanka jerked his head toward Lauren.

"I said *money*."

Daniel ducked into the tepee and came out with a satchel. He tossed it to the bandanna-clad Big Dog, who looked inside and pulled out a wad of money, then riffled through it. "Is this all you have?"

Tatanka flicked his head toward Lauren.

Big Dog ogled her.

"When do we get our next shipment?"

Big Dog smirked, then looked at the two bikers beside him.

The biker in back said, "Where's the money? You shortchanging us again?"

"Calm down, Tank. Let's hear them out." He raised his eyebrows at Lauren.

She shut her eyes. Her mouth moved but no words came out.

Big Dog pointed to the violin on the ground. "How much is that thing worth?"

Lauren remained silent but continued to mouth words.

Tatanka kicked her shin.

She squeezed her eyes tighter and winced.

"I said how much is it worth?"

"It's priceless."

The biker to Big Dog's left gestured at Lauren. "I think she's describing herself, boss."

Big Dog leered at her. "We'll take her."

"Do you want him?" Tatanka pointed at Doug.

Big Dog scoffed. "Who would want him? You take care of him."

Daniel tied Doug's hands behind his back.

"Boss, should we take the violin?" the unidentified biker said.

"Nah, I don't want that piece of junk."

Tatanka grabbed Lauren's forearm and yanked her from the ground.

"Hey! Easy on the goods," Big Dog said. "Bruiser, why don't you take her on that ol' Road King of yours."

"Naw, I'll take her," Tank said, then he kick-started his bike and revved the engine.

"You just hold your horses. Bruiser's bike beats yours for two-ups. But trust me, we'll all get a turn with her."

The musty smell of unbathed bodies lingered in the dark, dank tepee. Alone inside, Doug fidgeted, trying to work his hands free. His legs had been duct-taped to a stool, and he'd toppled onto his side in a futile attempt to free them. The voices outside stilled him.

"What should we do with him?" Daniel said.

"Let's just kill him," Tatanka said.

Doug's brow dampened.

"That'd complicate things," Daniel said. "Emma Red Cloud already knows we had the she-wasicu."

"Yeah," Tatanka said. "And we're not touchin' Emma Red Cloud."

"What about the stuff in his bag?" Daniel said. "And that stupid violin."

"I got my gun back," Koda said. "And here's his."

"Thatta boy," Tatanka said. "We'll add it to the stockpile. But let's get that bag outta here."

"Let's trash the phones," Daniel said. "The she-wasicu had one too. And that useless violin."

"Why don't we have some fun with him?" It sounded like Mato.

"I like how you think," Tatanka said. "Why don't you and . . . Koda. Yeah, Koda. Let's let our boy prove himself worthy to be called a Blood Warrior. Yeah . . ."

The voices faded.

*They must've walked away.*

The whining of a bow sawing randomly across violin strings tossed Doug's stomach. Group laughter followed it.

"This should be far enough," Mato said as he jammed on the brakes.

The tires screeched, and Doug fell forward in the back seat, banging his forehead against the headrest behind Koda. He took another breath through the tight gag in his mouth.

"I'll do the honors," Koda said. "Keep the motor running. It'll only take a second."

Blindfolded as well, Doug heard Koda's door open. Then Doug's door opened, and he felt a tug on his arm until his hip dropped out of the vehicle and hit something hard. His head knocked against Koda before he found himself on his side.

The engine revved. "Come on, what's takin' ya?"

Something thudded onto the ground. Koda slammed one of the doors shut. He yanked on the rope cinching Doug's hands a few times before scrambling back into the vehicle. "Let's get outta here."

A squeal sounded as exhaust fumes spilled onto Doug. His eyes watered, then he coughed. *Punks. How could Koda do this?* But at least they'd spared his life.

He moved his hands, and they came free. Koda must have cut the rope.

Reaching behind his head, he untied both the gag and the blindfold. A beautiful prairie surrounded him, but he had no idea where he was. It could have been anywhere from fifteen to thirty minutes in that vehicle. His pannier sat beside him. After taking a deep breath of fresh air, he removed the duct tape from around his ankles.

The pannier felt lighter. Sure enough, the guns were gone. But the pocket was unzipped. He fished his hand inside and pulled out one phone, then another, both unblemished. He powered up his phone. *Koda, you're a good man after all.*

"State Police."

"I'm on the Golden Prairie Indian Reservation and a friend of mine has been taken hostage."

"Are you Doug?"

"Yeah, how did you know?"

"It was already called in to us. Are you okay?"

"Yeah. I am. Emma Red Cloud must've called you."

"We've had a couple of calls, sir. One of them anonymous. Before we get cut off, could I confirm your number and identity?"

Doug gave the dispatcher his information.

"My friend is in a lot of danger right now."

"We're working on it, sir. Can you tell us what you know?"

"I was with her. Lauren Baumgartner is her name. She's from Virginia. A gang of young hoodlums down by the river on the rez handed her over to a motorcycle gang. Payment for drugs. The leader's name is Big Dog. And there's a Bruiser too. That's his name, I mean."

"You mean the bikers?"

"Yeah. And a guy they called Tank. They put Lauren on Bruiser's bike."

"Could you describe them to me?"

Doug scratched his head. "You know. Motorcycle thugs. Beards, tattoos, cuts, patches. I don't know. I was just trying to survive. Bruiser had a nose out of joint. Long, long beard. And"—Doug clutched his bicep—"big guns. I mean, huge."

"How did you escape?"

"They dropped me in the middle of nowhere, blindfolded, then sped off. The kids, I mean. I can't believe those punks get away with stuff like this. They should be locked up and the key thrown away . . . Except for the one named Koda. He's trapped . . . Haven't you guys investigated the gangs on the rez before?"

"We're in constant contact with them. It's an endless battle. And when one gets convicted—or murdered—two more take his place."

Doug's stomach turned. His own son could have ended up like one of them.

"We could have you look at photos of bikers, but with Sturgis, who knows where they're from. Did you notice any club patches?"

"All sorts. I couldn't begin to tell you what they were, though. There was a *1%er* decal on the bikes."

"Yeah, they all use those."

After a moment of silence the dispatcher said, "Where are you now, sir?"

"I have no clue." He looked around at the vast prairie. No road signs or any man-made structures. "Can you trace my phone's GPS and pick me up?"

"Is your phone location setting enabled?"

"Yes."

"We'll send someone out."

He glanced at his open pannier. "Oh—and they took my guns."

The prairie breeze brushed his face, an adjacent wheat field dancing in its wake. Doug pulled Lauren's phone from his pocket.

Jeffrey had called it. Three times.

He pushed the call icon.

"I thought I'd never hear back from you. Are you okay?"

"Hi, Jeffrey. It's Doug."

"Where's Lauren?"

"That's a good question."

"What do you mean?"

Doug sighed.

"What's going on?" A frazzled tone had crept into Jeffrey's voice.

Doug sighed again. "She's been—" And here he was supposed to keep her safe.

"Doug?"

"Abducted. Lauren's been abducted."

"What? By whom?"

"A youth gang, then thugs on motorcycles."

"Whaaaat?"

Doug moved the phone away from his ear. "Yeah, some punks here are peddling drugs and paying with pounds of flesh. It's horrific. Murders, suicides, violence. Absolutely tragic."

"You're telling me. How could you let this happen?"

Doug's stomach sank. "What was I supposed to do? I offered to take her place, but they wouldn't have me."

"Tell me what happened. The whole story."

Doug filled in Jeffrey for the next ten minutes, fielding a barrage of questions, most of which he couldn't answer.

"Look, I gotta go. Court reconvenes in two minutes. But I'll stay in touch. I promise. And thank you for being there."

Doug scanned Lauren's contacts and called Emma. Dead air.

A few minutes later a South Dakota State Police cruiser slowed as it approached.

"Could you take me to 289th?"

"Sure," the trooper said, "but could you narrow it down a little for me?"

"A vehicle was torched there earlier today."

"I know right where you mean."

"What do you know about Lauren?"

"I'm not handling that case and can't comment on it anyway since it's an ongoing investigation."

Fifteen minutes later the trooper slowed his cruiser as they approached a charred spot on the road. What was left of Koda's pickup had been hauled onto the adjacent grassland.

"A mile or two back," Doug said.

Shortly past the billboard Doug got out and located the strip of duct tape. He jogged through the field until he found their bicycles, then waved to the trooper as the cruiser turned around and sped away.

What now? And what was happening to his precious Lauren?

In Butte a group of white knights had come to their rescue. They'd had Christian icons all over their cuts, pleasant faces, and the polar-opposite spirit of the ones he'd seen today. Where were they now?

He'd taken a photo of one of those motorcycles. He scanned his phone until he found it. Enlarging the image, he read *Narrow Gate Bikers* below the prominent cross.

He googled it. Amazing. Their website even had a phone number.

A recording picked up:

"Welcome to Narrow Gate Bikers, where we work to uphold righteousness in the biker community. If you have a concern about an injustice or would like to leave an anonymous tip, you can do so after the beep. The fastest way to provide us with information is to send a text message to this number. Remember, God is in control."

Doug hung up and texted:

A friend named Lauren Baumgartner from Virginia has been abducted by a motorcycle gang on the Golden Prairie Indian Reservation near Crow's Foot. She was handed over to them in payment for drugs from a youth gang on the reservation. My name is Doug Zimmer, and we were traveling through by bicycle before all this went down. Any help you can provide would be greatly appreciated. Please text me back if you have any questions or leads.

He picked up Lauren's phone and called Emma. Still nothing. Before he hung up, a call came in from Jeffrey.

"Doug, I'm flying to Rapid City. I'll rent a car and find you."

"Exactly how will you do that?"

"Just keep the phones on. I'll call. See you later tonight."

# CHAPTER 39

Riding on a motorcycle would have been a treat under different circumstances. Especially out here. The storm had cleared.

But nothing about this joyride pleased Lauren. Where was she going and what would happen to her?

And what about Doug? And Koda?

At least her hair could grow back, but the kids had the audacity to whack her violin on the ground. And they'd taken her phone.

One of the bikers had a spare vest in his saddlebag, and they made her put it on, along with a pair of oversized sunglasses. Maybe she looked the part, but she certainly didn't feel it.

Exhaust fumes from the Harleys blatting in front of her ruined the otherwise fresh scents of the prairie, as did the odor emanating from the brute she was resting up against.

With no bars behind her to lean against or hang onto, she'd had no choice but to wrap her arms around Bruiser. She would much rather be hugging locals in Uganda who hadn't showered in a week.

Bruiser had more to hang on to but smelled far worse, a cross between the boys' latrine at the orphanage before its monthly sanitation and the dairy farm she cycled past as a child in Pennsylvania.

She peered around his shoulder at the vibrating dash, careful to keep her slippery-soled cycling shoes on the foot pegs. Wind smacked her face, and she almost choked.

Then she read the speedometer. Eighty miles an hour. It felt more like one twenty after traveling at ten miles an hour the past month. A bicycle helmet protected her then, but she wore no headgear now. It made no sense. She should have been afraid of a crash but was more concerned about staying on the bike and protecting what little personal space she had left—and other dangers that seemed more probable. Why couldn't she be clinging to Jeffrey, Lars, or Doug?

Worst of all, what if she had a seizure? Things had been so hectic she'd forgotten to take her medication.

At least Bruiser's weight stabilized the bike. And balance came naturally to her after well over a thousand miles on a bicycle. But when they leaned into the next curve, he kicked the engine into a higher gear. Her head snapped back and her arms squeezed him harder.

The road looked like any other on the prairie. Yet as they motored into the afternoon sun, she sensed they were backtracking the route she and Doug followed to the center of Golden Prairie.

When they made it to the Badlands, she could wait no longer. She tugged on Bruiser's shirt. "Can we stop?"

"I can't hear you!" he shouted.

She raised her voice. "Can we stop?"

"What for?"

"I need to stop. At a facility."

He nodded.

Several minutes later they rumbled into a ghost town with what looked like only one operating business, a convenience store. All four bikers turned off their engines.

Lauren dismounted and took a deep breath.

"Hey." It was Big Dog. He got off his bike and strode over, stopping inches in front of her. He lifted his chin, then pooched his lips. "You try anything at all in there, you're dead meat. Not to mention what we'll do to your friends back on the rez. You hear me?"

Lauren nodded once.

In rolled a pair of motorcycles from the opposite direction. The lead driver wore a vest Lauren would remember for the rest of her life. She'd seen it at the bar in Butte. A white cross drizzled with crimson red blood. A brother! With a biker body trained with much more than beer, burgers, and fries. His riding companion was a woman in her forties, similarly clad, and matching his fitness.

Before the man turned off the motor, he looked at Lauren, then stared at Bruiser, who straddled his bike while chatting with Big Dog.

Lauren hurried into the store.

The female motorcyclist followed her in, as did Big Dog.

Lauren hung her sunglasses on her shirt collar as she scurried to the lone restroom in the back wall. It was a one-seater.

Before she closed the door, the fit woman approached, the shiny red droplets on her vest glinting from the overhead lighting. She searched Lauren's eyes, bouncing from one to the other.

Big Dog stood in the far front corner with his arms folded, watching them.

Lauren closed the door and locked it.

As she pivoted to the toilet, she glimpsed herself in the mirror. Her heart skipped a few beats. What a ghastly hack job. She ran her hand through her hair, what little of it remained. If she ever got out of this mess, she'd need a better hairdresser. But that didn't matter now.

*Lord, help me.*

She didn't want to endanger a stranger, but could those Christian bikers be her only way out?

Someone rapped on the door.

"Are you okay in there?" It was a female voice.

"J—just a minute." Lauren's voice shook.

She should have said, *"No, I'm not okay. Those hulks have kidnapped me. Can you help me get away?"* But who else might hear her? "I'll be right out."

A lightweight object tapped the floor just outside the door, drawing her attention to the crack below it.

A business card slipped through with a metal disk the size of a bicycle-tube patch taped to it. Numbers were etched on the disk. Then came a thud from the sole of a women's biker boot.

Lauren stretched to pick up the card.

*Jessica, Motorcycling for Jesus. Narrow Gate Bikers. Upholding righteousness in the biker community.*

A lot of good that phone number would do without a phone to call or text it.

On the other side of the card, she read a handwritten note, *Wear this.*

As the toilet flushed, she pulled the disk from the card and slipped it into her bra. She secured the card on her backside, inside the waistband of her underwear. It would be more comfortable there. And maybe separating the two would double her chances of survival. Of course, she hoped she would be the only one to access them, but her nauseated stomach suggested otherwise.

When she opened the door, the woman smiled at her, then winked before passing her and closing the door.

Big Dog walked toward Lauren, then waved his arm. "Come on. Let's go. How long does it really take to use the bathroom? And put those glasses back on."

As Big Dog followed her toward the entrance, one of his gang was at the checkout paying for a carton of Marlboro cigarettes. "Smokestack, pick me up some Camels. No filters."

"Sure thing."

As the attendant turned to retrieve another carton of cigarettes, he eyed Lauren. If he only knew what was happening, maybe he would call the authorities. She could hope.

Bruiser and Tank stood behind Smokestack, a six-pack of beer hanging from each and every hand.

Big Dog nudged her forward. "Let's go."

Once outside, they stowed their purchases.

The Narrow Gate Biker stood, admiring Bruiser's bike. "Does your Road King have the heated handgrips on it?"

"Nah. Don't need 'em."

Before returning to his Harley, the Narrow Gate Biker nodded his head at the other bikers.

It went unacknowledged.

"Stupid Christian," Big Dog mumbled.

The four bikes rumbled back onto the highway.

Lauren glanced back.

Two motorcycles pulled out of the convenience store lot and headed in the opposite direction.

Lauren's phone rang.

Doug stopped his recumbent and pulled her phone out of his pocket. *Emma Red Cloud.*

"Emma, it's Doug. Are you alright? I tried to reach you earlier but all I got was dead air."

"I've been better, but I'm okay. Where are you?"

"A biker gang rolled into the campground and took Lauren. The kids dumped me outside of town, then the state police came and took me to my bicycle. I'm heading west, back to town. They're on the case."

"Not exactly."

"What do you mean?"

The receiver muffled, and Emma spoke garbled words to someone else.

"Hello?" Doug said.

"We'll pick you up. Are you on 289th?"

"Yeah. What's going on?"

"I'll fill you in when we get there."

"Who's we?" he said, but she'd already hung up.

Lauren squeezed her legs against the seat as the four bikes rolled off the main road into a wooded area, onto a narrow dirt road with tall grass growing in the middle before coming to a stop. A makeshift sign with a wooden stake read *Private Road*.

"Blindfold her . . . Never mind. I'll do it." Big Dog got off his idling bike and dropped the kickstand with one swift swipe of his foot. Then he rummaged through the storage bin behind his seat and ripped out a red bandanna.

After tying it around her face, he cinched it tighter than necessary, then knotted it.

"Why don't you tie her hands together around my chest." Bruiser laughed.

"You. Besides, she knows better than to try something stupid while we're ridin'. Don't ya, hon."

Lauren sucked in a shaky breath.

"We'll tie her up once we arrive at camp . . . until the party begins."

He rubbed her cheek with what felt like his thumb and forefinger, his skin rougher than sandpaper. "Purdy girl."

A moment later the motors revved, and Bruiser's bike began bouncing down the lane, leaning one way, then the other. To keep her balance, Lauren again had no choice but to hug Bruiser.

The exhaust fumes from the bikes ahead penetrated the bandanna in no time, but at least they masked the three hundred pounds of body odor sitting between her legs. With each bump in the road and the jostling that came with it, the discomfort of close quarters chafed her spirit.

Emma peered in the rearview mirror. "You said through the Badlands, right?"

Koda nodded. Then he placed his hand on Doug's shoulder. "Hey, I want to thank you." He held out his fist.

The look on his face told all. Doug mustered a smile, formed a fist, and bumped it against Koda's. Then he clutched Koda's arm. "Proud of you. But it's you who deserves thanks . . . How did you get out?"

"When we got back, the others had gone to make a delivery. Mato wanted to smoke weed, so when he went into the tepee, I took my fishing rod downstream . . . and draped my vest over this." Beaming ear to ear, Koda raised Lauren's violin case. "Once I was out of sight, I bolted."

"You're a brave man. We'll get you out of here somehow. And I sure hope we get to deliver that to its rightful owner . . . You're doing the right thing."

Koda had informed them of two hideaways the Blood Warriors had discovered while on trips to pick up drugs from the biker gang. They'd nosed around and stumbled onto the encampments, which represented intel in the event of the dreaded double-cross. Smart kids. Too bad they weren't putting their ingenuity into revitalizing the economic well-being of their people.

Maybe going there was a long shot, but what else could they do? Lauren's life was on the line. If the police weren't going to respond quickly, then maybe they could.

Doug yanked out his phone to check messages. An unidentified number had left this text:

> Thank you for contacting Narrow Gate Bikers. We have a team working on your case and are in contact with law enforcement. A suspicious group of four motorcycles was spotted with a female rider heading west from Scenic. We'll update you if we learn more.

Doug sucked in a breath. Then he read the message aloud.

"That's right where we're heading," Koda said.

Emma floored the accelerator.

Doug swapped his phone for Lauren's. Jeffrey had left a text message:

> Pumpkin Spice, do I ever miss you! Hope
> to see you soon.

Maybe he shouldn't have read it. But what if it had something to do with Jeffrey's travel plans? Or Lauren's captivity? Maybe he should forward Jeffrey the Narrow Gate Bikers update. But the poor guy would worry even more. Doug had his own angst as the empty pit gnawed inside him.

He swapped phones again and texted Jeffrey:

> Do you have any connections with the
> FBI? Biker gangs from who knows where
> and youth gangs on the rez are trafficking
> across jurisdictions.

The Buick flew past the bullet-riddled sign, leaving the reservation.

Doug looked down at his phone:

> Reached out earlier. Praying they listened.

# CHAPTER 40

"Gimme another brewski, would ya?" Big Dog said.

Bruiser belched.

Smokestack took another puff on his cigarette. "Comin' right up, boss." He went into the shack adjacent to the open pit.

Tank was flipping burgers on the grill.

The bandanna that'd been around Lauren's face now held her hands together behind her back. She was seated, but they'd also strapped her waist to a pole with a bungee cord. Any squirming only dug it deeper into her hips.

They'd at least offered her supper, but she had no appetite. Instead she'd resigned herself to ingesting the smell of hamburgers cooking over an open fire and then going without. They deserved no satisfaction.

It was dark, except for the light from the firepit and another inside the shack. Tank retrieved a lantern from inside, lit it, and set it on the picnic table.

It was also quiet, but for the macho banter from the gang members and an occasion snap from the firepit.

"What should we do with the babe, Big Dog?" Smokestack asked.

"He-he . . . He-he . . . . . . Ha-ha-ha."

Big Dog's deriding laughter continued unabetted, increasing in intensity until the others joined in.

When Big Dog's outburst slowed, so did the others'. "Smoke, come on. You need me to explain that to ya? Really?" His grin exposed a chipped front tooth.

A chill flashed through Lauren.

With no sounds other than fifteen more minutes of raunchy talk, including offhanded references to Lauren's body parts, the gang members sat at the picnic table with burgers on paper plates, a bag of chips between them.

Big Dog looked at Lauren. "Darlin', you sure you don't want none?"

"No thank you."

"Awwwww, ain't she *po*-lite," Big Dog said.

*You wouldn't think so if I could kick you where it hurts.*

The foursome, each with an open beer bottle, chowed down their burgers in no time. After seconds, then thirds, Bruiser let out a five-second belch.

Big Dog looked at him. "Oh?" Then he leaned hard to the left and sputtered gas from his hind end. "Take that! How 'bout another round, boys?"

Smokestack got up to go inside, then stopped and looked over at Lauren. "Want one?"

She shook her head.

Big Dog cracked a grin. "Well maybe she does." Then his head swiveled slowly toward Lauren as his smile widened.

As Smokestack returned, Bruiser sucked the last drop from his bottle and belched again.

Big Dog got up and walked over to Lauren, placing the mouth of his open beer bottle under her nose.

She held her breath and turned her head, but he moved the bottle under her nose again. She swiveled her head in the opposite direction and drew in fresh air.

Big Dog laughed. Then he clenched her jaw, brought the bottle to her mouth, and tipped it forward. "Now let's just give this a taste. It won't do you no harm."

As the beer splashed against her lips, she blew out, spraying it on her clothes.

Big Dog removed the bottle, drew back his head, and roared. "We need to loosen you up a little."

"Looks like she don't want none, boss," Smokestack said.

Lauren blew and blew until the beverage evaporated from her lips.

The foursome roared, then sprinkled in wisecracks.

The more they drank, the coarser the mockery.

She countered it:

*. . . Though I walk through the valley of the shadow of death, I will fear no evil. For Thou art with me. Thy rod and Thy staff, they comfort me . . . Surely goodness and mercy shall follow me all the days of my life, and I will dwell in the house of the Lord forever.*

Bruiser belched.

It was no use. She couldn't escape. Not physically or mentally.

After they tossed their plates into the firepit, Big Dog walked over to Lauren.

His breath reeked of alcohol as he lowered his face to hers.

She jerked her head back as he puckered his lips.

"C'mon now. We're not going to hurt you." He wrapped both hands around her jawbones and pulled her face to his, bloodshot eyes peering through her. "No, darlin', we won't hurt you."

He moved closer still.

His lips touched hers.

She squirmed, but he'd immobilized her head with his strong grip. She tucked her lips into her mouth.

He kept pressing in, the stubble of his beard rubbing against her skin.

"Easy now. Don't make this any harder than it needs to be."

"Boss, you need some help?" Smokestack said.

"No. But you can be next," he said over his shoulder, then looked back at Lauren. "Would you like me to untie your hands so you can . . . ah . . . get more comfortable?" He chuckled. "And take that smelly top off? Yeah, you got beer all over it. Of course, I could do the honors for you?"

Lauren's heart pounded. She couldn't let this happen. Even during her years of living in Africa, exposed to any manner of barbarism in the jungle, none of the locals had seen her naked. This wasn't the time to start. *Only my husband.*

"Shy, are we?"

"Leave me alone."

"I'm not going to hurt you. This is going to make you feel good. Real good."

"Leave me alone, I said."

"Now now . . . don't make this difficult. I'm perfectly capable of stripping you naked. And if I weren't"—he looked around at the others—"I have them."

"What kind of a man would force himself on a woman?"

He squinted. "You just need to be shown a little lovin', that's all."

Her mind was going numb, along with her body. Her stomach squeezed tighter than the strings on her violin. Maybe she should just give in. Hope to live another day.

*Lord, help.*

Then she remembered. They might beat her to death, but would that be any worse than yielding to an animal?

She nodded. "I can do it."

"That's better." Big Dog smiled. "Now we're talking. I knew you'd come around. They always do."

He untied her hands.

She grabbed the bottom of each side of the oversized vest she was wearing and pulled them away, each metal snap unfastening click by click.

Watching her every move, Big Dog's grin broadened as he slowly shook his head.

Then she reached for the zipper on her half-zip cycling jersey and inched it partway down. Leaning forward, she untucked the tail.

Big Dog's eyes bulged and his jaw dropped.

Rather than pulling the jersey over her head, she sat back, fiddled with the zipper to distract the men, and twisted her body—until the disk slipped out from under her top. It caught on the bungee cord around her waist. Light from the nearby lantern glinted off the metallic surface.

Big Dog reached down and picked it up. "What have we here?"

Smokestack blew out a long stream of smoke from the cigarette nested between his fingers. "What's that, boss?"

"It—it looks like a—a tracking device."

"Lemme see," Tank said.

Big Dog held it in his palm as the others huddled to examine it. He looked up at Lauren. "What is this?"

A chill flushed through her. "I—I don't know."

"Sure you don't."

"Boss, if that's a tracking device, we need to split and fast. Wanna get rid of her?"

"Ohhh no. I was just gettin' started with her. But you're right. Let's get outta here."

He threw the disk as far into the woods as he could, then tied Lauren's hands behind her back again. An extra tug sent a sharp pain through her wrist.

The men scurried around the campsite, packed, and loaded their bikes. Finally they released Lauren from the pole, untied her, and set her on Bruiser's bike.

She zipped up her shirt and fastened her vest. Then she reached around and felt her waistband. Still there.

Smokestack, cigarette dangling from his mouth, stopped before mounting his bike and cocked his head. "What's that?"

Big Dog looked at him with narrowing eyes. "What's what?"

"I didn't hear nothing," Bruiser said.

"I do," Tank said. "We need to go."

Big Dog turned to listen.

Smokestack yanked the cigarette from his mouth. "Sounds like a whole herd of 'em."

"Yeah, I hear it now. Approaching fast. Let's take the back road out. Then head over to the other place. Splash that fire out first."

In no time they were off. Apparently they saw no need to blindfold her on a pitch-black night.

# CHAPTER 41

Big Dog raised his arm, then waved. Bruiser's engine burbled as he let off the gas. He hit his brakes hard, Lauren pressing into his back until they stopped.

Big Dog turned. "Cut your engines, boys."

Stars peeked through clouds overhead. An owl hooted. A distant murmur grew.

"Boss, they're following us."

Big Dog looked at the others. "Let's keep going. Back to Rapid City. We'll lose 'em."

"I don't like the sound of that," Smokestack said.

"You have a better idea?"

"No, that! Can't you hear it?"

A faint wail of a siren chimed in with the distant roar of motorcycles.

"That ain't nothin'. Remember, this place is crawling with bikers. Don't let it spook ya." Big Dog fired up his engine and revved it before accelerating back onto the remote highway.

The others followed.

After several more minutes Tank pointed ahead of them.

Lauren peered over Bruiser's shoulder. Her heart leaped. Blue lights.

As they approached the cruisers—three of them—a trooper stood in the road and waved two orange stick lights, pointing them to the shoulder.

Big Dog slowed, circled in the road, and accelerated in the opposite direction.

Before Bruiser could turn, the trooper dropped his stick lights to his side and ran toward his cruiser. Another cruiser turned to pursue them.

Bruiser reversed direction with the others, their speed increasing by the second. As did Lauren's heartbeat.

She leaned harder into him and squeezed her arms around him. This was no time to check his speedometer.

What if an animal darted out in front of them? Or they hit a bad patch of blacktop? . . . Or she had a seizure? Maybe that wouldn't be so bad at this point.

The blue lights from behind began to flash on the pavement beneath them, growing in length and intensity, while the sirens increased in volume.

She peeked ahead. Solitary headlights—at least a dozen— shimmered in the distance. They clogged the oncoming travel lane, growing in size before commanding the full width of the road.

Her captors would either have to turn around—that wasn't really an option—leave the road, or stop.

Suddenly the blat of their Harleys paused. Bruiser's bike slowed with the others'. Then the drag of brakes thrust her deep into layers of back fat.

Big Dog swerved right. When Bruiser's bike did the same, a jolt rammed her underside. She bounced on the seat and tightened her squeeze on him. Ensuing bumps jostled them as wheat stalks brushed their legs.

On the gas, off the gas, again and again as they ran through muck from the recent downpour, mud splattering on Lauren's legs.

She looked behind.

The pulsating headlights of bikes winding through shaky ground were closing distance. Blue lights flashed from police cruisers roadside.

The motors ahead silenced one by one.

When she turned around, Big Dog was dismounting his bike. Then he raised a gun in the air.

Tank and Smokestack wheeled up to him, armed themselves, and took cover behind their bikes.

When Bruiser's bike was about to stop, Big Dog slung his arm around Lauren, his beer breath raising goosebumps on her neck. He dragged her from the bike, squeezing her against his hip as he positioned himself behind Bruiser's bike. Bruiser joined them, pulling a gun from his storage bin.

Apparently the weapons had curtailed the pursuit. The chasers were seeking shelter behind their bikes, idling motors moaning.

"You have no way out. Drop your weapons, stand up, and put your hands in the air." The command came from an amped megaphone visible above the hood of one of the cruisers before a floodlight blinded her. "You have nothing to gain and everything to lose by not surrendering now."

"We're not surrendering!" Big Dog shouted.

"Lauren! Lauren, are you okay?"

Her pulse quickened. *Doug!* His voice came from the other group of bikers in the field.

"Tell him you're okay," Big Dog growled.

"Yes. I am. I'm okay."

But she wasn't. Nothing was okay.

"They have her!" Doug yelled. "She said she's okay."

"We know you're holding a female in custody against her will. Kidnapping is a serious crime. We suggest you let her walk to safety right now."

"We're not getting out of this one," Bruiser said. "I think we should surrender."

"Not a chance," Big Dog said. "Not a chance. You're gettin' yellow on me, Bruiser. What's gotten into you?"

"She ain't done nothing to us. And she's not a fit for us anyway. Why don't you let her go?"

"Maybe he's right, boss," Smokestack said.

"What's wrong with you guys?"

"I'm walking." Bruiser dropped his gun, stood up, and raised his hands. "Not interested in doing any more time."

"You walk outta here, I'll shoot you in the back."

"In front of a buncha cops?"

"That's it," the megaphone blared. "Now walk slowly out of the field. Keep your hands in the air and we won't harm you."

"No, you're not that stupid." Bruiser stepped out from behind his bike, his torso sprouting from the wheat field like a fully grown tree with two massive branches reaching skyward.

"If I don't shoot you, those other bikers will."

The sirens of more emergency vehicles approaching sliced the cool of the evening.

"Boss, didn't you see the flag on the back of them bikes? It's them Christians."

"Yeah, the losers."

Bruiser took another step, then another, each successive step more confident than the last as his dark outline walked toward the blinding light.

"I know three of you are still there, plus the woman you're holding against her will. Who's next?"

Tank and Smokestack looked at one another.

"Not you too?"

Smokestack dropped his gun, lit a cigarette, then stood up, raising his arms over his head. He let out a few puffs of smoke as he began walking.

"I'm going too." Tank disarmed and followed, the light breeze sifting the cigarette smoke before it vanished into the darkness.

Big Dog's head snapped back and forth.

"God loves you, you know. Why don't you surrender before the consequences get any worse? He has a plan for your life, and this isn't it."

"Don't preach to me, woman."

"Lauren, we're going to get you out of there!" Doug shouted.

Big Dog raised his voice. "No you're not!"

He jammed the muzzle of his gun under Lauren's chin and pushed them to a standing position, Lauren in front.

"You get that gun out from under her face. She's done nothing wrong." The sound of Emma's voice warmed Lauren's heart, but these weren't Emma's people. Big Dog would never listen to her.

"Did your momma ever correct you like that?" Lauren said.

"Shut—"

"If you're part of the Christian bike group," the police said, "we appreciate the help, but please stay down. We don't want any of you getting hurt. You're in direct line of sight with the suspect."

A motor revved in response.

Lauren glimpsed movement in the wheat stalks to her left. "Do you really prefer to get shot?"

"It'll be you first, woman."

"I know where I'm going."

"You keep talkin' like that, and I'll get you there a lot sooner."

"There's nothing you've done wrong that God won't forgive."

He thrust the gun harder into her throat.

She gasped for breath. "O— . . . okay."

"You can't use your hostage as a shield anymore. We've got you surrounded. It's time to surrender."

As Big Dog pivoted to look behind him, his grip on Lauren loosened.

This was her chance. But what could she do with her hands tied behind her back?

Suddenly the surrounding wheat stalks separated, and a trooper lunged for the gun in Big Dog's hands, wrestling it away from Lauren's head. Another joined in the fight.

Lauren drove the cleat on her bicycling shoe into Big Dog's midsection, twisting it with all her might before she escaped his clutches.

Two other rescuers, one wearing Narrow Gate Biker cuts and the other in civilian clothes, leaped from the stalks of grain to help the officer subdue Big Dog.

Lauren took a giant breath and dropped her head.

Then a pair of hands gently cupped her shoulders from behind. "You're going to be alright."

It was Doug's voice. She collapsed backward into his arms.

He embraced her while rubbing one of her shoulders.

After he untied her, she squeezed him. "Oh, it's sooo good to see you. I didn't know if I would make it out alive."

The face of the Narrow Gate Biker was unmistakable.

His riding companion spread open some wheat stalks and climbed to her feet. "Sister, that was a close one. You need to start hanging with nicer people."

"Thank you. Thank you so much." Lauren hugged her. "How did you guys find us?"

The male rider leaned down and reached under the rear fender of Bruiser's bike, then held out something for Lauren to see. "We got a little concerned when we arrived at an empty campsite, so we went to plan B. You can be grateful they all went into the store. I won't ask you how the first sensor landed in the woods."

As the troopers walked away with Big Dog in handcuffs, Emma stepped forward. "Koda told me everything. He couldn't bring himself to talk with the police like he did with us—some bad history there—but he knew where the hideouts were and what was going down."

"Emma, thank you so much. And thank Koda too."

"You can thank him yourself. He's waiting in the car."

# CHAPTER 42

As Lauren, Doug, and Emma walked to her car, Doug's phone vibrated. *Not now.* But it could be Jeffrey.

Lauren continued explaining what had transpired since her abduction. The thought of what might've happened to her gave Doug chills.

When Koda stepped out of Emma's car, Lauren ran and hugged him.

Doug pulled out his phone. *Jeffrey Maddox.*

As the women caught up with Koda, Doug handed Lauren her phone, walked toward the field, and called Jeffrey.

"Hey, Doug, I just picked up a rental car. I'm on my way. Any news on Lauren?"

"*Great* news on Lauren. She's safe and sound. A little shaken, but she'll be fine."

"I can't tell you how much of a relief that is. I just—"

The phone went silent.

"Jeffrey?"

"I"—he sniffled and sucked in a breath—"I can't let her slip through my fingers ever again . . . I love that woman." His voice cracked.

Doug's stomach twisted.

"The thought of anything happening to her ripped my guts out. I can't get there fast enough."

"Well, keep it under seventy."

"Where should I meet you?"

"Um . . ." That was a good question. One he'd rather not answer. Or maybe give him an address somewhere in Wyoming. Doug might have given that serious consideration a few months ago, before his encounter with the Almighty. "I'll need to get an address for you. But head toward Crow's Foot on the Golden Prairie Indian Reservation. I'll text you the address when I get it."

"Do you have a few more minutes?"

Doug turned to see the women engaged in conversation with Koda, standing outside the car. "Yeah, just a few."

"I'll make it quick. I arranged a leave of absence. I'm going to . . . I'm going to marry Lauren. Like, right off."

A lead weight went *ka-thump* inside Doug's stomach and stretched it to the ground.

"I have a list with me—thought I could pick up these things out here to make it easier. I'm going to need a local contact to help connect me with the right merchants in Rapid City."

Doug cleared his throat. "I—I take it you haven't asked her yet."

"That's another piece of advice I need from someone who has been on the ground out here."

"What do you mean?"

"To make arrangements."

"Uh, well, what if she doesn't say yes?"

"I've been praying she will. I gave her mixed signals in the past and put things off. I'm now resolved. I'll never find a better woman than her. Not gonna put this off any longer."

"Don't you think she should weigh in before you—what's all this about merchants in Rapid City? Are you talking wedding setup?"

"Pretty much."

Doug felt nauseated. *How can this be happening?*

"Doug!"

It was Emma. Koda was running toward him.

"Hey, look, Jeffrey, I gotta go."

"Okay. Thanks for all you've done for Lauren. I can't thank you enough. I'm heading there now and will look for your text. And please keep this a surprise if you would. Thanks, Doug."

On the return ride to Crow's Foot, Lauren recounted the events of the past day. Koda asked most of the questions. Emma concentrated on the road, but shook her head as Lauren described what she thought could be the last day of her life.

Doug was particularly quiet.

"How did you get out of the encampment?" Lauren said.

Doug didn't respond.

"Yoo-hoo."

"Oh, sorry, what did you say?"

"How did you escape?"

"You're sitting beside him." Doug explained Koda's heroics and how the police and Emma had picked him up, then said, "It's your turn now, Koda."

Koda lit up as he lifted the violin case from between his feet.

"It's my violin!" Lauren took the case and hugged it. "Thank you!" Then she stood it between them.

A text message landed on Lauren's phone from Lars:

Please call when you can. I miss you.

Once the tingling inside her subsided, she texted back:

I will.

Rickety vehicles whizzed by in increasing numbers as they rode toward Crow's Foot, the most recent with only one headlight illuminated. Twenty minutes later, after dropping off Koda, Emma rolled her car into her driveway. The number on the mailbox read *426*.

Doug had already typed *313th Avenue* into his phone's text editor. He added *426* in front of it. Once he sent the text, Jeffrey would soon arrive.

Did Doug really want that? Regardless, he'd given his word. He swallowed hard and poked send.

Doug, Emma, and Lauren sat around the kitchen table decompressing. The children and their parents had gone to bed.

"I need to go freshen up," Lauren said.

Doug excused himself and went upstairs as she headed toward the bathroom.

She couldn't wait to hear Lars's voice again. She wanted to catch up on so many things. But she couldn't very well dial him in the bathroom. Or the girls' bedroom.

She returned to the kitchen, where Emma was clearing the counter.

"I'd like to make a phone call. Is there somewhere I can talk in private?"

"You can use my bedroom if you make it short."

"Twenty minutes. I promise."

Emma showed her to her room and closed the door behind Lauren.

She noted the time and called Lars.

"Hello, Lauren! So good to hear from you."

Her stomach fluttered. "Hi, Lars. How are you?"

"I'm fine. Where are you?"

"South Dakota. On the Golden Prairie Reservation."

"It's beautiful there. I've painted some of the landscapes. How are you?"

That was a loaded question. "I'm fine." With only twenty minutes she couldn't get into the details. Instead they talked about the beauty of her South Dakota travel.

Then she said, "I was glad to hear from you, but what prompted your text message?"

"I . . . I needed to talk." His exhale blew through the phone's speaker.

"About what?"

He didn't respond.

"Are you okay?"

"I—I thought about what you said. About my lifestyle."

"And?" She hoped she wasn't applying too much pressure, but she also wanted to make the best use of what time they had to talk.

"I went to church last week."

Lauren heart thumped. "With someone?"

"By myself. Lauren, it's like the sermon was for me."

"It can feel that way."

"I want to make some changes in my life, and I want to see you."

Lauren fumbled the phone and caught it before it hit the bed.

"Lauren? Did you hear me?"

"What changes are you considering?"

"I believe the religious types would call it penance."

"Do you mean *repent*ance?"

"Yeah. That's it. I mean, I need a fresh start."

Her heart raced. "God's all about second chances. He loves you, Lars, and has a plan for your life."

Lauren checked the clock on the phone. They were already more than ten minutes into the call. "Do you know a pastor who can help you?"

"No. Not really."

"Well, you should find one. I can help you with some basics, but you'll need follow-up counseling. I'm so excited for you."

"What should I do?"

"First, tell God you're sorry for your sins."

"I've already done that."

"Do you believe He came to earth as Jesus to shed His blood on the cross to cover your sins?"

"I'm trying to."

"When you come to believe that and ask Jesus to be your Lord and Savior, you'll discover the peace of God in your life. And eternal life when you die."

"Okay."

Her pulse slowed. Lars didn't sound ready for this. Maybe he didn't really believe it, or maybe he didn't understand. Perhaps he was having a hard time surrendering. Considering his family history, he probably found it hard to trust. Whatever the reason, they were out of time to explore it.

"Lars, I wish I had more time to talk, but what you've told me is encouraging. I would recommend you talk to a pastor. These things can take time to sort through."

"I have the weekend off. I was wondering if . . . I might come see you."

Warmth flushed through Lauren's chest. But it was too much to consider, especially with Doug around.

"I—I can't right now, Lars. I hope you understand. But I want to hear what happens with you. Promise you'll let me know how you're doing?"

"I will. Thank you for calling me back, Lauren . . . I really miss you."

"Take care, Lars."

The phone clicked.

*I miss you too, Lars.*

Doug, Lauren, and Emma reconvened at the kitchen table. There was so much to rehash.

Wolf began barking outside.

Soon a knock sounded at the door.

Doug looked over, knowing who was behind it, anticipating the end of something that had never really begun. He swallowed hard.

Emma got up, walked across the room, and opened the door a crack. "Who is it? Wolf, you be quiet." She peered out with her hand on the doorknob, her mouth open, cheeks hollow.

Lauren looked at Doug, both of them listening, but he stared toward the door instead. This couldn't be happening.

The faint sound was that of a male voice, but the words were indistinguishable.

"I see." Emma nodded several times to each of the murmurs from outside. "Just a minute."

She beckoned Lauren with her index finger. "There's someone here to see you."

"Oh?"

Wrinkles formed above the bridge of her nose. She looked at Doug.

Doug's chair scraped against the floor as he rose—"Excuse me"—and headed upstairs.

As Lauren reached the door, Emma pulled it open.

"Jeffrey? Wha—what are *you* doing here?"

Emma placed her hand on Lauren's shoulder but addressed Jeffrey. "Would you like to come in?"

"No, I think it would be better if we talked outside. But thank you."

Wolf whimpered, retreated to the doghouse, and lay down.

Lauren walked out the door and closed it behind her. The outside light came on.

Jeffrey was wearing shorts and a polo shirt. And he had no flowers or other gift for her. For that, she was thankful.

She folded her arms across her chest. "It's . . . it's good to see you, but . . . why are you here?"

"I'm so glad you're okay." He looked at her hair. "I can't tell you how relieved I am."

*How does he know? And what does he know?* "I'm a little relieved myself."

"Look, I know this is unexpected."

"I'll say."

"It's just that . . . I've been thinking. And . . ."

"Go on."

"Are you mad at me?"

Lauren exhaled. "No, I'm not mad at you. But the last few times you showed up unannounced—they didn't go well."

Wolf let out a sigh, his jaw resting on his paws, eyes heavy.

Jeffrey's lips curled down. "I'm sorry. I truly am. You have every right to feel this way."

Something about him was different. Maybe it was the look in his eyes. Contrition. Maybe his casual attire. Perhaps—and who knows how he pulled it off—making the effort to find her on one of the worst days of her life and risking rejection at the same time. On a Native American reservation in South Dakota of all places.

Her heart fluttered. Her mind told it to stop. "You say you've been thinking. What about?"

"You."

"Me?"

His eyes sparkled. "And us."

She cocked her head.

"I've finally figured it out, Lauren."

Her heartbeat increased. "What's that?"

"I—I can't live without you."

Water hastened to her eyes.

He stepped closer. "I don't want to lose you."

Her emotions were about to burst. But could she survive the deluge? So much had happened. So many things—and people—tugging at her heart. She'd taken her medication after arriving back at Emma's, but would this trigger her anyway? She should have told him her secret earlier.

His hands cupped her arms. "Will you marry me?"

She convulsed under an unstoppable torrent of emotion until her muscles went limp, collapsing in his arms.

Breaking her fall, Jeffrey held her close. "It's okay. It's okay."

Tears streamed down her face. This was too much. But she was still lucid. No seizure.

"I'm not bailing out this time. We're not getting any younger, and there's no more time to waste. I feel as though God has confirmed this to me. I'm wondering—hoping—He does for you too."

She nodded against his neck. She'd wanted to hear these words. Then another wave of emotion spewed out.

A minute later her arms clutched him harder.

He squeezed her.

Oh how she loved being in his arms. She remembered it well. Felt like she'd come home. But—

She'd been down this road with him before—under false pretenses. Doug was already clued in. Certainly Jeffrey had a right to know before making such an offer.

She let go. And swallowed hard. "There's . . . something I need to tell you."

"Wh—what's that?"

"I have a medical condition."

Jeffrey's forehead creased.

"I'm sorry I didn't tell you about this before. Most people know nothing about it, and I can usually control it with medication."

Jeffrey stood silent, studying her.

"But sometimes I have . . . I have seizures."

His eyes ping-ponged to each of hers. "We'll get through it. I told you I can't live without you, and that includes all of you."

"It may be hereditary."

"Well, there's no guarantee we can have kids." His dark-brown eyes did not waver.

Lauren breathed a sigh of relief and hugged him around the neck, then pulled away.

Seizures were one thing, but could he understand what she'd never told anyone, not even her pastors? Was he ready to hear it? Was she ready to speak it?

"I . . . I—"

He would never accept this. His very job was all about combating such ills. And if *she* couldn't accept it, how could he?

"I know you've been through a lot today. And I know this came as a big surprise. If you need more time . . ."

"I . . . I need to pray about this."

"I understand. I'll give you as much time as you need."

"Where are you staying tonight?"

"I'll find a place. Don't worry about me." He looked at the top of her head again. His brow furrowed.

"It's a long story. I'll tell you later because I don't want to keep a house full of people up all night. Okay?"

"Yes."

"Good night."

As they separated, they stared into one another's eyes.

"I love you, Pumpkin Spice."

She wiped her eyes and cheeks, then offered a weak smile. "I love you too."

Wolf groaned.

# CHAPTER 43

Lauren sat up and stretched. Maybe she could catch Emma for another 6:00 a.m. cup of coffee. Her phone showed *5:37*. She had managed to put herself back together well enough last night to avoid questions from Emma and Doug that she wasn't prepared—or didn't want—to answer. Doug had been aloof anyway, not engaging in conversation before an early exit to bed. He'd been through a lot too.

The comfort of being with people who cared about her made for a better night's sleep after such a harrowing experience. Plus Jeffrey had asked an important question—*the* question—without pressuring her for a response.

She'd prayed about Jeffrey's question before going to bed. Maybe that prompted one of her dreams, which seemed to bring clarity to her decision. It was another motorcycle group ride, but this one was not a nightmare. Three riders, but only one had a second seat on the back of his bike. Much like a contestant on *Let's Make a Deal*, Lauren faced a choice—seemingly an easy one.

But maybe it was just a dream.

Almost a year ago she'd jumped at the opportunity to marry Jeffrey. However, she'd entered a roundabout and taken a U-turn.

This time he sounded sincere and committed. Lighter on the romance, heavier on the urgency. She liked that. *Is this what God has for me?*

*Or is He working in Lars's life? Apparently, but for what purpose?* With Lars's background, he might know how to handle her secret.

*Then there's Doug, steady and reliable. And now as pure-hearted as they come. He brings a sense of security and joy.*

She walked down to the kitchen, sat at the table, and opened her phone. She googled "Bible verses about choices."

Partway down she found a familiar passage—Proverbs 3:5–6:

> Trust in the LORD with all your heart,
> And lean not on your own understanding;
> In all your ways acknowledge Him,
> And He shall direct your paths.

She believed that. Always. It made sense. And took the pressure off.

Nothing else popped out until Proverbs 11:14:

> Where there is no counsel, the people fall;
> But in the multitude of counselors there is safety.

It was time to ask for input.

As she bowed to pray—

Emma opened her bedroom door. "Good morning!"

"Good morning, Emma."

"Let me fix us some coffee."

"That sounds great."

Emma poured water into the coffee maker. "You had quite a day yesterday."

"It ran the full gamut of emotions. I'm wondering . . . Do you have a few minutes to talk before the others get up? In private?"

"I would be glad to. Let's go into my bedroom. I'll come out and get us coffee when it's ready."

The two went into Emma's bedroom, and Emma closed the door. They sat.

"What's on your mind?"

"Jeffrey proposed to me last night."

"I thought he might've."

"I'm torn. I feel like God has shown me some things, put other men in my life. I . . . I'm confused with my choices. Jeffrey seems dead serious this time. He's waffled in the past, but now he said he can't live without me."

"Oooo, that says a lot."

"I also feel close to Doug. And Lars—he texted me yesterday, and we talked on the phone. He wants to see me."

"This all sounds good. But I can see why you would feel confused."

"Yes, it's like three options, and I have to choose."

"Don't you mean four?"

Lauren rubbed her chin. "What do you mean?"

"You don't have to choose any of them. And you shouldn't if none of them fits you."

"I've wanted to be married for so long, to have kids of my own, to start a new life."

"If that's the case, then don't you really have only one choice?"

"What do you mean?"

Emma studied her. "Has Doug or Lars asked for your hand in marriage?"

"Oh. You're right. But what if they do—or would?"

"Just a minute. Cream?"

"Yes."

A moment later Emma returned with two cups of coffee.

"How did you feel last night when Jeffrey proposed?"

"Overwhelmed. But today I feel much better."

"Yesterday was an unusual day, and it's no wonder you were overwhelmed, even if you hadn't gotten a surprise visit with a marriage proposal attached." Emma sipped her coffee. "You said you're religious. Which direction do you think God is pointing?"

"I think if I trust Him, He'll direct my steps."

"I could believe that. You seem like such a sincere person. I think your future can be bright with whatever decision you make about Jeffrey's proposal. In your way of thinking, God can bless that decision either way. You have promising options. But based on what you said earlier about wanting to be married and have children—and I say this not knowing him—it sounds like that's what Jeffrey is offering you."

Lauren looked at her and nodded.

"And you know him better than the others. You have more history with him." Emma looked toward the closed door and took a deep breath. "You asked earlier if there was any way you could repay me. Don't make the same mistake I made. Don't let independence . . . or fear . . . make the decision for you."

"Hmmmm." Lauren placed her hand on Emma's. "Oh, Emma, I'm so glad we talked."

It was another restless night. Doug had slept maybe three hours.

Lauren had seemed scattered when she returned from talking with Jeffrey. It had to have been him, though she hadn't let on. And he left without coming inside. Maybe the conversation didn't go well.

Doug checked his phone. No messages. He texted Jeffrey:

> Was that you last night?

Yes.

> How'd it go?

Not sure.

*What's that supposed to mean?*

Yesterday helped put Doug's feelings in context. Lauren was a keeper. Any man would be a fool not to snatch her up.

But it also seemed like she was overwhelmed. If he told her how he felt about her, could she even make a rational decision after all she'd been through?

And then there was Jeffrey. They'd been engaged before, and Lauren had said they'd always love one another. Did he want to get into the middle of that? Could he even get her attention? He sure didn't look like Jeffrey, nor did he have age on his side, although he could teach Jeffrey a thing or two about people. The young fellow was so ambitious he tended to lose sight of their feelings. He didn't realize most of them processed life slower than his supersonic speed.

Still, becoming more transparent with Lauren wouldn't be fair to her. If Doug loved her, he needed to give her space and see if things would fall into place. She would probably call it waiting on God's will.

After an active breakfast with the kids, Lauren escaped down the street for a walk. She texted Maggie to see if she had time to talk.

Her phone vibrated.

"Hey, Maggie. Thanks for calling."

"Hi, Lauren. This is a perfect time to talk. How are things going?"

Lauren guffawed. "You would not believe what's happened."

"All good I hope."

"It is now, but things got crazy yesterday. A biker gang took me on a not-so-joyride."

"Oh my."

"God worked it all out."

"He always does. What's on your mind?"

"Jeffrey showed up again."

Maggie hesitated. "There's a strong pull between you two, isn't there?"

"Yes, I think you're right. He proposed."

"Well, Lauren, that's wonderful. Or don't you think so?"

Lauren slid her fingers through what hair remained on the top of her head. "I'm not sure what to think, Maggie. You remember our conversation about Lars. And Doug and I have reconnected on the road too."

"Isn't Lars out of the picture now?"

"He texted me yesterday. Before Jeffrey's proposal. It sounds like God is working in his life, and he wants to see me."

"You mentioned Doug. How's he doing?"

"He's doing great. We've shared some meaningful times on our bicycles."

"These all sound like positive developments, Lauren. What are you thinking?"

"I'll always love Jeffrey, but he's bailed out before. He said this time is different."

"Dear, are you afraid? Of making a commitment?"

Lauren stopped walking.

Maggie went on. "These connections with Doug and Lars have been serendipitous, but I wonder if they translate to day-to-day living. And that's what Jeffrey is asking for, I do believe."

"Maybe I am a little afraid."

"Does this have anything to do with losing your father, dear?"

Lauren teared up, then sniveled into the phone.

"I'm sorry. I didn't mean to upset you."

"No, I needed to hear this. I think you're on to something, Maggie."

"Dear, God is the Father who will never abandon you, whether intentionally or not. You have a firm enough foundation with Him to risk loving someone at a deeper level than you do now. That's what marriage is all about."

"I see what you mean."

"The day I married Brother Jim, I shook like a leaf. I had no idea what I was in for. But it was the second-best decision I ever made. God was in it. And He's used our marriage to grow our roots deeper into Him. And one another. It's not easy, and there are no promises for success. But if you both have a relationship with Jesus and keep your eyes on Him, you have nothing to fear.

"Like love, marriage is a choice. It's possible God could bless your union with any of these three men. But He can't if you don't move forward. One of them may work out better, but you'll never know which one. You can only choose one—that is, if they all propose to you . . . Or . . . you can choose none. Listen for that still, small voice inside you. Then follow it."

"Thank you, Maggie. Like I said, I needed to hear this."

"We'll be praying for you."

# CHAPTER 44

With his arm around Lauren, Jeffrey stood tall and looked out over the knoll where Koda had almost ended his life. "Spectacular! What a view! This is so much better than a stuffy office in DC."

The wheat danced in the breeze, the sun illuminating it golden yellow. A patchwork of fields in the distance reminded Lauren of Gram's afghan, though the pallid yellows were more fitting for a baby's blanket.

"You took me by surprise yesterday." Lauren clutched his hand.

"I owe you an apology for my on-again, off-again behavior. I'd already been struggling with the thought of losing you. But when Doug told me you'd been abducted, I was crushed. God used that to show me how deeply I felt about you and what was truly important in my life."

"All things working together for good."

"Exactly."

Lauren grabbed his other hand as they faced one another. "I've learned things too. I went on this trip to experience a great adventure before marrying, but I think I was also running away. There's a part of my past that makes me fearful of getting close and losing someone who is dear to me."

"Your parents?"

"Yes. But God is there for me. I just need to trust Him. He's never let me down yet."

"And He won't. Nor will I, with His hand guiding us."

Lauren smiled. "I so want to have your babies."

His dimples deepened, the white of his teeth slipping out from between his lips. "Is that a yes?"

She looked away, then down.

She couldn't this time. Not without him knowing.

But she hadn't even been able to tell Maggie . . . or Doug, even with as well as he'd handled her medical condition.

Despite the sun beaming overhead, a curtain dropped around her heart. If she told him, he wouldn't understand. How could he? An upstanding lawyer who fought for innocent victims rather than defending the guilty.

*Guilty* was the word for her. She knew it. She didn't need him to tell her.

*But what if . . . ?*

This might be her only chance. She was so close. How could she not?

It was time to level with Jeffrey, for better or worse. And with herself.

"I—I terminated a pregnancy."

The glee poured off Jeffrey's face like soapsuds in a shower. A somber stare replaced it.

"What did you say?"

Even though she knew God had forgiven her, would Jeffrey? Why should he? Even she couldn't forgive herself.

"Abortion?"

The word hung in the air like stench from an open sewer pit on a 90-degree day in Uganda.

Her worst fears were coming to fruition, and she'd exposed herself for the hypocrite she was.

Jeffrey pulled his hands away as he stared into the distance.

"I'm sorry." What else could she say? She folded her arms.

He scanned the horizon, then his eyes glazed over. "Why didn't you tell me?"

It was sinking in. And of course she should have told him. But she hadn't. Her stomach roiled.

"I can't believe it." He turned his back to her and stepped away. "Why oh why didn't you tell me?"

Guilty again. But with nothing left to lose, she at least owed him an explanation. She pulled in a deep breath.

"I was twenty-one. And scared. And he—" It was so hard to dredge this up. She drew in more air.

"But you're so . . . pure. So much more than me. Who was this guy?"

"It was a date at college. After my parents died."

Jeffrey scratched the back of his head. "Consensual?"

"Yes, I mean, no. Well, not really."

"Lauren, I'm just asking what happened."

"Things got a little too hot and heavy. And I . . . I lost myself in the moment and . . . I gave in."

Jeffrey froze.

"Did you hear me?"

"Yeah, I heard you. Why have you been holding all this inside?"

*He doesn't understand.*

As Lauren doubled over, tremors began to shake loose years of masked sorrow and regret like an avalanche on a mountain peak.

Jeffrey stood there as the emotion poured out. Then he finally stepped forward and cradled her in his arms.

Jeffrey and Lauren sat in his rental car, looking out over the vast prairie.

"The nurse at the clinic said it was just a blob of tissue. I was all alone. He wanted nothing to do with me or my problem. I should've known better, but I made a mistake I regret to this day."

"You're not alone."

"What do you mean?"

"We've all made mistakes we regret."

She nodded. Her pulse slowed.

"A client once told me, 'More women than we know are carrying around burdens of guilt and grief from past abortions. They're not allowed to talk about them.' I just wish you'd have told me sooner. I could've helped you."

Lauren grimaced. "I'm sorry. I truly am."

"'One in five have had an abortion,' she said. 'Women of child-bearing age in America.' So you're not alone." He thumped the butt of his palm on the steering wheel. "Come on."

Jeffrey exited the car, then retrieved something from the back seat.

Lauren climbed out.

He reached out his hand, and she clutched it as they walked toward the edge of the knoll.

"Now, where were we?" he said.

"Are—are you saying . . ."

"I'm sure you've already taken this up with God. If I can't forgive you, why should He forgive me?" He looked over her shoulder. "And, to be perfectly honest, but for the grace of God, I could've been on the other side of this. I'm not without my own mistakes."

Lauren's jaw dropped. She studied his glazed look. "Care to share more?"

"You already know I was no angel back in the day. Before Jesus rescued me. But those days are over and done with, totally forgiven . . . that is"—he cupped her shoulders and looked into her eyes—"if *you'll* forgive *me*."

"Are you asking me to?"

He hung his head for a moment. "Yes, I guess I am." He dropped to one knee, then peered up at her. "I should have asked you to forgive me before . . . Going too far with other women back in the day was also a sin against my future wife—something I should make amends for . . . Whether you're my future wife— that's up to you. But I'm sorry, Pumpkin Spice. Honestly, I am."

A lump formed in her throat. She kissed the top of his head.

He rose and yanked a pink T-shirt out of his back pocket. "I still think this will look good on you."

She smiled and pulled it on over her cycling jersey.

"*Stand Tall.* Look at you!" He smiled. "Wish I'd gotten one myself."

"Pink's not your color."

He swallowed her giggles in his arms.

Moments later she pulled away and tilted her head. "I love you, Jeffrey Maddox. And I . . . I forgive you."

"Does that mean you still want to have my babies?"

Lauren's heart pounded. "If I can. Well, you know what I mean."

"Yeah, it may take a miracle at our age."

"I believe in them."

"I can't live another day without you." He reached into his pocket, pulled out a red velvet box, and opened it. The diamond solitaire sparkled in the sunlight. "I love you, Lauren. Will you marry me?"

She nodded, a tear trickling down her cheek. "The sooner, the better."

A text message came through from Jeffrey:

> Could you give me the name of someone
> who can refer me to local resources?

Doug shook inside. She must've said yes.

After he gathered himself, he sent back Koda's phone number. Then he texted Brother Jim:

> Got time to talk?

His phone vibrated.

"Thanks for calling."

"We've been thinking about you. How are things going?"

"I feel like I've topped the summit and am now in free fall."

"Oh? What's up?"

"Yesterday Lauren was abducted by a motorcycle gang. It was touch-and-go, but she's safe now."

"This sounds like good news, Doug. What's troubling you?"

"I'm in love with Lauren."

"How is that bad?"

"Jeffrey is back in the picture and has every intention to marry her. Like, right now."

"I see."

"How could God let this happen?"

"You're looking at this as if a tragedy has occurred."

"Pretty close to it."

"Would it be a bad thing if Jeffrey and Lauren married?"

"It feels like my gut is turning inside out."

"Doug, you've been down this road before. You know marriage isn't easy, especially in the early years. Lauren has never been married before."

"But she's so mature. So committed to her faith."

"God will work this out. Last time I checked, He's still in charge. I know you've made Him a priority."

He'd contacted Brother Jim for a little understanding. This wasn't what he expected. Nothing inside him suggested everything would be okay. He wiped his palm on his pant leg.

"Talk to me, Doug. What are you thinking?"

"It's not so much what I'm thinking but what I'm feeling."

"What are you feeling?"

"Heartbroken."

"Is God asking you to step aside? And you're discouraged because you thought a deeper relationship with Lauren would complete you?"

"I don't know. Isn't it possible that God's plan is for Lauren and me to be together?"

"I suppose it is. Are you prepared to ask Lauren to marry you?"

Doug swallowed. He hadn't considered popping the question right now. And Jeffrey had probably already done it.

"You ask good questions, Brother Jim."

"From what I've seen, Lauren is a wonderful woman. But she's not your Ruth. You would be starting from scratch."

The dull ache in Doug's chest intensified.

"This is a time to lean into your faith, Doug. To seek God's guidance and not get out in front of Him. He knows what's best. Our own vision is limited to what we see right in front of us. That's why it's better to clasp His hand and let Him lead."

Doug took a deep breath.

"You may feel like you're free-falling, Doug, but God won't let you crash. Sometimes we need to let our emotions do their thing and hang on for dear life. They'll come back around."

"Thank you, Brother Jim. I appreciate your wisdom."

"If you walk with God through this trial and it's His will for you and Lauren to marry, it'll happen. I can say that because I'm pretty sure Lauren will do the same thing. If it isn't His will, He'll have spared you more pain and have something far better for you on the other side."

"That's hard to believe, but if you say so."

The extended silence suggested Doug ought to follow up, but he could only listen to his broken heart.

"Doug, do you have another minute or two?"

"I do."

"I wanted to update you on our suicide prevention ministry. We're planning a launch next month. We have some donors lined up and a list of prospects to contact."

"Wow. That's exciting. You don't mess around."

"This has been on our hearts for years . . . Doug, we could use your help. It's not going to pay great, but the benefits are out of this world."

Doug's anxiety drained from his soul like the muscle pain from his body when he began coasting down Bozeman Pass. "Really?"

"I know you're at loose ends still being on the road, but we could use you anytime after the first of the month. I just need to know before then so I can make other plans if you're not interested."

"No. I'm interested. It's not that. Let me think about this and get back to you."

# CHAPTER 45

Lauren paced in front of a window in Emma's living room, with Jeffrey seated in an overstuffed chair close by. Emma sat with Tashina at the kitchen table. Doug was upstairs.

As Lauren watched the kids playing tag in the yard, she called her brothers, Jamie and then Nick, with her exciting news. After hanging up, she thought of someone else.

"Maggie, guess what? Jeffrey and I are getting married this weekend!"

"This weekend? Oh, Lauren, that's wonderful. I'm so happy for you . . . Jim, Lauren and Jeffrey are getting married this weekend. Hold on, I'm going to put you on speaker. Where are you getting married?"

"Lauren, we're so happy to hear your news."

"Thank you, Brother Jim. I feel like I'm walking on air."

"I'll bet you are," he said.

Lauren crouched and leaned into Jeffrey so he could hear the other side of the conversation. "We're getting married on the reservation. I know it's a long way and short notice, but we'd be remiss if we didn't at least extend an invitation."

"Thank you. That's very kind of you."

"Lauren, do you have someone to officiate the service?" Maggie said.

"We haven't gotten that far yet."

"Jim, do you have any commitments on Saturday? It is Saturday, isn't it?"

"Yes," Lauren said.

"Dear, we would need to get there first. And then back before the Sunday service."

Jeffrey leaned closer to the phone. "If you have Saturday free, we'll fly you out and back."

"Oh I wanna go!" Maggie said.

After a pause Brother Jim said, "That could cost you a lot of money given the timing. Are you sure? It may even be hard to find a flight."

"I'm sure. I have friends . . ."

"Thank you for the offer. That's very generous. We'll get back to you."

After Lauren disconnected, she ran her hand through her hair, then froze. "Oh, my hair!"

"I know a hairdresser who works miracles," Emma said. "I'll set something up."

"Thank you—because my hair sure needs a miracle."

Doug looked at the display on his phone.

"Hi, Brother Jim. You must've heard the news."

"Yes, and I just wanted to check in to make sure you're doing okay. I know this must be a struggle for you."

"I'm okay. Went for a ride today and that helped. I kinda knew it was coming to this."

"But not easy for your emotions to accept?"

"How'd you know?"

"Doug, I hope you'll be able to find it in your heart to be happy for Lauren and Jeffrey. It may take time, but I think you'll get there."

"Yeah."

After a long pause Doug said, "I've had a chance to think, and I want to take you up on your offer. I think it's the open door I need right now."

"Oh, Doug, that's an answer to prayer. Thank you. We'll have time to work out the details later."

"I appreciate your confidence in me. What's your vision for the ministry?"

"First and foremost is to help people struggling with suicidal thoughts. Montana has a big problem with suicides. We want to expand our reach elsewhere too . . . Plus Maggie and I also have a heart for what we see going on in war-torn countries. So many innocent people are caught in the crossfire. We'd like to find a way to help refugees, as long as the government and our own funding issues don't stand in our way."

"Wow, Brother Jim. I had no idea."

"We love Montana but would like to get outside of Missoula. I think that'll help my successor at church and allow Maggie and me a clean break for what God has next. Somewhere in the region. Maybe a place that would allow for temporary housing for people in recovery or displaced. I don't know what, where, or how, but God does."

It was halftime at Koda's basketball game. He'd been added to one of the squads of the outdoor summer league. Lauren slipped out of the bleachers, leaving Jeffrey and Doug to discuss how Koda's team could make up a twenty-point deficit.

Landing on a semi-private spot behind the concession stand, Lauren looked up the number and pressed the call icon. Heads of wheat across the street drifted in the breeze as cattle grazed in an adjacent pasture.

"Lauren! Hello. What a pleasant surprise."

"Hey, Lars. I wanted you to know that Jeffrey and I are getting married."

"Back on again, huh?"

"Yes. We're getting married on Saturday."

She waited for a response but none came. "Here . . . Lars? Are you there?"

He cleared his throat. "Yes. I'm happy for you, Lauren. And for your fiancé. He's going to be a very happy man . . . if he isn't already."

"Thank you, Lars. That means a lot—"

A call came in from Maggie. She let it go to voicemail. "How are *you* doing?"

"I took your advice and searched for a counselor. Everything pointed to James Covington at New Hope Alliance."

A chill tickled Lauren's spine.

"We set up an appointment."

"That's great, Lars. You're in very good hands."

After hanging up, Lauren listened to Maggie's message. Warmth washed through her body.

She returned to the park bleachers. The second half was about to begin. She, Jeffrey, and Doug acknowledged Koda's wave from the bench.

"Brother Jim wants to perform our ceremony. He moved appointments to do it. That was so kind of him."

"Great," Jeffrey said. "I'll make the flight arrangements."

"That sounds like Brother Jim," Doug said.

"If my college buddy, Gary, flies out, we'll already have a charter for the Covingtons."

"I wonder how Freddie is doing," Lauren said to Doug. "Do you think he'd come too?"

"Maybe. It's early yet since his surgery, but I can check. It sure would be good to see him again."

"I know it's a long way, but I also know you stay in touch with your sister, Carmen. Maybe she'd like to come."

"That's kind of you. Thank you."

Jeffrey laughed. "Don't let her fool you. We just want some guests." He elbowed Doug.

"Are your parents coming?" Doug said.

"Highly unlikely. Mom's gone, and Dad and I aren't that close."

"You'll love the Covingtons. They are so caring."

"That's what Lauren tells me."

"They want to set up a center for recovery victims and refugees. It's more than a suicide intervention ministry."

"Really!" Lauren said. "I wonder if they're aware of the old Montana Children's Home in Twin Bridges."

Jeffrey and Doug looked at her.

"I toured it coming over here. It's for sale. It needs a ton of work, but I could see it as a retreat. There are a lot of buildings. The setting is so beautiful."

"I know a few people who would invest in a ministry like that," Jeffrey said.

Doug set his hand on Jeffrey's shoulder. "You give me their contact information, and I'll call them."

Lauren and Jeffrey turned to Doug with quizzical looks.

"I took the job."

"Oh, Doug. That's wonderful," Lauren said. "I was hoping you would."

Jeffrey's forehead creased. "What job?"

"Brother Jim offered Doug a job raising funds for the ministry."

"That's great. Congratulations!" Jeffrey stuck out his hand.

Doug squeezed it. "I think I can make more of a difference at this job than my last one in sales."

"Totally!" Lauren said.

"Did you ever make contact with the FBI?" Doug said to Jeffrey.

"I did."

"A motorcycle gang peddling drugs kidnapped Koda's mother," Doug said. "She's either dead or trafficked."

"Trafficking has become epidemic. Rest assured, I'll follow up on this."

"I wonder how his sister is doing," Lauren said.

"Me too. That family has been through a lot."

"What happened?" Jeffrey said.

"Running with a gang," Doug said. "Not sure if they're on the rez or off."

# CHAPTER 46

Jeffrey and Brother Jim stood near the far edge of the knoll. Only three days earlier Lauren had pedaled this grade in a frenzy as Koda caught one last glimpse of this beautiful spot before almost ending his life.

*Thank You, Lord, for intervening in Koda's life. And thank You for Jeffrey and his kindness to fly in Brother Jim and Maggie. They're such precious people. And thank You for the people who traveled so far on such short notice.*

She clutched Doug's arm as they walked forward to the sound of the "Bridal Chorus." Playing a portable keyboard, Tashina led four of Emma's adopted grandkids, singing the lyrics Lauren had penned for them:

> "Here comes the bride,
> Fresh off her ride,
> Pure as a white dove and waiting for love,
> Long uphill climb,

> Redemption time,
> New season dawns as their music spawns.
> No more alone, the two become one,
> Serve hand in hand, this cord of three strands,
> Their prayers fulfilled,
> As God has willed,
> Let us not forget, how their needs He has met."

They repeated the verse as Lauren and Doug walked down the aisle.

She never thought this day would come. But if it had, she would never have expected this setting. It was more worthy of beginning a new life than ending one.

The sun shone through a clear blue sky, warming her face. Lush wheat bent in the gentle breeze, fanning the flames of love aloft.

Jeffrey stood ramrod straight, teeth gleaming, coal-black, wavy hair coiffed.

Emma had lent Lauren her wedding gown, a size too big but fitting perfectly for this day.

The day before, Emma's hairdresser friend trimmed Lauren's hair into the perfect pixie. She'd never had hair this short, not even in grade school. While it wasn't what she'd have chosen to wear for her wedding, it could be a blessing if it lowered the temperature underneath a bicycling helmet.

Maggie, Emma and her entourage, Gary and Jeffrey's cousin Mark, and Jessica and three of her fellow Narrow Gate Bikers dressed in cuts smiled as Lauren walked forward. Freddie and Doug's half-sister, Carmen, continued trading words with one another behind cupped hands.

Lauren's two brothers, one of them confined to a wheelchair, were unable to make it, but had sent beautiful flowers that sat on the ground on either side of Jeffrey and Brother Jim. Lars had sent flowers too. *How sweet.*

And there stood Koda, his mother hanging on his arm, her sunken cheeks and sullen eyes struggling to remember how to express happiness. Koda's hadn't forgotten. With his chin raised high, he was beaming. Based on the arrests made after Lauren's harrowing ride with Bruiser, the FBI had obtained enough information to bust a few more thugs and rescue some women.

Lauren looked at Doug, but he didn't return her gaze. He'd been such a good friend. No one on planet Earth would make a better escort.

To the right, two loaded bicycles leaned against Emma's LaCrosse. Multicolored tissue flowers clung to the spokes, along with streamers soon to be flowing from the rear panniers. A sign attached to the back rack of one bicycle read *Just Married*. The sight explained why Koda had asked to borrow her bicycle yesterday, although he scarcely had time between shuttling people from the airport. Several of Emma's many adopted grandkids had their hands over their mouths but couldn't hide their coy glee as they watched Lauren from the corners of their eyes.

She couldn't imagine Jeffrey would ever have agreed to a honeymoon on wheels, with his demanding occupation, his schedule, and his conventional ways. But when she looked at him, his grin widened, then broke into a chuckle.

She wrapped her arm tighter around Doug's. Had her father been here instead, would he have been shaking like Doug? She glanced at him. He merely looked forward, his chin held high, but with what looked like water forming in the corner of his eye.

They had almost reached Brother Jim and Jeffrey. The others drew in behind them. It was time to hand her over. Doug's stomach somersaulted again.

He'd never had a daughter, but this wasn't that. The lump in his throat was too large, the breath in his lungs too faint.

There were no other Lauren Baumgartners in the world. And there'd been no mold to break or lose. Someone much like his beloved Ruth, yet unique in her own way, brought to him for a different reason and another season.

Somewhere along the trail Doug's heart had been pierced. The seeping now bled. A delightful blend of caring and compassion, faith and fun, virtue and vitality would soon hang from someone else's arm. *Till death do they part.*

Why did this have to end?

Yet, another door had opened. He would end his tour sometime in the next few weeks, relocate from Los Angeles to Montana, and begin a new life as a fundraiser for Big Sky Hope for the Heart. Based on Brother Jim's strong expression of interest, Doug would begin seeking investors who might be willing to resurrect the old children's home in Twin Bridges. He was looking forward to it, even as his emotions struggled to let go.

He gathered himself and took a deep breath. He clutched Jeffrey's right hand and squeezed, but he couldn't hazard another look into Lauren's hazel eyes. Instead he yielded her arm to Jeffrey's and dropped his head. He didn't want to sour their special occasion, but his emotions had commandeered him and threatened to spill over their banks.

Brother Jim, forever the solid rock, looked forward at the empty prairie and asked, "Who gives this woman to be married to this man?"

Doug gulped. He looked at Brother Jim and managed, "I do," his voice cracking. That wasn't the "I do" he'd anticipated.

Then Lauren leaned forward and kissed Doug's cheek.

Without looking, he could feel the others examining his every move. He backed up and stood among them. Someone touched his shoulder. He glimpsed Carmen, then looked down.

He attempted to swallow the lump, then tried again, to no avail.

"We have gathered here together in the presence of these friends and God Almighty to unite the hearts of Lauren Faith

Baumgartner and Jeffrey Aaron Maddox. If anyone objects to this union, may they speak now or forever hold their peace."

Doug's heartbeat quickened. Why did Brother Jim have to include that? There were only a handful of people, and they were new acquaintances. Surely none of them would deny happiness to this couple.

Of course Doug objected. At least his heart did. The breeze cooled the sweat forming on his brow. His heart pounded.

Yet his head told him to get out of the way. This was good and right. Jeffrey was younger and more vibrant. He and Lauren had their whole lives in front of them. They shared a stronger foundation of faith. Their kids would be world-changers. This was meant to be.

Doug's love for Lauren, however, would not be defined by what he did on this day. His love for her would never be quenched. But neither would it demand its own way. It would last as long as he had breath, expressed with a respect for what God was doing here on her special day, hope for what He would do in the future.

The silence persisted. Why wasn't Brother Jim proceeding with the service?

Doug looked up. Brother Jim was staring at him, scanning his very thoughts before looking back at the couple.

"Very well then. This is most unusual, but the bride is providing the special music today." Brother Jim motioned his palm toward Lauren before announcing, "I know you won't be disappointed."

Koda stepped forward with her violin, apparently no worse for wear despite the rough treatment at the hands of the thugs down at the river.

Lauren had played Bach's "Jesu, Joy of Man's Desiring" several times at other people's weddings, but never on her own behalf. Her confidence in Jesus fortified her skillful and emotive play. For she would always love Him first and most. He loved her enough to answer her prayers for someone special. She would endeavor to love Jeffrey as Jesus loved him, to submit to him in obedience to her Lord and Savior. Such a noble, intelligent, and motivated man deserved her respect. She would leave his shortcomings to the Lord and attempt to do the same with her own.

She loved the lyrics to this song. They came to her as she wielded her bow across the taut strings.

> Jesu, joy of our desiring,
> holy wisdom, love most bright;
> drawn by Thee, our souls aspiring
> soar to uncreated light.
> Word of God, our flesh that fashioned,
> with the fire of life impassioned,
> striving still to truth unknown,
> soaring, dying round Thy throne.

*He who covers his sins will not prosper. But whoever confesses and forsakes them will have mercy.*

—Proverbs 28:13

# DISCUSSION QUESTIONS

1. Who were you hoping would win Lauren's heart? Were you surprised by the outcome?
2. Discuss the opening scene. Identify a few reasons why Lauren and Jeffrey's lunch date ended the way it did. How might it have ended differently?
3. What are constructive ways to fill a void left by the unexpected death of a loved one?
4. Do you know someone who might be suffering from father hunger? What characteristics or behaviors do they exhibit?
5. How can you help a person who lacks parental role models? How can you help restore their ability to trust?
6. How would it make you feel if you discovered that an acquaintance had Lars's issue? How would you react to him or her? What would you say?
7. How would you try to help someone who was struggling with Lars's issue? What does the Bible have to say about it?
8. What do you think about the plight of Native Americans? What can the government do to make their lives better? What can you do?

9. Why do motorcycle gangs exist? What can be done to prevent the crimes they commit?

10. Which US president would you consider adding to Mount Rushmore and why?

11. Why did Lauren keep her deep, dark secret buried for so long? How did it affect her?

12. Do you know someone who harbors Lauren's secret? If so, please have them check out the *Forgiven and Set Free* Bible study by Linda Cochran. There are also groups that offer support in working through the issue.

13. Do you have a question about the novel that you would like to ask me? If so, please email me at tim@timbishopwrites.com. I would love to hear from you.

## PLEASE POST A REVIEW!

Help other readers discover *The Road Unveiled*. Reader reviews are invaluable to a book's reach. For quick access to the review sites for *The Road Unveiled*, use the QR code below or go to https://t2m.io/V2JWZJ1U. And thank you for telling others about the book.

# Acknowledgments

My prayer warriors are crucial to my writing success. Not only do they offer encouragement through their presence and prayers, they instill accountability. I'm grateful for their ongoing support.

My editors blessed this project with loads of experience in Christian publishing. Vicki Crumpton rode in with a passion for bicycling, a much-needed saw, and spare boards. Amanda Varian patched faulty construction while sanding, and John David Kudrick applied the final coat. Thank you all for making me a better writer.

Between editing rounds, MacKenzie, Mikayla, and Somie critiqued the work in progress, prompting revisions to touch readers more deeply.

No one can enjoy a book if not drawn to it. That's where Micah Kandros comes in. He designs book covers that make readers want to look inside. Thank you, Micah, for your appealing artwork.

Due to this novel's sensitive content, self-doubt became the most challenging part of writing and publishing it. The book production process is about finding fault—questioning whether content will resonate with readers, balancing the pace, strengthening the writing, identifying plot holes, and cleaning up mistakes. I couldn't do this without encouragement. Heartprint Writers' Group knows how to dole it out. Thanks also to beta readers Anna Bottoms, Rev. Brian Haggerty, Fred Ludwig, Justin Rudnick, and David Socoby. They found problems but also offered ample encouragement. William Moore, a photographer from southwest Montana, reviewed scenes set in his vicinity and called out inconsistencies. I can't thank these people enough. The same goes for whoever helps launch this book.

Debbie Bishop is much more than a beta reader, although she's that too. In addition to offering input on anything I ask, she cheers louder as I approach the finish line. I'm so thankful she is in my life.

Finally I couldn't and wouldn't do any of this without God. Story ideas pop into my head, often when I'm in bed, and I jot them on the notepad in my nightstand drawer. I consider them downloads from Above. I'm grateful for what God has taught me through my life experiences and helping people online. He also blessed me with a mother full of sacrificial love for her children, love for words, and wisdom. He allowed Debbie and me to bicycle some of the roads Lauren and Doug have. Sharing curated nuggets with readers is a blessing I don't take for granted. I'm hopeful God uses them to touch lives.

# About the Author

After a thirty-year career in business, Tim Bishop left his corporate treasurer position, married his dream girl, and embarked with her to parts unknown—on bicycles. Ten thousand miles later, the first-time newlyweds have written four books about their cycling adventures. Their devotional, *Wheels of Wisdom*, won four first-place book awards. *Publishers Weekly* dubbed it "a road map for life."

Tim's first novel, *The Persistent Road*, won the Ames Award in General Fiction. The award acknowledges excellent books that encourage living a courageous and obedient Christian life, especially under challenging circumstances. The audiobook edition of *The Persistent Road* was selected as a Selah Award finalist.

Tim volunteers as a coach for a ministry that reaches people who are dealing with challenging life issues. He has written numerous articles for various Christian content providers.

A graduate of the University of Maine, a CPA, and a three-time Maine chess champion, Tim and his wife, Debbie, live in Middle Tennessee.

For a free ebook, subscribe at TimBishopWrites.com

Read Tim's monthly newsletter for email updates, articles, truth on issues of the heart, meditation moments, and giveaways. And listen to his *Wisdom from the Heart* on your favorite audio platform.

Follow @TimBishopWrites

# Order Book 1 Today!

# Books by Tim and Debbie Bishop



## Presenting the Winner of Four First-Place Book Awards

At last. A devotional with adventure. And more than just a little. While bicycling over 10,000 miles throughout America, midlife newlyweds and hope coaches Tim and Debbie Bishop glean 52 life lessons from the open road in their award-winning *Wheels of Wisdom*.

"Impressively well written, organized and presented . . . compelling, informative, and thoughtful." –*Midwest Book Review*

"Sound biblical principles presented in a practical, experiential way." –Rabbi Eric Walker, host of *Revealing the Truth*

"Those looking for a road map for life can get directions from the Bishops." –*Publishers Weekly*

## More Life Lessons

After pedaling thousands of miles throughout America, Tim and Debbie Bishop offer eight powerful life lessons from the seat of a bicycle. With wisdom gleaned all the way from a twilight ride up an Idaho mountain to a bicycle shop in Ohio, *Metaphors in Motion* provides enlightenment for your own travels through life.

## The Story Behind the Stories

After fifty-two years of life, Tim and Debbie Bishop finally found in each other that special someone they'd been searching for years to marry. In only ten weeks they moved from marriage proposal to embarking on a cycling adventure of a lifetime. Read their inspiring story *Two Are Better* and travel vicariously across America on a bicycle.

9 798986 012551